ELLE

D0953977

Also by Emma Mars

Hotelles

ELLE

Room Two in the
Hotelles Trilogy

EMMA MARS

TRANSLATED BY ALEXIS PERNSTEINER

HARPER PERENNIAL

NEW YORK • LONDON • TORONTO • SYDNEY • NEW DELHI • AUCKLAND

HARPER PERENNIAL

Photograph on pages iv–v by ilolab/Shutterstock, Inc.

HarperCollins books may be purchased for educational, business, or sales promotional use. For information please e-mail the Special Markets Department at SPsales@harpercollins.com.

FIRST EDITION

Library of Congress Cataloging-in-Publication Data has been applied for.

ISBN 978-0-06-227419-9   *5658 9715 04/15*

15 16 17 18 19 OV/RRD 10 9 8 7 6 5 4 3 2 1

"It is a silly idea to place one's happiness in the hands of another, and yet women's lives are none other. Condemned to perpetual dependence, women are subjected to a fate that is imposed upon them, they endure the consequences of it, and when those consequences crush them, they are the ones who take the blame."

ALEXANDRE DUMAS—*MEMOIRS OF A BLIND MAN*

ROOM TWO

Paris, the First Days of June 2010, a Hotel Room in the Middle of the Afternoon

Our haven. Our home.

That is what room number one, the Josephine, became when I took refuge here in my tattered wedding dress. When Louie opened his arms to me. Maybe it has lost some of its luster under room service trays and rumpled clothing since we first moved in. But its charm has also become subtler, with our sighs reverberating through its walls day after day, our moans dripping to the ground and collecting on the parquet, an ephemeral and invisible army that only we can sense. Not that we let anyone else come in.

Outside, spring is in full blossom. Summer, fall, and winter passed like a dream. Close your eyes, open them. Bam! Already gone. An entire year went by before we could even think of going back to Rue de la Tour-des-Dames. The renovations at Mademoiselle Mars's old house will soon be completed. Louie has been dreaming of this restoration for ten years. He's so excited, he's on the verge of exploding; he's champing at the bit. I've been using all my wiles to quiet and temper his excitement. I like arousing his senses in a way that calms and soothes his nerves.

As we wait to move into our new house, we are savoring the sunny days through the curtains of our room. Over the course of these past months, we have tamed each other, like two animals, two wild beasts nestled up together. Hungry to learn the other's secrets, avidly seeking out sensitivities and subtleties in our bodies, genitals, and souls, we have explored each other in careful detail. We walk around naked. We've barely left this room, with the exception of Maude's burial. We hardly ever even open the window. We like to revel in our combined musky scent and grow drunk off its perfect blend.

But I have not forgotten David and his lies. I have not erased the memory of my mother or her painful death. I have not emptied myself of my past; I have filled myself with Louie. He has flooded my every crevice. He has conquered me. Absolute ecstasy, absolute sweetness, absolute desire for the absolute and for self-abandonment.

I HAVE NO IDEA WHAT day it is. And I have even less of a sense of how others are living, down there, in the streets. I have been cut off from everything these past months.

Our world is sweet, tender, studded with love and occasional interruptions in the form of room service brought by Ysiam, our mischievous accomplice these early days of our bliss. Every ray of light promises to illuminate us for all eternity. And we bask in the natural warmth, languid and hungry only for our bare bodies.

Half asleep and bathed in light, I feel Louie's hand, a horny snake on the verge of biting, slip between my thighs and crawl toward the origin of its temptation. He skims over my quivering crotch. Slowly, reflexively, my legs open. He smiles, satisfied. Three fingers flutter over my genitals, coaxing a first pearl of fluid. If he had to, he would wait for me to be ready, but I am always ready for him. He knows it. He takes advantage of it, and I can't get enough of it—or of him.

I moan enough for him to understand. I stretch out on my back like a cat, offering a complete, pictorial, original view of myself. I have definitely changed. I no longer fear his gaze, and I abandon myself to him without an ounce of restraint. No matter the position, the lighting, the angle. No matter my curves, which have gotten more abundant with our siestas and inactivity. I keep my eyes closed. Since he wants me now, while I am still half asleep and in this state of lethargy, he'll take my groggy sweet surrender. His hands touch me where the sun has left my skin hot and silken.

When I feel his tongue on my labia, it is too late to push him away. Is this what I want?

He is usually more attentive to the space surrounding my pink button. This time, he presses the sticky candy button directly with the flat of his tongue, as if to test its elastic resistance. I like this. I like when he tries new things, when he rewrites and transgresses our rules. I like when lovemaking is unpredictable. My flesh candy trembles and swells. He has a sweet tooth. He wants more. Me, too. I paint his lips with my nectar.

Blindly, I grab his index finger and hastily insert it inside me. He seems surprised, then his finger gambols, drawing large circles against the walls of my vagina. They contract, spasm, irradiate with the coming joy. When he pushes his last digit deep inside, my cunt blooms around his wrist, accepting it.

"Keep going . . . yes, like . . . !"

I don't have time for any more words. His member has now replaced his finger. I blink in gratitude. Through squinted eyes, I can make out his torso, which is rocking up and down over me. He seems less lean than usual. More muscular. But that's probably just an effect of my sleepy state and this orgasm that has started rumbling deep inside of me. I'm on the verge of exploding. His penis is less precise than his finger, but the way he fills me satisfies my desires. It is swelling and pumping more violently. With each withdrawal, it longs to return. Our lazy bodies, like bread hot out of the oven, are slowly crashing into each other. This is not one of our great romps. It is slow and rejuvenating. We are savoring each bite. Sex like this is vital, primordial, nourishing. Nothing is too intense for us. And yet sweet gentleness emanates from us.

"I'm going to come . . . ," he says, underscoring his first spurts of semen.

I, too, am on the verge of surrender, and I cry:

"Come!"

I open my eyes wide as he starts to release a flood of fluid. I want to admire him. All of him. I invite his eyes to lose themselves in me. Each time our bodies come into contact, I feel his desire branding me. I want image and sound, scent and touch of burning skin to become one.

More than anything, I want to admire the shape of his long muscles and read his latest coiling tattoos. His living alphabet. How I love to see his arabesques rippling all around me.

But I don't see them . . . His left shoulder is blank. So is his inner arm. I am just about to push him away when at last I see his face. He is smiling brightly, triumphantly.

"David?"

I WAS TORN FROM MY dream by my own muffled cry. That was the first time I had dreamed of David in months. The sudden intrusion of his brother did not surprise Louie, and it didn't seem to bother him either. He took me in his arms and rocked me, dissipating the effects of the dream, which he could see in my incredulous eyes. Ghosts from our past were of no concern to him; his kisses no longer had a rival. He was the indisputable winner. I was all his. Who would doubt that?

1

MAY 10, 2010

The first image I had of that night was a black carriage led by two chestnut horses that shimmered in the streetlights. Its arrival on Rue de la Tour-des-Dames hinted at the old-world theme Louie had chosen for the evening. A cluster of men in top hats and tails descended from the carriage. They were laughing loudly among themselves when one of them missed the running board and fell, splayed out, over the sidewalk.

As I neared Mademoiselle Mars's house, I was able to admire the guests and their extremely sophisticated attire. I was underdressed since the only instruction Louie had given me was to arrive at our new home at ten p.m. Sharp. Almost everyone was wearing a costume reminiscent of the Romantic era, although a few had opted for clothing from subsequent decades.

I noticed two young women in pink dresses with cap sleeves, gossamer corollas that went to their ankles, and plunging necklines that showed off their slender shoulders. They skipped over the cobblestones, obviously delighted to wear such costumes.

A FOOTMAN GREETED ME AT the entryway, wearing livery and holding a candelabra. I felt as though I were traveling into the past. Someone must have warned him that I wouldn't be dressed according to the evening's code because he addressed me by my first name:

"Good evening, Mademoiselle. You must be Elle."

"Yes."

"You will find your dress in the cloakroom on your left," he said, pointing as he stepped back to let me inside.

"Thank you."

"There will be someone to help you get dressed."

Inside, a crowd of uniformly black tailcoats and an assortment of colorful dresses were already gathered. A young woman with two clusters of curly black hair pinned above her ears grabbed hold of me. I didn't even have a chance to look for the evening's host.

Despite the dim candlelight, I was able to make out the magnificent decor, which had been restored to its original specifications. From what I could tell, it was well worth all the years and money that Louie had poured into it. I recognized the neo-Pompeiian style of Duchesnois House next door, although it had been taken to an unparalleled level of refinement. Everything, down to the smallest floral frieze, was trimmed in gold. And no ceiling was left unadorned with reproductions of classical instruments, lyres, auloi, and harps, all trimmed with birds of paradise. Some of the finishing touches had been added since my last visit.

"Do you like it?"

As I was lacing the pink silk corset he had chosen for me, and before putting on my matching satin dress, Louie's sensual voice whispered in my ear. And with it came the now familiar notes of vanilla and lavender that I'd come to associate with so many memories and the promise of pleasures to come. I felt his breath brush over the stray tendrils that had fallen from my expertly crafted bun. I had been living with Louie Barlet for months, and his presence alone still had this incredible, earth-shattering power over my body, mind, and most secret thoughts. I was still trembling when he placed a soft hand on my shoulder. I felt like I was burning up.

"Tell me . . . ," he insisted. "What do you think?"

Was he talking about my dress, the perfect restoration of our home, or this party, which was the most extravagant housewarming I had ever seen?

"Yes, it's wonderful."

"Just you wait . . . This is only the beginning!"

He swung me toward him like a doll, bringing me face-to-face with the embodiment of that promise. At last I saw him, his stance as regal as his wounded knee would allow. He was supremely elegant, the perfect embodiment of every Romantic fantasy, in his dandy's costume: a tightly belted night-blue redingote that flared at the waist, a gilded vest and brooched silk scarf, cream stirrup pants, ankle boots, and gaiters.

He noticed me admiring him and quickly corrected me:

"Of course, I wasn't talking about myself . . . but about everything that awaits you here."

Whenever he became overenthusiastic, he reminded me of his brother. But I kept that thought to myself. Instead, I smiled, kissed him on both cheeks, and then said, as I curtsied:

"I understood, milord."

Over the past several months, I had played along with all of the fantasies that Louie had imagined for us. I was never reluctant, nor did I ever decline. And although we'd rarely left the Hôtel des Charmes, we hadn't confined ourselves exclusively to the Josephine, our beloved room number one. Depending on his whims, Louie and I had explored rooms devoted to other courtesans: Mademoiselle Deschamps, Kitty Fisher, Cora Pearl, Valtesse de la Bigne, and Liane de Pougy.

In each room, I had been introduced to one aspect of sexuality. It wasn't about abandoning myself to other lips and other hands, nor about relinquishing my precious lover to foreign mouths, but about immersing ourselves in an atmosphere of intense sensuality. I had discovered the pleasure of making love in front of others, in proximity with other bodies, in unison with other genitals seeking to fuel their own bliss. From insatiable lovers, we had become avid libertines. We had no taboos, but also no perversions. In a natural progression of things, the couples who shared our bed had begun to replace the illustrious courtesans and lovers from the past.

TWO YOUNG WOMEN IN CORSETS crossed the hall, giggling, falsely timid and bare-bottomed. They were soon followed be a pair of erect rods. It dawned on me that those nights at the Hôtel des Charmes had been rehearsals for tonight's grand show.

"You should know, Mademoiselle, that today is March 21, 1827," Louie said, interrupting my licentious musings.

"Very good," I replied, playing along. "And why that date?"

"Because that is the day when Anne-Françoise Boutet, a.k.a. Mademoiselle Mars, inaugurated this magnificent Palladian villa decorated by Visconti."

"Luchino . . . Visconti?" I cried, struggling to believe such an anachronism.

"Darling!" he scolded me with another electric kiss on my

neck. "1827! Louis Visconti, the architect. Not Luchino, the filmmaker."

His tone was proud and affected as his arm swept over the room. Had the remodel been completed on time, I am sure that he would have wanted to celebrate the event on the villa's actual anniversary. But there had been a delay of almost two months.

"So I'm guessing that she threw an incredible party, and that you want to replicate it?"

"And how!"

He thumped his cane into the marble floor as he spoke. I had never seen this one before, and I admired the embossing of an imperial eagle on its knob.

"Imagine the most dazzling masquerade ball of the early nineteenth century!" he exclaimed, looking as though he himself had traveled back to that glorious past. "The cream of society is in attendance: princes, marchionesses, foreign ambassadors, and all of the neighborhood's renowned artists— Sand, Chopin, Musset, Berlioz, Delacroix, Scheffer."

"Okay, but what was so extraordinary about that? Gatherings like that must have been fairly common, I should think."

"Come, I'll show you."

He grabbed my hand, and since my wardrobe mistress had just inserted the final pin into my Marquise de Sévigné–inspired bun, I had no other choice but to follow him. He was in such an enthusiastic hurry that his usual limp had practically disappeared.

When we arrived at the massive reception hall, whose three arched bay windows looked out onto an English garden, he pointed first to a generously stocked buffet and then to the dance floor on the other side of the room, where several couples in costume were attempting a quadrille being played by a chamber orchestra in the opposite corner.

"Do you notice anything special?"

"Sorry, no . . ."

"And yet something important is missing."

"Really? What?"

"Put yourself back in that era," Louie said, his eyes brightening. "Custom had it that game tables were set up at soirees for the men. They would give one or two dances to the women and then go off to another room to take part in their *real* passion. While their dates waltzed, chatted, and nibbled, the men challenged one another to backgammon and faro. But on that infamous night of March 21, 1827, there was no such thing. Mademoiselle Mars refused the men that prerogative."

"Okay . . . but what was so subversive about denying these gentlemen their games?"

"Well, that night they were left with nothing to do but attend to you women! Believe you me, revolutions have been fought for less!"

To better illustrate what he was saying, Louie led me into a small adjoining room, which was to be our dining room. There against the floor was a gigantic and very old kilim, whose cost I could hardly even imagine, and on top of which were strewn cushions as big as mattresses. Several couples were already lounging on them, their costumes fanned out around them.

I immediately recognized the two performers who had given each other so much pleasure in a black-lighted hotel room on my second rendezvous at the Hôtel des Charmes with Louie. They were larger in real life and just as wild about each other. Their sixty-nine, which was more exciting in person, was a source of fascination for several people leaning against the wall.

"Hmm," I whispered. "I'm not so sure that these fine gentlemen would have *attended* to their companions like that back then."

"Oh, but they would have. Parties often grew wild behind the scenes. Like tonight."

We watched as another couple paired off. I recognized the statuesque ethnic woman from Belles de Nuit's catalogue, the woman who had made me come with the handle of a fan. I had given her a nickname that seemed to suit her better than ever: the Vine.

"Who is that?" I asked, thrusting my chin in her direction.

Louie seemed amused by my question and gave me a knowing smile.

"I think you know her already."

"Yes," I agreed, hiding my embarrassment. "I meant, what's her name?"

"Salomé."

My eyes took in the other attendees. Who were all these people? Who were the people in Louie's circle of intimates? Whom else would I recognize—based on the size of his member, or the curve of her breast? Did he have any real friends? Or just partners in debauchery, as he had been an instrument in his brother's schemes?

During our period of voluntary house arrest, Louie had rarely gone out, attending only a few dinners and cocktail hours to which I had not felt like accompanying him. Instead, I'd spent that time with Sophia, whom I had been neglecting. During that time, we never appeared outside in the world together. We never went out with friends or attended concerts. Our bodies and souls had been completely devoted to our love. We had been putting off the demands of conventional relationships, but that night, our identity as a couple began to take on a social shape. Until that night, we had been lovers; now we were becoming a couple with social attributes. Louie, I sensed, was eager to be alone with me again.

SUDDENLY, HIS ELEGANT AND FIRM hand grasped my corseted waist and drew me into his side, his eyes gazing deeply into mine.

"You look magnificent."

"Thanks. You're not so bad yourself."

I pretended to inspect him from head to toe.

"Magnificent." It was a word that David would have used. The younger of the Barlet brothers might appear in my dreams or in an expression, but for me, he belonged to the past. Those days—our abandoned wedding plans—were like a shadow; they weren't a real threat.

And yet, not one day had gone by without my thinking about a wedding. A different wedding. A union that would be based on infinitely deeper feelings, which time and proximity had nurtured, and which were no longer bound by my childhood fantasies. Despite his material wealth, his powers of seduction, and thousands of other qualities that I'd discovered over the course of our lazy afternoons, Louie was not exactly a Prince Charming. He was opaque and complex, and the life he was offering looked nothing like the quotidian with David— first-class, hermetically sealed, without any highs or lows.

Louie guided me to a free cushion, unbuttoning his jacket with one hand.

"No, wait," I stopped him.

"Why? Are you uncomfortable?"

"No ..."

"Shall we ask them to leave?"

"No." I smiled. "It's not that."

None of the lovers seemed to have noticed our conversation. The protean mass of sirens was otherwise occupied, with mouths, genitals, hands, and voices swelling in a common moan.

"What's wrong, then?" Louie asked.

If he had taught me one thing in the time that we had known each other, it was to beware of convention. To laugh in the face of custom and subvert tradition for the sake of our pleasure, in which we partook whenever and however we pleased. It was easy to uphold these principles when we were in our room. Our love nest brimmed with pleasure of all kinds. But it was quite another thing when we were in the real world.

I didn't know what to say, so I let myself collapse onto a giant cushion. Louie was kind enough to pull it away from the group, quickly understanding my childish posture as a plea for conversation and not an invitation for petting. He sat beside me, seizing my face between his hands.

"Elle . . . what is it? This wasn't how you'd imagined our homecoming, is that it?"

"No, honestly . . . I promise you, it has nothing to do with that. Everything is . . . perfect!"

An orgasm's crescendo gave substance to my statement of appreciation. In fact, the young woman's pizzicati of drunken yeses corresponded so well with my words that I was having trouble containing my laughter.

"Is the thing you can't tell me really that funny?"

"Actually, it's very serious."

"Well, maybe it would be best to save it for later." He bristled, rising to return to the ballroom.

I reached for his coattail. I didn't want him to leave my side.

"No! Stay. What I have to tell you is . . . very simple. And it primarily concerns you."

"Okay. I'm listening."

I made a modest sweeping gesture over the sublime scene he had created for us. Such a miracle implied money, education, impeccable taste, and good relations.

"As you know, I don't have anything to offer, not like this."

"Wrong," he corrected me. "You are the owner of a magnificent home in Nanterre-Ville."

I didn't like jokes that involved my late mother or her dearly acquired estate, however modest it may have been. In fact, I avoided the subject altogether and had already postponed a meeting several times with Master Whurman, Mom's notary, who wanted to finalize the details of my inheritance. I was the sole beneficiary cited in my mother's will.

"What I meant was, outside of my humble self and my feelings for you, I have nothing to give you."

"Don't underestimate your *humble self*," he murmured playfully.

"Stop . . . I don't even have a job!"

We had both been fired from BTV several months before. My termination had been easy to justify. After all, I had disappeared from the set at the end of *Culture Mix*'s premiere. Mine had been an immediate termination without severance pay, in compliance with the terms of my trial-period contract. I hadn't even had to go back to Barlet Tower to collect my things. Chloe, David's assistant, had had them sent to the address they had on file for me: 29 Rue Rigault in Nanterre.

For Louie, who had been an employee and shareholder at

Barlet Group for nineteen years, and whose brother was the CEO, things had not gone as smoothly. Although he was delighted to finally be free of his family's empire, Louie had had no intention of jumping from the dynastic ship in his swim trunks and without a lifeboat. The financial negotiations orchestrated by his lawyer, Jean-Marc Zerki, a young wolf in the Parisian legal world, had lasted weeks and had resulted, after much pain, in an arrangement that included a lot of zeros. Suffice it to say, my lover would be comfortable for the rest of his life.

If we got married, and Louie knew this as well as I did, I would also benefit from that thick and gilded cushion.

"So?" he replied. "Everything that I need, everything that I have ever wanted, is here. In my arms."

His reference was obvious. He was paraphrasing the words to the song that had been playing the first time we'd made love, one year earlier.

And it wasn't just a passing reference. I knew the symbolic weight that Louie placed on music, images, and all manner of signs that surrounded us and were constantly resonating and echoing our emotions.

At last I asked the question that had been on my mind, realizing that I couldn't wait another second to give voice to what was scratching at my throat, my chest, my gut, my sex:

"So, then . . . do you want to marry me?"

He stared at me for a long moment, which he stretched out unbearably, suppressing what soon blossomed into a gigantic smile. I recognized his tell: the dimple on his cheek that lets me know if he's lying or hiding something, and that sends me into raptures. He reached to stroke my hair but was thwarted by my meticulously constructed coiffure and instead settled his hand on the nape of my neck, which he gently, tenderly stroked.

"Annabelle Lorand," he growled, his voice hot and muffled, "you blasted little woman . . . Tell me . . . how long have you been planning this?"

That was Louie when he felt backed into a corner: he could reverse the situation with a single smile, a single well-chosen word. I sighed like a damsel and hid my blushing cheeks in the crook of his neck.

"Yes . . . I mean, no. I mean, for a little while now."

When we were intertwined in each other's arms in room number one, when I was pressed into his torso and his sex was lost in mine, I didn't think about it. But after only a few instants in the social world, I began to see our age difference as an obstacle. And my childish stammering didn't make me feel particularly mature.

"Kudos, you surprised me. And here I thought I was the one who would be impressing you tonight. You've definitely beaten me at that game."

"You haven't answered my question," I retorted; I wasn't going to let him off the hook.

"Do I have to give you my answer tonight?"

He was a picture of composure. In fact, he seemed to be enjoying the situation: the power it was giving him, the way I was hanging on his every word and anxiously waiting to hear one devastating or wonderful syllable.

"Umm, yes," I said.

"Has no one ever told you that in our culture, it's the man who typically asks the woman of his choice for her hand? And not the other way around?"

"No. Just like no one seems to have informed you that it

isn't customary for a man to steal his brother's fiancée on the day she is to be married. In our culture, that is."

His kiss seemed rushed and forceful. What discomfort was he trying to hide? What shameful reply was he trying to suppress?

After a few seconds, our lips detached themselves, and he seemed to have regained his composure.

"In that case, my answer is yes."

I was stunned. So it was that easy? One had only to ask? That was how to get the most exquisite, most tender, most loving and spirited man to choose you?

"Yes? . . . *Yes?*"

Had our engagement plans titillated the couples around us? A thundering yes, an ecstatic and throaty cry, the moans of men and women blending and becoming one—the room swelled with these sounds, as if to contradict my sense of anxiety.

Louie did not seem bothered by this incongruous situation, and he continued in the same self-assured tone:

"Yes," he confirmed, as though it were obvious. "We could have the wedding in a few months. What do you think?"

"A few months?" I asked, surprised.

I couldn't help seeing the delay as a sign of doubt on his part.

"No offense, but hasty decisions have not exactly served you in the past."

His remark more than stung. It reminded me of the person living next door, someone I, for my part, had been desperately trying to forget. But could Louie wall off his brother from his life? And could I really ask him to do something like that?

"True," I said, trying to calm myself down.

"In any case . . . we'll need at least that long to complete your education."

I thought he was kidding and shot him a wide, sarcastic smile. His expression quickly set me straight. He wasn't being facetious. Quite the opposite, in fact. I had rarely seen him so serious.

"My education . . . You mean . . . ?"

"Your erotic education, yes." He finished the thought for both of us.

His jaw contracted, an involuntary twitch that demonstrated how much this subject meant to him. It wasn't an idea that had come to him out of thin air. It was a philosophy, a way of life for him.

"We haven't already completed it?"

I was referring to the past few days, months, and even before that, when he was still just a ghost haunting my thoughts as well as the rooms at the Hôtel des Charmes, where I had abandoned myself to him and his delicious accomplices.

"That was more of a crash course in fundamentals."

Who did he think he was to look down on my knowledge of the erotic arts? I was perhaps new to the game, but I wasn't exactly scribbling with crayons, was I? Could I be that bad? Or was he accusing me of the same sensual shortcomings that his brother had once attributed to Aurora, my doppelganger?

My neck stiffened, and he withdrew his hand.

"Really? Just the fundamentals?"

"Yes. Don't take offense, but your real education is only just beginning."

I straightened and uncrossed my legs, preparing to leave.

A sidelong glance toward the door gave me an unrestricted view of Salomé's whip, which rippled over her partner's body.

She was like a panther stalking her prey. The man lying beneath her couldn't wait any longer. His member, which looked gigantic, extended toward her in excited jerking movements, and his tip was bouncing off her flat, amber belly like a rubber ball. Compared with her, I felt pretty inexperienced. Who wouldn't, in the face of such mastery?

"What's next? I'm curious . . ."

"As in any pedagogical journey, it will include a blend of theory . . ."

The reading he had assigned, I supposed.

" . . . practice . . ."

With him, he meant. And, on that front, it seemed to me that we had made a lot of progress over the past several months.

" . . . and, finally, exams to test your knowledge."

"Exams?" I exclaimed. "You want me to take an SAT in sex?"

"I was thinking more along the lines of a series of practical tests."

"What kind of practical tests?" I asked curtly, still sulking.

He hesitated, sweeping his gaze over the couples nearby, focusing his attention with keen interest on what he must have seen as expert examples of doggy-style and fellatio. Then he faced me again, his eyes gallantly boring into mine:

"Hmm . . . A bit like what we have here tonight. In fact, this could be considered the first in the series."

"The first . . . ," I breathed. "How many are you planning on administering?"

"I don't know. The number isn't important. The important thing to notice is your progress. What do you think?"

A normal girl—me, if I weren't so madly, stupidly, blindly in love with him—would have rejected the whole idea, leaving him alone with his poor man's *Arabian Nights*. I should have gone on the offensive and rebelled against his rule, but I gave in, resigned:

"Yes . . . I guess it's a good idea."

Another rite of passage, like his commandments the year before. And what else would he have in store for me after this? More castigation? More punishments? More orgasms? At least he had limited the number of rendezvous at the Hôtel des Charmes to ten. I couldn't help but notice that he had avoided setting an exact number of lessons, no doubt so that he could draw out my education as long as he deemed necessary and delay my coming-of-age indefinitely. To be sure, he hadn't made this education a precondition for our wedding—it was more of a preliminary. But it was obvious that he wouldn't abandon himself to me completely until he had the feeling that he possessed me in my entirety.

He must have read the fear in my eyes because, as he wrapped me in a protective embrace, he quickly added:

"Hey! Don't worry. I'm only thinking of your pleasure. And by no means am I reneging on the answer I've just given you."

"Guilty"—that was the word that crossed my mind . . . Louie felt guilty about his younger brother. It didn't come as a surprise, but it was the first time in months that I had noticed signs of guilt in my lover. When Louie had stolen his brother's bride-to-be, he had broken an agreement and revived a conflict that time and all of David's triumphs had laid to rest. Worse still, when Louie had stolen me, the doppelganger, David had effectively lost Aurora for a second time.

Louie needed to forget his disloyalty toward his brother by throwing himself into new games, new forms of intoxication. I was to be the bottle from which he got drunk, even if it meant breaking me between his hands.

"And it's up to us to make it fun."

"Fun . . . ?"

"Yes! We can write about all of our experiences in our Ten-Times-a-Day."

In the secrecy of room one, the notebook detailing my erotic thoughts had quite naturally become a space of common expression.

My desire for you is absolute.

Ever since Louie had written those words, we had been exchanging fantasies, desires, dreams, and memories in the shape of missives. Our source of inspiration was our bottomless reservoir of mutual desire.

"Why not?" I granted, reluctantly.

"Yes!" he cried, trying to persuade me. "Don't you see? It will all make sense in the notebook. And we'll transform these little tests into an authentic literary challenge."

He rambled on for several long minutes, as passionate as ever. He was convinced that this was the beginning of an important project, one that would unite us and help us defy the effects of time on desire.

I didn't know what to say or do that could curb his enthusiasm. Sadly, though my feelings for him were unchanged, I did not share his excitement. Louie's love was not something that he gave halfway. I'd known that since the beginning. If he chose you, you were his. And he wouldn't relent until he had conquered every bit of your intimacy, vanquishing it like virgin territory. He made fun of his brother's thirst for domination, but in many ways, that personal attribute was something the siblings shared.

I WAS SAVED BY SOMEONE I recognized in the doorway: David Garchey, my future husband's protégé and featured artist at the Alban Sauvage Gallery. Despite his provocative work, the young man had a timid demeanor. And his limp wave from across the room of naked bodies seemed farther away than it really was.

I stood abruptly and went to greet him, putting on my social smile as though we were old acquaintances.

"Hello! I'm so glad to see you again!"

My exaggerated enthusiasm made him even more ill at ease.

"Hello," he replied, extending a soft and moist hand.

Louie hurried behind me and seemed vaguely offended. Slipping a possessive hand over my ass, he offered these words of advice to the young artist:

"I leave you with my chef d'oeuvre, my friend. Take good care of her."

Then he went to attend to the new arrivals, leaving me with the shy kid, whose new haircut hid a good part of his chubby face.

"Do you have any upcoming shows?" I asked in an effort to make him feel more at ease.

"Yes. Soon. In a couple days, actually."

"At Alban's gallery?"

"Yeah. He's a big supporter of my work—he and Louie."

Hearing a kid who had only recently grown out of puberty call his pornographic form of provocation "work" was startling, to say the least. But I didn't let myself get distracted.

"I know. Louie gets deeply invested in some topics."

He must have grasped my meaning because he flushed and changed the subject:

"Especially now that he's a majority shareholder in the gallery," he was quick to specify.

That was the first I'd heard of it. I kept my annoyance to myself and instead asked him about his work, knowing full well that any artist worthy of the name only really cares to talk about him- or herself. I had no doubt that this awkward kid belonged to that category:

"What medium are you working in now? Inflatable toys still?"

"No, no . . ." He scowled, noting the undercurrent of sarcasm. "My new installation is very video-oriented."

"Really? What kind of films?"

"More or less in real time, captured using a webcam . . ."

"Interesting," I said to be nice.

" . . . or, like tonight, surveillance cameras."

"Tonight?"

His furrowed brow told me that he had said too much and that he didn't know how to fix it. He no doubt considered keeping me happy—I was, after all, his patron's fiancée—an essential part of his job.

"Yes, we can see everything from the control room."

He was blinking wildly: second blunder. His third, even, if I counted his reference to Louie's recent stake in the Sauvage Gallery.

"You've piqued my curiosity!" I simpered, breaking into a weird high-pitched laugh. "Will you show me?"

"Okay . . ."

He was quiet for a second before he realized that I was

patiently waiting to follow his lead. Crossing the living room, now filled with coats, bustiers, and crinolines, he drew me toward the foyer, where a small door hidden under the main staircase took us into the depths of the house.

The fact that he was the first person to give me a tour of this part of the house was perhaps not ideal, and when we reached a heavy reinforced door that opened onto the basement, I felt a shiver run through me. Down there, the decor was sober and modern, a stark contrast to the remodeled floors above, which had been restored to their original patina. We walked through a gray and soulless hallway, whose only adornment was a set of electronic cords. At the end of the corridor, we were greeted by a second metallic door that opened onto a room furnished with a computer console and over a dozen monochromatic screens.

"Here we can see almost everything that's going on in the house."

The porch, the entrance, the living room, the dining room—where we could see couples embracing—the library, the kitchen, the garden, and even our future bedroom: not a room was missing.

But that is not what caught my attention.

"Are you recording everything?" I asked, vaguely gesturing toward the wall of screens.

"No, just the ones where you can see the red lights blinking."

In other words: the entry, the living room, the dining room.

In the upper left-hand corner of this mosaic, two of the screens were black.

"What about those? Can we turn them on?"

"I don't know . . . ," he said, clearly uncomfortable.

"Come on," I encouraged him. "It must be something fun."

He obeyed like a zombie, his trembling finger pressing a sequence of buttons. I instantly recognized the rooms. They didn't belong to Mars House but to its neighbor, Duchesnois House. The first screen showed the Pompeiian living room, which was empty and plunged in darkness. The second was a shot of David's bedroom. It was not much better lit, but I could make out the distinct image of two bodies pressed against each other. They changed positions on the bed with a kind metronomic regularity, as if they were being timed. I had no doubt as to the man's identity—I recognized his athletic build and the silk armband on his left arm—but I had to wait a moment longer, as Garchey cleared his throat in embarrassment, before I caught a glimpse of the lithe creature in David's arms.

Suddenly she lifted the curtain of blond hair from her face, and I got a clear view of Alice Simoncini's ecstatic smile. David's former mistress, whom he had once rejected, was now back in her prince's good graces.

2

A few days earlier . . .
in early May 2010

In truth, that night was not my first visit to Mars House. You will perhaps recall the time my cat, Felicity, ran into the yard, and I knocked on the house's royal-blue door, which Richard, Louie's chauffeur, answered and then quickly slammed in my face. Back then, I had only caught a glimpse of a gigantic construction site. It was nothing like the splendor you can see here today.

But there was another time a few days before Louie threw his transtemporal ball to mark our official move-in date. I was just entering *my* foyer for the first time when I heard a familiar voice:

"Holy crap . . . This is insane!"

I didn't need to turn around to know who was cursing her amazement. Sophia came to stand beside me and take in the dazzling sight before us. Not all of the furniture had yet arrived, nor was anything in its proper place. In this near-empty space, we were therefore able to admire the exquisite restoration.

"Isn't it, darling?" I joked.

"And here I'd thought the house next door was too luxurious."

I remembered her childlike reaction during her first visit to Duchesnois House.

"Yeah. Well, let's just say that here I don't intend to hang out in sweats or flannel pajamas."

"No kidding," she agreed. "You're going to have to rethink your wardrobe."

"Like I need an excuse!"

Her eyes made a panoramic sweep over the decor.

"Yeah, but this time you're going to have to do your shopping in a museum, as opposed to the Galeries Lafayette!"

She had no idea . . . particularly in light of the ball Louie was planning. She wasn't invited. Past relations between my best friend and the man I loved had been rather peculiar.

From behind us, a deeper voice joined our oohs and aahs.

"Damn! You're not in Nanterre anymore, girls."

Holding his helmet, his leather jacket unzipped, Fred Morino, my ex, had arrived at almost the same moment as Sophia. He was nodding his head like a dog in the backseat of a car, admiring the magnificent building and whistling through his teeth. He and my best friend had never gotten along when we were going out. But ever since the catastrophe that was my wedding day, an event during which they had allied themselves in order to support me, they had remained in contact. I suspected that "checking in on how Elle is doing" was only a pretext.

Over Monacos on café terraces and occasional phone calls "just to see how you're doing," a friendship had blossomed between them. And the motorcyclist no doubt hoped for something more, somewhere in the back of his mind. For the time being, their relationship had remained at the level of friendship, and I was glad to see it. Who wouldn't want the people they cared about to become friends?

After hugs and congratulations, they helped me carry a few boxes and bags I had brought with me from the Hôtel des Charmes into the house. Monsieur Jacques, the hotel's concierge, had kindly lent me an old truck. I had also made a detour to the house in Nanterre, where I had grabbed some clothing and old papers.

"This isn't the Paris that people like Fred and I know either," Sophia remarked, underlining the social chasm that separated them from my new life.

I have always liked moving day. It's a time to hang out with friends, to reminisce, to leave old memories behind, and to look toward the future. That was why I had declined Louie's repeated offers to hire professionals. A couple of enthusiastic friends, a few hours, affectionate digs—that was all I needed.

"Are you sure?"

"Yes! Honestly, what are friends for if not to do some heavy lifting from time to time?"

Honestly? The level of camaraderie that day exceeded my expectations. And having them there as I moved into my new life was really comforting. It was something I found myself missing sometimes with Louie's intensity. Loving and being loved by Louie Barlet was a strong gust of sea air; it was savage, exciting, completely mad. It was nothing like the gentle wind one typically expects from everyday, more ordinary relations.

"Will you give us a tour of your castle?" Fred asked, visibly impressed by his surroundings.

To be honest, Louie hadn't given me the keys until that very morning, and I hadn't had much time to see the house. While looking for a place to put all my boxes, I had even come across a door to the basement that none of my keys would unlock.

"What do you think your man is hiding in the basement? A dungeon?"

Coming from Sophia, this hypothesis had nothing to do with medieval architecture. Ever since I had told her about my man's erotic fantasies, and since she herself had been witness to them during a joint expedition to the Hôtel des Charmes, she had been teasing me about them.

The fact that, from her perspective, I had gone from something of a virginal angel to the submissive in a BDSM relationship was a never-ending source of surprise and delight.

"If that were the case, don't you think we would have already tested all of the equipment!"

"Yeah, I still want to see⁻"

"In your dreams!"

In terms of dreams, our bedroom suite was a masterpiece. Here more than anywhere else in the house, Louie had paid scrupulous—almost maniacal—attention to the details of the original design. He had consulted an impressive number of documents from Louis Visconti's time to achieve an exact historical replica. For the moment, it was the only room that had been completed. Nothing was missing, not a single piece of furniture or tiny detail. Here, one could admire faithful reproductions by master craftsman Patrick Bénard: an antique-looking bed that was raised on a platform, a low cabinet decorated with porcelain medallions, two mahogany armchairs, two other chairs made from the same species of wood, one large mirror, a barber's table embellished with Egyptian heads, and, finally, a chandelier. In addition, there was a red marble chimney flanked by gilded bronze sconces.

"Well, well, Madame la Marquise," the cheeky Sophia exclaimed. "You won't be making babies here but gold ingots!"

Neither Fred nor I laughed—she was right. In fact, I had been wondering what would become of our unbridled, light-hearted, spontaneous sex life in surroundings such as these, which came with centuries' worth of baggage. Of course, there was that old theory according to which our illustrious predecessors had left traces of their erotic activities in the walls of the rooms we now inhabited. But had those memories been able to survive all the layers of plaster and fresh paint? What was left of Mademoiselle Mars's sighs?

The more I thought about it, the more a dungeon seemed like a potentially good way to keep our libidos intact, a way to avoid being suffocated by all the gold and sumptuous wall coverings.

THE DOORBELL RANG—THIS WAS THE first time I'd heard it—drawing me out of my thoughts. I made my way to the ground floor to play my new role as mistress of the house. Behind the blue door, leaning against the column on the left of the porch, I found Armand, who was holding a pet carrier.

"Hello, Elle."

I hadn't seen him since my abandoned wedding day, when I'd made the imprudent decision to return to Rue de la Tour-des-Dames before going to meet Louie at the Hôtel des

Charmes. I could still hear him calling after me, in my soiled white dress, a barefoot runaway bride: "Elle! Come back!"

A vexed meow from Felicity put an end to my flashback. In any case, what would he have said to me that day? What words could have changed my mind? What could have extinguished my love for Louie?

"Hello, Armand," I said, "I . . ."

I didn't know what to say. He was in David's service and therefore in the opposing camp. A camp that had seen fit, moreover, to send Louie the bill one month later for our aborted wedding. The elder brother, being a gentleman, had paid every last cent, without a word of complaint, including Madonna's cancellation fees.

It was an enemy camp all right: David hadn't even shown up to my mother's funeral, nor had he made any efforts to present his condolences. No card, no flowers, no messages of any sort. Not even a text message. Nothing to indicate that he felt anything for my suffering. Louie, on the other hand, had been extremely attentive and supportive, listening for as long as I'd needed him to listen, finding the right words of comfort, knowing also when it was best to keep quiet and let me cry—into his neck or on his shoulder.

"I have Felicity here for you."

"Thanks," I said, seizing the hard plastic crate.

"I'm sorry, I didn't want to balance the books on the day you moved in . . . but David wanted everything taken care of as soon as possible."

"I understand. Don't worry about it."

"Felicity has been having a hard time. Last week, another one of her scuffles produced a victim."

"A victim?" I inquired, to be polite.

"An old piece from the Ming dynasty that belonged to David's father, Andre."

David could afford to replace such trifles. I wasn't going to get worked up over something like that.

"Annabelle, I don't know how to say this . . ."

He was twisting his old wool cardigan like a little girl playing with the hem of her dress.

"So don't say anything," I said, my tone more bitter than I had intended.

"We are divided by circumstance, in spite of ourselves."

I was so touched by his demeanor that I hardly noticed the black sedan pulling up behind him.

"I know—"

"What I mean is, even though I understand David's anger, I still care for you."

"Yes, it's normal that you would still care for Louie," I said.

"Not just Louie," Armand insisted. "You, too."

As he said this, he took me in his arms. His brief and awkward hug was so sudden that I almost dropped Felicity's crate. Annoyed, my cat meowed. He released me at the sound of someone calling, almost yelling, from the street. Then, two car doors slammed and two elegant persons stepped out of the luxury vehicle.

"Armand!"

It was David—in an immaculate suit, his chin cocked, his eyes as dark as the sky was clear—together with Alice, who was blonder and more statuesque than ever.

I turned my attention away from Armand for a moment and quickly searched through my handbag, looking for the key to Duchesnois House. I had kept it all this time, waiting for the right moment to return it to its rightful owner. But I wasn't looking forward to facing David, and I had even considered slipping the key into his mailbox.

Once I had found it, I tried to press it into the butler's hand, but he refused it. With a blink of his eyes, he seemed to be saying: *Keep it. You never know.*

From behind the old man, standing only a few paces away from us, David started barking again. The master's patience was clearly being tried by his servant's insubordination. He didn't even so much as glance in my direction.

"Armand!"

This latter slowly turned, a weary look in his eyes.

"Sir, please don't dawdle," David said, his tone softening. "The neighborhood isn't what it used to be."

Then, he grabbed Armand by the shoulders, as if recovering something that belonged to him, and led him to the gate of the house next door. Still, he said nothing to me.

Behind them, as if she were lugging her bag down Avenue Montaigne like a schoolgirl, Alice was wearing a triumphant smile. With each sway of her hips, as she teetered in ridiculously high heels over the cobblestones, she seemed to be saying, *Look, all of this is mine now,* until at last she disappeared into the house next door.

"Come on," I whispered to my cat. "Let's go inside."

I found my two sidekicks in the foyer.

"You okay, hon? You look pale . . ."

"Yes, yeah, I'm fine."

"Did you see a ghost or something?" Fred pressed.

"Kind of . . ." I grimaced.

"You ran into David! Don't tell me he was the one to bring you the creature?"

I concentrated on freeing Felicity from her crate, hoping we could soon move on to another topic of conversation.

"Yes . . . And no, he wasn't the one who brought Felicity. Armand was."

"I've always found him sketchy," Sophia asserted.

"Why?" I asked, surprised.

"Dunno. Just an impression . . . For instance, on your 'wedding' day"—she made air quotes with her fingers—"when everyone found out that you wouldn't be coming . . ."

"Well, what is it?"

"I don't know. He almost seemed relieved."

"That's probably because he figured it would be less work if the caterer just took the untouched food back with him," Fred speculated.

"Ha!" My friend laughed. "Wait, has the big boss fired you yet?"

Sophia's question was intriguing, and I was glad to have their attention off me. Fred worked as a sound guy at BTV, and the fact that he was still there was something of a mystery. He had kept his job well after Louie and I had been fired, and there was no sign that he would encounter the same fate. Every morning he went into work expecting to be called into a fateful meeting. And in the evening, he would return home, as safe in his job as the day before. Everyone was really happy with his work. And his coworkers, who apparently knew about his past with the ex–future Madame Barlet, called him "the miracle."

"If you want my opinion, I think he just forgot about me."

"It's possible," I agreed.

"Remember that time I came to see you in your office, right before you were fired, and he mistook me for an intern? So then for him to remember that I'm your ex . . ."

"At least in the meantime you have a job and a paycheck at the end of the month," Sophia whined. Her job prospects as a dancer were especially desperate of late.

"Oh, I'm not complaining!"

"And yet the people who work for the Barlet Group have their fair share of horror stories! Am I right?"

Louie's voice surprised us all. None of us had heard him enter. I quickly went to greet him with a kiss but kept myself from pressing my lips too hard. As I've said: I was not yet accustomed to public displays of affection.

Although Fred was grateful to my beau for having taken him out of the ranks of the unemployed, relations had cooled between the two. I suspected it had something to do with Louie's new role in my life, one that used to belong to Fred. My ex wasn't jealous anymore. I could tell he had gotten over our breakup and moved on. But there was still some tension between us.

"Well, for me it's not exactly slave labor . . . ," Fred said, downplaying the situation. "I've known worse."

Fred was in an awkward position, one that made him something of a double agent. He was both our friend and David's employee, and he had access to the goings-on at the Barlet Group—something that Louie could legitimately envy these days. And Louie was not ashamed to take advantage of the situation:

"What's new at the station? Is David still flirting with his Koreans?"

"You know, I don't know all the secrets. The only major piece of news these days is Simoncini's return—"

"Alice?" I cried, a little too vigorously.

"Although no one knows what she'll be doing exactly."

"He'd already found someone to fill her former job," Louie confirmed.

"Yes . . . Apparently it's been musical chairs in management."

"Some girls at least get compensated for sleeping around!" Sophia moaned.

Alice's haughty look a few minutes earlier now made sense.

"They haven't made any official announcements, I suppose?" Louie asked.

"No. Rumor has it that David is organizing a small press conference, more for gossip magazines than business journals."

"Where is it supposed to take place?"

"Not at the tower—otherwise everybody would know about it."

The doorbell rang again, interrupting him midsecret. I went to the door, where I saw Ysiam's sweet smile through the window. The bellboy from the Hôtel des Charmes was holding a large manila envelope, and I noticed that he wasn't wearing his livery, which meant that he had come to see us during his free time.

"Hello, Mademoiselle!"

"Hello, Ysiam. Please, come in."

He declined with a timid gesture, thrusting the envelope toward me.

"Oh, no, no. I'm just here to give you this."

"That's very kind of you, thanks."

He quickly left, and my two assistants went back to work, this time with some help from Louie, to the extent that he could help, what with his bad leg. Together, we would be able to get everything done in no time.

But before returning inside, I stayed at the door for a

moment and mechanically opened the thick envelope. For the past several months, I had been having my mail forwarded from Nanterre and Duchesnois House to our room at the Hôtel des Charmes. As thoughtful as ever, Monsieur Jacques had apparently taken the initiative to have my mail brought here.

I quickly sorted through the stack, which contained a number of bills, ads, and promotions. Nothing interesting. However, the last envelope caught my attention.

Mademoiselle Lebourdais
The Hôtel des Charmes
55 Rue Jean-Baptiste Pigalle
75009 Paris

There had no doubt been some sort of mix-up. I didn't know of a Mademoiselle Lebourdais who worked at the Hôtel des Charmes. She was probably a secretary or an accountant, someone who didn't come into contact with the clientele.

Without paying it any more attention, I set the envelope on a small mahogany table, thinking I would return it to Ysiam the next time he came by the house.

Felicity, who had just gotten back from her reconnaissance mission, was now rubbing herself against my legs and purring with contentment, as if to say, *We're going to be happy here.* I wanted to believe it, too.

3

May 12, 2010

M y man may not have determined the exact number or nature of the tests he had in mind for me, but I knew that I would be judged according to my own initiative and ability to meet his demands. The more I could surprise him, the more points I would score. The closer I got to the end of my studies, the more completely Louie would belong to me, the more he would be mine, a prisoner in my arms, my loins, my sex, all of which were open wide in anticipation of him.

AS I WAITED FOR NEW episodes in this sexy saga, I began acquainting myself with life in Mars House. As opposed to the house next door, where David had taken care to combine old and new elements, here it was difficult to feel at home. It was so sophisticated and imbued with so much history. It would probably take several months before I would start to feel comfortable here. Thank God Sophia was taking any excuse to see me. Her presence alone was convivial, and it was definitely helping me acclimate.

"Engaged!" she exclaimed, slack-jawed, when I told her of my plan.

"I mean, we're not going to throw a big party or anything."

"Yeah, I got it, but still . . ."

Surprise, joy, and a hint of jealousy—a range of emotions crossed her face.

"Oh, speaking of engagements . . . you haven't seen the best this year."

"What is it?"

Drawn to the sound of our voices, Felicity had come into the little living room, the same room where I had seen Louie's guests going at it the night of our housewarming party. My cat rubbed herself against my legs, then climbed up to my knees.

"Do you have an Internet connection in this castle yet?"

"Yeah." I shrugged. "We can't live completely in the nineteenth century."

"Where's your laptop? I have something crazy to show you."

I went to find it, displacing Felicity, who looked annoyed to be thrown off the soft cushion of my legs. I opened my computer.

"Okay, now type 'David Barlet + Alice Simoncini,'" she instructed.

"Now what have they done?"

A memory of the black-and-white real-time video of the two lovers came back to me in waves. Ever since our housewarming, the metallic door that opened onto the basement—the Dungeon, as Sophia had dubbed it—had remained hermetically shut. Had David Garchey mentioned his blunders to Louie?

"You'll see. Go on, type!"

As soon as I entered the words into the search engine, an impressive number of results appeared on my screen. The first of them included a vignette of photographs showing the two lovebirds embracing tenderly on a sofa I knew too well.

"Now, click on a video."

"Which one?"

"It doesn't matter; they're all the same. They sold an exclusive story to *Paris Match*. It's been online since this morning."

"To *Paris Match*? But I thought they were going to do a small official press conference."

"Exactly . . . That's what's so funny. Click, girl, click!"

Which is what I did, my index finger trembling, feeling more curious than worried.

After an ad for a family minivan and a shot of the famous weekly magazine's logo, I immediately recognized the setting: the living room in Duchesnois House. There was no doubt about it. Alice looked like an Amazon. She was sitting in an erect position, her legs folded beneath her, her blond mane smoother than ever. Clearly, someone had done her hair and makeup. Even David, who for once was not wearing a suit, was all smiles in his light-pink shirt—unbuttoned to show off his clean-shaven chest—and he looked more suntanned than usual.

Suddenly we heard the interviewer's voice:

"David Barlet, tell me, why are you speaking out today, with Alice at your side?"

"Quite simply to make our relationship public. And to show the world that—"

"That it's serious." Alice, all cleavage, completed his sentence.

They then leaned in toward each other and exchanged a quick peck.

"May I ask how long . . . ?"

" . . . we've been together? It's been five months."

"Soon it'll be six," the buxom creature added. "Right, kitten?"

Alice's smile widened as she pinched David's nose, the kind of gesture typically reserved for private moments.

It wasn't just ridiculous, and a little indecent; it was totally grotesque.

"In that case, you won't mind if I ask whether or not you have any *plans*?"

"No, I don't mind," David said. "We're planning on getting engaged, very soon."

"That's great news," the interviewer gushed from behind the camera. "My congratulations."

"Thank you!" they replied in unison, closing the gap between each other in an impeccably timed embrace.

A few shots showed the two in various rooms throughout the house. Here they were acting busy; there they were clasping what looked like expensive jewelry around each other's wrists; here they were exchanging little kisses; and there he was putting his arm around her waist. Then we were abruptly brought back to the living room, with a close-up shot of "kitten."

"I believe you'd like to make another announcement, David . . ."

"Indeed. Alice is not only the woman I love; she is also a media professional, one of the brightest I have ever met in my career. In fact, those who know us know that that's how we met."

"At BTV, where Alice used to be the director of marketing, is that right?"

"Director of international marketing," Alice corrected in a pinched tone.

"And in a few days, she will officially become my right-hand woman at the Barlet Group's flagship station, with the title of Assistant General Director. I know that with her help we'll be able to push BTV up to the position it deserves."

"Which is to say?"

"The premier news station in Europe."

Forgotten: her shocking offense with Christopher Haynes. Expunged: her blunt dismissal. That they were both able to have such amnesia while facing the camera, without so much as blinking or stuttering, showed some serious acting talent.

Sophia reached toward my laptop and clicked pause.

"Isn't that insane?"

"Yeah . . . ," I agreed, torn between shock and laughter.

"You should see how people are reacting on social media! Everyone is talking about them—and not in a good way. Public consensus seems to be somewhere between ridicule and shock. Fred even told me that the unions want to hold David accountable for the damage it has caused to the Barlet Group's image."

"I'm not surprised . . . ," I breathed. "But I don't see why David would sacrifice so much with such a farce."

And yet the marriage proposal that he had planned for me, with its catalogue of clichés bordering on poor taste, had shown me that this man was not afraid of being corny and over-the-top. And that, even though he was an important businessman with all manner of fancy diplomas and bank accounts, he was more than capable of acting like a tacky vacationer in fluorescent beachwear.

"I mean, it was clearly her idea. Did you see how much that bitch was gloating?! She could hardly contain herself! She looked like a kid who had just won a stuffed animal from a claw machine!"

She was right. And yet I couldn't help but see the work of my ex-fiancé in this pathetic display. I couldn't shake the inexplicable impression that, although this ridiculous show was surely meant to dazzle the masses, it also had something to do with our fiasco the year before, and that David had not gotten over it. And the more he tried to pretend otherwise, the more I was convinced that these public displays were really addressed to me, and me alone, the woman who had had the gall to reject him. Above all, it seemed, he wanted to throw his new life in my face, to shout for all to hear that he had moved on.

Who did he think he was fooling?

I REFUSED TO TAKE THE bait. I had no intention of dueling this two-bit Napoleon and Josephine. Still, to put distance between our past and our future, Louie and I needed to formalize our engagement. Even if we kept it private. Even if it remained a secret. Perhaps some sort of engagement party, after all . . .

Yes, I needed to organize something soon. And that is how, with the thought of the imperial couple in the back of my head, I had the idea of Malmaison. But not just any version of Malmaison . . .

"WHERE ARE WE GOING?" LOUIE inquired, blindfolded, as I pushed him into the backseat of the limousine. "May I know what you have in store for me today, Mademoiselle?"

"Absolutely . . . not, darling. What would be the point of the surprise if I told you in advance?"

Delighted by the fact that I was suddenly taking charge, he relinquished his cane and obediently held out his wrists to be bound.

"Richard," he said in a joyful tone, "don't tell me you're in on this?"

Oh, yes, he was, and in more than one way. Ever since I had officially become a part of his employer's life, Richard the Chauffeur had relaxed around me. To say that we were now friends would be an overstatement, but I saw that he made himself available to me and was completely devoted to his boss. When I'd presented him with my plan, he'd therefore been more than accommodating. My idea was to kidnap Louie and take him to Empress Josephine's room on the second floor in the north wing of Château de Malmaison. We had to take great care so as to avoid revealing our final destination to our *victim*.

LOUIE'S HIGHLY REFINED SENSES AND acute faculty of deduction wouldn't make things easy.

"We're entering a second tunnel, with a bridge between the two . . . ," he guessed aloud as we drove out of Neuilly-sur-Seine. "Wait . . . we're going to Malmaison, is that it?"

As we had previously agreed, Richard and I were not answering his questions. This was not supposed to be a game of hot and cold. He had already guessed too much.

What he could never guess, however, was that Richard had gone into his address book and found some very relevant contact information. A few phone calls—to National Napoleon Museums, Rueil-Malmaison's town hall, management at the Malmaison Castle Museum, and a handful of other officials and factotums whose palms we greased—and the castle was ours. When we pulled up to the estate, the gates magically opened.

The main building was all ours until the next morning.

Naturally, we had had to sign a number of releases and pay a hefty deposit in case of any damage. However, no one expected there to be any problems, of course.

"Gravel! We are driving over gravel!" Louie exclaimed.

The limousine was in fact driving through a wide driveway lined with conical thujas, English oaks, and a variety of wild and domestic flowers.

I was also on the verge of blossoming, my senses were on the verge of exploding wildly. The seeds of desire that Louie had spent the past year planting in me were ripe and ready to burst forth. The role of pleasure master came with a number of responsibilities, and my stomach had been in knots for the past several days, but that only heightened my desire and fed my lascivious imagination.

"You be quiet, Monsieur," I whispered sensually into Louie's ear. "You be quiet . . . or I will have to punish you!"

This titillating promise made him smile: he knew that the wait would be long and hard but that the rewards would be equally intense.

He stepped out of the car, still blindfolded, and we guided him through the main courtyard to the building's turquoise entry.

The foyer was flanked by thick columns of pink marble. We turned right, passing through an elegant billiard room, and then pushed open a double door onto a stairway that led up to the second floor. Richard the Chauffeur and I had already explored the castle in order to ensure that everything went smoothly on the day of my surprise. This was the day.

The first floor was laid out in an L-shape, and the empress's bedroom was located next to its crux. We walked left around the outside of the circular room before arriving at its stunning mirrored French doors, whose reflective surface made the sixteen-sided canopy room seem immense.

I helped Louie step over the wooden partition meant to keep visitors on the side of the room with the windows. I then sat him down on one of the red sofas, both of which feature an embroidered uppercase *J* in gold thread. Atop an Egyptian pedestal table in gold and mahogany sat a bottle of chilled champagne and two flutes, along with an assortment of petits fours, macarons, and calissons—a reminder of the ones Louie had once given my mother, Maude.

"Are the games over yet? May I take off my blindfold?"

"Wait, no! Just a minute . . ."

I dismissed Richard—he disappeared with surprising stealth, considering his build—and drew the thick curtains before undressing. There would be no striptease this time. The surprise I had in store for him went beyond the purview of a basic stripper.

I checked one of the gigantic mirrors to make sure that the ink hadn't smeared and then gave Louie the signal he had been dying to hear.

"You can open your eyes."

He stared at me in silence for a long moment. He was visibly delighted with what he saw.

"My flower . . . ," he breathed.

It's true, I was his flower. And what a flower! Interlacing stems running up my thighs, a burst of pink and red rosebuds blossoming on my stomach and breasts—the whole thing, arabesques and bright colors, made my curves comelier than they had ever been before.

And if now I could accept that title—his flower—which at one time I would have found inane or too big for me, it was because I had opened up to him during our months spent in the greenhouse that was the Hôtel des Charmes. There, our love had blossomed and my body had learned how to tame the vigorous life coursing through him.

I had spent that same morning with Sophia, who had carefully painted the various patterns we had chosen together onto my body. She had taken great care in drawing the arabesques of the stems and the delicate petals. Thanks to her painstaking attention to detail, she had transformed my entire body into a gigantic bouquet.

First hour, undo the bouquet

With the help of a cotton towel and a moisturizing cream, Louie spent the first hour unveiling me, unearthing me from layers of paint, erasing the flowers that covered my body, one by one. Sophia's experience with face paint and costumes in the dance world had come in handy. She had chosen an ink that disappeared with the first wipe of a cloth, the kind that practically evaporated when it came into contact with the milky cream. I could tell by the concentrated look on his face that Louie was in awe of my body, and as he slowly uncovered my skin from the verdant envelope, it was as if he were discovering me for the first time.

"And after?" he asked, concerned, though he had only just started working on the vast field of my torso and breasts.

"After? We still have nine hours to pleasure each other."

"You're going to make love to me like Josephine, is that it?"

I couldn't pull one over on him.

Josephine de Beauharnais had made Malmaison into the perfect showcase for her floral passions. An Eden as lush as her native Martinique.

My man's gestures were gentle but methodical. He approached each area of my anatomy with the sensitivity of an archeologist uncovering a treasure, using his towel like a paintbrush. The touch of the soft cloth made me shiver, and I almost moaned at times. As he uncovered each zone, it quivered and opened itself to him like a new petal trembling in gratitude.

Second hour, inhale my flower's perfume

When he reached between my legs, toward my dewy lips, I pushed his hand back. We had all night. I wanted our delicate preliminaries to last as long as possible. Tonight, we would be as patient as gardeners. We would let our desires grow with the night, drawing from the rich soil of our fantasies. We would avoid rushing things and laying it all to waste. We would respect our natures.

"Smell it . . . speak to it."

He took me in his arms and carried me to the bed—I had been told to be particularly careful with this piece of furniture, which the museum's curator had assured me was original to the house, and in which Josephine herself had slept. Louie set me down on my side and placed his face between my thighs.

He buried his nose in my rose and spent a long moment breathing its scent, savoring its crude perfume, which was a blend of sharp and musky notes. I had taken care only to clean it with water these past few days. That way my natural odor prevailed.

"I love smelling you . . . I could stay like this for days," he confided for the first time.

So I wasn't alone in fetishizing the scent of our intimate parts. This discovery filled me with a new confidence. No longer would I fear him catching an odorous whiff. We could sniff each other like two curious dogs, and we could even express ourselves freely on the subject.

Louie didn't know it but, in addition to the reading list he had prescribed, I had gotten my hands on other very instructive works that I'd found during a solitary trip to La Musardine. These included a book by someone called E.D., a mysterious author from the 1900s, who wrote an erotic gem called *Odor di femina*.

The short novel follows the trajectory of a man who grows tired of sex, which he finds bland and odorless, and moves to the countryside in search of authentic scents.

"I wish I were a perfumer and could distill your nectar into a perfume," Louie murmured.

As if to convince me, he gave up on eloquence and plunged his nose into my vulva. He buried his face in me like a puppy, smearing himself with translucent and odorous fluid, raising his head for a second to sniff the scent that now clung to his upper lip, and then diving back into me to further enjoy my secret fragrance. As he pleasured me, he grew madly intoxicated by my scent.

Third hour, erase my petals

Labia majora, nymphae, perineum . . . the abandoned children of female pleasure. What man will give those mucous membranes the attention and know-how they require?

Mine. My man.

His finger pads, so silky. The tip of his tongue, so precise. He worked to give my fleshy folds what they deserved. A woman's vagina is a complex plant. No man can claim to understand it if he has not spent time with it, if he has not taken a moment to carefully explore its innermost recesses, its nooks and crannies, the entire moving, changing, expanding, dilating, lubricated structure, which hardly ever looks exactly the same. It takes time and patience. We had the former, and he the latter.

Every now and again, he rolled a fold of flesh between

his index and middle fingers, working his way up toward my clitoral hood, before reaching its base and then turning back toward my anus. Each journey of his fingers produced a wave that radiated through my vulva.

Increasingly, I felt a need for him to penetrate me, there, without delay, even if it was just with a finger or two. But again and again, I found the strength to resist, and I tried to concentrate on the delicate and intense sensations.

We had been engaged in preliminaries for three hours, focused on the fusion of our bodies. Even the most subtle, most localized of touches brought them closer together than ever before. An electrical current ran through us. And although the room had been plunged in darkness for some time, our features and shapes obscured, we had not thought to turn on a light until now. I would have preferred candlelight, but because of the wallpaper, it was strictly prohibited.

The light was a bit harsh for our taste, though at least the fixtures were hidden in folds of red satin. Louie was so focused on my slow-blossoming flower that he found in it a new source of wonder.

"It looks like it's making its own light!"

Like a phosphorescent flower, my vagina seemed to give off an iridescent light. And when Louie raised his head between my thighs, he was haloed by my inner glow.

Fourth hour, gather nectar from my pistil

We massaged each other's bodies as one tends to the nourishing earth. Shoots of pleasure such as we had never experienced began to spring forth. Sensation shot through every part of our bodies, sometimes concentrated in a particular area, sometimes spread out over the whole—nipples, lips, bellies, asses, tongues.

Our desire had grown too strong, and it seemed to me that it was time to relinquish control. We would leave our calm and polite gestures behind, and give free rein to a desire that had until now been structured and tended like a French garden.

Pointing to my clitoris, I commanded him:

"Tend to it . . . Suck it."

He was better at it than anyone, better even than he had ever been before. He took his time with every step, and it was so pleasurable that I could hardly even stand it.

First, he began by softly licking my outer fold, under which I could feel my sensitive button impatiently coming to life. It seemed as though my clitoris was growing in direct response to his touch. With each moist brush of his tongue, it swelled a bit more, like the time-lapsed image of a flower blossoming.

"In your mouth. Put it in your mouth," I begged, after several long, delicious moments.

He pooched his lips and began sucking my protrusion, first slowly, then faster and faster, unconcerned by the suction sound he was making and that was driving me wild. He wasn't treating it like a simple piece of candy. Each time his lips closed around my clitoris, his tongue caressed it, kneading and pressing into the glans itself. The maneuver had to be executed so quickly that it didn't always work. But each successful attempt sent a shock up through my genitals and into my loins, forcing an irrepressible moan through my throat.

I came at least three or four times during this fourth hour. Between orgasms, Louie gave me just enough time to catch my breath, and my clitoris just enough space to calm down, before touching me again, attacking my senses in a determined effort to exhaust my body in every way possible. Good seed planted in fertile earth with proper watering and just the right amount of sun: it all made for the most beautiful flower of pleasure.

Fifth hour, massage his stem

I didn't want our engagement party to be all about my pleasure. The castle was shrouded in darkness, and nocturnal animals had begun to play their symphony, when I decided that it was time for the flower to take care of her gardener.

Louie was still wearing his clothes, which I calmly stripped off, layer by layer. When at last he was naked, I kissed each of his many tattoos, growing drunk off their ink, inhaling their permanent designs as he had erased my temporary garden. I felt him shudder at the touch of my lips.

My lips. During our voluntary captivity in the Josephine, he had written an ode to them, penning a poem in a literary form I had never heard of before: the blazon. Popular in the Renaissance, the blazon is a short poem that pays homage to one part of a woman's anatomy. I was his model, his muse. And in just a few minutes of staring at me in rapt attention, he'd composed this:

Lips pressed to my body
Lips melted into me
Lips that never fail, never miss
Lips so fleshy they're swallowed in a kiss
just when they thought they were free
Lips, flowers of thy being
Lips, eternally blooming
Lips, affixed to me and to my being
Lips I'll never release
Lips, try it, if you please!

I may not have had his way with a pen, but I did have those two strips of flesh that he loved so much.

Echoing each verse, I pressed my lips wherever they urged me to put them. I wetted them and planted them on him as if to suck up more nectar. My little trick was driving him wild, I could tell. He, who was usually so calm, was writhing in delight and hungry for more.

When at last my lips closed around the tip of his penis, I thought he might suffocate. He opened his mouth wide, as if gaping for air.

"Yes . . . ," he managed to growl.

My lips had been in his service for a year, and Louie was fully aware of what they could do once wrapped around his swollen gland. He was familiar with the sensation of my mouth squeezing over his shaft and wetting his entire member, down to his testicles. And yet, that night, I managed to surprise him. I had imagined all manner of variations, thousands of original ways to mold my lips to his member. My lips pumped, sucked, swallowed, until they seemed to become one with his virility.

"Careful," he warned in a hushed cry.

I didn't want him to come in my mouth. Not this time. I quickly drew back, grabbing his ass and pressing him against my torso.

His sperm burst forth, fertilizing my chest. Where Louie had earlier erased black floral motifs, he had now drawn a white design. The blotch of semen slowly formed petals on my skin, extending between my breasts and into the crook of my neck.

Sixth hour, make a bed of flowers

The sixth hour was one of mutual effusion, freer movement, and more staid positions. It was already late, and we were flagging. In order to combat such waves of exhaustion, I had planned a few innovations into our program for the evening: all subsequent positions now had either to be named after a flower or to look like one. With hardly any transition, we tried one evocative position after another: the lotus, the rosebud, the orchid, and the vine. This last one had us stretched out against each other, our arms and legs inextricably intertwined.

The vegetal was not, however, simply a question of nomenclature in this singular way of making love. Rather, it was located in the fluidity and extreme languor of our movements. The way in which Louie was thrusting himself into me was neither hurried nor violent. He penetrated me, but at the surface, at my inside's edge. His touch was an envelopment. His spasms, a response to the nectar rising in him, in me.

Making love to someone for a whole hour, in an almost immobile embrace, while suppressing a growing need to orgasm is an intense challenge. I was aware of my partner's most subtle movements. The combination of desire and pleasure was overwhelming.

The sixth hour was magical. As in nature, nothing was lost. The pleasure felt by one fed the desire of the other, the cycle constantly renewing our mutual ardor.

From time to time, I simply contracted the muscles of my vagina around his penis. Or sometimes, I let myself feel his sex pulsating inside me like a pumping heart. If I had been able, if I had had the energy, I would have written him a blazon of my own.

Seventh hour, nourish the earth

I'd forgotten that Richard had committed to staying on the premises. It was he who knocked on the door to the adjoining room, the empress's so-called ordinary room, before ducking in, with eyes veiled. He had brought a silver tray with cups, a large coffeepot, and a variety of cakes and dried fruits.

"A little snack?"

We welcomed his proposition with grateful sighs. He left his offering on the small Egyptian pedestal table, where he picked up the remnants of our last meal and quickly departed. Greedily, and without saying a word, we ate.

Once we were lying on the bed again, framed by two gigantic golden swans, I thought we would sleep for a little while. But he pressed his mouth to my ear, and I sensed his desire to express himself in flowery words.

"I love you . . ."

I hadn't been wrong. Whereas David used to overdo it with his declarations of love, Louie was miserly with his emotions. This may have been the first time.

"And I love your surprise."

The first sentence was like a trophy. And the second was fertilizer for our games to come. Since he liked it when I was creative, I silently vowed to myself that I would take every possible opportunity to surprise him. In reply to his tender admissions, I covered him in kisses, wound my legs around his, and let my hands wander to his backside and sex.

I don't quite remember what we said next. I know that the topic was more serious, and that we specifically addressed our wedding. Louie mentioned a prenup and also referred to the one David and I had signed. Ours, like that earlier one, had been drawn up by Master Olivo.

Yawning, I had just enough energy to ask Louie to have it sent to Master Whurman, Mom's notary.

Some plants do more than blossom. Some have thorns.

Eighth hour, resist the change of season

The eighth was the most difficult hour, and despite vast quantities of coffee, we struggled to stay awake. Outside, a pink hue had descended on the plants. They were so beautiful, so impatient for the night to end, so thirsty for the sun's light. I reflected on the notion that these would be our last hours of confinement. We had spent months ripening in the shadows, first at the Hôtel des Charmes and then here. It was time to come out into the light.

For now, and in order to avoid the chill of dawn, I decided to plunge my hand inside of myself. I gathered enough fluid, which was neither too viscous nor too sticky, to spread all over my lover's body, everywhere I thought it should go: his cheeks, forehead, neck, chest, even his mouth, which greedily licked at my fingers. I did not leave out his temples or the crease behind his ear, since I knew from experience that a few drops there were sure to stimulate him elsewhere.

After I had finished, he did the same with his seminal fluid. It didn't offend or disgust me. Rather, I was overcome with a sudden desire to drink this concoction straight from its source.

Ninth hour, delight in the advent of spring

Louie's eyes were fluttering. He was on the verge of surrendering when Richard lightly knocked and then appeared in the half-open door, followed by a more slender figure.

"The young lady you've been waiting for is here," he announced in a low voice.

"Thank you. Send her in, please."

I recognized the young woman and her military cap, which she had been wearing when I had paid her a visit at her shop, Dragon Tattoo, on Rue du Roi-de-Sicile.

She herself had many visible tattoos, including some on

her arms, the tops of her hands, and her neck. Her soft features contradicted an otherwise masculine look.

"Hello," she greeted us with a faint smile.

"Come in, Stéphane, come in."

Stéphane, like the famous French actress Stéphane Audran.

Louie was just shaking off his lethargy and seemed only now to have noticed our visitor.

"Stéphane?"

He knew her well. Her agile hands were the ones that had so expertly drawn some of his most beautiful tattoos, notably the interlacing roses on his left shoulder.

"What are you doing—"

"Tsk, patience, sir!" I commanded.

The khaki-clad tattoo artist unwrapped her tools, which she checked for sterility and proper functioning. When everything was in order, she asked me:

"Whom should I start with?"

"With me, if you don't mind."

"I thought you weren't interested . . . ?" Louie interjected.

"I wasn't, at least not as an individual project. But . . . this is different."

"What do you mean?"

No need to give more of the surprise away. He understood what I had in mind, even if he couldn't guess exactly which form my idea would take.

Rather than answer him, I stretched out on my back, naked, and offered my pubis to Stéphane. She then started shaving me. Soon all that was left was a small line of fuzz on the edges of my labia.

Louie didn't know whether to applaud or protest. I had definitely surprised him!

The needle made its first contact with my tender skin, which is so delicate in that particular spot, and I squealed, a sound I quickly suppressed. All I had to do was get used to the piercing but manageable pain.

Louie peeked over the tattoo artist's shoulder, curious as a child, eager to see what was slowly, point by point, taking shape before his eyes.

"What is it?" he couldn't help asking.

"Hold on . . . You'll see."

"A feather?"

No. It was a simple petal, pointed at the bottom, full at the top, hollow on the left, thick on the right, and subtly veined in shades of gray.

Stéphane worked quickly, and less than fifteen minutes later, she shot Louie an inquisitive smile.

"Your turn?"

I nodded, a gesture meant as much for the tattooed as the tattooer, and Louie, who was always so sure of himself, who was so secure in his authority, lay down without a word.

As she had done for me, Stéphane shaved his pubic hair in monk-like silence. She plotted her design, an exact replica of the one she had just traced on me, with a measuring tape. The only difference: his petal was turned upside down, with the point at the top and the rounded part at the bottom.

"Is that what I think it is?" Louie asked, as the artist added the finishing touches to his reddened skin.

"I don't know," I teased. "What do you think it is?"

After Stéphane had completed her task, and a soothing balm had been massaged into our raw skin, I lay on top of Louie, as softly and gently as possible, and inspected our abdomens to make sure that it had all turned out how I had imagined.

It was perfect. When our bodies were united, the two petals formed a single sphere, with Louie's masculine yang indissociable from my feminine yin. Now our two forces were joined; they were complete. In order to recompose the sensual whole that we had become, we'd need to combine these two energies.

AND IN THAT MOMENT COULD it be that I saw him cry? Or had I fallen asleep?

4

May 15, 2010

Madame Barlet, you're a very busy young woman these days! How long have we been trying to set up this meeting?"

The man in the black suit who was holding out his hand to me was a sixty-something Don Juan with thinning, slicked-back hair. And despite his barely concealed reproach, he was almost too affable and exuberant for his profession. But, then again, nowhere is it written that a notary can't be nice to his clients. He pulled out a tired old club chair for me before taking his place on the other side of his desk, in a brand-new leather chair. Whether he had intended it or not, his message was clear: here, he was the only one who was supposed to make any money.

"I know, I'm sorry . . . Anyway, I'm no longer Madame Barlet. I now go by my mother's name, Lorand."

His smile disappeared, and he put on his glasses to inspect a pair of thick folders resting on his desk blotter.

"Yes, yes, yes . . . of course. We have two files to review, is that it?"

"That's right," I agreed.

"Maude Lorand's estate, which her daughter, Annabelle *Lorand*, is to inherit . . ."

"Yes."

" . . . and a marriage contract drawn up by my colleague in Paris, Master Olivo, between yourself, Mademoiselle Lorand, and Monsieur Louie *Barlet*."

As he waited for my assent, he raised a thick eyebrow and looked like a dog waiting for a sign from his master.

"That's right."

"Perfect, perfect, perfect. Now we're already clearer on everything."

He should have already been clear as to the purpose of our meeting. Master Whurman had been Mom's notary since forever, and the file concerning her estate had been collecting dust.

I still smarted where Stéphane the tattoo artist had inked me three days earlier, and although the pain was not too strong, whenever the soothing balm I rubbed over the wound dried, it reminded me of that wonderful night. It was enough to assuage my mounting irritation.

"In accordance with your instructions," he went on, "I have proceeded with the sale of your mother's primary asset, namely the house located at 29 Rue Rigault in Nanterre, of which she was the sole proprietor. And you are now its sole inheritor. As my clerk informed you over the telephone, we have received a firm offer on the house, and if you agree to the terms, we will sign the preliminary papers today."

"Okay, I agree," I mumbled.

"Good, good, good," he said with a reassuring smile.

I wondered if he always repeated terms of approval in threes, or if that was his way of comforting a young woman who was so clearly distraught.

"We will take care of it, then. You can sign the related documents in a few minutes in the office next door. While you're waiting . . ."

He had removed his glasses, and his laid-back and slightly lascivious expression had changed.

"I feel it my obligation to warn you. You are about to receive a lot of money. And experience has shown me that such sums are more quickly spent than earned."

Was this a reaction to my monogrammed handbag? Did he take me for a fashionista who would drop all of her mother's money on something as frivolous as trendy clothing? Or maybe he simply thought of me as any other girl of my age: young, impressionable, surrounded by parasites and moochers.

"I'm perfectly aware of that."

"Excellent!" he exclaimed—just once this time. "If you'd like, I would be happy to advise you on some sound investments."

So that was his angle. And I'm sure those investments would have included a generous cut for him.

"Thank you, but I already have an idea of what I would like to do with the money."

"Ah, ah, ah" was his tripartite reply, his jaw suddenly tense. "And what is that, if you don't mind my asking?"

"I'm going to buy an apartment in Paris."

The apartment that I never could have bought when I was with Fred. The one I had given up the idea of when I'd gotten engaged to David, and then in the early days of my relationship with Louie. The one I had imagined for years and years. I had decorated every last detail of it in my mind, had rolled imaginary paint over its walls.

"Hmm," he said, sulking. "Your inheritance is indeed considerable, but with the market as it is, don't expect to be able to afford much in Paris."

"I'm not very demanding."

Had he just blushed, or were my eyes playing tricks on me in his dark office?

"Which is to say?"

"I'd be happy with a studio or a one-bedroom."

"Okay, okay, okay . . . I understand now," he said, delighted. "You're interested in making a real estate investment, I gather?"

"Yes . . . mostly."

Why else would I be purchasing a studio in Paris, I who had just moved into a several-thousand-square-foot house? It had been a dream of my former self, a symbol of independence and success. A year earlier, I would have been elated at the thought of such a purchase. Circumstance had since made the dream obsolete. But only in part. I wouldn't live there, but knowing that I, little Annabelle from Nanterre, owned a piece of property would shore up my dismal self-confidence, at least temporarily.

"That's a wise decision."

The notary blinked three times in approval.

"Nevertheless," he added briskly, "considering the other issue that concerns us today . . ."

He tapped the second file under his left hand three times.

" . . . I must ask you this: Do you wish for this new property to figure into the estate mentioned in the marriage contract?"

"Err . . ." I hesitated. "Doesn't it have to?"

"Right, right, right. But your contract defines community property in terms of assets acquired after your marriage. Everything that you possess *before* that time will be your exclusive property. It is very clearly stated here."

"I understand completely, Master Whurman," I said firmly, and then, to remind him of the moral duties related to his profession: "And if that property is to remain one hundred percent mine, even after the wedding, then why would I hide it from my future husband?"

He squirmed in his chair, a ridiculous movement that ruined his charm and aging good looks.

He hid himself behind the file, licking his index finger as he turned the first few pages.

"I also have here the draft of your marriage contract with Monsieur *David* Barlet." He emphasized the first name to avoid any confusion. "Master Olivo sent it over with the one between you and Monsieur *Louie* Barlet."

"The first contract isn't valid," I asserted, my tone shriller than I had intended it. "I didn't sign it with my usual signature."

I congratulated myself again for my presence of mind when I had scribbled my name in such a way as to nullify the contract. Master Whurman stared at me for a moment and then cleared his throat in a particularly revolting manner.

What was so wrong with my situation that this representative of the law thought it best to advise me to lie by omission to my future husband?

"Yes, yes, yes . . . I know all that. I only bring it up because, well—"

"Well, what?" I interrupted, annoyed by his virginal trepidation.

"Umm, well, if you look closely at both documents, you will notice an anomaly."

He handed me the first page of both contracts, the one between David and me from a past life that was now happily over and the one that symbolized my future bliss with Louie. Could they be more different? Could the contrast be any sharper?

"And? What am I supposed to be seeing here?"

He pointed with his glasses to the line on each contract that listed the birth date and place of each brother.

"There. Nothing strikes you as odd?"

I scanned over both pages, not noticing anything at first; then it became clear. I couldn't believe it.

David Barlet: born January 5, 1969, in Saint-Servan, 35400, in the department of Ille-et-Vilaine.

Louie Barlet: born May 18, 1968, in Paris, 75015, in the department of Paris.

"According to these contracts," he went on, "there were only seven months between David and Louie Barlet's respective births. Louie first, then his brother, David. Seven months later, Mademoiselle. Seven. Not nine or twelve or eighteen. Do you understand?"

I had never been pregnant, but I understood the biologically improbability of Louie and David being from the same mother.

"There must be some mistake," I asserted.

How had I not noticed this detail when Armand had asked me to review my marriage contract with David a year ago? Admittedly, I had put it off for a while, and when I did finally sign, it had been with reluctance. I suppose it is not all that surprising that I had overlooked this piece of information.

Master Whurman was now chewing on the end of his glasses and looking doubtful.

"Maybe it's just a . . ."

These few words were enough to open our conversation to sordid speculation, and I did not want to go there.

"Listen. I lived with David for several months. I saw his driver's license and passport with my own eyes, and I can assure you that he was born on January 5, 1970. That makes him one and a half years younger than his brother—no miracle there."

"Good, good, good. If you say so—"

"I do say so!" I practically barked, so difficult was it to contain my feelings at that moment.

"I just wanted to spare you any unpleasant surprises or inconveniences . . . in terms of inheritance, for example."

I curbed my feeling of exasperation and replied in as curt a tone as I could manage:

"I can handle this situation and its complexities on my own, thank you."

"I'm delighted . . ."

"Me, too."

" . . . and I suppose, then, that your future acquisition will belong to your estate, and yours alone—that is, if you purchase it prior to signing the marriage contract. Am I correct?"

It took me just a second too long to answer, and the notary caught a glimpse of the uncertainty I felt.

"Isn't that right, Mademoiselle?" he insisted.

"I . . . I don't know. Let's see when I've found an apartment, I guess."

I shivered. I couldn't believe the expression of doubt that had just come out of my mouth. My mouth, which only a few days before had been devouring Louie, his mouth, his body, his sex, his soul. The verdant cocoon of Malmaison, our feverish flowering, seemed so far away now. Thinking this, I felt a tug from the raw skin around my tattoo and I winced a little.

All I had done was defer my decision, but my reply was ambiguous, which Master Whurman took as proof that he had gotten under my skin. Yet as far as the notary was concerned, I figured denial was my best option.

The notary nodded and smiled discreetly, but I noticed a derisiveness in his expression that someone in his profession ought to have been better able to conceal.

As he walked me to his clerk's office, where I was greeted by a surprisingly young and attractive woman, Master Whurman squeezed my shoulder and offered some paternal advice:

"You're right not to rush into anything. Take some time to reflect . . . People tend not to spend enough time on preliminary research."

Was he talking about my future studio . . . or the Barlet brothers' past and my imminent wedding?

I was still reflecting on the ambiguity of what he had just said when I noticed that he had gone back to his lair, like a crab scuttling back under its rock.

HAPPILY, OUR BRAINS ARE CONSTANTLY editing reality, in a process not unlike the work of a film editor in postproduction. In memory, the ordinary experiences of everyday life are elided in favor of the critical and the intense.

That May 15 was one of those important moments. I don't remember exactly how I got from Master Whurman's office that afternoon to a foyer that smelled of potpourri at eight o'clock that evening. The charming little building was located in the 12th Arrondissement near the Palais de la Porte Dorée and run by two very gracious Englishwomen.

"Hello. Someone is expecting me in room number fifteen."

"Fifteen," confirmed the short-haired brunette in a thick British accent. "Yes, your friend is already here. It's on the second floor."

DURING OUR LAZY AFTERNOONS IN the Josephine, I had told a very intrigued Louie about Sophia's rendezvous in complete darkness with an anonymous client. He'd been surprised to learn that the man had continued seeing her after the agency that had put them in touch, Belles de Nuit, had closed.

What had started out for Sophia as an exciting engagement, an appointment that stood out from the humdrum of her usual missions, had become an obsession. In fact, if the mysterious man had not on several occasions threatened her with disappearing, she no doubt would have tried to unmask him. She would have suddenly flooded light into the room where their secret acts took place, a room that was always kept pitch-black. The man whose member smelled of strawberries or raspberries had come to haunt her libido, which was already replete with wild fantasies, and she would talk to me about him for hours on end. Meanwhile, she kept putting off making any sort of commitment to Fred, and my ex-boyfriend was beside himself.

"ARE YOU THERE?" I WHISPERED, pushing open the second entry door to room fifteen.

Two doors were an essential component in this fantasy. There was no other way to enter a room without seeing and being seen, without even the thinnest strip of light making its way in, too. Only in a room with a second door located just a pace away from the entrance can one control the elements that come into it—though no system is exactly perfect.

I assumed that the hotel had been chosen for this reason, since I couldn't think of anything else that would justify going anywhere but our beloved Hôtel des Charmes, especially a place so far from our house.

"Come . . . ," he breathed from a corner opposite the window.

No, I'm wrong. That's not what he said. I remember it now. He was fastidious about maintaining the illusion of anonymity between us. He didn't utter a single word the entire time that we were in that room. He had even neglected to wear his usual cologne for the occasion. In other words, I was bereft of the usual cues that one uses to identify another person. All I had were my hands and my trust in him. Nothing else could certify that it was actually he in that pitch-black room.

His silence was commanding. And in the darkness, I barely made out his motionless shadow on the méridienne facing the bed. His eyes must have adjusted to the darkness while he'd been waiting for me to arrive because I felt them examining my silhouette and watching my furtive entrance from across the unlit room. Without saying a word, I undressed, careful not to rush anything or burst the ethereal bubble in which we were trying to float. Wordlessly, I lay across the bed, whose sheets he had already turned down. I remained stretched out there, my ears and nose attentive.

When I caught a sweet whiff of his skin and heard a gentle rustle as he opened his legs, I realized that he, too, was naked. Other sounds began to fill the room: a jagged breath, sustained rubbing, then a gentle hiss that I could only interpret as a spurt of seminal fluid. He was already on the verge of coming. Hearing him masturbate without being able to see or touch him seemed to me like the most delicate of invitations. This might have seemed crude if we had been able to see each other, but in the darkness it was a ballet for the senses, which delighted in taking turns at discovering which would perceive something first. It was like a game of cat and mouse.

Thanks to this arrangement, I began to hear things for the first time, things that I had always relied on my eyes to see: I heard his foreskin retract over the tip of his penis and then revert back to its initial position; I heard his frenulum extending to the point where it began to cause him pain, and I heard him let out a brief moan in response; I perceived his half-open lips and the saliva he spread over his fingertips; I then noticed his hand enveloping his convulsing, mauvish member.

Despite the distance between us, my nose perceived the smell of his sex, which grew stronger and more pungent with each stroke of his hand. I could sense his imminent pleasure.

I did not wait to be told to touch myself. Without his gaze upon me, I lost all of my inhibitions. I spread my legs wide, without a care for decency. Usually I hated masturbating so openly in front of him, but now I abandoned myself to it. I rubbed my vulva in large circular movements. I pinched the swollen summit of my clitoris, knowing that he would take his turn to do the same, though less expertly than I. I boldly sunk three fingers into my soaking cunt, though not in a way that invited him to take their place. I did want him to fill me, but only when I was ready. I didn't want to rush these delicious preliminaries. I continued to touch myself, drunk on the dizzying fragrance of our two sexes.

The shock of his gland on my face instantly drew me out of my sensual reverie. I wasn't so much annoyed as surprised. I had been so engrossed in what I was doing that I hadn't heard his footsteps across the carpet as he'd approached me. Nor had the sound of his breath registered as it did now. It felt like a light mist in the night, first touching my neck, then my pelvis, then my breasts.

I threw my mouth forward, opened my lips wide, and stuck out my tongue—a kind of homing device thrust into the darkness. I gently licked his swollen flesh, once, twice. I was suffocating with desire. I would bite into him if he accidentally came into contact with my teeth. But he sent himself deeply into my throat, diving into the abyss, and together we moaned in pleasure. We were both relieved to have at last established contact between our two planets, which had been separated by what had felt like eternal darkness.

I let him slide in and out of my throat a few times. Sometimes he went a little far, almost provoking my gag reflex, but I didn't mind. I loved feeling him grow bigger and bigger and wondering what proportions I could handle. That was my power: blowing up his member like a balloon, commanding this ever-expanding universe of pleasure. I was a goddess, the only woman capable of giving him eternity.

When his shaft began to contract and his tip to tremble, I grabbed hold of his hips with all my strength and fought against his reflex to withdraw. I wanted his sap in my throat; I wanted to drink his Milky Way, to feast on his raining cosmic matter. He immediately understood and plunged one of his middle fingers into my avid vagina. We knew what to do without even looking into each other's eyes, and we let these supernatural forces guide our actions, neither one of us polluting the environment by breaking the primordial silence.

I moved my free hand from my incandescent meteorite— the image made me smile—to his heavy scrotum, which was beating rhythmically against my chin, and then to the black hole of his anus, which, less than a light-year before our joint orgasms, gladly welcomed my index finger. Louie hiccuped in delight.

I BELIEVE THAT WAS THE first day that I sprayed him. A large translucent squirt of fluid flooded his hand and the sheets below. My vulva contracted strongly, holding his middle finger prisoner for a moment. Then, when at last I released him, he came, spurting his white lava into me. His semen melded with my mucus in a sticky blend of pleasure and love. I drank it all as if it were nectar. I even smacked my lips, savoring the taste.

Collapsing onto the sullied bed, we each placed a hand on the other's intimate part. We were the happy owners of a piece of heaven.

5

MAY 18, 2010

United by the sacred bond of tattoo artistry.

That is what Louie and I were now. We were also chained to each other sensually, a subservience that grew with each passing day. Yes, I preferred ink to diamonds as a symbol of our engagement. Engagement rings hadn't brought me much luck in the past . . .

I wondered if David had reused Hortensia's ring, the one he had given me, in his proposal to Alice. I admit to having compulsively checked gossip rags for photos in which her left hand appeared. I finally found one: her ring finger was still naked. Strange. Or perhaps David was saving the ring for a more official ceremony than that joke of a video—one that would still be the talk of journalists and members of the paparazzi, of course.

THE NIGHT OF OUR ANONYMOUS rendezvous, I agonized over whether to grill Louie on the anomaly that Master Whurman had pointed out to me. It was nothing, a simple mistake . . . but I couldn't stop thinking about it. His birthday was in just two days; it would be easy to broach the subject . . . and I was so tempted to do it. In the end, I gave in. Curiosity kills, you see—that is, when it doesn't drive a person mad.

"May 1968 . . . a pretty interesting time to be born," I began, feigning distraction.

As was the case every year, the media was predicting a spring season reminiscent of '68, in terms of social movements. Politicians and union leaders of all political persuasions were making big predictions on the potential pros and cons of such a movement. One such person was currently pontificating to that effect on the television. Louie was only half watching, his attention absorbed in an art magazine.

"I guess . . . hundreds of thousands of people were no doubt born in 1968. Of them, several tens of thousands came into this world in May. I am not exactly unique."

"That's true . . . but not everyone in the world can tell such fascinating anecdotes about the day he was born."

On May 18, 1968, the strikes had already been going on for almost three weeks, and service stations had run out of gas. Since he did not have a car with any gas in the tank, and since there were no taxis to be had, Andre Barlet had requisitioned a little delivery tricycle from one his newspapers to transport Hortensia to the clinic. And it was in that same carriage that, forty-eight hours later, he had brought his wife and child back home, to the astonishment of passersby. It was such a comical sight that some of the Barlets' neighbors had taken out their cameras to immortalize the moment. The event was archived in the family memory, becoming one of those highlights that someone retold whenever there was a lull in conversation at family gatherings.

"I guess it was kind of out of the ordinary," he admitted.

"Look at David, for instance . . . ," I insisted.

"What do you mean?"

"I don't think anyone has any amusing anecdotes about births that took place in January 1969."

He didn't react, so I tried again:

"January '69 must have been a completely ordinary month. Especially the fifth of January, since it was just four days after the New Year."

He didn't even look up from his magazine as he corrected me, his tone almost too calm:

"January 1970. Not '69. David was born on January 5, 1970," he said, his tone icy.

He was supposedly reading, but I could have sworn that his pupils remained absolutely frozen as he pronounced those words.

"'69, you're sure?" I pressed, without raising my voice.

"Yes, David was born on January 5, 1970. I *know* my brother's birthday."

His firm tone only half convinced me. Yes, in theory, there was nothing to dispute.

I could tell that it would be no use addressing the question head-on, and that I wouldn't get anything out of him in the immediate present.

"Right, '69, '70 . . . same thing," I said lightly.

"Not really."

He stood, threw his magazine on the coffee table, and quickly changed the subject, his tone suddenly playful:

"Tell me, Mademoiselle Historian, where can we find our Ten-Times-a-Day?"

His question caught me off guard—that had clearly been his intention—and I couldn't find anything better to say than:

"In our room, isn't it?"

"No, it's not. I looked for it earlier and couldn't find it any-where in the house."

I still wasn't used to using that word to designate the palace that was now our permanent residence. "House." Did Sleeping Beauty talk about her castle like this: *Come on, guys, I'm sick of hunting the dragon. Let's go back to the* house?

From a confined space at the Hôtel des Charmes, a com-fortable and cozy cocoon, whose every inch had been saturated with our shared pleasure, to the gigantic lodgings where we now lived. The place certainly had plenty of charm, but no one had set foot here for a long time. Too long.

"Oh . . . When we left the Hôtel des Charmes, didn't we say that you would take care of it?"

I didn't want to reproach him, but that had been our agree-ment; I remembered it perfectly.

"Yes, well, that's just it. I'm wondering if I didn't leave it in room one."

"I see . . . Well, I'll drop by the hotel later and pick it up."

"Great," he approved. "In the meantime, we can use some filler sheets, if you want."

"Okay. But I thought you were the one who wanted to write something."

We hadn't established any clear rules for our notebook. It hadn't been necessary. So long as we'd been living in room one's seventy to eighty square feet, our Ten-Times-a-Day had passed back and forth naturally between us, between lovemaking ses-sions, siestas, and occasional bouts of cleaning. There had been no need to plan. We'd each written in the book whenever it had struck our respective fancies. All shared events and sensa-tions could therefore be found within its perforated pages, in either his handwriting or in mine—and sometimes in both.

"Actually, I wanted to reread a few passages."

We had not yet done much of that.

"Oh, okay . . . why?"

He advanced toward me, firmly took me in his arms, pressing our tattooed pelvises together, his eyes shooting into mine, and said:

"Because I am over the moon about your recent progress, Mademoiselle . . ."

He had enjoyed our engagement party at Malmaison as well as our blind rendezvous. I could see it in the way he was suppressing a smile; he looked as though something sour had blossomed in his mouth. I silently celebrated the fact that I'd been able to surprise him so well.

" . . . and I wanted to compare today's Elle with past Elle."

"Just you wait," I said enigmatically, "until you see tomorrow's Elle!"

I cocked my head, as if offering my neck to his lips, and then lunged at his neck and planted a kiss directly on the spot where Stéphane had tattooed a rose bud. I loved placing my lips on his tattoos. They quenched a thirst in me, and in return I breathed a bit of life into them.

"Hmm . . . intriguing."

This little game we were playing was not innocent. It was May 16, two days before his forty-second birthday. The implicit promise of my words wasn't lost on him. No subtitles were needed.

"I hope you're intrigued! You can torture me all you want these next two days, but you won't get anything out of me, darling!"

"Only two days?" he teased, sinking his teeth into the nape of my neck.

"Ouch!"

I'll let you in on a secret: I had worked with Ysiam on his birthday present, which would be a continuation of our Edenic night. An urban version of it, one might say. I had rented all the rooms at the Hôtel des Charmes for the night of May 18. My plan was that we would explore each room, each an embodiment of a male fantasy—or at least what I imagined were Louie's fantasies.

My intention was not simply to exhaust my lover and future husband's desires; I wanted him to see the extent to which this gallery of chimeras also reflected my own fantasies. I would be satisfying him by fueling my own sensual imagination. Would he be able to see this change in me? Would the master notice his student's growing sexual agency?

LOUIE AND I WERE DRESSED up, arm in arm, when we arrived in front of the Sauvage Gallery on the night of May 18. Its window seemed tame: a series of blank screens formed a depressing gray wall that faced Rue de Sévigné, to the indifference of passersby.

"That's your little protégé's shocking installation? A bunch of black screens?"

"Patience . . ."

He pulled me inside, where we were greeted by Alban Sauvage, who was as voluble and affable as I'd remembered him. He was also just as bald as before, with the same beard, but he was now wearing a new pair of very fashionable glasses, which succeeded in hiding neither his excitement nor his feverish energy.

"This is going to be killer, my friends! Killer! The minister's office told me that she would be dropping by. And absolutely all of the media will be here. Even *Time* magazine's French correspondent is coming."

The crowd of curious visitors was still sparse. As for me, I still hadn't figured out what this show was about. The walls were lined with more screens than in the window outside. They, too, were lifeless. The only difference between these and the ones that looked out onto the street was a series of signs on which were printed the names of cities from all over the world: London, Tokyo, Sydney, San Francisco, Rio de Janeiro, Moscow, Rome, Johannesburg, Shanghai, Calcutta, Berlin, Stockholm, etc. "More or less in real time, captured using a webcam . . ." David Garchey had alluded to his show during our housewarming party.

So this was his big idea? To give touristic snapshots of the world? Who did he take us for?

"Are the girls ready?" Louie asked, worried, his hand on my waist.

With those words, he pointed to a large black curtain at the back of the gallery behind which there appeared to be a small stage.

"They're just finishing their makeup. They'll be in their places in ten minutes," the gallerist informed him.

"Perfect."

"Is there going to be a performance?" I inquired, my curiosity suddenly piqued.

"Kind of . . ."

Louie wanted to keep his surprise a secret, which I could understand. For him, contemporary art should be like electroshock therapy. It should use all means necessary to devastate the spectator. And after such an initial shock, the spectator must then be given the means to come back to his or her senses and decode the social critique contained in the work's conceptual soup.

"Oh, oh!" Alban caught sight of a group at the entryway. "New victims have arrived. I think it's time."

Art gallery regulars have a kind of radar where timing is concerned. Inevitably, as soon as the first petits fours have been brought out and the champagne glasses been arranged and filled with dancing bubbles, they will at last make their entrance.

"Is David around?"

David Garchey, of course, the star of the evening. The person upon whom Louie's place in the art world depended—and vice versa.

"If he's still where he was five minutes ago, then he's in the bathroom, throwing up his vodka orange juices."

"Do you mind getting him?"

Among the new arrivals figured Rebecca Sibony, the owner of Belles de Nuit, an escort agency for which I had once worked. She was blond, thin—almost gaunt—and she was wearing an elegant fuchsia pantsuit. I hadn't seen her since that time Sophia and I had gone to her home one June morning the previous year. It seemed like another era. I left Louie to his duties and went to greet his former mistress.

"Good evening, Rebecca. It's been a while . . ."

"It has. And I'm delighted to see how much conjugal life suits you. You look fantastic."

As she complimented me, her eyes examined the extremely fitted Chinese dress that accentuated my slim waist and ample hips. Louie had given me the dress for this occasion.

I couldn't help but hear a hint of bitterness in her tone. She had once hoped that she and Louie could be a couple.

"Thank you."

This was followed by a long and uncomfortable silence, during which a number of memories flashed through my mind, in particular that extremely familiar way in which she had spoken to Louie, in the recording that Fred had made of one of their telephone conversations: "My Lou," "You know I'm here for you, my Lou. All of me." And here she was again tonight, there before him.

I had often considered the relationship between these two. I liked to believe that I knew the full story: at first, Louie had played David's game; then, he sincerely fell in love with me and concocted a plan with his former mistress to persuade me not to marry his younger brother. But that version of things didn't take everything into account: I was Aurora's doppel-ganger, and Aurora was the first love of both brothers. Ever since I'd made that discovery . . . well, I had simply stopped torturing myself over it. What did it matter? After all, I now lived with the only man I had ever loved.

"Do you know what they have in store for us?" Rebecca asked.

She pointed at the black screens, and suddenly, as though an invisible ear had taken her question as a signal, they all flickered to life. First, we saw a kind of test pattern, then a number of rough images that looked like choppy pictures taken by webcams from all over the world. Slowly, we began to see underthings, boxers, thongs, pubic hair of various hues and textures, and different colors of skin.

After several seconds, the true content of the installation became clear: about four dozen sets of genitals from both gen-ders, of all ages, races, and colors appeared in a live and larger-than-life tableau.

The most curious element of this installation was the collection of colorful cords that ran across the ceiling from each screen, converging at the back of the gallery, where they disappeared behind the curtain that was still hiding the small stage. Together, these cords looked like a network of rainbow-colored tentacles.

"Good evening, and welcome to the Alban Sauvage–Louie Barlet Gallery."

It was official. My man had been inducted into the snobbiest, most exclusive club on the planet: the world of contemporary art galleries.

Alban, who was very much in his element, had taken the microphone and was weaving through the densifying group of gallerygoers.

"Louie and I are delighted to welcome you here tonight to see David Garchey's new work, *Permanent Sex*."

He then blabbered on for a few minutes in conceptual, philosophical gibberish, with about as much seriousness as if he were announcing the engagement of an English prince to an R&B singer, before handing the microphone to the ghostly white artist with the long bangs who seemed to have emerged from nowhere.

The young dandy took the microphone, turned his back on the audience, and addressed himself to the screens as though they were physical people:

"Okay, touch yourselves, please," he said in English.

All at once, in a perfectly synchronized movement, as many hands as there were genitals wandered toward the naked anatomy.

"Now . . . go ahead and jerk off," David Garchey said encouragingly.

Then, with the same level of synchronization as before, they all began to masturbate. Only then did I notice that there were as many women as men, and that they were arranged in alternating order—one man, then one woman, and so on—as a good hostess does with her guests at a dinner table.

As the anonymous participants stroked themselves, each manifesting pleasure more or less loudly, the colorful cord attached to each screen grew brighter and brighter. Soon, it felt as though we were in a nightclub with garish, rainbow-colored neon lights.

I hadn't noticed that Alban was standing next to me until he whispered into my ear:

"It's a reflection of the level of pleasure each participant is feeling, based on the resonance of his or her voice. The louder they are, the more pleasure they feel, the brighter the corresponding light and color."

"That's it?" I asked, disturbed by how corny the whole thing seemed. "To transform your gallery into an orgasming nightclub?"

"You have no idea . . . Their moaning is also being converted into musical notes by a program like Auto-Tune. And the whole thing will be mixed live. We just have to wait until they've reached a certain threshold of volume."

As he spoke, David Garchey began coaxing his good little pleasure soldiers in order to reach the necessary level of sound:

"Harder . . . harder, please, you guys!"

The more the participants moaned, the more the crowd in the gallery stirred. Everybody was looking around to gauge how others were reacting and craft an appropriate response. Some had trouble suppressing disgust; others could not contain their laughter.

I caught Rebecca's attention and asked her in a low voice:

"Is the minister of culture really coming to see . . . *this*?"

She raised a helpless eyebrow, which was so blond and so sparse that it was almost invisible. The first notes of atmospheric, orgasmic music began to play over the speakers. The sound had just enough rhythm to elicit head nodding. I figured this must be a piece being written in real time, the sum of the sighs that David Garchey was harvesting from all over the world. The thrust of the show had been staked on this misguided idea: that gallerygoers were expecting just another provocative installation, but that in reality they would be treated to a musical performance, a riot of sensations that would be composed in real time.

Meanwhile, the black curtain was raised, revealing three dancers wearing flesh-colored, almost transparent bikinis, which was more erotic and scandalous than if they had been completely naked. Despite the commotion created by this new revelation, I instantly recognized Salomé, the ethnic woman. Then Peggy, Sophia's infamous friend, the one who had worked for a time as a Hotelle at Belles de Nuit and who had once lent me her convertible bug. And Sophia herself. All three were swaying their hips with lasciviousness, pouting and batting their eyelashes as they tried their best to coordinate their movements to the dubious harmonies being created by the cosmopolitan masturbators.

"I'm delighted to have worked so hard to instill in these girls a modicum of decency . . . ," Rebecca lamented, her teeth clenched.

"Did you know about this?"

"Of course not!" she cried. "I could never approve of such . . . filth!"

Louie could have hired any girl for his little show. Anyone who was desperate enough and who had enough guts. But not Sophia. Not *my* friend! Not for this kind of show!

"Sophia is a real dancer," I said, defending my friend. "She's an artist, not—"

"I know, I know!"

On stage, my friend started doing a striptease, which consisted of her unhooking her bikini top. She stared at a point on the horizon, clearly embarrassed and avoiding eye contact with the audience.

For their part, Louie, David Garchey, and Alban seemed satisfied with the audience's stupefaction, and they were smiling at the dancers like three kids. The guests didn't know whether to listen, rinse their eyes, or think about what all of this might mean. Most of them simply looked incredulous and uncomfortable.

"Okay. I'm outta here!" I said, as I headed for the exit.

Based on the brouhaha coming from the street, I understood that this spectacle was being played on the screens in the gallery window—I wondered if the pedestrians could see and hear everything, the music included.

Once outside, I was able to confirm my hypothesis. Shots of the three dancers were interspersed with those of the various genitals from all over the word. It was all live, the masturbation—everything—in the middle of the street.

Had they all gone mad?

I CAUGHT SIGHT OF LOUIE running after me as he pushed through the crush of media and guests. Then, I heard police sirens screaming through the streets. They were headed toward us. Louie, with Alban at his side, still hadn't reached the door when two plainclothes cops—whom I recognized by the orange armbands on their left biceps—appeared.

"Police . . . police—let us through, please."

They weren't so much trying to get curious onlookers to disperse as they were working to clear a path to the entry. The scene was so surreal that instead of leaving, as I had intended to do just a moment before, I remained frozen in the street amid astonished passersby.

Addressing the man blocking the way, the eldest of the two police officers, a balding blond with a cropped goatee, demanded curtly:

"Are you the man in charge of this mess?"

"No, why?" he replied flaccidly.

During this time, the officer's colleague, who was as thin and dark-featured as the other was athletic and blond, took several pictures of the front of the gallery with a large reflex camera dangling from a strap around his neck.

"I am!"

Louie had sprung forward from inside the gallery, as quickly as his knee and cane would allow. He was wearing his public smile, the one that looked nothing like him, the one that hid his dimple, and he cordially extended his hand:

"Louie Barlet. I am in charge of legal affairs at the gallery."

"Captain Lechère . . . ," the officer replied, ignoring Louie's hand.

"May I ask to what we owe the pleasure of your presence, Captain?"

"Are you joking? Have you seen the mess your little screening has caused?"

He pointed an accusing index finger at the screens. And at that precise moment, two sexes—one male, the other female—

appeared over a five-foot diagonal expanse. The girl's vagina, into which two fingers had been inserted, looked as though it were on the verge of coming.

"Listen, I don't expect you to understand or appreciate . . . ," Louie said, stiffening. "But this is art. High art, at that."

As if to contradict him, the screens suddenly went dark, both in the window and inside the gallery. Alban, who was running in all directions, had obviously gotten scared and unplugged everything.

The cop eyed Louie with scorn before firmly replying:

"I forgot to mention this earlier: I am a member of a squad whose mission is to protect minors. I am therefore not concerned with whether or not this is art. But I can tell you, Monsieur, that showing genitals in action like that on a street that is located less than six hundred fifty feet from a middle school is considered a violation of children's rights. And it is punishable by time in prison."

The last word hit Louie hard, leaving him speechless.

The man with the camera joined his superior and withdrew a pair of handcuffs from his jacket. A wave of indignation rose through the crowd.

"Could you tell me what's going on?" Louie asked, his tone grave now.

"Oh, it's very simple, we are going to take you in for questioning."

With those words, the dark-complexioned officer approached Louie, the cuffs open and aimed at his wrists.

"Wait . . . I'll come with you. I don't think those will be necessary."

"That's kind of you, but I'll decide what's necessary."

He nodded, signaling to his fellow officer that he could

proceed. Louie took a step back, then let himself be cuffed without resisting. In no time at all, the policeman had bound Louie's wrists in steel bracelets behind his back. He then pushed my fiancé toward the nearer of two police cars, whose lights were still flashing blue.

I may have been angrier with Louie than I had ever been, but that emotion was overwhelmed by a wave of fear. I felt a knot of concern in the pit of my stomach. I didn't want them to take him away from me like a delinquent. My stomach began to palpitate in strange, spasmodic convulsions that extended to my pelvis and sex like a series of tsunamis. My body was rejecting his being taken from me.

These successive abdominal pains tore me out of my torpor. Pushing through a curtain of anonymous bystanders, I finally spoke up:

"Captain!"

"Who are you?" barked the bearded blond as he brusquely turned to face me.

"I am his fiancée."

"And?"

"May I ask who alerted you?"

"Excuse me?" he said, pretending not to understand.

"Don't tell me you just happened to walk by the gallery. The exhibit had only just started when you arrived. Someone must have informed you. Am I mistaken?"

Someone must have ratted us out, I kept myself from saying out loud.

He squinted and offered a laconic reply:

"A group of concerned parents."

"Parents?" I asked, surprised.

"Victor Hugo middle and high school is located just down

the street, Mademoiselle. According to article 227-24 of the penal code, exposing minors to pornographic material of any sort is punishable by three years in prison and a seventy-five-thousand-euro fine. Sex shops and other adult locales are not allowed anywhere within six hundred feet of a school. That is the law."

"But this isn't a sex shop. It's an art gallery!"

"All I'm saying is you have to be cautious about certain things when it comes to this kind of *art*."

I was about to argue with him, to unravel his by-the-book worldview, when I felt a friendly hand on my shoulder. It was Alban.

"Drop it!" he whispered in my ear. "You're only going to make things worse for him."

"But we can't just let them take him away like that!"

"Drop it, I tell you. Personally, I've already been through this kind of thing at least a half dozen times over the past ten years. He'll be okay. Don't worry."

My gut did not agree.

I watched as the officer forcibly pushed Louie into the back of the Peugeot, the rose on my fiancé's neck disappearing, suddenly wilted, into the cage.

"They'll keep him a day or two. They'll try to scare him, but I promise it won't be too bad," Alban tried to reassure me, sharing his personal experiences. "Anyway, for now you have a right to a lawyer during the interrogation."

"A lawyer? What lawyer?"

"Zerki," he replied casually. "Jean-Marc Zerki. Louie's lawyer. You don't know him?"

The name had come up when Louie was dismissed from the Barlet Group, but I had never met the man. And I suspected he wasn't up to date on all of my future husband's current news.

"Actually, Louie asked me to give this to you."

The bearded gallerist handed me a flat key with what looked like an infinite number of tiny notches. This kind of key was typically used to open multipoint locks or reinforced doors.

"What does it open?"

"No idea. He told me you'd know."

"But when did he have time to give it to you?"

"Just now. When he saw the cops get here."

"Okay . . ."

I considered the key with suspicion.

"He also wants you to get your notebook from the Hôtel des Charmes. He said you should lock up anything that could be 'too hot.' Those were his words. Again, he said you would understand."

As soon as he heard the police sirens, Louie had anticipated what would happen to the gallery and to him, its representative. He had entrusted Alban with a few instructions for me so that I could manage the fallout. We had put sex at the heart of our relationship, and now I had to hide it all, for fear that it could be used against us in a court of law. It seemed so absurd, so unjust. Another uppercut suddenly tore through my pelvis.

"Elle! Elle!"

The sound of footsteps, followed by a familiar voice.

During the commotion, Sophia and her friends had left the stage. My friend had hastily thrown on a very short robe and was now rushing toward me, ashamed and concerned by everything that had happened.

"Elle, let me explain . . ."

Without thinking, I bolted. Despite the crowd and my tight dress, I cleared a path and ran. There were people everywhere, crowding the narrow one-way street. I didn't know where I was going—down Rue Saint-Antoine, more or less toward the Seine River.

I just wanted to flee. I wanted to erase the image of Louie's rose as he was being taken by the police. I wanted to erase the scent of his cologne, which still lingered over the cobblestones. All I wanted to think about was the memory of our two bodies together. I didn't want the rest, those awful feelings and images that kept trying to ruin everything.

Everything was ruined, starting with my present—the surprise I had planned at the Hôtel des Charmes that was supposed to take place that night.

6

The district of the Marais plays a central role in Paris's geography and history. Orthodox Jews live in the area surrounding Rue des Rosiers, the gay community and artists can be seen all over the neighborhood, and well-connected people of all stripes are known to wander its streets—it makes for a motley crowd.

What I find special here is that although this is one of the most central neighborhoods in Paris—it is spread out over the 3rd and 4th Arrondissements—it is not nearly as pretentious as one might expect. In its own way, it is more reminiscent in character of a less central part of the city, a homier, more modest area. Despite its prestigious monuments, its wildly expensive apartments with exposed beams, it still feels accessible, spontaneous, some would even say working-class. You can get falafel or a pastrami sandwich at any hour of the day. You can talk to any of its residents without getting that disagreeable feeling that they're looking down on you—as they will in the very aristocratic 8th and 16th Arrondissements. The Marais is such a wonderful mix of memory and modernity, heritage and the avant-garde, the chic and the cheap. It is one great amal-gam, and has been for some time. The heart of Paris has heart. And it never ceases to surprise and enchant me.

WHY AM I TELLING YOU this? Because I got to know the Marais when I was still a suburban girl. Belles de Nuit had its offices there, and Sophia and I used to spend almost as much time in that neighborhood as we did near Drouot. We loved its narrow streets filled to the brim with boutiques and bars.

When I began looking at studios for sale—the day after my meeting with Master Whurman—the Marais seemed like the natural place to start. One-bedrooms were out of my price range, but if I limited my ambitions to a studio—with the bed-room, living room, dressing room, and dining room all between four walls—then my dream of owning an apartment in the neighborhood was reasonable, given my budget of a little over three hundred thousand euros, what was left of my inheritance after taxes. I saw several dark, run-down, horrible places before I came across an adorable little nest, located on the seventh and second-to-last floor, no elevator, on Rue du Trésor, a cobble-stone, tree-lined, dead-end street with excellent bar terraces. I hadn't yet made an offer, and the real estate agent was already putting on the pressure with an old adage of her profession:

"At this price, in this street, you won't find anything else like it! It has just come on the market, and believe me, it'll go fast. I'm showing it to two more people this afternoon."

"I can pay cash," I said, happy for once to be able to flex the muscle that my savings afforded me.

"When you say cash . . . ?" Her eyes lit up.

"I can pay the full asking price. I'll have access to the money in a couple of days. I won't need a loan."

"Including the notary fees?"

"Let me recalculate, but I think so."

The price was steep: the death of my mom. But wasn't it Maude who used to urge me to preserve my independence? She who had always fought for her own, at a time when women had so little. After my father's death, no man had had power over her again. She had undoubtedly had lovers, but the master of her house had always been her. My mother was not a militant feminist. She was a free woman. A woman who never let anyone tell her how to live her life.

SO WHILE I WAS FLEEING the Sauvage Gallery, Sophia, and the misfortune that had befallen Louie and our recent engagement, I instinctively veered right on Rue du Roi-de-Sicile, toward the apartment I planned to purchase. As if, through some miracle, the bill of sale would already be signed, and the keys would appear in my hands.

I was nearing the Dragon Tattoo—Stéphane's female-run tattoo shop—when I noticed that Sophia was still chasing after me. Barefoot, her robe half open, revealing her naked stomach and opulent chest, she was gaining on me. That cursed Chinese dress was slowing me down!

"Stop! Elle, stop . . . shit!"

I didn't want to hear anything from her. I pressed forward, despite the risk of twisting my ankles in my high heels.

The next time I heard her voice call out to me, Sophia seemed farther behind me. She had stopped running.

"Stop . . . It wasn't Louie's idea . . . I was the one who begged Alban to put me in the show."

I froze. Sophia was standing half naked and drawing attention to herself in the middle of the street. Only later did the preposterous idea cross my mind that passersby must have taken this for a lesbian spat.

I considered for a moment the few steps separating her from me, but she was the one to close this distance. She took me in her arms and led me—I was as lifeless as a doll—toward Layover in Lebanon. I remembered the place from the time I had met Rebecca there a year earlier. It was there that I'd first learned of Louie's feelings for me.

We collapsed, exhausted—we hadn't been jogging in Bois de Vincennes for a long time—and Sophia ordered two teas and an assortment of pastries.

"You mean to tell me that Louie had nothing to do with it?"

"Nothing, I swear. Peggy is a mutual friend of David's and mine."

"A friend of David's?"

"David Garchey," she quickly clarified. "She mentioned the show to me after he had talked to her about performing in it. She thought it was funny. But I wasn't supposed to be in it. They thought that you guys wouldn't like it. I was the one who begged David and Alban to let me do it."

"For God's sake, Soph . . . you're so much better than that."

She stared at me and readjusted the folds of her robe, which the waiter had been eyeing. He set down our drinks and sweets, and left with a crude smile.

"Wake up, Elle! I'm worth what people are willing to give me. Do you think I'm happy about having to do that kind of thing? You don't think I might have higher aspirations than to shake my ass for a bunch of stuck-up snobs? Honestly, they're no better than the nasty men who go to peep shows. And at least those men don't hide behind some idiotic, pseudointellectual crap when they want to get their rocks off."

"Then . . . don't do it."

"Oh, great! You tell that to my landlord. Tell that to my banker. To the credit card companies. Tell that to the asshole checkout guy at the grocery store, shit!"

"What checkout guy?"

"The guy who forgets to scan my tampons if I let him peek at my breasts while I'm paying."

I didn't know what to say. I had already offered several times to give her some financial help, but she always declined, saying that my charity, however nice, wouldn't fix her problems. It wasn't just cash she needed but a real job, a stable situation, a reliable source of income. She did not need to add to her mountain of debt.

"It's easy for you. You went from your mom's house to David's house, and from David to Louie. Remind me, when was the last time you paid rent? Or bought groceries? Or had bills to pay?"

That was unfair, mean even. She realized it as soon as the words came out of her mouth, and her look was one of contrition.

"Sorry. I didn't mean that."

"I know," I said, more coldly than I had intended.

I drank some hot tea to suppress the sob I could feel forming in my chest. I did not want to break into tears in front of her. I managed to compose myself.

"Anyway, that's not the problem between us."

"What do you mean?"

"You're still not over the fact that I slept with him before you did."

With him, Louie. This was the first time the subject had ever been broached between us.

"That's not true," I said, defending myself without much conviction.

"It's completely true, and you know it."

If our aim was sincerity, then she had just scored a point.

"Okay . . . I'll admit that it wasn't nice finding out that my boyfriend had screwed my best friend before he and I had even had our first kiss."

"So you he *kissed*, and me he *screwed*. Thanks."

"You weren't Sophia on those nights," I argued. "You were a Hotelle."

"True. And what's done is done. Even if I'm sorry . . ."

Louie didn't share her opinion.

That is why he wanted us to make love in every place that had once meant something to each of us. Particularly those where we had experienced intense love.

He thought that our respective pasts, including our biggest mistakes, could be covered over with new erotic memories, which we would make together. He wasn't talking about forgetting. He had been careful to use the expression "covered over," as if he were speaking of a shroud.

So, a few days earlier, he had taken me to Café des Antiquaires on the pretext that he wanted to attend an auction of early nineteenth-century furniture at Drouot next door. I didn't have any bad memories in that cozy café on Rue de la Grange-Batelière. What I liked about that place was simply its familiarity, after all the time I had spent there with Sophia. But that was enough for Louie: he wanted to transform the place for me, for it to be imbued with sensual meaning.

"Drink your coffee, then go to the men's room," he had commanded, in all seriousness.

"Why not the ladies' room?"

"Because there are always more people in the ladies' room. Also, men would never complain about a couple messing around in one of the stalls."

"Are you sure?"

"Absolutely, Mademoiselle. Worst-case scenario, the guy will listen in on the noise we're making and masturbate in the stall next to ours. With a woman, nothing is sure. She might tell the owner."

Was he speaking from experience? Had he already done this before? Or had he ever been the voyeur getting off on two adventurous lovers?

I obeyed his orders and chose the larger of two stalls in the men's restroom. As is the case in most Parisian cafés, the facilities were run-down, and the smell of urine overwhelmed the artificial floral scent of some cleaning product.

About two minutes later, I heard a limp over the restroom tiles, then a light knock on the wooden door in front of me.

"THREE SHORT KNOCKS, FOLLOWED BY two long, so you know it's me."

THE KNOCKING PATTERN CORRESPONDED TO our plan. He slipped into the cramped space, and I noticed that he must have left his jacket on the back of his chair—a smart but risky move.

"WE WON'T HAVE MUCH TIME," he had warned me.

THAT WAS TRUE. MY HEART was pounding, and my head spinning. My whole body was on high alert, as he had said it would be. The fear of being caught made the space feel even smaller and more uncomfortable. It became clear to me that coitus such as we had known it would not be possible here. So I dropped to my knees, unzipped his pants, and withdrew his cock, which instantly hardened, a drop of liquid pearling on his tip.

"YOU WILL SUCK ME MORE avidly than ever before."

"Oh really?" I had smiled mischievously. "And what makes you so sure?"

"You'll see."

I SAW . . . HIS PULSATING member growing in the darkness and its eagerness to dive into my lips. His face tilted forward, tense with desire. His hands pressed into the walls of the stall to avoid swaying or falling down on top of me.

I smelled something, too. The specific scent of his sex was stronger than the others. My man's aroma. My dominant male marking his territory, conquering it from all those who had been here before.

So this was danger? To feel him be so impatient, so vulnerable? I did not go into details with him this time. I did not explore the folds of his foreskin with the tip of my tongue, which is what I usually liked to do. I simply formed the roundest shape with my lips that I could, making them wet and juicy as I sucked him. My movements were fast but smooth. They were loud. And saliva frothed at the edges of my mouth as though I were a dog lapping up the contents of her dish. I was thirsty for him.

"I WILL PROBABLY COME IN your mouth; you should prepare yourself for that."

PRETTY SOON, IT BECAME CLEAR that release was imminent. He was gripping my hair, pressing my forehead into his abdomen, thrusting his member deep into my throat. His breath grew heavier and heavier.

The restroom door banged, and I froze, his dick still half inside my mouth. Louie suppressed a moan during the time it took for the unsuspecting guest to relieve himself in a neighboring urinal. *Don't move!*, my lover said to me with his eyes. The guy was taking forever to pee. I wondered what he looked like. Was he young or old, handsome or not so much? And his penis?

"AND WHAT ABOUT ME?"

"You? You'll touch yourself, darling."

AND THAT IS WHAT I did. Reaching up my dress, I pushed my panties to one side and slipped two timid fingers into the folds of my soaking vulva. The entire area surrounding my genitals was so sensitive that I had trouble containing vocal expressions of pleasure. The man relieving himself suddenly cut short his stream of urine and asked:

"Hello? Is there someone there?"

His question was greeted with silence and he didn't insist. I thrust my middle finger into my gaping vagina. Liquid flooded my hand. I even think that a few drops of fluid fell onto the grimy concrete floor. Louie devoured me with his eyes. From his dominant perspective, I was barely visible. The image of his cock in my mouth was probably forefront in his line of sight. The juxtaposition of images—my lips so vivid and the rest of me hidden—was the height of excitement, it seemed. And being forced to remain immobile was almost more than he could take.

At last we heard the sound of the sink, then the paper towel being torn off the dispenser with force, and then the anonymous guest left the restroom without a second thought to our presence. I fingered myself with renewed vigor and re-adjusted my left leg so that I could reach even deeper inside. I could now caress my most sensitive regions, the ones that re-acted to even the slightest touch. A little mound of flesh grew more and more engorged with every passing motion. A soft vibration emanated from it, shaking my entire body.

I hardly noticed when Louie started moving back and forth again inside my mouth.

"AND DO YOU THINK WE'LL be able to come?"

THAT IS EXACTLY WHAT WE did. At the same time, or almost. His semen spread through my mouth like milk cloud-ing a hot beverage, and I swallowed his thick and rich liquid in greedy, gluttonous gulps.

The little puddle beneath me had grown. With a strong arm, Louie helped me stand and grabbed hold of the hand that had been digging into my innermost depths. He put it in his mouth and hungrily licked it clean.

Clearly, the menu at Café des Antiquaires would never be the same for us.

SOPHIA'S VOICE WOKE ME FROM my reverie:

"But you know . . . if Rebecca hadn't given me that mission with him, the two of you might have never met."

"How do you figure that?"

"They didn't want me to tell you—"

"Who do you mean by 'they'?"

"Rebecca and Louie."

"Why?"

"Lord knows," she breathed, her eyes gazing at the ceiling. "All I know is that the first night I met him, he saw the picture of the two of us I had as the background image on my phone. Of you and me."

I remembered the picture. It had been taken at Café des Antiquaires one night when we had needed a morale boost. Sophia had taken it herself with an extended arm after we were already well lubricated.

"At one point," she continued, "my phone rang, and our picture lit up. Let's just say that he and I were in a position that forced him to see it. And then he immediately asked if he could look at it."

"That's it?"

"No . . . he also asked who you were."

"You mean . . . he saw me before we ever met? And before he saw my picture in the Belles de Nuit catalogue?"

"Yes. And even before the mission when you met David. The night I'm talking about took place about a month before that night with the HEF alumni."

Or early March 2009. More or less four months after I'd started as a Hotelle. I guess the Barlet brothers did not consult Rebecca's catalogue every day—or perhaps she had managed to filter their access.

Until then, I had made a concerted effort not to think about Louie's feelings for the deceased Aurora. He had intimated that he'd once loved her. But he had made it a point not to overstate his feelings for her, insisting that Aurora's choice— David over him—had been a relief.

But what were his true feelings? How had he really felt

when he'd seen Aurora's doppelganger for the first time, when he'd seen that photograph?

"He fell in love with me before his brother did," I realized out loud.

"Yeah, I think so," my friend agreed. "And if there is one thing you should never doubt, it's the sincerity of his feelings for you."

"Do you think so?" I asked.

"I was there when he first laid eyes on that picture. I saw what he felt. Louie is not in love with a ghost. He's in love with *you*."

"But that wasn't me. It was a picture of me."

A picture of *us*, I thought, both my doppelganger and me.

"Maybe . . . but he really seemed bowled over. Love-at-first-sight kind of thing."

And yet he had let his brother have me. He had been an accomplice in that twisted plan, whereby David was to marry me while Louie initiated me in illicit games. And, like David had, he now loved a woman who looked exactly like the woman with whom he had been in love twenty years earlier.

I drove these troubled thoughts from my mind. After all, Louie had taken all kinds of risks for me. Starting with the reawakening of a fraternal quarrel that had been dormant for decades.

Noting my melancholia, Sophia must have guessed that her revelation was a slippery slope because she quickly changed the subject—although this new topic was not much lighter:

"Any leads on the work front?"

"Nothing. With all that happened, I think David has done everything in his power to kill my reputation."

"You never know," she downplayed.

The strident sound of a percolator ripped through the room, and I waited to respond. When at last calm was regained, it was accompanied by the smell of fresh coffee and spices.

"No, but . . . when people you have never met tell you over the phone that you're not what they're looking for in terms of their 'standards of professionalism,' I think it's fairly obvious what's going on."

"True . . ."

"And I don't know if Fred has already told you, but I asked him if I could get a copy of my one episode of *Culture Mix*."

The show that was supposed to be my big debut on television but that was never broadcast.

"And?"

"Guess what the people in the archives at BTV said?"

"I have no idea."

"That the demo, the rushes, the test shots, and even the casting tapes had all been erased—on management's orders. End of story. It's like my show never even existed. Even in its early planning stages."

"At least it's all out in the open."

"Yeah. I mean, the problem is that I'm back to where I started, with just as little experience as when I first graduated. But with the addition of a lost year on my résumé."

AS WE WERE LEAVING THE Lebanese lunch spot, we saw Stéphane smoking a cigarette on the sidewalk across the street. She was absently leaning against the window of her tattoo parlor, partially obscuring the logo—three female silhouettes in white above the shop name, DRAGON TATTOO, and accented by three orange flowers.

She noticed us and waved.

"Hey. How's it going? Tattoo hurt much? Been using the ointment?"

"Yeah, everything's fine. But I don't think I'll be getting another one anytime soon," I said, smiling.

"Your man is braver than you."

What did she mean by that? Had Louie already scheduled his next tattoo in his Alphabet Man series?

He was really secretive about it, preferring to unveil each new letter as a surprise.

Rather than put Stéphane in an awkward position, I pretended I knew what she was talking about:

"Yeah, he's obsessed. By the way, he said you had some new stuff to show me."

"I've just finished the sketches for his next tattoo. Do you want to see them?"

The small waiting room was mostly taken up by a large sofa. We sat there, and she withdrew a number of drawings for different tattoos from a folder marked *Louie Barlet*.

My man's new tattoo would depict large waves crashing into a series of foam-rimmed rocks, from which would emerge two uppercase letters: *S F*.

"'SF'?" Sophia asked, surprised. "Louie is a fan of science fiction?"

"Umm, not to my knowledge. His literary tastes are more traditional."

"'SF' like 'Semper fidelis,'" Stéphane informed us.

I was bothered by the fact that this tattoo artist knew more about the symbols and messages that were important to Louie than I did. But I hid my frustration in favor of satisfying my curiosity:

"Isn't that the army's motto? Or some police force's?"

I couldn't help glancing at Stéphane's military cap, which she seemed to wear in all seasons and for all occasions.

"It's been the motto of the American Marines since 1883," Stéphane confirmed. "But that's not why he has chosen those initials."

"Really? Why, then?"

"Well before the Yanks got their hands on it, 'Semper fidelis' was already being used as the motto for a French town."

"Which? Saint-Félicien?" Sophia joked. She seemed to be as curious as I was.

The tattoo artist pointed a well-manicured index finger at the rocks and waves.

"Saint-Malo. In Brittany."

Aurora's resting place, at Rocabey Cemetery.

7

May 19, 2010

I have never known how to say no to Sophia. She has always been like a big sister to me, the one I never had. I've always had to think seriously about even her most foolish plans for adventure before eventually refusing. Ever since we first met in college, it's been like that. Everything seems more interesting, more intense, when Sophia is the one suggesting it.

But my heart was anything but eager for adventure that night . . .

"COME ON, IT WILL HELP take your mind off things," Sophia argued, though without much conviction.

I thought of my relationship with Louie, which was like an erotic construction site, where equal parts of sexual tension and emotions were used as cement.

On the ground floor of 24 Rue du Roi-de-Sicile, the former address of the now defunct Belles de Nuit, there was a sex shop called Dollhouse. Despite having frequently walked by the place, I had never been inside. Sophia, who was a regular, wanted to fix that, and in spite of her limited resources, she had offered to buy me the latest gadget in sex toys, which a well-known maker of condoms had recently put on the market, and which women's magazines had been heartily endorsing: app-controlled vibrating panties.

"What's the point?" I asked, skeptical and trying to dissuade her.

"You put it on one night when Louie is gone, Louie signs onto the app . . . and I swear, hon, you'll see the point!"

"That is, if I ever see him again alive," I said in a melodramatic tone.

I was having trouble hiding my worry. And a weird present wouldn't be enough to make me smile.

LATER THAT NIGHT, AFTER SOPHIA had gone home, Alban sent me the address for the child protective services branch of the police force. It was housed in the police headquarters of Paris, at 12 Quai de Gesvres, or about fifteen minutes away on foot. But once I got there, a dreary looking state worker stationed at the prison door informed me: (1) that they closed the doors to the public at four thirty p.m.; (2) that those under questioning could not receive visitors, even during opening hours.

Louie was no longer a tax-paying citizen like any other. He was now "under questioning," a potential criminal. And the whole idea made me shudder.

IRONY OF FATE: I HAPPENED to find myself on Rue Jean-Baptiste Pigalle, at the entrance to the Hôtel des Charmes at ten o'clock. The hour of Louie's and my past rendezvous there. Remarkably, Monsieur Jacques, the tall-statured and slightly over-formal greeter, could not be seen from his usual perch at the reception desk. He was no doubt attending to something upstairs. Instead, I noticed Ysiam's comely smile from the street.

As soon as he saw me, the young man started frantically rummaging through the varnished compartments behind him. In place of a hello, he handed me an envelope, with a pained look on his face.

"I'm sorry, I haven't had time to bring this to you directly."

The envelope was, in effect, bulging. It had already been four or five days since Ysiam's last visit, when I had given him the letter addressed to Mademoiselle Lebourdais.

"That's okay. I'm not expecting anything urgent. However . . ." I hesitated.

"Yes?"

"Louie thinks we forgot a notebook in the Josephine."

I had almost referred to it as room one before I remembered that only Louie and I called it by that name. It had a symbolic place in our hearts, memories, and sexes. A capital place. For everyone else, it was the Josephine, a room on the second floor of the hotel.

"What does the notebook look like?"

"It's silver. With spirals. Have you seen anything like it?"

"No. And if someone on the cleaning staff finds it, he or she gives it to me immediately."

Although his choice of verb tense in French was not perfect, his meaning was unambiguous: no one had given him our Ten-Times-a-Day. Although I was not surprised, the fact that we couldn't find the notebook filled me with worry. All of our intimate moments were recorded there, in vivid detail. And while I feared the idea of some third party riffling its pages as if it were his or her own bed, I couldn't even bring myself to imagine what might happen if someone with dark intentions got his or her hands on it. It was imperative that I find it.

"Okay. Do you mind if I have a look?"

"Now?"

I could have sworn I saw his swarthy skin blush.

"Yes. Is there a problem with that?"

"Umm . . ."

"It's occupied, is that it?"

"Yes," he affirmed, with a look of relief.

"Okay, I understand."

It had had to happen eventually. Since we'd left, room one had once again become a room to rent like all the others. Anyone, lovers or others, could rent it. The room was, in a way, like a Hotelle: it went to the highest bidder.

"Will you let me know if someone finds it?"

"Yes, of course, Mademois-Elle. I can also go and look when the room is empty."

"Thank you, that would be nice."

Sometimes he mashed together the form of address with my nickname, creating a kind of portmanteau: Mademois-Elle. It was delightful.

"Oh! And Ysiam . . . ," I added, just as I was about to leave, "don't mention it to Monsieur Jacques. There's no reason to bother him with this."

I SLEPT FITFULLY THAT NIGHT alone in Mars House. Whenever I finally drifted off, it was short-lasted and agitated, with haunting dreams that startled me awake again. I endured this cycle for seven or eight hours, feverish, my nightgown drenched in sweat.

I primarily attributed my feeling of agitation to Louie's absence. To my missing him. To that fear that any woman would have at night alone in such a large house. And also to my worries over his current legal situation. But above all, the agitation within me was the result of something much simpler: this was my first night without him in a year. My whole body was used to his being there, to the heat of our bodies commingling. I had grown accustomed to curling up to him, and my curves longed for his angles. The sad events of the day had amputated him from me, and like someone who has lost a limb, I could still feel his phantom presence.

THE NEXT MORNING, STILL GROGGY, I called everyone I thought might have news on Louie: Alban, Sophia, David Garchey, Rebecca, even Peggy. No one knew anything. The gallerist insisted, however, that I take down Jean-Marc Zerki's number. But I decided against calling Louie's lawyer. I didn't want to hear him talk to me about the situation in matter-of-fact lawyer-speak, regardless of whether what he had to say was good or bad.

I made do with sending him a text message in which I introduced myself and asked him to keep me informed of any developments. His response was terse: "Okay."

I also kept myself from contacting Ysiam. I didn't doubt for a second that if the nice Sri Lankan bellhop found anything, he would be quick to inform me. I had nothing to do but glumly kill time. Nothing, except that absurd pair of vibrating panties—but what good would they do me if Louie ended up in jail? There was also that key that Alban had given me.

I turned it over and over in my hand, as if it were a strange and novel insect. As I contemplated the key, the thought occurred to me that such a specimen could only open a modern door, a high-performance, ultra-resistant, top-security door. With the exception of the gate separating our home from the street, the shape of whose lock didn't look like it matched, there was only one door in the whole house that met the criteria.

I quickly found myself at the base of the main staircase. The reinforced door that led to the basement was locked. I hadn't seen it open since I'd followed David Garchey through it on the night of our housewarming. I slid the long, narrow key into the keyway of the cylinder lock. It met no resistance. I turned it twice to the left, and a triple click told me that the pins were in alignment. The lock was open. I lowered the door handle, reached to turn on the interrupter at the top of the stairs, and made my way down to the depths of the old building.

In the video room at the end of the gray corridor, all the screens were off. I found that reassuring—Louie was not as much of a voyeur as I had feared—but the reason for his having given me this key was no clearer. What did he expect from me?

Speaking through Alban, Louie had asked me to find our notebook at the Hôtel des Charmes. He had also added, more evasively, that I "should lock up anything that could be 'too hot.'" Did he want me to hide sensitive documents here, like our Ten-Times-a-Day? It didn't make any sense. If they came to search the place, the cops would have no qualms about opening the reinforced door. Moreover, what exactly was to be considered "too hot" in Louie's vast collection of erotic documents and curiosities? Which of these texts or images could be compromising in the prudish eyes of the courts?

Unless perhaps he wanted me to do the opposite: not hide what could incriminate him here but find something that could set him free.

On the vast electronic control panel pocked with lights and buttons, I noticed a red button that was larger than the others and on which was printed a half-erased *Power On-Off*. I pressed it and a number of colorful lights flashed on. Several menus appeared on a small liquid crystal display that looked to me like the command center. I used a wheel located beneath it to select *Files*. I figured that this must be the system's memory, a kind of hard drive with backed-up files. There were a number of subfiles with abstruse numeric titles. Some looked like they could be dates, but most didn't seem to adhere to any particular logic.

I randomly selected one among them, and a screen on the wall of monitors in front of me lit up. Black-and-white images appeared. They were in some ways familiar. I immediately recognized one of the rooms that Louie and I had frequented at the Hôtel des Charmes, the Kitty Fisher, named for the famous English courtesan who was immortalized by Giacomo Casanova in the 1760s.

The girl on the screen was a young blonde, barely twenty, long and lean—though also with a well-endowed chest. The image was a high-angle close-up of her mouth, one that paid homage to her skills as a fellatio artist. I pressed the fast-forward button—the rapid playback for the video made the two characters look like ridiculous puppets—until I got to the part when the man ejaculated on her face, decorating her plump cheeks with white stripes. Even though I was shaken up, I noticed something important: the clip had a date and time stamp—05/12/1997 23:52.

This film was also far from being the only one of its kind. I opened the files one by one. Each clip was taken in a different room, but it was always filmed from the same tilted angle that made the cameraman into a faceless hero in an orgy of soft- and hard-core pornography. Indeed, depending on the ambiance and period of the room, our man indulged himself in soft-core and hard-core, with one partner or many, with and without accessories. I also noticed that the clips got more intense with time. One of the more recent videos, dated summer 2005, was almost unbearable to watch. In it, our protagonist shoved an unimaginably large dildo—three to four times the size of a normal penis—in and out of a petite Asian woman's vagina. The girl squealed in pain—or was that pleasure?—and the whole point of the bit seemed to be for the actor-cameraman to use the monstrous sex toy to elicit ever sharper, ever more desperate cries, unless this was a tribute to one of those X-rated Japanese films Louie had told me about, where a female victim of male aggression reenacts the shameful scene as loudly as she can. Bit by bit, the disproportionately large black object became covered in a kind of white froth that grew thicker with each thrust. And despite being disgusted, I felt a new sensation grow inside me.

But the most exciting film for me was the one in which our mysterious lover was paired with a young brunette with light skin and long hair, a girl who looked like me. The similarity was disconcerting, the way she moved beneath the man's weight, the sound of her wails of pleasure. Did similar physiques have similar ways of orgasming?

When she climaxed, a long, drawn-out series of spasms that seemed to possess her body and raise it from the sheets, the girl was lying on her stomach, her legs spread wide, and the cameraman was stretched out on top of her. I remembered that this was the same position in which I had found myself when Louie had made me come for the first time one year earlier. There was an awkward movement of the camera, and then a new angle: a close-up of the couple's thighs and asses, their sexes joined. Then, a final cry, and the anonymous cock quickly withdrew and covered a still very excited vagina with spurts of translucent fluid. The sheets were drenched. She had just ejaculated, much as I had a few days earlier in that pitch-black hotel room.

ONLY AFTER I HAD SEEN over a dozen of these movies, all from different times between the early nineties (around 1992) and the year 2007, did I at last allow myself to wonder: Who was this man? Who was the man behind the penis? Who was penetrating this great variety of women whose only common traits were their youth and physical attractiveness? Oh, when it came to the women, there was no mystery. In the more recent clips, I had recognized some of Rebecca's girls. And it was not much of a stretch of the imagination to conclude that this compulsive lover had done his shopping in the Belles de Nuit catalogue.

As for the man . . . who else but *my* man, Louie, the sex addict, the man accustomed to high prices? Who else could it be? Although its view was skewed by the camera angle, although the dim lighting made it grainy and pixelated on-screen, that penis seemed familiar. Still, I couldn't be sure if the penis I saw on-screen was always the same penis, nor was I absolutely certain that it belonged to the man I loved.

It didn't help that the man never made a peep in any of these films. Only his partners moaned, screamed, whined, and sometimes even vocalized—"oh yes!" and "God, yes!" But he had been careful not to make a sound, not to be seen, not to be recognizable in any way. He was clearly concerned with remaining anonymous. Had he gone so far as to edit his voice out of the soundtracks?

If it really was Louie in those movies, then it confirmed my suspicions as well as David's spiteful allegations: for many years, apparently, Louie's intimate relations had almost exclusively been with professionals, Hotelles provided by Rebecca through her agency. Had she given him a special rate? Had it been free?

One question in particular was nagging me: Why would a man who was so handsome, so interesting, so wellborn and rich, limit himself to transactional relationships with no future? The question engendered another, more concerning thought: Why had this commitment-phobe changed his routine and principles of radical independence when he had seen that picture of me on Sophia's phone? Had I cured him of his obsession with sex simply by looking like Aurora? Or, as my friend had insisted, was there something else about me, something truer, stronger?

During my exploration of the contents of the computer, I found a program to delete all the files. My finger hovered over the button as I considered my options for several long minutes: Should I erase them, as Louie seemed to have suggested I do? Was I to get rid of these troubling remnants of my future husband's past?

"Well, well, girl, what are you doing here? The upstairs not enough for you anymore?"

The sudden intrusion of Felicity, all whiskers and curious to explore an area that was usually off-limits, decided things for me.

I was looking for you, she seemed to purr at me as she climbed onto my lap.

I gave up on making any decisions that I could regret and shut everything down. The screens went dark, and I grabbed my favorite ball of fur and climbed upstairs.

MARS HOUSE, MY HOME WITH Louie, seemed to me like a movie set or a magician's stage, where every nook and cranny might reveal new secrets about this man.

Where were his secrets buried? Did he lock them in his desk like David?

No. What was most disconcerting, in fact, was that aside from the basement, nothing—no door, no drawer, no lock—put up any resistance to my thorough investigation that day. I wasn't fooling anyone, least of all myself, by pretending to explore the house in order to hide anything that could prejudice the courts against Louie. I had simply succumbed to my unhealthy curiosity, whose extent I had already encountered in the past and whose deleterious effects I had already experienced. It was my curiosity that drove me to spend more time searching through his office than through any other room in the house.

I was about to give up when I stubbed my bare toe on a piece of the parquet that was just barely coming loose.

"Ouch! Crap . . . that was stupid!"

I was cursing the construction crew and the fact that home remodels are never done with as much care as one might hope when a little pressure from my heel tipped up the narrow oak floorboard, opening a dusty hiding place. I leaned forward to see what was inside and made out a small white envelope, the kind used for invitations and announcements.

"What's that?"

I carefully withdrew it from where it was resting and

considered it for a while before daring to open its flap. Considering the paper's degree of discoloration and its wilted corners, I guessed that the envelope had not been buried in this wooden hiding place just yesterday. Finally, my chest heaving, I quickly pulled open the triangular flap.

It contained just one small, yellowed photograph with a scalloped border such as was common in the sixties and seventies. In fact, everything about the photograph—its faded colors, the pose of the people in it, their clothing—was reminiscent of that era.

The picture was of an adult couple standing on either side of a gaudy Christmas tree and, in front of them, two young children of about two or three years. At least that is what I was able to gather, given the condition of the photograph. Because although the bigger of the two children, the boy, David, was completely recognizable—David's features had hardly changed with time—I could not for the life of me identify the little chestnut-haired girl who was holding his hand. Her face had been scratched out with the blade of a knife or a pair of scissors. Whatever it was, it had almost pierced through the photograph's thick, glazed paper.

And even though their faces hadn't been massacred, the man and woman didn't remind me of anyone I knew. After having seen numerous pictures of Andre and Hortensia Barlet at Brown Rocks, their beach house, I knew that this was not them. Who were they, then? And what was David doing in this family portrait? Who was the girl with the mutilated face? And why had her identity been scratched out like that?

But above all: Why did Louie keep that snapshot hermetically sealed underneath a floorboard?

I turned the picture over to see if there was any kind of

inscription on the back that might give me some answers, but it was blank.

My next reflex: dig out my cell phone, launch its camera app, and photograph the picture so that I would have it archived in my device's electronic memory.

The little faceless girl had been brought out of her hiding place. And I was not going to forget about her.

8

May 20, 2010

Louie to be questioned for another 24 hours.
Will keep you updated. JMZ

That was the kind of text message that Jean-Marc Zerki sent to his clients or, in this case, to the future wife of one of his clients. No "hello," no "sorry," no trace of emotion or compassion. Strict efficiency. Professional and unfeeling as the penal code.

In any case, what could I have said if he had spoken to me with a bit more humanity? That I had spent the last day fretting alone in our three-thousand-square-foot castle? That I wasn't sure whether to spend the day crying or checking every square foot of parquet in said palace? That without Louie I felt hollow?

My mustachioed professor—you remember him, I've mentioned him before—used to tell his journalism students: "An image is an image. Ten images, now that's style. At least, that is, if you own it," he was always quick to add. So I could have said that I was tearing out my hair, as restless as a caged wild animal, that I couldn't eat, that without my man I was only a shadow of myself . . . None of that was true, and yet, in a literary sense, it wasn't very far off.

What Monsieur Mustache and all his wisdom couldn't have anticipated was the extent to which my missing Louie—in a physical sense—surpassed all other sensations. It was an erotic lack. Not only did my bed miss him, but also my mouth, my breasts, my buttocks, my sex—each part of my body was missing its male counterpart, along with all the sensual stimulation I had grown used to receiving every day. For the past year, we hadn't gone twelve hours without making love or participating in some kind of sexual activity, even if it was just sleepy genital touching underneath the comforter.

The discovery of those hidden videos in the basement should have dampened my ardor. Any sane woman in my place would have felt betrayed, degraded, demeaned, even though all of the tapes were from a time well before our relationship. Any sane girl would have run as fast as she could away from that libidinous monster, that sex maniac, that man obsessed with vaginas—I mean to emphasize the plural, *vaginas*, since multiplicity seemed to be an integral part of his addiction.

But I only desired him all the more. It burned like a fire inside me, expanding with every hour spent away from him. After all, had it not been his madness, his passion, his licentious desire that had attracted me in the first place? Isn't that what had drawn me to him, despite the taboo? I had crossed obstacles to lose myself in him, to lose all sense of reason, to become one with him. Could I really reproach him?

THAT DAY, I TOUCHED MYSELF for a long while, stretched out on our bed, dressed in his favorite underthings for me—a demi-cup bra and mini slip, both in a transparent tulle edged with pink satin. He had given me the set one night at the Hôtel des Charmes, and I imagine its price was inversely proportional to its surface area.

Right then, I didn't know what to do that could help him besides pleasuring myself. What else could he expect of me? Sex had become our special unspoken language, and I couldn't think of a better way to speak to him through the prison walls than to masturbate.

Still, this pleasure wasn't joyful. My fingers forcefully, almost savagely, thrust themselves inside me. I was masturbating in the same way that one angrily, impotently, slams a fist into a wall. My hand crashed into my vagina, hitting it violently. It dug inside me like a starving animal. And the few orgasms that I was able to draw out of myself in this brutal way were nothing like the ones he gave me. They reverberated through my body like a slap in the face. They twisted me around like I was wet laundry. They left me exhausted and gasping for breath. Afterward, I felt strangely bitter and satisfied.

"TURN ON BTV! RIGHT NOW!"

When Sophia called, the ring of the phone sounded like an order. I thought something bad must have happened. Or something big. And it was something important. I hadn't watched that channel since I'd left Barlet Tower. But I forced myself to press two buttons on the remote and turn to channel twenty-four.

"Is it on? Are you seeing this?"

I thought it would be a shot of Louie surrounded by a horde of journalists, with his robotic lawyer, Zerki, at his side.

Instead I saw the bland and unattractive mug of a balding fifty-something. *Antoine Gobert—President of PRSPS, Third District, Paris,* scrolled the man's name and title at the bottom of the screen.

I had never laid eyes before on this man in the sky-blue shirt and silk scarf. However, I did recognize Rue de Sévigné and, in the background, a street view of the Sauvage Gallery.

"Who is that idiot?" I asked.

"That idiot is the idiot responsible for your man's night with the cops."

"What's PRSPS?"

"I had to look it up online: Parents of Religious Students in Public Schools. Great, right?"

"Hold on . . . I'm trying to listen."

My ears were ringing with emotion. I turned up the sound so that I could hear what this affable person had to say:

" . . . situation is very clear: *we* parents will not tolerate it when disreputable people target our children with pornography. I don't care if they say they're defending modern art—I say that's a false pretense. And what's more, this happened just as these kids were getting out of school, in the same neighborhood where their school is located. That is the state of society today. If we don't speak up now, what next? Sex toys distributed in elementary schools? After all, they are toys, am I right?"

"There's an idea!" Sophia laughed on the other end of the line.

"Shh!" I said, wanting to hear what came next.

"So, if I'm understanding you correctly," the young voice of the reporter interrupted from the other side of the camera, "you will not be rescinding the complaint you've lodged against the Sauvage Gallery and its representative, Louie Barlet?"

"That is correct. We will rescind nothing."

"And yet the artist's show that you say offends you has been taken down, it—"

"That may be, but we cannot erase what our children have already seen. It's not as simple as taking paintings off the wall. What is done is done. And that is why we are seeking reparations."

"He speaks pretty well for an idiot," Sophia said as the program moved on to the next headline and Antoine Gobert's face disappeared.

I had thought the same thing. And also that I wished I could be in the interviewer's place.

Sophia knew me so well that this suggestion didn't need any prompting:

"Do you want to meet him?"

"What do you mean?"

"Well, so I've already called PRSPS's office, and I used my nice stewardess voice. And we have a meeting with His Majesty Antoine Gobert in two hours."

"Under what pretext?"

"The truth, or almost: that two journalism students have a paper due tomorrow morning. I really played up my girlish pout over the phone."

For the first time in days, I burst out laughing, and I approved her plan.

A HOT AND STICKY MIDAFTERNOON shower was just letting up when we got off the metro at the very bourgeois Rue de l'Arcade, a few steps away from the Madeleine.

A secretary with a gray bun asked us to wait a few minutes for "President Gobert" to grace us with his presence.

He was even uglier in person, his jaw at once prognathous and low-hung. It made his face look droopy, and me a little nauseated.

"Mesdemoiselles, please sit down," he said, pointing at two threadbare chairs.

His office was depressing and poorly lit. The walls featured various pious pictures and portraits of popes from the past fifty years. Even an end-of-life John Paul II looked friendlier and livelier than our host.

"I'm listening," he said, forcing a hideous smile. "I'm all ears, ask away."

"We would like to know why the show at the Sauvage Gallery bothers you so much," I began, innocently. "After all, it can't be the first gallery to do such a raw show on sexuality. In fact, if I recall, the Pompidou Center did an exhibition a few years ago called *Feminine/Masculine* that featured pieces that were at least as racy as what we're talking about now."

"You're perfectly correct, Mademoiselle. And I do not take issue with artists exploring a subject as fundamental as human sexuality or male-female relationships. People are free to practice their art as they see fit. I myself often go to museums, and I've admired nudes by Michelangelo and Botticelli. That is not the issue here."

"What is the issue, then?" Sophia interrupted, a little too aggressively. "Those children that you work so hard to protect also go to the Louvre. They've also seen breasts and statues with wee-wees."

The human toad in front of us stiffened in his chair and swallowed loudly before replying:

"You're mischaracterizing my position, Mademoiselle. It is not my intent to keep all traces of nudity from children. Not only can nudity be the subject of high art, as the examples I've just mentioned prove, but to try to hide it would be impossible. Nudity is everywhere today. Just turn on the TV, watch a movie, look at an ad. It has become a ubiquitous part of our society, and to a certain extent, we have to work with it."

"In that case, I don't understand," I fired back. "Why are you so against this art exhibit and the people backing it?"

He planted his cruel little eyes into mine, like a hook gouging into the throat of a fish, determined not to release me.

"Because this *art exhibit*, as you call it, was not simply a display of girl parts and boy parts such as children draw them on bathroom walls. Here, genitals were shown in action, and the way in which these images were juxtaposed gave an absolutely deformed sense of sexuality. Representations of sexuality ought to include respect for the other and engender a kind of mutual fulfillment. This *exhibit* was no longer art. It was pornography being played in the middle of the street!"

"Oh, right. Because you're so familiar with respect and fulfillment!" Sophia barked.

The allusion to his unfortunate physique and its obvious limitations in the bedroom was blatant. Sophia had barely kept herself from spitting more invective into his face, something along the lines of *Seriously?! Because, have you seen your kill-love face?*

Still, the game was up. The president of PRSPS saw through us. He began to stand, as though he feared for his safety, then sat down again and went on the offensive:

"Who are you really? And what do you want?"

"I'm Annabelle Lorand," I declared, unmasking myself. "And I would like you to reconsider your complaint against the Sauvage Gallery and Monsieur Barlet."

"And, pray tell, why might that be?" he asked, his tone now much sharper.

"Because . . ."

What argument did I have against him, besides my love for the man he was accusing?

" . . . because Louie and I are getting married soon. And I would prefer not to have to do it in the VIP section of La Santé Prison."

My sincerity barely gave him pause. He replied in a vindictive tone, his expression mean:

"Listen, I'm sorry, but I couldn't care less that our complaint has put a dent in your wedding plans. I'm not sure that you have grasped what is at stake here—"

"Oh, I understand. And I think that the public has heard enough from you. Now, I don't want you to persist in—"

"Excuse me, but what exactly do you take me for?" he boomed. "Do you think I'm doing this to get on television? To promote myself? Mademoiselle, a person with morals and convictions does not turn them on and off for the cameras. We will not sacrifice anything when it comes to protecting our children! Do you understand? Not a thing!"

"And according to you that justifies putting an innocent person in prison?" I cried.

"He should have thought of that before putting those heinous images in public view. Tears can't make up for such a ghastly display. That would be a little easy, now, wouldn't it?!"

This man was not going to let us off the hook easily. I even worried that my intervention may have hardened his position, and that he might try to draw still more media attention to himself. The opportunity was just too good for Gobert to pass up. And although Louie was less of a known figure than his brother, his name alone would be enough to catch the public's attention. Meanwhile, Gobert's moral stance was no doubt vindication enough for him.

"Let's drop it," Sophia whispered. "He's an idiot."

We didn't even give him time to show more indignation. A second later, we had left his office.

I WAS SO ANGRY THAT I declined Sophia's suggestion of a Monaco to lift our spirits. I went straight home to Mars House, where a surprise visitor was waiting for me at the door.

"Hello, Elle."

David, in casual attire—a polo shirt, khakis, and a cream-colored sweater around his shoulders. He seemed almost cheerful. He was as handsome and bright as he could be. Luminous, characteristically so.

"Hi . . . ," I yelped, my throat tight.

"I know my presence must come as a surprise . . . but I heard about Louie."

I raised my brow at him in irritation. What was I supposed to say? How else was I supposed to react to his concern?

"I wanted to tell you that I am sincerely sorry. And that if there's anything I can do to help you . . . I mean, help *him*. He's still my brother."

Despite the past. Despite the betrayal. Despite you and me, Annabelle, and your ultimate choice. But he didn't mention any of these qualifiers, even if I could read them in every syllable, every guarded expression.

"That's nice of you. But he has a good lawyer."

"Zerki." He nodded. "He is good."

"Do you know him?"

"I'm the one who introduced him to Louie, years ago. But

given the circumstances, he's going to need much more than a lawyer."

"What do you have in mind?" I asked, still on the defensive.

His smile widened. That expression could convert those with the most hardened convictions, motivate the apathetic, and win over all the undecideds. It was a politician's smile; I had often thought so when we were still together.

"First, let me take you to dinner. That will give me plenty of time to tell you all about my ideas on how to get my idiot brother out of this mess."

"You aren't dining with Alice?"

"Not tonight. She's entertaining her parents, who have come to Paris from the provinces to see her."

I didn't answer right away, letting my eyes drift off into Rue de la Tour-des-Dames, as if the correct response would come from one of the neighboring houses—for instance, the house that had once belonged to the famous actor Talma. He would have known how to act.

Louie would not have approved. But I felt relieved by this change in David's and my rapport. And while my feelings of guilt did not completely subside, they were lessened.

"Okay. But let's stay in the neighborhood," I suggested.

"If you like. There's that little Italian place on Avenue Trudaine."

"Perfect."

LA PIZZETTA LOOKED MORE LIKE a local dive than a gastronomic destination, but the crowd inside was an indicator of its popularity.

When we arrived, the waiter immediately led us to a reserved table near the kitchen and wine racks, which made me think that David had planned the evening before our discussion at Mars House. I didn't take offense and tried to put on a good face. I didn't want to rob him of his role as a savior, a superhero who had come out of his Batcave at just the right time. But nor did I want to be relegated to the role of the weeping woman in need of saving.

So I went on the offensive as soon as our two martinis arrived:

"What are your thoughts on Louie's situation?"

The image of David as a little boy standing in front of that Christmas tree floated in front of my eyes, superimposing itself over his adult self. But I wasn't able to get a clear view of both at the same time. And, faced with his impassive features, I decided against broaching the topic—at least for the time being.

"I don't want to worry you more than is necessary, but unfortunately, I think he's in bigger trouble than it looks."

His tone was serious but undramatic.

"Why?"

"Do I really need to spell this out?"

The waitress placed two steaming plates in front of us—we had both ordered tuna and asparagus paccheri—and whispered a barely audible "Bon appétit" before leaving us to our conversation.

"Listen, if you're going to speak in allusions and hints . . . ," I replied.

To show him that I was serious, I pretended to ignore my very appetizing meal.

He jabbed at his pasta and nodded his head, his eyes half closed.

"Okay. I guess it's not a secret: Louie is obsessed."

"Obsessed . . . ," I said, feigning ignorance.

"Annabelle . . . don't pretend, not with me. You know exactly what I'm talking about. Louie is a sex addict. He has a wandering penis. He is hypersexual, if you prefer."

"Okay, okay . . . I get it," I said, annoyed. "I understood you the first time."

"And it's been a while," he continued, in the same afflicted tone.

He had already given me this speech about his brother in the courtyard of the Max Fourestier Hospital in Nanterre. Back then, he had tried to pass the blame onto Louie for using Belles de Nuit as a private marriage agency. I remembered him saying: "He likes the chase, you see . . . Always on the hunt for fresh meat."

"What does that have to do with the present situation?" I asked insistently.

"Well, this isn't the first time his addiction to sex has gotten him into a dire situation."

He was exaggerating, or maybe not.

"Really? Give me an example."

"I have plenty. But I don't think I should be the one to—"

"Go ahead! Tell me!" I urged him. "Just one example."

He introduced a forkful of paccheri and asparagus into his mouth, taking his time to chew, then said at last:

"About ten years ago . . ."

"Yes?"

" . . . Louie was arrested for indecent exposure."

I didn't know what to say. Louie, the man I loved above all else . . . I was incapable of seeing him as one of those nasty men in raincoats who haunt schoolyards and expose themselves to unsuspecting little girls. The image didn't fit with the Louie I knew.

"What do you mean by 'exposure'?"

"Don't worry. Louie doesn't flash little girls."

The abject picture in my head immediately disappeared, and I was relieved.

"What did he do, then?"

"He was caught making love to a girlfriend in a car. It was parked in the middle of the street, in the middle of the day."

I couldn't help but smile. While I knew what the law would have to say about such an act, I had trouble seeing it as all that reprehensible. After all, it wasn't something that Louie and I wouldn't ever try. And though making love in an automobile was not yet on our list of accomplishments, this anecdote made me want to move it up on our list of erotic priorities.

"I know what you're going to say: that's nothing to write home about."

"True," I admitted.

"The problem is that, because of this kind of hobby, my brother already has a police record. And I can guarantee you that his past is not going to play in his favor."

"Has he ever been convicted of a crime?"

"No. In the past, he's gotten off with fines and stern warnings."

Fines, warnings, plural. I guessed that the car incident had not been a one-off.

I stared for a moment at the guests dining around us. Young men and women, all fairly good-looking and well groomed. I wondered if any of them added spice to their sex lives with the kind of activities we were discussing. Did they confine themselves to their bedrooms, or did they sometimes treat themselves to riskier behavior? Had Louie Barlet's type of libido become the norm or, without quite realizing it, had

I ventured down an oh-so-exciting and yet dubious—and illegal—path?

"What do you want, David? To warn me about your brother? To scare me?"

He sighed and placed a heavy hand on top of mine, which I withdrew at once.

"Elle . . . you and I, we're a thing of the past. We both agree on that. You live with Louie now. And I am going to marry Alice. I don't want to put any of that into question."

"We're still happy . . . ," I breathed.

"I just wanted to make sure that you were fully aware of the situation. Louie has gone too far in the past. And though I don't mean to frighten you, it will probably happen again."

"What do you mean by that?"

"Don't be naive, Elle. Louie is not just someone who collects porn and X-rated movies."

Sequences from the sex videos on Louie's computer flashed through my mind. His member diving into all those vaginas. His spunk spread across all those faces, those stomachs, those breasts . . .

David stared at me. His eyes tried to connect with mine, to create a sort of dialogue, which my blinking kept interrupting.

"He's a predator, Elle. A compulsive sexual consumer. And I'm sorry to say this, but as charming as you are, I have a hard time believing that he will be eternally satisfied with the same prey. It has never happened before. Why do you think he came up with the idea of creating Belles de Nuit?"

"To find you a new Aurora," I ventured.

"Wrong! Any private detective or online dating site could have helped him with that. For him, the girls were like livestock, and he helped himself to as much fresh flesh as his appetite demanded. At the time, he was insatiable, and I don't think that libertine clubs were able to fully satisfy him, what with their lack of privacy."

Insatiable. That was exactly the impression that I had gotten from the collection of pornographic videos I had seen on the wall of screens in the basement control room.

As for the agency, when I had asked Rebecca about it, she had been evasive, claiming she couldn't remember exactly which of the two Barlet brothers had initiated the Belles de Nuit project.

"You're the one with shares in the company, not him," I countered.

"On *his* request! And only out of my friendship with Rebecca. The poor thing was a wreck. Louie had just left her again for the umpteenth time. You can check if you want: Louie was the one who did all the paperwork; he was the one who trademarked the name Belles de Nuit at least a year before the business actually opened. The whole thing was *his* idea. Not mine."

I hadn't noticed the background music before, but suddenly it became more present in the room. I don't know why the restaurant owner had decided that this was a good time to turn up the volume. The speakers were playing bland pop-rock, the kind favored by housewives and sales reps, a nostalgic flow of sound that gave the impression that some deranged DJ had taken our memories and was spinning them together on the mixing table of life.

I was caught off guard by the first notes of the next song. "More than this," sang Bryan Ferry in his velvety voice. This was one of the first songs that Louie had played for me at the Hôtel des Charmes. It was on his ideal soundtrack for making love.

"Ask Rebecca," David insisted, ignoring my mental absence. "She has already had the experience—"

I shook myself out of it:

"Except that Rebecca was never the object of your perverted games."

"Neither were you," he said defensively as he patted some sauce off his lips with his napkin.

"Are you saying that you had nothing to do with the rendezvous Louie arranged for me at that hotel?"

"Nothing," he affirmed unblinkingly. "I never asked him to . . . to pervert you as he did."

This version of things directly contradicted what Louie had confessed to me on the eve of my wedding day, in the Chevalier d'Eon room. In his version, he had only been executing a plan conceived by his younger brother.

Above all, this new version contradicted a number of troubling clues: Louie had known secrets on what I liked in bed, things that only David could have told him. At least that's what I had believed all these months.

But recently, other information had begun to erode my sense of certainty, namely the camera in the bedroom at Duchesnois House. Louie could have used it to watch me with David from the basement of the house next door. What if David was telling the truth? What if Louie had been the only one behind the sensual trap into which I had fallen?

"You need to open your eyes: the only person who has been using sex as a weapon is Louie."

More than this. Always more sensations. More mistresses. More pleasure. More extreme experiences. Always more sex, in all its forms. I didn't want David to be right, but I had to admit that everything he was saying fit with the Louie I had gotten to know over the past year. I wasn't so blinded by my love for him as to be unaware of these aspects of his personality.

"Not as a weapon," I said, defending my fiancé. "He has never tried to hurt me—never."

Was I so sure about that? The sharp cries of the petite Asian girl were still ringing in my ears.

"That's even worse!" he erupted in a whisper as he scanned the room to make sure that no one was listening in on our altercation. "He's like a kid with a gun where his dick should be!"

I was surprised by this kind of vulgarity from David. It was so unlike him.

"Classy," I said, pretending to be offended.

"You know exactly what I mean: all he cares about is pleasure, especially his own, and he doesn't give a damn about hurting anyone in its pursuit. Rebecca isn't the only person who's had to pay the price, believe me."

Sophia? Salomé? Who else? How many girls had been drawn in by his aura and then sacrificed on the altar of his orgies, like expiatory victims in some obscure and esoteric ritual?

"Go on, tell me. I'm interested," I urged. Suddenly nauseated, I pushed my untouched plate away from me with a disgusted hand.

He leaned closer toward me and continued in a very low voice, his tone conspiratorial:

"Fine . . . Okay, I've frequented Hotelles, too. You know that . . . I mean, I didn't make it a habit or anything."

"Get to the point."

"A girl I saw once poured her heart out to me. With a little encouragement, she told me that she had spent over a dozen nights with Louie."

Was she in any of the videos? What did she look like? I muzzled my curiosity and signaled for David to continue. Meanwhile, the waitress took our plates, visibly annoyed that we hadn't finished our meals.

"She said she'd found some of his notebooks. In them he apparently kept detailed accounts of all his conquests, including the most shocking ones."

The ancestor of our Ten-Times-a-Day, I realized, containing my anger. A primitive version of the anonymous notes he had sent me over the course of several weeks, before the beginning of our secret relationship.

Until then, David's revelations hadn't been very shocking. But I was scandalized by the idea that Louie wrote about any girl who agreed to a quickie or a one-night stand. I thought I had been the first!

"Hmm . . . To each his own, I suppose," I said between clenched teeth.

"That's not all. The young woman also intimated that Richard—that's the name he used back then for his ephemeral encounters—posted the best passages from his diary on the Internet. And that sometimes he included pictures he had stolen from his partners. Risqué photos, according to her."

An icy shiver ran through me.

"Have you ever spoken with him about these rumors?" I asked, leaping to my man's defense.

"Of course. At first he denied everything. Then he admitted to it. But he downplayed his actions and swore that they'd been the result of youthful folly, that he hadn't 'done any of that' for a long time."

It sounded like what a junkie would say to a judge or his doctors. I had known that sex could become an addiction, a poison that was as destructive as any drug, but I couldn't bring myself to see Louie like that. It couldn't be true!

"Have you seen these Internet postings?"

"No. But I don't see why that girl would have made up a story like that."

Although I couldn't deny Louie's passion for all things related to sex, I had never considered him sick. He was too meticulous about it, too refined. His approach to intimacy was cultured. He put soul and intelligence into it. None of that cohered with the image David was painting of a compulsive monster, someone whose thirst for novelty and numbers could never be quenched. Louie didn't seem dependent on sex. For him, it wasn't a substance without which he would be totally lost. Rather, it was a way of life. I took the reading lists he had given me as proof. If he were really hypersexual, how could he have survived the period of sexual deferment in our relationship that he himself had imposed?

"Is there anything else you want to know?"

. . . There was the way he had drawn out our mutual desire, over an almost unbearable length of time. There was his refined art of foreplay preceding the grand finale. He had been patient, had taken his time. That didn't fit the profile of a violent and ravenous sex fiend. He didn't act out of an irrepressible need, throwing himself on his prey to quell his hunger. He wasn't someone who could never be satisfied. That was not Louie. Not with me, in any case.

"Elle . . ." David gently shook my arm. "Is there anything else you want to know?"

"No . . . No, thanks. I'm okay." I immediately changed my mind. "Actually, there is one thing."

"Yes?"

"Tell me: Were you born on January 5, 1970?"

"Yes, yes . . . of course I was."

His face contracted into a hard mask. Here was the captain of industry. The man capable of firing any one of his employees with a simple Post-it note—that anecdote was true; a number of BTV employees had confirmed it, including Albane.

"Not in '69?" I insisted.

"No, in '70. You know that. Why are you asking?"

"Hmm, nothing. It's just that, on our marriage contract . . ."

He was playing nervously with his glass, the rosé threatening to slosh over its side.

"Yes?"

"Your birth date is listed as January 5, 1969."

"That's ridiculous!" He dismissed the idea with an irritated gesture. "It must be a clerical error."

The same excuse I had used when speaking with Mom's notary.

"People don't know how to do their jobs in this country anymore. Even copying a simple date has become a big deal . . ."

I wasn't interested in his bitter rant. It was clear that he wasn't going to tell me anything more.

Nodding vaguely, I cut short his litany of complaints on contemporary society—yet another iteration of a common conversation these days bemoaning French weariness, laxness, laziness; apparently France was letting itself go, and as a result many of my fellow citizens were moving abroad. I placed my napkin on the table, signaling that I was done with dinner and with asking questions.

It seemed that David was also eager to leave, as he had already stood to pay and was moving to the bar to wait for the credit card machine to become available.

Outside, a spring evening slowly fell, city bikes and couples arm in arm filling the streets. It was going to be a nice night. Two chic and slender specimens wandering past storefronts shot me a look of pity. To them I was a painful sight: I was alone at my table, my head slumped between my hands, my eyes on the verge of tears. After what I took to be a brief attempt to cheer me up, they walked off; a long ray of sunshine hung around them for a moment, and then they disappeared into a shadow, as if being absorbed into the tender night.

It was a beautiful night for a romantic dinner, I thought. A perfect night for a lovers' stroll. And I had spent it with my ex, listening to him tarnish the man I loved. David said he was trying to help me; all he had done was make the burden of my dark thoughts a little heavier.

WHEN WE ARRIVED AT OUR twin doors, we took leave from each other without so much as a word. Once inside, I resisted the urge to go down to the basement and activate the surveillance cameras on Duchesnois House. What good would it do? I had already seen David and Alice being intimate. And that was about as appealing to me as I had been to that couple at the restaurant.

Instead, I sulked on my bed. Felicity joined me, also in need of warmth. A cold current of air rushed through the half-open window. But that is not what chilled me the most. I was troubled by thoughts, images, words. And the contours of the portrait David had painted for me were growing sharper.

Suddenly, I straightened, startling my cat and ejecting her from the bedspread.

"My computer, crap . . . Where did I put my computer?" I scolded myself before finding it partially hidden under a pillow.

I raised the screen, and it immediately lit up. After entering my password, I went online. I paused as I considered what to enter into the search engine. What to type? What were the right words? I tried several combinations, erasing them one by one, before I finally decided on this:

diary + sex + Richard

Since that was the name he supposedly used on his one-night stands, I figured it was the best option. Google did not agree with me: none of the many results looked relevant. The first one referred to the tumultuous love affair between Richard Burton and Liz Taylor. The second was an anonymous erotic novel called *Diary of My Sex*—I noted its title for possible future reading. The third entry, *Diary of an Escort Girl*, was obviously a fake, a false confession, probably the work of a professional writer to attract visitors to the site and sell advertising space.

"Stupid . . . ," I said aloud to myself. "Why would he hide?"

So long as he kept the Barlet name under wraps, why dissimulate the rest of his identity? And: Why use a cover he had invented for dates with Hotelles, since that would surely send a smoke signal to the next escort?

I reentered my search terms, replacing the first name:

diary + sex + Louie

The links that I had already seen in my first search were now second and third in the results. The first, however, was the only one that caught my attention. It was all summarized in the header, in biting reality. I was submerged by a giant wave. It choked me and drowned the cry of rage welling up in my throat.

ELLE & LOUIE—Diary of Passionate Eroticism
elle-and-louie.leblog.fr/index.html

May 10, 2010 ¯ Elle & Louie is the diary of an erotic and passionate relationship, told in careful detail. Readers can score the intimate solutions that the couple . . .

9

May 21, 2010

I had suggested Café Marly for want of a better idea. Seeing each other again in the place where we had last met made obvious sense. François Marchadeau approved of this choice, and we planned to meet there that very afternoon. However, convincing him to see me again had not been easy. The journalist was a friend of David's and had more than one reservation when it came to me:

"Let me be clear: I'm agreeing to see you, but I haven't forgotten what happened a year ago."

He was referring to the aborted wedding—François was supposed to be David's best man—as well as the secrets I had pried out of him on his old friend.

For his part, David wasn't an idiot. He'd known exactly where I'd gotten my information, and their friendship was now hanging on by a thread. Or, rather, the string of a tennis racket: the two men settling the score with twice-weekly smashes and passing shots.

"I'm not asking you to forget."

"In any case, I don't know what I can do for you . . ."

"David thinks that you can be very useful to me," I bluffed. "I mean, to his brother."

"You've seen David recently?"

"We had dinner together last night."

"Really?"

"Really . . . You can check if you want . . . Only fools refuse to bury the hatchet."

That was total nonsense, but I loved using popular adages and mixing my metaphors: *That's the pot flying off the handle. Don't throw kettles in glass houses.* The more ridiculous the expression, the more I felt exonerated for using such commonplaces.

Marchadeau was the kind of person who appreciated this sort of humor. I felt him smile from the other end of the line before he confirmed our meeting time.

I ARRIVED FIRST AND STOOD under an arcade facing south, the midafternoon sun inundating the crowded terrace. I had trouble finding a table and ended up settling for something small and poorly situated—near the Passage Richelieu.

A copy of *Le Figaro*, a notoriously conservative daily, was lying on the table, which was still smudged with coffee and sugar. Aside from the main international and economic headlines, a question at the bottom of the page caught my attention: *Sex and art: Is anything off-limits? (story on page 12)*. I feverishly tore through the broadsheet and at last came to a quarter-page portrait of Antoine Gobert, who looked as ugly and smug as he did in person. In the associated column, the president of PRSPS decried what he called "the cancer of pornography." Unfortunately, now I saw the full impact of our intervention at his office. The man seemed more determined than ever to wage his moral crusade against "pornographers who present sexual violence to our children as a simple pastime." Louie was named specifically, along with the Sauvage-Barlet Gallery, which was described as a primary offender. The timing of these attacks on Louie could not have been worse.

This garbage was making me sick, and I tried to settle my mounting disgust with a cold Monaco. I was here out of duty and to meet the man who was suddenly standing in front of me.

"I know I've said it before . . . but you look ravishing."

The journalist appeared in a halo of blinding light, a white shirt and cream-colored Panama hat—a very casual ensemble for a weekday. Still, he looked good, charming even, if you liked a certain traveler chic. In any case, he wore it well.

"You've said it before, but I don't mind," I simpered.

He withdrew the red chair with off-white topstitching from under the opposite side of the table and slumped into it with all his weight and an arrogant ease that brought to mind all Parisians of a certain level of comfort in life.

I didn't wait for him to order anything before pointing to the newspaper, which was still open to the ignominious page.

"Hmm . . . What am I supposed to say?" he asked after scanning the article. "That I disapprove of this man's moral scruples?"

"I'm not asking you to support everything Louie does. I'm asking you to help us counter this campaign that's dragging him through the mud."

He raised his eyebrows, perplexed.

I didn't hold it against him. Based on what I had learned the night before, I knew that Louie could handle things on his own, no matter the mire in which he found himself.

I hadn't read all the notes published on the Elle & Louie blog, but what I had seen had mortified me. Most of the posts were faithful, word-for-word transcriptions of our entries in the Ten-Times-a-Day notebook. The one that had disappeared from our room one. But that wasn't the worst of it. The worst was the voting system, whereby readers were asked to grade each of the scenes described in the post, from one to five stars. Louie's informal tests these past couple of weeks had therefore been submitted for public evaluation. And my performance had been graded each time as if I were a filly at the racetracks. I will spare you the racy, and at times filthy, comments. Suffice it to say, there seemed to be no moderator after they were posted.

It was not only degrading and humiliating; it was a violation of our privacy. Of *my* privacy. I felt exposed, as though I were naked in a shop window for all to see. I was like the genitals that had been displayed at the Sauvage Gallery. And although I was allergic to Antoine Gobert's puritanical morals, I did agree with him on one point: some things shouldn't be shown, not to everyone. Especially not when the person being thrown to the lions has been kept in the dark. Louie, my love; Louie, my man, my passion; Louie, whom I would adore no matter what he did; Louie, who delighted me, disturbed me, made my head spin—Louie was the man who had just betrayed me.

That is, unless this was another game, a final ruse to test the strength of my emotions. Hadn't he already given up so much for me—including his relationship with his brother? His relationship with his family? And what about me? What had I given up? By which sacrifice could he measure my love for him?

I decided against telling Marchadeau about the site for the

time being. David Garchey's show, Gobert's lawsuit, Louie's reputation—that was already quite a lot.

"David promised I could help?"

"No . . . ," I admitted. "I'm coming to you on my own."

"What do you think I can do?"

"I don't know. Publish something that could raise the level of the debate—an expert opinion, something."

I thought for a moment before suggesting:

"Something along the lines of: The job of the avant-garde artist is to upend social convention, and the use of sex in the most innovative art works has always acted as a particularly effective lever of vast social change, with an impact that goes far beyond the bedroom," I improvised. "In a sense, sex in art breaks through the glass ceiling of social conformism and disrupts class stratification. A ban on such forms of artistic expression might put us face-to-face with obscurantism."

A spark in his eye told me that he liked how I'd put things.

"Not bad . . . 'Sex breaks through the glass ceiling of social conformism.'"

"Yes, I mean," I said, modestly, "I'm not going to teach you anything about how to put that kind of piece together."

He took more distance, his expression reverting back to neutral.

"However . . . ," he grumbled, "I don't see what I can do for you. *The Economist* is not exactly an opinion magazine. Besides, I am but a lowly associate editor. In the press today, if you want to play Zola, you had better check with the shareholders first. Otherwise, you can look forward to being unemployed."

In other words, no. An irrevocable no, and I saw that there was no use arguing.

Still, his look softened, becoming almost friendly, and I

understood that he wasn't against me. He was just trying to protect his own interests. Hadn't he said something about an unstable family situation the last time we'd met?

"Speaking of employment," he went on, "I hope it hasn't been too rough for you after everything that happened at BTV."

He was obviously being polite. There was no way he didn't know about David Barlet's scorched-earth tactics.

"Let's just say that doors haven't exactly been opening for me . . ."

"I can imagine . . . ," he replied, dipping his lips into the beer that an aproned shadow had just placed in front of him.

He placed his sun hat on the table and considered me for a moment in the same way that someone assesses merchandise, sipping his hoppy, cool, and frothy beverage.

"Would you consider writing a column for my magazine?"

"I'm not following. I thought you said there was nothing you could do for me."

"I'm not talking about your love-driven mission for your man. It's very touching, but there's nothing I can do for you in our periodical. But now that I see you, I'm envisioning something for *you*."

"For me?"

I had asked the question with the candor of Walt Disney's version of Alice, when the Mad Hatter and the March Hare wish her a "very merry unbirthday." He must have thought of the scene, too, because he replied, tit for tat:

"For you. What would you say about starting out with a column for the online version of *The Economist*?"

"A column? On what?"

For print journalists, the regular column is a high accolade. Typically, those admitted into the very exclusive circle of news magazine columnists are very experienced writers, notable authors, researchers, university professors, editors, or press magnates—all respected intellectuals. I may have been a neophyte, but I knew that basic rule.

"I was thinking of a kind of anonymous journal: 'The Private Life of a CEO on the CAC 40.' Or something like that."

"The cack?" I asked, my tone blonder than usual; I was so surprised by the offer.

"The C-A-C 40, Elle, the CAC 40."

He took another sip from his beer as he patiently waited for me to take the bait.

"You want me to keep an anonymous diary on David's private life?"

"Not exactly. It won't be a society column. David manages to appear in those without any outside help."

That was a clear reference to the ridiculous interview a few days before.

"What, then?"

"Ambiance pieces, with a kind of embedded quality. The daily life of a powerful man, his typical day, his worries, his faults, his obsessions . . . his doubts. All that from the point of view of the woman with whom he shares his life."

"One problem: I left David over a year ago. You know that."

"True. But you probably got to know him better than anyone else has over these past several years. And you can always embellish a little, extrapolate from your past to create an account that could still be relevant today."

His proposition was disconcerting. I gazed absently at the bunches of tourists converging in front of the Louvre's glass pyramid; then at last I refocused my attention on him.

"I'm sorry, but . . . I don't understand what's motivating

you. David is your friend. Why would you want to do this to him?"

"I don't want to do anything to or against him. David won't be named explicitly, and the details will be modified to protect his identity and the identities of his intimates."

"What's the point, then?"

The smile he had been wearing ever since he'd broached this topic widened.

"Contrary to what you may believe, this project is actually good for him. Even if the public can recognize who he is. *Especially* if it recognizes him."

"I don't see how my revealing what cereal he eats or the reason for his stomach cramps can help regild his public image," I said.

"David couldn't give a damn about public opinion. And if you asked me, I'd say he's right."

"Whom is he targeting, then?"

"You've no doubt heard of GKMP?"

"Yeah . . . ," I said limply and unconvincingly.

"It's South Korea's premier private television company. Sort of the Canal+ or HBO of Southeast Asia."

The infamous Koreans, the ones David had spent so much time wining and dining when we lived together. I had almost started to think that they were fictitious, an alibi for other, more secret activities. After all, I was living proof that he was almost as likely as his brother to treat himself to certain costly services.

"Well . . . David is preparing a merger between the two companies. The negotiations have been going on for so long that rumors have been circulating for several months already. Still, you didn't hear it from me."

"And where do I fit in?"

"David is doing everything in his power to keep the Barlet Group from being eaten up by the other company. There's always a risk of that in such large-scale capitalistic exchanges. He's working to keep the deal as equitable as possible. And in this kind of war of economic nerves, any and all messages to the market count. Including those that relate directly to the CEOs of the two companies. To be clear: it's now or never for him to shine in the media. To be portrayed in a favorable light for his investors, if you prefer."

That explained the song and dance with Alice. As well as François Marchadeau's idea for a column. An idea he might have gotten directly from his old friend.

"I understand . . . but why not do it yourself? You've known David for a lot longer than I have. And you don't have the same . . ."

"Liabilities?" he suggested.

"Yes."

"That's true. But I've never eaten cereal with him at breakfast, nor have I taken care of his stomachaches. For this kind of article, style and experience count a lot less than authenticity. The reader wants to feel as though he or she were living in close proximity to the personage in question."

My phone, which was sitting on the table, started to vibrate. Sophia's face appeared on the screen.

My interlocutor apparently had no qualms about peeping into my private life and was craning his neck to catch a glimpse of my friend's pretty face and chocolate curls.

"Who's that?"

"My best friend."

"Really pretty."

I pressed the virtual red button, rejecting the call. Sophia's smile disappeared at once.

"Listen . . . I don't think it's a good idea right now," I professed.

"Think about it. You don't have to give me your answer right away."

"It's not a question of time."

"It is for me. The Barlet-GKMP merger is supposed to take place within the next few weeks. Maybe sooner. If you take too long to decide, my magazine won't be interested."

"I understand that."

"In that case . . ."

He reached for his Panama hat, and he was just about to stand when I seized the opportunity:

"Speaking of David . . . did you know that he was born on January 5, 1969, and not in 1970, as it is published everywhere?"

He looked taken aback by my question.

"Excuse me?"

"In our marriage contract, David's birth date is listed as January 5, 1969, and not 1970, as I had always thought."

"It must be a mistake."

"Are you sure?"

"Completely sure. He and I filled out our enrollment papers at HEF together. I saw him write out his birth date on the form with my very own eyes."

François Marchadeau was smart enough to know that his testimony proved nothing. Nothing besides the fact that David always wrote the same year for his birth date whenever he had the opportunity.

But I didn't insist. Not for now.

"Oh . . . You're right. The notary must have made a mistake."

THAT NIGHT, MARS HOUSE SEEMED emptier and drearier to me than ever before. Had it not been for Felicity's presence, the house would have almost felt hostile. Unlike Louie, I did not take comfort in the house's ghosts and the stories of its former inhabitants. Despite the charm of our abode, its undeniably beautiful restoration, it usually felt like a museum, and I a simple visitor to be ushered out before closing.

I HADN'T HAD A CHANCE to check into what David had insinuated over dinner. As I had done the night before, I sat on the bed, my cat stretched against my side, my computer on my lap. The list of registered companies, which I had consulted a year before, confirmed his first assertion: Louie had been the one to register Belles de Nuit, on February 13, 1992.

The website of the INPI, in charge of patents and trademarks, vindicated David again: a certain Louie Barlet had registered the name Belles de Nuit under the very broad classification number 41, a hodgepodge that included educational services, job training, and entertainment, as well as athletic and cultural activities. As David had suggested, this, too, had been done a year before the agency had opened its doors, or in April 1991.

There was no doubt. Although David had ended up with a stake in the company, Louie, and Louie alone, was the person who had created it.

But why? Had lechery been his only source of motivation, as his brother had intimated? Had the search for a new Aurora simply served as a cover for his unquenchable thirst for debauchery?

I leaped out of bed and dressed. I felt assaulted by my surroundings, the idyllic decor that I hadn't chosen. It was suddenly unbearable, as if each detail, the tiniest frieze, the thinnest layer of gold or paint, threatened to reveal some new truth about Louie, one that I wanted neither to see nor hear. As I was leaving the house, it occurred to me that my present fiancé, like his predecessor, had, unthinkingly, imposed his lifestyle on me. Because, well, who would refuse such luxury, such history and beauty, particularly when one had nothing? But which part of me had chosen this place? Would I have wanted to live in one of these mansions if it had been up to me? Was this really me? If he had asked me, wouldn't I have preferred a fresh slate? A modern and functional apartment where we could have written our own story? A beautiful and new tale, one without the weight of past loves?

I felt the supreme need to take refuge in a familiar place. To curl up in welcoming sheets. To let my eyes wander over a friendly ceiling. The house in Nanterre had been sold. And my Parisian apartment was still in its dream stage. Honestly, there was only one place where I knew I would feel at home: the Hôtel des Charmes, room one, the Josephine.

10

MAY 25, 2010

His hands unhooked my bra slowly and with attention to detail. No sudden movements. No signs of impatience. I could tell that he derived pleasure from the sight of me. He liked to look at me—a mysterious and fragile being. He slipped the two bra straps off my shoulders, the pearly pink lace falling soundlessly to the floor. He drew his torso against my back and buried his nose into the nape of my neck, a few stray tendrils fluttering under his hot breath like a butterfly with wings outstretched, his palms gripping my breasts, pulling them up against gravity.

"I never want to move again," he murmured into my ear.

"I know . . . Me neither."

Immediately contradicting his last words, he released my chest and grabbed my hips, the curves of which seemed to expand in desire with each touch of his hands. All men are sculptors, you see. We women never tell them that enough. We do not sufficiently valorize their ability to mold us with an embrace, to fashion us, to play up our faults and transform them into voluptuous forms. I hadn't lost weight over the past year, not by a long shot. We had been sedentary, and there was all the room service Ysiam had brought us. Yet my body had been so kneaded, so prodded, so loved by Louie, and with such ardor, that it felt more beautiful than ever before. No longer was it a source of discomfort or embarrassment. His caresses had given it meaning where once there had been none. No longer was it sterile. Rather, it blossomed; it lived for him. And in return, my body gave me pleasure such as I had never known. My body: I had hated it, then learned to tolerate it, and now I loved it. My curves anchored Louie's desire. They were the sails of his fantasies. The bow of my pleasure.

Rushing through the bulge of my buttocks, his right hand slipped between them, spreading my two damp and engorged lips. A middle finger introduced itself inside me, probing my vagina with curiosity. Was it ready for more? Moist enough? Had its walls parted easily? Did it long for further inquisitions? He circled his finger around as if to spread it wider, pressing into my mucous flesh, which was soft in places, rough in others, and increasingly sensitive.

Without realizing it, I arched my back and tilted my pelvis, offering my backside to him. We had already done a lot of experimenting and found that standing positions were best for us. Something about our respective heights and shapes predisposed us to such acrobatic feats. There exists a taboo, even among partners who are open with each other: not all bodies are suited to one another; they aren't all made to enjoy the full array of sexual positions.

Louie once told me about a theory related to this very issue in the *Kama Sutra*, the work of reference on the art of lovers. According to it, everyone—each man and each woman—has an animal totem based on the shape of one's body and genitals: bull, horse, or hare for men; elephant, mare, or doe for women. Among the nine possible combinations of totems, two are said to be unfavorable matches since they represent the most dissimilar attributes (horse and doe, hare and elephant); four are said to be mediocre matches; and the three combinations of equal partners are said to be the most favorable matches. Was he a hare or a bull? Was I a doe or a mare? I don't know. But his long and slender member was perfectly adapted to my vagina, particularly in difficult positions.

He thrust his pubis into my backside, his rod diving into me. One of his hands gripped my waist. The other clutched my shoulder. He moved himself in and out of me with the self-assurance of someone who knows he is welcome, anticipated, desired; he was the lord of this fiefdom. Each time he pushed into me, my body widened and the delicate balance of our cathedral of flesh trembled.

But I didn't want him to go gently. Not because I worried about disappointing him, but out of my own need for satisfaction. I liked feeling him deep inside me. He lanced right through me and stroked the threshold of my uterus. His forays into me could never be too energetic, never too deep.

"Harder," I exhorted softly.

Then I felt him bend his knees to find an angle that would propel him with one single thrust through the endless boulevard of my sex. Deep, deep into my moist and hot night. I couldn't suppress my voice after this subtle change of position.

"Yes! Yes!"

Sometimes I also yelled out his name, the two words becoming one, a synonym for pleasure: *"Louie-yes!"*

Finally, what happened when he took me like this happened. The outline of an orgasm hit me so hard, with a series of muted explosions radiating from my vagina and through my belly and thighs, that I lost all control. I felt myself totter and my legs shake. I tipped forward, trying desperately to keep his sex inside me, to hold on to his back or buttocks. I fell heavily onto the bed, crushed by my partner. He didn't give me a second of rest before thrusting deeper into my wide-open cunt, which was offering itself to him wholly, freely. I loved the feeling of his weight on my back. I loved that he filled me so well. Sometimes, he opened my legs. Others, he slipped a thumb or wet index finger into my terror-stricken anus—although my sphincter always let him in on his first essay. Still other times, his hand wandered down my stomach, wedging itself between the sheets and my bush, where it found and tickled my clitoris. The conjunction of the two attacks got the better of me within a few seconds. Once again, he instantly made me explode in pleasure.

"Ohhhh . . . Louie . . ."

IN THIS ROOM, LOUIE AND I had dozens of memories like this one, all recorded in our Ten-Times-a-Day, all posted on his blog—which I consulted again that night, shaking with rage and desire. If we could have, we would have replaced the swatches of purple fabric with mirrors, and we would have contemplated the two unbridled lovers carving their names into the surface of the glass. *Elle & Louie.* That was how I liked to consider our two names. Not in the context of some sordid website for lonely masturbators.

I think I touched myself while half asleep and dreaming of our past escapades. I was the only who could rightly do so.

LATE THAT NIGHT, I WAS suddenly overcome with hunger and called room service. Ysiam picked up the phone, and ten minutes later, he was the one to deliver my club sandwich.

"How are you Mademois-Elle? Are you happy to be back?"

Was it that obvious? Did my expression betray the happiness I felt being back in this room, *our* room? The sweet bellboy had arranged for me to have the Josephine, despite the fact that it was already booked. I think I could have asked him for roast moon for breakfast, to use one of Mom's expressions, and he would have found a way to get it for me.

When it came to our Ten-Times-a-Day, however, there was nothing he could do. And my own searches of the room had been in vain.

"Very happy to be back," I said, nodding my delighted head. "And starving!"

I attacked the layered sandwich, savoring each crisp and delicious bite. Ysiam hadn't skimped on the avocado—one of my sinful pleasures—and I was grateful.

"I take the opportunity, I bring your mail," he added in his approximative French.

He handed me a manila envelope.

"Monsieur Jacques wants to know how long you're staying."

"No idea for now," I replied in a distracted tone.

I was already scanning the mail—mostly bills and ads—when I noticed one that was addressed to the following person:

Émilie Lebourdais
The Hôtel des Charmes
55 Rue Jean-Baptiste Pigalle
75009 Paris

That same woman, and now with her first name. The same mistake . . .

"Clearly someone is insisting on confusing me with this person."

"Oh . . . Sorry."

He took the envelope from me, his tone contrite.

"Do you know who that is?"

"No," he replied, looking sincere. "I mean, I believe someone who takes care of her bill. But I never seen her."

"Ysiam . . . Would you do something for me?"

His fluttering lashes confirmed his devotion to me.

"Yes."

"If Monsieur Louie calls or stops by at the reception . . . don't tell him that I'm here."

"What if he asks to come to the room?"

"Tell him that it's been rented to someone else."

He slipped away as discreetly as he had arrived, refusing the ten-euro bill I offered, his smile almost offended.

I HAD WRITTEN LOVE AND breakup letters in the past—not many, but enough to know how to categorize them, including the short note I'd written David in Nanterre, the day I'd fled our common future.

The message I drafted for Louie that night, in the room that had seen blossom my love for him, belonged to neither category. It was neither a declaration of love nor a good-bye note. To be sure, I still loved him, and I didn't want to let our recent misadventures ruin the sentiment we had forged together over the course of a year. But what exactly was the basis of such sentiment? *We never truly examine our motiva-*

tions behind sharing our lives with one man or one woman. That is something I had once written to my ex-fiancé. Had I truly examined my motivations behind sharing my life with Louie? Or had I let myself be carried away by that powerful wave of emotion originating between my legs? What exactly was my love for him based upon? What was the soil that nourished it? Was I capable of analyzing it under the microscope of reason? Or was I no better than those lobotomized women who succumb to the first orgasm that comes their way? Was I simply an orgasming doll—dazed after a few horizontal sessions?

Sex had become such an important part of my life that it was difficult, even now that we lived together, to determine what else united Louie and me. "Sex is capital, but there comes a time when even the best lay in the world can't make you forget that your bills are due," Sophia had once said. Her form of philosophy may have been simplistic, but it was spot-on. Our problem wasn't paying bills but finding meaning for ourselves as a couple. To me, this seemed at once less critical and more fundamental.

Because if the cement that bound us together began to crack—the Elle & Louie blog being an important cause—what would remain of and between us? The dubious circumstances under which we'd first met, the early days of our relationship—our history wouldn't be enough to keep our flame alight. Relationships are perhaps built on mythologies of themselves, but there comes a time when the myth begins to fade, wilt, and fall apart. Where does love find its strength then?

Lacking inspiration, I scribbled a few hasty lines to Louie, a string of clichés and commonplaces that were beneath me, beneath us.

My love,

If you are reading this message, then the police must have released you. Please do not take these words or my absence as signs of repudiation. You know that I support you completely in your struggle.

But after the stress of these past few days, I am in need of a break. A breath. We haven't left each other's side since the eighteenth of June last year, when we checked in at the Hôtel des Charmes. I suppose I need some air.

Some transparency, too. I don't mean to reproach you, but so many opaque screens still separate us. There are still so many shadows, many from your past, that weigh on our present lives.

New tests, you say? A new course to become a perfect lover? Know that so long as you haven't opened your heart and answered my questions, I won't participate in such things any longer. I love you. I am on your side. Please, be on mine. On ours. Do not be afraid of my judgment, just as I am not of yours.

> *Elle, yours and madly in love*

The next morning, I placed the letter in an envelope and entrusted it to Ysiam. He said he would deliver to Mars House within the hour. I had been careful not to mention the Elle & Louie blog. Too direct. Too painful. I wanted an explanation from his voice. I wanted him to look me in the eye.

In the meantime . . .

"Hello, this is Mademoiselle Lorand. I visited a studio on Rue du Trésor the other day. I was wondering if it would be possible to sign a provisional sale agreement today?"

"Today? And . . . you're okay with the price?"

"Yes, I am."

"You should know that I've already received an offer."

"For how much?"

"Seven thousand euros below the asking price."

"That's not a problem. I'll take it for the asking."

"Really? Are you sure?"

"Completely," I said firmly.

She asked if she could make a phone call, and in less than a half hour, she confirmed that we could sign the papers that day. The seller accepted the offer, and since all the necessary deeds and inspections were in order, nothing prevented the sale from being processed quickly.

Since the notary's office was located on Rue Vieille-du-Temple, a few steps away from my future apartment, I spent the hour before our midafternoon meeting at the terrace of TrésOr, the large brasserie on what was soon to be my charming dead-end street.

I had asked Sophia to meet me there. She soon arrived, with a strange look on her sun-kissed face. Her first Monaco of the day didn't even succeed in changing her expression.

"You okay?" I asked. "You seem a little off."

"Your man just called me."

Ever since Ysiam had delivered my message, Louie had been harassing me, too. He alternated between leaving voice and text messages, demanding an explanation. He begged for a meeting. I hadn't replied to any of his attempts to contact me. I may have been the one who needed answers, but I wasn't ready for a confrontation. How could I be sure of his sincerity? How could I be sure I wouldn't again be taken in by his charm? I was defenseless when it came to him, more fragile than a house of cards.

"And?"

"And I wouldn't say he's happy that you fled at the first sight of cops."

"When did they release him?"

"Today, early this morning."

And yet Louie hadn't been worried about me until he'd received my letter. Only then did he start sending me worried and sometimes even spiteful messages.

I was also surprised that Zerki, his lawyer, hadn't informed me as soon as his client had been freed. Clearly, the lawman thought little of my place in Louie's life.

"Did they charge him with anything?" I inquired.

"No, not for now. But his lawyer thinks they will soon. Our *friend* Antoine Gobert hasn't been helping our cause."

On the table next to ours, I noticed a newspaper affixed to a wooden rod—a sign that this periodical was for the use of the brasserie's guests. I grabbed it and leafed through its pages.

"Listen, Elle . . . I know none of this is any of my business—"

"You're right, it's not," I said, my tone colder than I'd meant it.

"But I think you should go home. Regardless of the reason you ran away, Louie deserves an explanation. Don't you think?"

What had he said to convince her to play Mademoiselle Mediator and plead his case? Had he promised her a new striptease gig? I kept my depressing questions to myself and explained to her in simple and direct terms the nature of my problems: the tests, all the videos, David's revelations . . . and, above all, that blasted blog.

"Even when I was a Hotelle, none of my clients treated me like that," I confided.

"You said it yourself: they were clients. The relationship was contractual. Most of the time, that protects us."

"Right, so since Louie is my man, and since he isn't paying me, he has the right to do whatever he wants with my image? He can tell the entire world how I get wet or how I give head? Is that what you're telling me?"

I must have been talking loudly because a couple with a child sitting a few tables from ours shot me an outraged look. They were visibly scandalized by what I was saying.

"Of course not . . . ," Sophia said, trying to calm me down. "But I'm sure he saw it more as a kind of game between you two."

"A game! He should have at least let me know that we'd started playing."

"I suppose that for him that was part of it."

"For me to stumble across the blog?"

"Yes . . ."

Admittedly, that sounded like the Louie I had come to know over the past year. He was the one who had hidden behind a mask and inside a black latex suit. The one who had found thousands of little tricks to draw out my desire for him during our rendezvous at the Hôtel des Charmes. The one I loved.

But I longed for another man. For a Louie without the mask. I thought I had found him these past several months, the real Louie, naked, stripped of all the artifice. The man I loved.

I shuddered. I had run out of arguments. My trembling skin remembered his hands, sometimes with such acuity that it almost felt as though they were sliding under my clothes and all over my body.

"Speaking of, he gave me a message for you."

I wasn't listening. My eyes had stopped on a full-page

article announcing the merger between the Barlet Group and GKMP (Global Korea Media Properties). The rumor Marchadeau had told me about was no longer a secret. In fact, the article was full of details, including the estimated value of the shares to be exchanged: two billion euros. The journalist added that thanks to this savvy financial sleight of hand, David Barlet's personal fortune would almost double. The merger was not just profitable for the two companies. Their CEOs, who were both discussed in separate boxes—the Korean on the left, the Frenchman on the right—would also personally benefit.

"Hey! Are you listening to me?"

"Just a sec . . ."

Without raising my eyes from the newspaper, I held an index finger in the air, signaling my need for a few moments of silence and patience. I glanced at David's portrait and looked more carefully at the biographical details printed in a salmon-colored box at the end of the article. The first line mentioned his date of birth. Here, it was listed as January 5, 1970. The official date. The one that David had always cited. The one that both Louie and François Marchadeau had confirmed when I'd asked them.

"What is it?" I asked, at last raising my nose from the article. "What message?"

"He wants you to meet him tonight. Not at your place. Out."

"Did he say where?"

"No. He said you would know the place and time."

The Hôtel des Charmes. Ten p.m. Where and when else?

"I'm not going," I said without hesitation.

Incredulous, Sophia widened her eyes. She often over-acted, but this time, I could tell that her surprise was sincere and spontaneous.

"Why not? You don't want an explanation from him?"

"I do. But not there. Not like this."

I didn't want him to use his erotic power to thwart my questions. The Hôtel des Charmes? No, more like *his* charm, his power over me whenever we found ourselves in remotely intimate situations.

THE MEETING WITH THE NOTARY was a brief formality. I signed the documents in a state of partial stupor. Hello, thank you, perfect, of course, as soon as possible, delighted, good-bye—I limited my conversation to functional and terse expressions. This was probably the most important meeting of my young life, and I hurried through it as if it were of no consequence.

My mind was elsewhere. Malmaison, for example. With its clusters of roses immortalized by the painter Pierre-Joseph Redouté. Amid the interlacing petals and thorns, where Louie and I had committed ourselves to each other a few days earlier.

In Nanterre, too. Because it was thanks to Mom's money, the fruit of a lifetime of work and sacrifice, that I was able to own property—and on a whim. Money, that thing that takes patience and persistence to amass, but that can disappear in the blink of an eye.

I KNEW LOUIE WAS PROBABLY hanging around the Hôtel des Charmes, so I forbade myself from returning before it was quite late. I saw a double feature at the movie theater at the Halles—I don't even remember which, I was so distracted. After eating a kebab, I spent the next several hours in an

Internet café on Boulevard de Sébastopol, right next door to a libertine sauna with a finely carved wooden front door.

From my seat, I could see the entry and watch as couples of all ages discreetly made their way inside. Then I saw them leave several hours later, their hair still wet and their smiles wide. I found one to be particularly touching: a girl, young and brown-haired, who looked a little bit like me, was accompanied by a man who was older than her, like Louie. We could have been one of those couples, sighing, moaning.

Their formula for happiness seemed so simple, so proverbial. I wondered if I, too, should dilute my suffering in the frothy fervor of sex.

I alternated between watching these people and researching the Barlet-GKMP merger. Websites were divided between purely economic coverage of the merger and society gossip—David and Alice's engagement. Randomly, I kept being guided to that video that had made them the laughingstock of social media. The hype surrounding the video was dying down, but my heart started racing when I saw what was presented as a new development in the soap opera of David Barlet's private life: *Engaged and already cheating?* The question served as a caption to a picture that had apparently been taken secretly with a smartphone. It was blurry and poorly framed. Nevertheless, I easily recognized David and me at La Pizzetta, but nothing about our expressions was remotely untoward. Based on the camera angle and the various elements present in the foreground, I deduced that this picture had been taken from a table at the other end of the restaurant, no doubt near the bar. If Louie somehow saw this amateur shot, he would be furious.

I decided to change computers and found a place in the Internet café where my screen couldn't be seen by anyone else.

An intuition, I suppose. Or leftover caution.

I typed the blog's URL in the address bar and its home page appeared almost instantly. I noticed that the site's design had been improved since my last visit. The title was now accompanied by an erotic black-and-white image of two nudes embracing over a background of rumpled sheets. But what really caught my attention was a blinking red button labeled *Live*. Was this a hidden advertisement? One of those links set up by con men to steal your credit card number?

Moved by an unhealthy sense of curiosity that has always driven me to open locked doors—my "journalist side," as my mother would have said—I decided to click. A second smaller window opened. Inside the pop-up window, a loading icon appeared. After a few seconds, an image replaced the icon. At first, it was too dark to make out anything; then, bit by bit, it became clearer.

This time, I didn't need a caption to tell me where the action was taking place: the Marie Bonaparte room. At least Ysiam had followed my instructions, preserving our sanctuary, the Josephine, our room number one. *Our home.*

As for the two interlaced bodies that glowed with pleasure and sweat, the man thrusting vigorously against the posterior of his partner, who was on all fours: I had no trouble identifying them either. That magnificent ass, round and tan, so perfect that it seemed to have been crafted from a computer algorithm, belonged to Salomé. Her backside swayed in the same lithe movement that I'd noticed at our housewarming party. It was her trademark. The man penetrating her, his slender sex extremely erect, was concentrating all his energy on this single focal point. With each intromission, he looked like he was going to come inside her. This man was my future husband. Yes. Louie. Him.

11

MAY 29, 2010

Sometimes, everything conspires against you. At others, everything seems to fall into place at such a stupefying and exhilarating pace that you can't believe your good fortune—and you keep waiting for the other shoe to drop.

The purchase of my studio on Rue du Trésor went off without a hitch. The property was a recent inheritance, and the two beneficiaries both wanted to sell it as quickly as possible. Another stroke of luck: the apartment was vacant and empty of any furnishings, which meant that I could move in almost immediately—a few hours after I'd signed the final paperwork, or two days after everyone had signed the provisional sale agreement. Typically, none of the parties involved in a sale of property agree for things to move so quickly. The notary especially tends to be very cautious, and is bound by law to respect a minimum cooling-off period of seven days.

"How much?"

The morning after my evening in the Internet café, I had forced my way through his office door on Rue Vieille-du-

Temple and fended off his Cerberean secretary. This notary was markedly more decrepit than Master Whurman, but just as venal.

Still, his virtue could not be bought at any price. He played up his scruples and sense of ethics in order to raise my bid:

"How much for what?" he asked, feigning innocence.

"To shorten the cooling-off period."

"Mademoiselle, one cannot negotiate with the law!"

"Right, I know . . . but how much?"

He let his gaze wander over the stack of files on his desk before at last raising his eyes to me:

"We both agree that this arrangement will remain between us . . ."

"Of course, absolutely. My lips are sealed."

"Good, good, good . . ."

Did all notaries have the same verbal tick? He pursed his lips and then said quietly:

"In that case, one percent."

"A one percent addition to your fee?"

"That's right."

Or about three thousand euros, to be exchanged under the table, illegally, from my pocket to his, then from his pocket to his coffers, without ever coming into contact with a bank or the tax department.

"Okay," I agreed.

That same day, driven by a furious and unrelenting energy that muted my sadness, I stopped by my bank. After getting a cashier's check for the notary, I wanted to withdraw the maximum amount of money that I was allowed.

"Two thousand euros a week? I can't take out more?"

"No, I'm sorry," the bank teller apologized. "That's your withdrawal limit. If you want to raise it, you'll have to make a formal request."

"How long will that take?"

"About one week—there's a cooling-off period."

The Kafkaesque absurdity of the situation made me want to burst out laughing.

In situations such as this one, David can be a useful asset. I sent him a text message, and he agreed to loan me the remainder of what I needed: one thousand euros in cash, which I could pick up at the reception desk in Barlet Tower. This new friendship with my ex-fiancé was somewhat surprising. To be sure, he'd been quick to fill me in on all the nasty gossip surrounding Louie, but I also got the feeling that he sincerely wanted to protect me and make amends.

Since I happened to find myself in Nanterre—a rare occurrence these days—I made a detour to see Mom's old house. After all the sorting I'd done and the giant garbage bags I'd put out on the curb, the house was almost completely bereft of her presence. I still had my memories, but they were orphans now, too—without so much as a bauble or decoration to cling to.

I had been putting off this visit to Nanterre for several months. I was surprised to see flowers at Mom's grave. In fact, her plot was fairly well tended. It was clear that some thoughtful person had been taking care of her. And since I couldn't imagine who else, I thought of Laure Chappuis and her fragile silhouette bending over her old friend's tombstone, faithfully filling in for me, ingrate that I was.

Suddenly, I broke down. I had only just taken a seat on the icy marble of a neighboring tomb when all the rage that had been propelling my actions instantly evaporated. I cried like an open faucet, in an uninterrupted flow, without hiccuping or pausing. For how long? I don't know. It seemed like hours. I missed my mom. This was the first time I'd been able to admit it to myself. I missed her common sense, her love for me, her rose perfume. I couldn't pinpoint a single ingredient that I missed most—I missed everything about her.

If she had been there, she would have known what to make of my situation. I was sure of it. Not only would she have tended to my wounds, she also would have understood exactly what kind of game Louie was playing. She would have explained the nature of his tests, as well as which of his fantasies I should refuse and which I could accept for my pleasure. She would have tried, with her attentive presence, to fill the visceral void I felt in his absence. Even more, she would have done everything in her power to make sure our relationship, our love, was as simple and beautiful as she had ever hoped for me.

Was Louie the predator that David had described? After all, hadn't he made me his captive at the Hôtel des Charmes? My tears slowly began to dry, and between two loud sniffles, something occurred to me: Louie was the male version of the Amazons in *Secret Women*, the book he had given me to read a year earlier. Hidden from sight, the book's heroines made a group of men into their sex slaves. Sensual slaves, like I was for Louie.

"Do you know why plants never grow near graves, Mademoiselle? With the exception of weeds, that is . . ."

An old man in a hat had appeared from the periphery, at the outer limit of my field of vision. He was wearing an unseasonable beige raincoat and a pair of corduroy pants that reminded me of Armand. In his right hand, he carried a large overflowing watering can. A smile rippled like a wavelet over the surface of his crumpled face.

"Do you know why?" he repeated.

I eyed this intruder from behind a layer of dried tears. He was clearly moved by my sadness and looking for a way to distract me.

"No . . . ," I admitted.

"Quite simply, because tears contain too much sodium chloride. Too much salt. Plants cannot grow in salty earth."

"That makes sense." I sighed.

"Just visit the Dead Sea and you'll see what I mean. Have you been?"

"No."

"You still have time . . . In any case, if you want flowers to grow here, you can't cry like that. The cemetery is the worst place to cry, if you want my opinion."

How could I tell him that I wasn't crying for my deceased mother but for myself? How to compare the futility of my sadness with the soundness of his recommendation?

I watched as he made his way through the rectilinear pathways. He stopped in front of a tombstone to water the anemic geraniums that had been planted in the gray and rocky earth at its base.

THE NEXT TWO DAYS WERE a slightly crazy succession of errands and purchases: pick up the envelope David had left for me; have several keys copied and give a set to Ysiam—I don't know why, but I trusted him; buy a bed, a dresser, and bring all the linens and dishes I'd left in the Nanterre house over to my apartment; set everything up in my studio, whose walls were freshly painted but still white and mostly blank; put my name on the mailbox; fill the single kitchen cupboard with provisions; clean the floors and windows; change a faulty lightbulb.

Collapse on my bed and contemplate the ceiling, which had a long crack like a smile welcoming me home. *My home.* Stretched out on the comforter I had just removed from the packaging, I repeated those two words to myself over and over. I couldn't believe it. I stayed like that for several hours, one ear listening to the sounds of my new neighborhood, the other smashed into the pillow. *My home . . .*

That wasn't quite true yet, and I was now a stranger in Mom's house, as well as an occasional visitor in Louie's mansion.

Louie had sent a dozen more messages, all of which I'd ignored. I read the ones Sophia had sent, though I didn't reply to those either. What was I supposed to say to something like this, for example?

Fred and I are a thing. Happy.
Call me, I'll tell you all about it. Soph.

My ex and my best friend together. I couldn't bring myself to be excited for them, not really. My happiness was more reasoned than genuine. To be honest, I didn't really feel much of anything.

That night, after heating some ready-made dish on the stove, I turned on the television. It was the news hour. The show was just beginning. Sports: UEFA had just chosen France to host the European Championship for men's soccer in 2016. In India, Naxalites were claiming responsibility for a train derailment, one hundred fifty casualties. Then, suddenly, a familiar face drew me out of my torpor.

" . . . My brother's choices shouldn't reflect onto the Barlet Group, which he left more than a year ago to pursue other activities. Regardless of my personal feelings concerning his conceptions of art and the artworks he is defending, I do not think it would be appropriate to express them. All that I can tell you today is that neither I nor the Barlet Group condones creations that put our children at risk."

David was being prudent and putting distance between himself and his older brother. Considering his position and his role in the company, I could understand why. But I didn't agree with it. I was disappointed by his overabundance of caution. I had expected more from the man who had spontaneously come to my aid. Unless his motivations hadn't been so pure . . .

"You're stating that you have no affiliation whatsoever with the exhibit *Permanent Sex* then?" the reporter asked.

"None. You can check. I wasn't even invited to the opening."

"Yet some people say that your company holds stocks in production companies that make pornography and, moreover, that those companies use illegal workers . . ."

"Listen, if you're referring to the Delacroix affair, then I have no comment. The courts will rule on that. Thank you."

David immediately disappeared into Barlet Tower, which appeared in the camera's field of vision like an immense phallus.

The apelike face of the presenter reappeared, and the program continued with a skillful tie-in:

"The Delacroix affair, which was mentioned in our last report, is back in the news. Stephen Delacroix, a financial analyst hired by the Barlet Group to diversify its investments, was involved in trafficking adult film actresses from Eastern Europe to work illegally in France. Delacroix, who has been charged by the court of assizes in Paris, is now on the counterattack. His appeal will be heard in a few weeks. He still maintains that senior directors at the Barlet Group, and David Barlet himself, mandated his participation in East-X Productions. He claims that he was asked to turn a blind eye to the women's legal statuses as well as their labor conditions.

"Beyond the legal aspects of this affair, we have investigated some of the infamous networks involved in trafficking from Eastern Europe. Who are these young women from Romania, Bulgaria, and Poland? Who is organizing their illegal entry into France? Is the work that they do for these production companies a form of prostitution? *X-Rated: Networks from the East* will air later this evening. We would like to warn you that the images in the excerpt we are about to show are not suitable for a young audience."

That explained why David had been so dismissive with the interviewer. Considering his upcoming economic marriage to GKMP, he already had enough on his plate with the Delacroix affair. The last thing he needed was another scandal. Louie could handle his erotomaniacal troubles by himself; it wasn't *his* problem. This disloyal thought sent a twinge through my stomach.

I was watching the blacked-out faces on-screen with a distracted eye when my phone buzzed from its spot on the comforter. A new text message from Rebecca Sibony.

Louie is really worried about you.
Where are you? Call him.
Or call me.
   R.

Louie was worried? Louie was so concerned about me that he had to comfort himself in someone else's vagina? My thoughts were arrested for a long moment by crude images and filthy words. I had trouble erasing them from my mind. I knew that Salomé had once been one of his regular Hotelles. She was the kind of professional who had a client base rather than random dates, which tend to be uncomfortable and more dangerous. Rebecca never mentioned it, but some of her girls had been held against their will, beaten, and made to participate in violent or degrading acts.

I wondered if Salomé had remained his mistress during our reclusive year at the Hôtel des Charmes. I had never accompanied Louie on his outings, and he easily could have gone to see her. My Internet connection was not yet set up, so I couldn't watch their video again. If I closed my eyes, I could still see a few scraps of them together, a few fleeting images. Now that I thought about it, the fact that the blog was primarily video- and image-based surprised me. Louie, the Louie I knew and admired, was a man of words. And yet here he was suddenly mute. Here he was an ordinary exhibitionist who cared more for obscene images than textual grace. This betrayal of his personality bothered me as much as his betrayal of our engagement. As a way of keeping the bond between us from becoming stretched beyond repair, I tried to imagine how we would have described the scene between him and Salomé in our Ten-Times-a-Day:

He lay on his back, and she approached him slowly, quietly, like a wild animal, her small breasts pointing toward his growing member. The movement of her perfect ass set the rhythm for the coitus to come. It was the metronome of her sensuality. It swished from one side to the other, fluid, supple, like a Weeble with an internal source of movement.

She didn't attack him right away. She took her time. While the man's hands sought out her tumescent nipples, she gently rubbed her humid vulva over his rigid shaft, which lay taut over her lover's hairy abdomen. She tortured and teased his distended cock with her humid labia, bathing him in her fluid, beginning first with his scrotum, then his blue veins, then his delicate frenulum, and at last the base of his mauvish glans.

If she hadn't placed her palm over her partner's mouth, gagging him, he would have begged her to finish. But she drew out this torture until she herself could no longer stand it, until her engorged clitoris needed the relief of the man beneath her. She was so in control of the movement of her pelvis—it was a gift, really—that she didn't need to use her hands to insert his member inside herself. Her vagina was eager, hungry, and it absorbed his penis instantly. She didn't move right away. Instead, she compressed the walls of her sex around the visitor. Each time she squeezed, he closed his eyes and sighed. She waited to make sure he kept them closed before beginning her dance. Then, she started expertly rocking her sumptuous backside, a nonchalant, agile movement. The man grew drunk with passion and soon felt himself overcome. "Stop . . . Stop, I can't take it anymore," he cried in a smothered moan.

MY PHONE VIBRATED, ABRUPTLY INTERRUPTING my dream, which had started to excite my lower abdomen.

Rebecca was being persistent. I ended up sending her a terse message:

Let's meet. Where and when?

After all, who better than a girlfriend from Louie's youth to shed light on him and the complex mysteries of his personality? The tiniest crumb of sincerity, the slightest of anecdotes, would be a relief, given my state of distress.

I KNEW THAT REBECCA LIKED to meet in the capital's touristy hotspots, so I wasn't surprised by her choice of place. I hadn't set foot in Printemps, with its imposing stained glass cupola, since I was a child. Mom and I had once taken the RER train to Boulevard Haussmann for a tour of its big department stores. This chef d'oeuvre, created by master glass-worker Brière, hadn't lost any of its luster or power to fascinate. As I waited for Rebecca, I sat on a bar stool in the tearoom under the dome and contemplated the thousands of stained glass panels.

"It's beautiful, isn't it?"

Rebecca appeared, wearing a black suit with cream top-stitching and looking as classy as ever, despite the closure of Belles de Nuit.

"It's amazing," I agreed.

"Did you know that during the war, the glass panels were removed one by one, to save them from being bombed? It wasn't until 1973 that people remembered where they'd been stored."

"I had no idea."

"Mmm-hmm . . . ," she replied as she lowered herself onto a bar stool next to mine. "But you didn't come here to listen to me tell you stories about Art Deco in Paris."

True. As soon as our frothy cappuccinos arrived, I told her about what David had revealed to me concerning the origins of the agency. Information that I had since verified, as I was sure to add.

She pursed her thin lips. I had her cornered, and she didn't even try to deny the facts.

"David presented the creation of Belles de Nuit to you as the cause of all Louie's troubles . . . I understand why. But it was only really a consequence."

"A consequence of what?"

"His regrets."

"For Aurora?"

"Obviously. She was their mutual obsession for twenty years."

No one—not Louie, David, or even Rebecca—had ever described this sentimental rivalry in such simple and direct terms.

"There's only one way for a man to drown his sorrow and not be consumed by frustration."

"Sex?" I asked.

"Not just *sex*," she said, emphasizing the last word. "An abundance of sex. An orgy of sex! A woman who can't have the man she desires more than anything will eat chocolate and watch vapid movies with her girlfriends. A man, on the other hand, will screw any woman capable of making him forget the one that got away."

"Quantity to compensate for the lack of quality."

"You could put it that way . . . ," she said, laughing softly.

Rebecca's explanation didn't reveal anything new about Louie's motivations, but it did put things in a new light. He wasn't sick. He was a man in despair. The thought was reassuring, and it relieved some of the pressure I felt in each of my organs whenever I thought of Louie's secrets.

"I don't understand why he was so destroyed by a woman he never had. How can someone be broken up for so long over a person who was only ever a mirage?" I wondered aloud.

"You're wrong. She was more than a fantasy for him."

Speechless, I let my attention wander for a moment longer over the rain of colors falling from the cupola above.

That contradicted what Louie had told me, that Aurora had chosen David, the winner of their father's competition, and that they had gotten married. End of story, if I believed him.

"Before or after Aurora and David were married?" I asked at last.

"Before *and* after."

Something Louie had said suddenly came back to me, a little speck of truth in the dark and compact mass of his lies: "She even cheated on him without the slightest remorse." He had forgotten to mention that it had been with him.

Rebecca swallowed a few sips of her sugary beverage, a thin mustache of cream adorning her upper lip.

David was bent on painting his brother as a deviant because he had himself been a victim of that behavior.

First with Aurora and now with me.

"I suppose you agreed to meet because you had other questions?"

She was right. I carefully described the hateful blog and the videos posted on it.

The creases in her face deepened, revealing wrinkles she'd so carefully covered with foundation. She seemed surprised by these revelations.

"That kind of display . . . It doesn't sound like him," she said, her expression doubtful.

"I know. But there is little doubt. The text comes directly from our notebook."

"True . . . ," she admitted. "Still, I find the idea of Louie *cheating* on you strange."

She emphasized the word "cheating" as if to imply that she considered it a poor choice to describe Louie's actions. I remembered the drawing of the tattoo that Stéphane had shown me the night of Louie's arrest: Semper fidelis. Forever faithful. The irony of the message was not lost on me. Given recent events, I couldn't understand the meaning behind the dictum. It was absurd.

" . . . I mean, with a girl like Salomé," she added, interrupting my thoughts.

"Why do you find that so surprising?"

"First, because she was never really his type . . ."

And yet he had been with the beautiful ethnic woman the very first time I had met him, the day when—although I would have been loath to admit it back then—I fell irremeably in love with him. Perhaps he considered her an escort, in the strictest sense of the word—a woman with a spectacular body whose presence at his side during public events added to his prestige. Because, to compare the two of us, I was nothing like that flawless tigress. Like many men, Louie made a distinction between women he liked to parade around and women he liked in his bed.

"Really?"

"Salomé loves conflict. And she has never tried to hide her more than pronounced interest in Louie."

"So if he wanted something on the side, something discreet and inconsequential, he wouldn't seek out a girl like that."

That is exactly what worried me. Why would he choose her unless it was a move in some perverted game between us? Couldn't he have found someone else from Rebecca's still vast pool of girls?

I really had to insist to convince Rebecca to give me Salomé's address.

"'Salomé' is a pseudonym," she informed me. "Her real name is Véronique Duclos."

Much less exotic, I noted.

"If she asks how you got her name and address, don't mention me, do you understand?"

Was Salomé/Véronique's wrath so terrible? After leaving a worried Rebecca, I made my way to the RER train line A, then transferred at the Halles station, where I took line B toward Saint-Rémy-lès-Chevreuse. Line B was a perfect example of the endemic problems and overcrowding of the transportation system as it sprawled out into the suburbs. But as luck had it, the train got me to my destination of Bourg-la-Reine without a hitch.

Salomé's building was a five-minute walk from the station, and it wasn't long before I was pressing an intercom button with her name on it:

"Hello . . . It's Annabelle Lorand. Elle," I announced.

This was met with silence, then an electronic buzz. I was soon standing in front of her door, on the second floor of an affluent building

"What the hell are you doing here?" she asked.

"I'm here for Louie."

"Why? He's your man. You wanted him, he's yours."

I reached to stop her from closing the door on me.

"Did you know he might be facing prison time?"

"Yeah . . . I'd heard that. What does that have to do with me?"

"He's published some things online that concern you . . . and they might be used against him in a trial."

"What kind of things?" she asked, her tone softening a little, her expression suddenly more attentive.

I let her think for a moment before trying my luck:

"May I come in for a few minutes so I can show you?"

She stared at me, hesitating, then smiled, opening her door wider and stepping aside to let me in. It was a one-bedroom apartment decorated exclusively with Swedish furnishings. It could have been in a magazine under the heading "How to Make the Most of a Small Apartment."

In the living room, she pointed to her laptop, which was turned on and sitting atop her polished glass desk:

"Make yourself at home. But hurry up. I have to leave in fifteen minutes."

I logged on to the Elle & Louie blog. The video I had seen was now filed in the archives. I clicked on the play button and the horrible sequence of images began to flash across the screen.

Salomé's haughty demeanor vanished. She could not deny that, of the two bodies on-screen, the female, lascivious, feline body was hers.

"When is this dated?"

"I watched it live . . . four days ago."

"That's impossible."

"Why?"

"Because that film is at least two years old."

"Two years?"

"Yes. For your information, I haven't slept with Louie since you two have been together."

Was she bluffing? I didn't detect any of the telltale signs of lying on her face: her gaze was not turned toward the ground; she was not blinking excessively, not biting her lips; she wasn't sweating, and she didn't look at all overheated.

"How can I be sure you're telling the truth?"

Without a word, she turned toward the screen, attentively watched a few seconds' worth of video, then suddenly clicked stop. Frozen on the screen was an image of Louie, his back toward us and at an angle that revealed his left side. His entire back was blank, the nape of his neck, and . . .

"You probably know better than I . . . Look at his left shoulder."

There was no inscription!

"Your man had a rose tattooed there over a year ago, am I right?" she asked, her sense of self-assurance regained.

I caught a trace of contempt in her familiar way of calling Louie "your man," but I took the phrase as the sweetest of officializations. If Salomé thought so, then it was because he was mine.

"Right . . . ," I stammered.

"Then explain to me why a video taken four days ago would show him without a tattoo there."

12

Along time ago, I first noticed the melancholic effect of the RER train on my mood. The frequents stops, the close succession of tunnels and stations, the premature slackening of speed, the steady *rat-a-tat-tat* of the wheels, the strident squeal of the breaks, the lazy and annoying ring of the doors closing, the sleepy silence of the train cars outside of rush hour—all these things make me drowsy, and I'll find myself in a daydream somewhere far, far away from the urban landscape. Only the RER has this effect on me.

As I made my way back home, my thoughts pitched strangely back and forth. They slid from hope and relief to a sense of unbearable affliction. I couldn't get Salomé's last words to me out of my head: "Then explain to me why a video taken four days ago would show him without a tattoo there."

If Louie hadn't slept with his former mistress recently, then why had he posted that video on the blog?

I felt like one of those imprudent girls who make love to strangers without protection and then fear that even a minor cold is a sign of infection. Like those girls, I was waiting for what seemed like a life-or-death answer. Positive? Negative? I was anxious to know.

More and more travelers boarded the train as it rolled toward the capital. Meanwhile, other thoughts entered my head, like what Sophia had said a few days before: "I'm sure he saw it more as a kind of game between you two."

What if this was all just a game? A kind of language, a dialogue he was trying to establish with me, from a distance? What if he was unable to speak sincerely with me when we were together? Everything made sense from that perspective: he was sending out beacons, signals to provoke me. Perhaps these were cries for help. And I was acting like a child, getting upset and turning my back on him at the first sign of hardship.

David had asserted that sex for Louie was an addiction. But wasn't it more of a mode of communication, the only one available to him? The only one he had mastered? In that case, shouldn't I consider the long series of tests he had put me through—the blog being the latest and most hurtful—as his slightly brutal way of establishing contact with me? His way of pushing the limits of our exchange beyond words or even caresses? Couldn't sex, when it was elevated to the level of art—a sophisticated way of relating to another person—couldn't it be a form of telepathic communication between beings? A way of speaking beyond words, beyond bodies or even pleasure?

If that was true, then he wouldn't be relinquishing his strange mores anytime soon. And I needed to prepare myself for a lifetime of experiences, some of which would be a kind of hazing. Was I prepared for that? Could I handle feeling the virus of his perversity proliferate in me, day after day, and with all the associated side effects?

No, because if I was going to accept this singular dialect,

then I needed him to speak to me in simple terms, without all the frustrating mind games. I just wanted his arms around me, his skin stretched over mine like a fresh sheet, his lips glued to mine, breathing life back into me, giving me confidence in him again.

TWO PIECES OF GOOD NEWS awaited me at my studio: my Internet connection had been activated, and David's full birth certificate was in my mailbox. I had ordered it from Saint-Malo's town hall while I was at the Internet café on Boulevard de Sébastopol the other night. Thanks to the previous year's wedding plans, I had all the information necessary for such a request: his first and middle names (David Marc Albert), his date of birth (I used the dubious one, January 5, 1969), and the surnames, first names, and birth places of his parents. That was all I had needed to have his birth certificate sent to me.

Identity theft didn't seem like a very difficult task. With a few basic details on David's life, I could easily obtain all manner of official documents. After I had confirmed my doubts, I called Master Whurman:

"Hello, this is Mademoiselle Lorand. I'm calling to speak with Master Whurman regarding my marriage contract . . . No, I don't want to cancel it."

What had given him such an idea? Did it happen often? Or had I, the young woman who had canceled her wedding plans with one man only to get engaged to his brother, become a laughingstock behind the closed doors of his office?

"I just wanted to tell you that I do *not* want the studio I've recently purchased to be included in my estate . . . That's all."

I had been so obsessed with David's date of birth that I hadn't taken time to inspect the rest of the document. I was simply scanning over it when something caught my eye: *Father and mother unknown.* I read the phrase several times, focusing on each locution, reviewing each word, as if to better understand its true meaning. Father . . . mother . . . *unknown.* The full thrust of the sentence resided in this last word.

"Of course they're known!" I cried aloud to myself.

I was tempted to call David, or the town hall in Saint-Malo, to set the record straight . . . But who really knew for sure, besides David and Louie? Or Armand and Rebecca, whose accounts of the Barlet brothers' childhood were difficult to verify?

And yet, there it was, on that piece of paper, in all its harsh truth. The puzzle was fairly simple to reconstruct, but I had trouble picturing everything, and it took me several minutes before I came to the following conclusion: if David had been born to unknown parents, and if everyone had agreed to present him as the legitimate son of the Barlet couple, and if today he was able to wear the Barlet name like a medal . . . it was because Andre and Hortensia had adopted him. Did David know?

It was a violent realization—a shock. I remembered the photograph I'd stored somewhere in my smartphone. Two children, one of whom was David, standing with a happy adult couple. Two unknown persons. Two unknown *parents*? But if that was them in the photograph, then they couldn't be completely unknown, could they? I looked more closely at the picture. It was difficult to tell, but there was something familiar about the man and the woman. They didn't show any signs of being a romantic couple: no hands around waists; their hips did not touch; there was no physical contact between the two bodies at all. They maintained a respectful distance from each other. Godfather and godmother? Temporary foster parents?

Among all the things I was learning that day, this last piece of information tipped the scale with its ominous weight.

I WAS FINALLY ABLE TO log onto the Elle & Louie blog from my studio. New notes abounded. Not so new for me, since they had all been taken from our Ten-Times-a-Day. Our erotic adventures at the Hôtel des Charmes weren't published on the blog in chronological order, but according to various thematic groups: all entries concerning sounds and words were in one group; a little further down, our chapters on scents could be perused.

Rediscovering these descriptions of our bodies embracing in room one was almost moving. If I closed my eyes, I could feel myself shiver each time Louie's hand brushed over my skin—a wave of intensity that always radiated well beyond the initial zone of contact. The palm of his hand could make my neck and shoulders quiver when he touched my stomach; and when he pinched my nipple, I felt my flower spontaneously blossom and pearl with dew.

But I was revolted by the thought that what should have remained between those four walls and confined to those pages had been posted, uncensored, to the wilds of the Web. At first it had felt like rape. But then, after tracking the blog's development and popularity—it was already one of the most visited sites in its category—I mostly felt dispossessed. Stripped of my own life, of my own pleasures, of my sweet orgasms. I was experiencing one of the disadvantages of fame: I belonged to everyone but myself. But I was by no means a star. It wasn't glitter and fame that I was feeling, but the abject sensation of anonymous hands slowly replacing those of Louie, squeezing me, frisking me, like crazed shoppers on the first day of a sale. A reduced-price item, that is what he had made me.

I FINALLY CALLED SOPHIA. EVEN when she annoyed me, even when she did stupid things, even when she was so selfish as to be happy when I was not, there was no one better to lean on. She alone knew how to bring me down to earth, to make me face reality, and to fight the irrationality of my hopes and fears. After briefly delving into her blossoming relationship with Fred, she lent me a very attentive ear.

"If you really love him, and I know you do, you have to help him," she said after listening to me for a long spell.

"That's easy to say . . . ," I lamented. "But how do I do that?"

"Don't get too involved in learning about every detail of his erotic indiscretions, hon. It will only come back to bite you, and you won't be able to change anything about how he treats you."

"But I don't want to change him!" I cried.

I wanted him to shine, to burn, to be free to express his desires, whatever they were. I wanted his perfect hands on my imperfect body, again and forever. I needed him now more than ever. I needed the contact of his body against mine, to erase all my doubts.

I hadn't left David—a man lacking in sensuality if ever there was one, a man shackled by his responsibilities and his image—to chain myself to the same tedium. Louie's sexuality was a raging river that sometimes overflowed but whose strength offered me an eternal journey with an ever-changing landscape.

But my friend was right: as soon as I had asked Louie to marry me, his behavior had intensified and he had veered toward more extreme forms of expression. Perhaps I was mistaken, perhaps my charges against him were misguided, but that is what I had come to believe.

"You do want to change him a little . . . You don't like seeing him get off on the Internet with girls that look like models. And you won't be able to put up with it over the course of decades."

"True . . . What do you suggest, then?"

"Regardless of what gave rise to this specific behavior now, it has to be tied to his childhood or his youth."

Now she was playing therapist. When she was first choosing a major in college, I remembered, she had agonized between history—which is how we met—and psychology. "If dance doesn't work out for me, then I want to help kids in bad situations," she had said, "you know, like be a school counselor." Six years later, she was gyrating her body in peep shows, and she barely ever saw children, except when she jogged past families in Bois de Vincennes.

"If I were you," she continued, "I would look into that photo and David's birth date. There is clearly something to dig up there."

Among all the new elements of this saga, the thing that interested her most was our protagonists' past. For her, Louie's relationship with Aurora when the men were young was probably a particularly sore point in the web of passion and resentment between them. Contrary to what Armand had intimated, the issue of which brother would inherit his father's seat at the head of the Barlet Group seemed more secondary to me now, in terms of their rift. There was something from before that time; something deeper, too.

"I thought I needed to investigate Louie . . ."

"Louie, David . . . You can see as well as I that the two are intertwined. The two faces of the Anus god."

That was one of Sophia's best qualities: she knew how to be

funny in the most serious of situations, though I could never tell exactly if she was doing it on purpose.

"Janus, Soph. It's Janus, the two-faced god!" I laughed.

"I know! I spotted him in the gallery when I went to visit the National Assembly. What do you take me for?"

I was contemplating something I had intuited earlier: we would never be able to understand or change the behavior of either brother without first inquiring into the origins of their life as siblings. The inconsistency in their birth dates had made that clear.

"If you want my opinion," Sophia continued, her voice more serious, "you can only love someone if you really know him. Otherwise, it's a lie."

One second she was a comedian, and the next a philosopher.

"You say that, and yet you're going out with a guy you once told me wasn't reliable," I retorted.

"First of all, I've never said that I'm in love with Fred. I just like him, that's all. And second, truly knowing the other person is only the first step."

"What's the second, if you please, Dr. Sophia?"

"You have to accept him the way he is," she replied, ignoring my sarcasm.

"Are you kidding? You just said the opposite of that two minutes ago!"

"That's not true. I said that you don't have to put up with the effects of his true nature, particularly as it pertains to your relationship with him. But he has to sense that you know and love him. You have to be prepared to handle some of his unconventional behavior. Not all . . . but some."

She was right. What better way was there to prove my

love for him than to shed light on his shadowy zones? When I finally knew everything about him, my declarations of love would be more honest. I would know the truth behind each tender word, be it raw, frightening, or painful. The idea sent a shiver of relief through my entire body that bore into the depths of my pelvis, where an ache had formed in Louie's absence.

There was a risk associated with diving into Louie's depths. With David, I had wanted to know more, to peel back the layers of his past lives. And what I had discovered had turned out to be more painful than wonderful.

So I made a commitment to myself. I wouldn't make anything formal with the elder Barlet brother before I had shed light on his past and on the nature of his relationships with his brother and the deceased Aurora. Being Aurora's doppelganger, I could allow myself a little leeway to look into her past with the Barlet family, couldn't I? I gave myself the right to be an archeologist of her history. Of *their* common history, all three of them.

There would be no question of marriage before I dug up all the vestiges of that loaded past or investigated every fossilized feeling, every skeleton of love and hate. It was my turn to set the terms of this relationship.

I tried to convince myself that no part of me was motivated by revenge. I wasn't setting up obstacles to watch the man I loved crash into them. On the contrary, I hoped that my investigation would help free everyone involved. One day, I was sure of it, Louie would be grateful to me. He would understand that my intentions had never been to humiliate him but to make his spirit, his heart, his body all equally accessible.

I HAD MADE MY DECISION, and there was no point staying cooped up in my apartment, feeling worried and sorry for myself. Saint-Malo and its purifying fresh air, Saint-Malo and its well-kept secrets were waiting for me. A quick Internet search explained a detail about David's place of birth that had been eluding me: "Saint-Servan, City of Saint-Malo." The small village of Saint-Servan, formerly the Gallo-Roman settlement of Aleth, is known for its immense villas and Solidor Tower. It features a large, rocky hillside overlooking the bay, with a view of verdant landscapes and its neighboring city, Saint-Malo. Saint-Servan was once a vast port town, renowned throughout the region and the country. In 1967, it was merged into Saint-Malo. But for years after, and no doubt out of force of habit, the former town appeared on the birth certificates of all those born there, despite the fact that it had been demoted to a neighborhood. The custom continued until 1969 (or 1970, depending on which version of things one chooses to observe), as evidenced by the document I had in front of me.

A discreet *knock-knock* at my door tore me from my thoughts and plans, which consisted for the most part of stuffing everything I would need for a short trip to the coast into a duffel bag. My first visitor! It was probably no one, a salesperson or a neighbor, but I still felt a surge of emotion as I opened the door, my heart pounding. Whenever someone used to knock at our door in Nanterre, Mom used to ask, her voice raised: "Who's there, the 7:45 stranger?" It was a reference to a French television show from before my time, in which small-time celebrities tried to guess the identities of two people who were barely more famous. A simple and popular game. My mother used to love it. I didn't understand why until years later: each time a person's identity was revealed, she secretly hoped it would be a person whom she had once known long ago.

As chance had it, my visitor that night arrived at precisely quarter to eight.

"Can I come in?"

His voice was much less composed than usual. In fact, his whole attitude—spine hunched, head bowed—expressed a distress and lack of self-confidence that I had never seen in him before. His cane featured a new knob that was molded into the shape of a Gorgon's head, whose serpentine hair fell in shiny threads onto the dark wood. He seemed to be relying on this accessory more than ever to keep him upright.

"What do . . . ," I stammered, my gaze lost beyond the line of his shoulders. "Who gave you this address?"

I had only hung up the phone with Sophia a few minutes earlier. I had trouble believing she was the culprit.

"Master Whurman. Actually, not him, his clerk."

I remembered the young blonde with the updo and the graceful neck.

Louie must have gone there in person and worked his charm, thanks to which she had no doubt gladly revealed my real estate venture.

"You know the best part? Her name's Claire Leclerk, and she's a notary's clerk. Isn't that something? She's a walking, talking pun."

"Mom used to work with an accountant named Ila Cheatem."

"Seriously?"

"It's true."

It took a trivial joke like that, an elementary form of humor, to ease the palpable tension between us.

He suppressed a laugh, then suddenly grew serious as I opened the door a crack.

"Come in," I said at last.

He took a few steps forward and then stopped in the middle of the room, his eyes sweeping over the still mostly empty space. He could have offered a polite compliment—*It's cute*; *It's charming*; *It's so you*—but he refrained from all commentary. Meanwhile, I was having trouble containing all the questions boiling inside me.

I realized now that I wouldn't get any answers from him directly, except through my own capacity to peer into his character and pluck them out unbeknownst to him. Making him talk would be of no use to me. Interrogating into his past, however, plunging my head into the crosscurrents of a tumultuous sea with an unstable skyline—now that would bring me closer to him. And that was the route I had decided to take. As sweet and as beautiful and sincere as his words might appear on the surface, they would never be more than false buoys, broken or punctured life jackets that would inevitably let me down.

So I didn't mention the videos on his computer console. Nor did I say anything about the blog, or even of Salomé and their video performance. And I was especially careful not to bring up the primary piece of evidence in my investigation, about which he had already lied to me: the mere seven months that separated his birth from David's. Why kill myself trying to make him talk, why give him an opportunity to lie to me again, when his body—his only tangible truth—was there before me, radiating that febrile heat with which he could so gently burn me?

Before he left, disappearing into the night, we didn't exchange another word. This time, it wasn't a game. It was a necessity. We were starved of each other, and reproach would have dulled our senses. What person thirsting for sincerity can turn down a drink from the corrupt waters of his or her pleasure?

I dragged him to my new bed and started undressing us. He let me lead him and was surprising docile, considering his past role as the supreme master of our desires.

After he awoke inside my mouth, long and hard, moist with impatience, I lay down on my stomach, offering myself to him in just the way he liked to take me: crushed, subservient. My backside arched toward him, begging to be opened, separated by his soft hands, pressed for its juice like a piece of fruit. But as his glans made its way through my thicket of hair, hesitating against my soaking vulva, agitated in a way I had never experienced, I was seized by a strange idea. In the past, I had avoided this inevitability, claiming a natural reticence, emphasizing the intensity of pleasure by other means. In the end, I had transformed the idea into a goal or a reward, both for him and for myself.

So that there was no ambiguity as to my intentions, I moistened an index finger with my mouth and inserted it into my tense and restive rosebud. At first, I could only manage a knuckle. Then, as my brown eye started to dilate, my whole finger. Each immersion of my finger raised my posterior, as though a string had been tied to my pubis and an invisible crane were lifting me toward invisible heights. Louie was immobilized, fascinated by this new scene.

I repeated the action with my fatter and longer middle finger. But nothing could have prepared me for the shock, the incomparable wave of bliss striped with pain that crashed through me when his member entered me. The tip of his glans forced its way through first, fighting against the resistance of my sphincter muscles. Then my canal slowly sucked in the entirety of his shaft, like a snake digesting its prey. After the initial tear, I experienced the exhilarating sensation of being filled like a laundry bag. I was beginning to understand why men used such vulgar terms to describe this rare delicacy, and also why it had such a terrible reputation among us women. My body almost rejected his rod on several occasions. But Louie's full weight was now on top of me, and I couldn't escape his grip.

Nevertheless, he waited several minutes before amplifying my sweet torture with slow and cautious movements in and out of me, seeing to it that this was pleasurable for me, too—and not just torture. I was almost suffocating. The lower region of my body seemed like a powder keg on the verge of exploding, and I couldn't decide if that was an agreeable sensation or not. Then, as though he sensed my hesitation, Louie seized my hand and slid it under my belly. The order was clear. I began with a few light strokes, but with his cock rushing into my tight orifice, I concluded that I had better get serious. He could take care of my dorsal, and I my ventral. My clitoris had never felt so hard and elastic between my fingers. Each time I pressed it, the little ball of orgasmic rubber resisted and rebounded. It seemed to echo the rocking movement of my posterior.

Did my cry of joy come when he spewed his hot and heavy lava into my entrails or when my discharge pricked my front side like an insect? Did I call out his name? Did he bellow mine, his mind scattered and grateful?

13

MAY 30, 2010

Only later did I understand the utility of my surrender. Regardless of what I did or of my future discoveries about him, I didn't want Louie to see me as his enemy. By offering him my ultimate bastion, and by allowing him to experience pleasure there, where no one had been before him, I was exonerating myself of future misdeeds. Since I was opening myself up so completely to his desires, wasn't it only fair that he let me deflower the innermost recesses of his personality? On the scale of mutual compromise, didn't my beautiful hips weigh at least as much as his mysteries?

HIGH-SPEED TRAINS DO NOT ALLOW for the same kind of reveries as the RER. I spent the first few minutes reflecting on our sodomitic evening but soon fell into a downy sleep, the train carrying me through the night. Looking for answers, if not a solution, I had caught a last-minute TGV headed for Brittany from the Gare Montparnasse.

I had been careful not to alert Louie to my travel plans. I hadn't even told Sophia, never mind Fred or Rebecca. I didn't want to hear their warnings, their empathetic expressions of worry, their voices of Cassandra. I owed it to myself to keep my mind free and clear—and not to confuse it with contradictory advice and admonitions from my friends.

After two hours of fitful sleep punctuated by announcements and screaming children, I sensed the high-speed train come to a stop in Rennes. Over the course of just a few minutes, the cars emptied themselves of two-thirds of their passengers, and when we took off again, our pace was slower, bumpier—better adapted to this stretch of ill-kempt railway. The movement of my fellow passengers lugging their suitcases stirred me out of my torpor. Soon, I was fully awake. The train car grew calm, the silence only interrupted from time to time by high-pitched screeches.

There were only a few of us now, stretched across the violet seats. I stood to visit the restrooms, which were finally vacant. Lowering my panties, I considered myself for a moment in the speckled mirror. I was the same as a year before and yet also so different. I could have sworn, for instance, that my breasts were a little fuller. Was this the result of age, or was Louie, and his pinching and prodding, to blame?

I hadn't lost any weight, but my face seemed slimmer, its contours better defined. It had more character, as if it had slowly integrated some of Louie's features into itself—a mimetic marvel of love. I wondered if in return I had given his face some of my youth and roundness.

One last detail caught my attention, and although I tried not to see it as yet another sign of trouble for us as a couple, it still worried me: three weeks after Stéphane had inked my tattoo, my petal was starting to disappear beneath a small tuft of hair big enough to disguise my Mount Venus and its discreet rumbling. Soon, like a forest animal hiding under the canopy, the design would be completely invisible to the eye. All that would remain of this mark of our love would be our memory of it.

These observations, along with the fresh memory of the previous night's reckless abandon, gave me the immediate desire to put pen to paper. Or, rather, to type out my thoughts with the virtual keyboard on my phone, which was in constant communication with a cloud-based notebook that I used for personal reflections.

I didn't fear my phone being hacked or my writing being fraudulently appropriated. Yes, in that sleepy train car, with the rhythmic rattle of the rails beneath us, a project was born. I needed an outlet for my doubts and stress—the Ten-Times-a-Day notebook had died when Louie had appropriated it—so I decided to write a book, a memoir to be exact. A record. And it is thanks to that sudden impulse that you are reading these pages now.

I sensed that the subject of my book would lead me toward unknown territories. My book would tell this story, mine, a story about a woman who uses her body to extract secrets from the men that she loves, secrets that enslave them. This is a story about how sex can become a truth serum.

I drafted the first words, then the first lines, and soon almost an entire page as the train made its way toward the coast: *I have never belonged to that category of women who see all hotel rooms as identical, all one and the same, each an anonymous space without any character or personality. A kind of cold tunnel with a uniform interior, offering standardized comfort for the night.*

THE SKY IN SAINT-MALO WAS heavy and glum. Its annual international book and film festival, Étonnants Voyageurs, had ended a few days before. Thanks to the conjunction of these two factors, I was able to book a room as soon as I arrived, in a brand-new hotel, and with a view. Walking down the wharf, I welcomed the region's tonifying air and each gust of wind, which smelled strongly of kelp.

The main room was L-shaped and decorated like a starkly modern lounge. The atmosphere contradicted the first chapter of my book. Nothing was more impersonal than this room, and I had trouble imagining any past inhabitants. But I didn't care. I was exhausted, and as soon as I had tucked myself under a thick comforter, I was overcome by a deep sleep that lasted all night. My dreams were mixed with memories and took place in another room. Dream after dream, I found myself in room one, replaying all of our favorite positions in a kind of oneiric *Kama Sutra*. In one dream, my partner's precise thrusting in doggy-style brought me to completion. In another, we were lost in an endless 69, each of us bringing the other to the brink of satisfaction, torturing each other, deferring our mutual pleasure ever longer.

After a few hours of such dreams, I awoke, my inner thighs moist and my pelvis palpitating with unsatisfied desire.

"GOOD MORNING, MADEMOISELLE. WOULD YOU care for tea or coffee?"

The young woman leaning over my breakfast table smiled weakly at me, doe-eyed. She literally seemed to be hanging on my reply.

"Tea, please."

"You're lucky. It's nice out this morning."

Bright sunbeams danced around her slim silhouette. As for my good luck . . . I had trouble sharing her optimism.

"Yes . . . ," I agreed, without enthusiasm.

"Is this your first time in Saint-Malo?"

Crap, this was one of those employees that hotel chains hire for their ability to adhere to the rules of customer service. The ones who dutifully memorize meaningless acronyms throughout their training: G(ood morning/afternoon/evening), W(elcome), W(hat can I do for you?).

"No. My family is from here," I lied. Then, to avoid further questioning, I asked: "Do you know what time town hall opens?"

"Yes. On weekdays, at eight thirty."

Her training clearly hadn't accounted for tourists who were only interested in local administration, and she left me alone. She came back with a heavy metallic teakettle and poured hot water into my cup without uttering another word.

AT LEAST HER INFORMATION HAD been good. At eight thirty sharp, I arrived at the majestic courtyard of Saint-Malo's town hall—located inside the fortified town's Renaissance-era château.

"What do you need?"

The city employee seemed to me like the exact opposite of the hotel waitress. She was short, old, brown-haired, and about as surly as the other had been affable. No acronyms or other niceties, here. Just a direct question and her eyes surveying me from behind crooked glasses.

Undeterred by this woman's attitude and determined to pursue my investigation of the Barlets, I handed her the birth certificate that her office—perhaps even she herself—had sent me.

"Hello . . . Could you please tell me if this document corresponds to the original?"

"What is it?" she asked in a disgusted tone.

"It's a copy of a birth certificate."

"That's not you, is it?" she asked, pointing suspiciously to the name.

David Barlet—unless one was truly blind, it would be difficult to believe that that was my name.

"That's my future husband."

"Hmm . . . Do you have proof?"

"I can show you our marriage contract."

I had had the foresight to bring along all the official documents I had in my possession, including those that were no longer relevant. She scanned the page on which we had signed, the one where I had provided a false signature. Satisfied, she then disappeared without saying a word. She reappeared a few minutes later, dragging her feet and her decrepit carcass, weighed down by several decades of paperwork and boredom.

"It matches."

"Everything? Even the parents, the—"

"Like I said, it matches," she interrupted, as sharp as the edge of a sheet of paper. "No two ways about it."

I didn't want to get on the bad side of this counter clerk.

"Thank you, you've been very helpful," I said, with deference.

I pretended to take my leave, then came back.

"I don't mean to take advantage of your kindness—"

"What is it?" she barked.

At this hour of the morning, I was the only person there. Prolonging my visit wouldn't inconvenience anyone, except, that is, her and her obvious desire to take a nap on her pile of papers.

"Do you also keep death certificates?"

"Yes."

"Would it be possible to check on a name?"

"What name?"

"Delbard."

"Is that a family member?"

"No . . . ," I admitted, short on lies. "It's the mother of my husband's ex-wife."

She contemplated me for a moment, her eyes clouded and menacing. But even if she considered my request illegitimate, I could tell that she would give me anything I wanted if it meant getting rid of me.

"Do you know the first name?"

"Sorry . . . ," I said, shrugging.

She started typing furiously; then suddenly her pudgy fingers froze:

"Do you have any idea when this death occurred?"

"It could have been any time between the early seventies and now."

"Well, that's helpful," she grumbled sarcastically.

I searched my memory for anything that could help her, anything that I could have gleaned on my last trip to this area. I only came up with this:

"Delbard must be her married name."

"And her maiden name?"

"No idea. But her husband's first name was Jean-François. He died in 2005, if I recall."

"Jean-François Delbard, the notary?"

She raised a curious eyebrow.

"Yes."

In a provincial town of this size it wasn't surprising for a city employee to know the names of notable residents. After another period of tapping into a partially erased keyboard, she said, her voice atonal:

"I have a Florence Delbard, maiden name Montroriser. She married Jean-François Delbard in 1965."

"That's her!" I exclaimed, with a little too much enthusiasm.

"But according to my records . . . she's still alive."

She announced this as though it would come as a disappointment to me. And yet it was the best news I had gotten since I'd begun my investigation. Finally, a key witness to the youths of David, Louie, and Aurora! Finally, someone close to them who wasn't dead.

I didn't want to try her patience, so I refrained from asking her for a recent address. But fate was on my side, because when I searched an online directory on one of the computers available for free use in the lobby, Florence was in it.

IMPASSE DES TILLEULS WAS A small, rather unremarkable dead-end street in the residential quarter of Paramé, about a mile east of Saint-Malo's city center. The weather was mild, despite a northerly wind, and I decided to follow the coastline on foot. Since the coast faces north, even when it is nice out, like it was that day, the area is exposed to cold winds, which temper the heat in summer months and exacerbate the chill throughout the rest of the year.

As I walked, I admired subtle variations in the sea's color, which, depending on the light and the water's distance from the shore, ranged from an almost translucent emerald green to a somber and metallic gray-green.

Number 7 was a small duplex that looked exactly like all the neighboring buildings, with their granite walls and slate roofs. I rang the bell for two long minutes, to no avail. And I didn't notice any movement, however slight, inside the house. I tried my luck at number 5. A small woman in hair curlers and an apron eventually opened her door.

"Hello, Madame," I greeted her with my warmest smile.

"Are you the young lady with the association?"

"No. I was just here to visit Madame Delbard, your neighbor. But apparently she isn't home . . ."

"Oh, that's possible. I don't see her much."

Apparently reassured by our initial exchange, she came down her front steps to get a better look at me through the gate. She didn't hide her surprise or the curious look in her eyes.

"Are you family? A niece?"

"Yes," I bluffed.

"Did you tell her that you'd be coming?"

"No . . . I just thought I'd stop by."

"It's too bad that you've missed her. She almost never leaves the house . . . except to visit her husband in Rocabey, of course."

She was referring to the cemetery—I knew because I had been there the year before with Sophia and seen the Delbard family tomb.

I thanked her profusely before leaving, fending off her questions, and headed toward Rocabey. This time I took an internal route that was largely protected from the strongest gusts of wind, passing through wide bourgeois arteries lined with early twentieth-century villas. Overhead, small clouds streaked through the clear sky as fast as falling stars.

As soon as I set foot inside the cemetery, with its granite workman's shed, I recognized the gravedigger. He was a man in his forties with bushy sideburns and hands that seemed permanently connected to an orange wheelbarrow. I waved, and he approached me at once.

"What can I do for you, little lady?"

He didn't seem to recognize me from my previous visit the year before.

"I just wanted to know if there's a Barlet family tomb here."

"Barlet? Like the Barlet I keep seeing on TV these days?"

He seemed almost to be exaggerating his rough, country voice.

"Yes," I confirmed.

"Let me see . . ."

He withdrew a small notebook from the breast pocket of his raincoat and began scanning it with a finger on his left hand, licking his fingertip as he turned each page.

"There . . . Barlet. E17. It's over there." He pointed a dirty index finger toward his left. "I'll show you, if you want."

He shot me a toothless smile and guided me through the geometric maze of paths, without ever letting go of his wheelbarrow. He was like Charon with his ferry. But it didn't seem as though his quotidian dealings with the dead had disconnected him from the living. His enthusiasm for being a guide was evidence of his affection for living things. I saw him delicately avoid stepping with his giant galoshes onto an earthworm that was inching its way over the muddy earth. I thought to myself that he must have to step aside often, considering the density of creeping critters in this place.

"Andre and Hortensia Barlet," he announced, pointing to a sober tomb whose gold lettering nevertheless left no doubt as to the status of its occupants.

"There are only two?"

The man leafed through his moth-eaten notebook with his gruff fingers, then raised his kindly head to me.

"Yes . . . They must not be from here. Usually, you'll see several generations of the same family in one plot."

He was right. Once they had amassed their fortune, the Barlets had chosen Saint-Malo as their summer residence. But, as Armand had once told me, the family was originally from a region farther south, near Nantes.

The tomb only mentioned the years in which its occupants were born and died. Not the day or the month. But one detail was striking: both husband and wife had died in the same year, 1990.

"You wouldn't by chance know the exact date of their death, would you?"

"Hmm . . . Yes. It's unusual."

"Why?"

"They died on the same day. July 6, 1990."

"Are you sure?"

"Unless the little ladies over at town hall were telling me stories."

"The city employees?"

"Yes. But I don't know why they would do that."

I thought back to the rude reception I had received that same morning from the woman at town hall, and I had no trouble imagining her playing mean-spirited tricks on this simple man.

However, if what she had told him was true, then Andre and Hortensia Barlet must have died from the same cause. And it must have been an accident, a tragic event, since it had taken the lives of two distinct individuals. I remembered that Armand had been very evasive when it came to Andre and

Hortensia's deaths. I also noted that it had taken place just six months after Aurora's death. Were the two episodes related? Or had fate struck David and Louie twice that year, cruelly, blindly?

"The date must be correct," I said, reassuring him. "Do you know how they lost their lives?"

"No . . . I was only eighteen at the time, and I didn't pay much attention to the news."

His gaze wandered over my jean-clad backside, as if to illustrate his point—and prove that he was not entirely indifferent to my charms. But it was done with such naïveté, such astonishing spontaneity, that I didn't take offense.

Ever since Louie had first grazed my body with his eyes, then his hands, I'd been getting more attention from men. Louie's attraction for me had opened the way for other men's latent desires. I didn't respond, but that didn't stop the constant flux. Over time, I had gotten used to it, feeling at once annoyed by the attention and a little flattered. Still, in spite of it all, I didn't feel any more confident as to my influence over men than when I'd thought I was invisible.

My purse started vibrating, putting a stop to these reflections. It was a message from Louie. I had hoped it would be a message expressing his love or his gratitude for the night before, but instead it contained the following practical information:

Elle & Louie
User Name: elleandlouie
Password: hoteldescharmes

As a kind of declaration of love, he was giving me the account information to his blog so that I could publish posts, too. Did he really think I was remotely interested?

Aside from the libidinous gravedigger and me, the cemetery was deserted. Not surprising, really, for a weekday morning. Then I noticed a small silhouette making its way through the graves. It was prudently dressed in a faded yellow raincoat.

"Okay . . . If you don't need anything else, I'll leave you," my guide said, his tone vaguely disappointed.

"Yes . . . Of course. And thank you."

"Have a nice day!"

He treated me to another toothless grin and walked back toward the entry, his hands still clutching his wheelbarrow. Soon he was swallowed by rows and rows of gray marble.

The yellow raincoat continued its progression forward; then it stopped, not far, it seemed to me, from the Delbard tomb. As I drew nearer, I was able to make out the hooded form more clearly: a petite blonde in her sixties. She must have sensed that I was coming toward her because she raised a frightened eye in my direction and quickly retraced her steps back through the rows. At last, I called out to her:

"Madame! Madame, please!"

As I called out to her again, she quickened her pace and looked like a terrified sparrow. From behind her, I distinctly made out her hand's gesture of denial, as if she were swatting a fly or an unseemly image.

"Madame Delbard?"

14

Put yourself in her place for a moment: Your daughter, who has been dead for more than twenty years, suddenly reappears in the cemetery where she was buried! Neither time nor the worms have altered her appearance. She hasn't even aged. On the contrary, she looks just as fine-featured and young as when you knew her before her death. A perfect ghost—but just as dense and embodied as the original, and who speaks and chases after you when you try to flee. A ghost who has all the characteristics of a living person. She is much better than some ordinary phantasm; she is a double!

"Madame Delbard . . . I would like to speak with you."

Short and rather plump, the woman in the yellow raincoat wasn't moving very fast. I was soon close enough to grab her arm.

"Let go of me!"

"Are you Florence Delbard?"

"What's it to you?" she barked.

She hadn't denied it, which I took as a sign that she was indeed who I thought.

She was seized by a small convulsion, although it wasn't strong enough to wrest her arm out of my grip. But she turned to face me, and I could finally look at her more closely. She couldn't have been more dissimilar from her daughter—and myself. She was short, round, with blotchy skin, her face squashed on both sides and reminiscent of a rugby ball. She had an unflattering bowl cut that framed and highlighted her puffy and less than charming features.

"You don't know who I am . . . but you do know the person I resemble, don't you?"

I loosened my grip, convinced now that she wouldn't try to run away, her curiosity being stronger than her fear. My assessment was spot-on, but she didn't say a word. Instead, she stared at me in amazement, her eyes wide and red with unshed tears.

"Aurora is dead," she stammered, as if to convince herself of it.

"I know. And I don't mean to scare you—"

"Then why are you here? Who are you?"

She still had her guard up, but I saw that I had begun to chip away at her mistrust. If I didn't want her to disappear, I would have to steer our conversation toward familiar terrain and hook her in with details:

"My name is Annabelle. Annabelle Lorand. I met the Barlet brothers a little over a year ago. Actually, they found me. I think you know why they were interested in me . . ."

She didn't say a word, but her eyes blinked in astonished assent.

"I almost married David. And now I am about to marry Louie. But before I do . . . I would like to ask you a few questions. It won't take long. I promise."

Her gaze wandered over the maze of pathways, as if she

were searching for a magic exit that would suddenly present itself for her escape, like the rabbit hole in *Alice in Wonderland*. At last, she decided to accept my invitation, with a contrite smile:

"Okay . . . but only a few minutes."

Avenue de Moka was poorly named—there were no cafés, bars, or brasseries in sight. Florence Delbard led us up three or four streets toward the train station. We ended up in an ordinary café called Relais that had a bottle-green awning and a sign advertising some obscure brand of beer.

Seated in front of our coffees, we spent several long minutes in silence. Florence Delbard looked like she was still on the defensive. I sensed that she would leave should even the slightest pretext present itself. One wrong word or painful evocation and she would clam up, and then it would be impossible to get anything out of her. Each word out of my lips would have to be carefully weighed, but the element of surprise would also play an important role. Topics would have to be broached in a roundabout way, not head-on. After a sip of hot coffee, I ventured:

"She didn't look much like you . . ."

"Excuse me?"

She looked as though she'd been torn from a dream.

"Aurora and you . . . you didn't look alike."

"We didn't," she agreed, visibly pained.

I quickly tried to soften this brutal approach.

"Did she look like your husband?"

"No . . . No, not really."

This confession piqued my curiosity, but it was clear that any forceful attempts to draw information out of her would backfire, and I knew I wouldn't get a second chance.

The sun, which had disappeared for a few moments behind a group of clouds, reemerged, bathing the café's windows and our adjacent table in light. In the bright rays, her eyes looked more brilliant than before. Her tears hadn't dried as I had thought. I could see that she was on the verge of bursting into tears, which would drown out any chance of my hearing her testimony.

"Sometimes, looks skip generations. For example, I—"

"That wasn't the case for Aurora," she interrupted. "We adopted her."

She reached into her bag for a handkerchief embroidered with purple flowers and discreetly dabbed at her eyes.

Adopted. That *was* the only logical explanation. Adopted, just like David had been by the Barlets.

I think Florence Delbard saw that I was refraining from blurting out what I was dying to ask. That I wanted her to say what weighed on her heart, at her own pace and in the order that she saw fit. I had simply prodded open her memory; the rest was up to her.

"Jean-François and I couldn't have children. At the time, the kinds of fertility treatments that are available today simply didn't exist."

I remembered having seen a televised documentary a month earlier about Amandine, the first French test-tube baby—born in the early eighties.

"We wanted a baby . . . ," she added. "There was no other choice but adoption."

"I see . . . Although the process must have been simpler back then than it is today, right?"

I was picturing a utopian image of clean and well-cared-for orphans, an abundance of perfectly combed blond heads and little faces waiting for their future daddies and mommies, in some verdant and halcyon French province. That was how I imagined adoption must have been before.

"Oh no, that's not true . . . not if you wanted to adopt an infant in France. We were approved very quickly, after only a few months . . . but it took three times that long to find a child that corresponded to what we were looking for. We wanted to adopt a baby who was less than three years old."

"How old was Aurora when you . . . *met* her?"

"She was seven. She had been abandoned several years earlier in the orphanage nearest Saint-Malo."

"No one had chosen her before?"

"No. And yet, if you had seen her at that age . . . she was so cute!"

It was easy for me to imagine young Aurora's face: all I had to do was remember my own childhood photos.

"Why not, do you think?"

"I don't know. Like I told you, most adoptive parents want very young children. After the age of three or four, a child's chance of adoption drops, and it is not uncommon for someone like that to be stuck in an orphanage for years."

"Is it possible that she spent time in foster homes?"

"Some children have that experience, yes . . . But she wasn't one of them; Saint-Broladre would have told us if she had."

Saint-Broladre was the name of a small town about twenty miles from Saint-Malo, between Cancale and Mont Saint-Michel. Back then, the region's main orphanage was located there.

"What were you told about the circumstances of her arrival?"

"Honestly . . . not a lot. In those days, there were rules to restrict the kind of information that could be provided to a child's new parents. We weren't given a complete picture of her identity or even the circumstances of her arrival in the orphanage. All we were told was that she had been there for five years. We accepted it, even though she was older than we had initially hoped."

Five years! Five interminable years. Five years in a dorm, with no privacy or love. Years during which child psychologists all agree that a person's character is formed. Decisive years for the people we will become.

"When you first saw her, what was your impression? Psychologically speaking, I mean. She wasn't disturbed? Aggressive?"

Armand and Louie's descriptions of her—her depression, her borderline personality disorder, her frequent crises—were taking on new meaning . . .

"Not really, no. Actually, she was a rather sweet girl. Always happy, always eager for anything. A little angel."

That profile didn't fit with someone who'd spent five years in an orphanage, nor with the image of the disturbed young woman that the Barlets had described to me.

Had Aurora been pretending with her new parents, out of a fear of rejection? Or had something, some event, stirred up her past traumas? Had her relationship with David and Louie, including the fraternal conflict that she had inadvertently reactivated, pushed her to extremes?

The morning was drawing to a close. I could smell it in the wafts of bay leaves and braised meat coming from the kitchen. I could see it in the glasses, whose liquid contents changed color. A group of workers from the neighboring construction site—the library across from the station—burst into the café, laughing.

"Hey, Z," a man with a Portuguese accent shouted, "which one's your woman?"

We were the only two women in the eatery, and Florence Delbard quickly turned peony.

"He told me he preferred blondes!"

Their laughter redoubled at the idea that their friend could prefer the older of the two of us.

One of the men, the eldest of the group, his face emaciated and his hair graying, perhaps the infamous Z, approached us and bowed his head:

"I'm sorry, Mesdames—"

"That's okay," I interrupted, forcing a smile.

"They're just trying to unwind. A man died on the site last week."

But I could see that this explanation didn't put my interlocutor at ease. If the man hadn't been blocking her, she would have bolted for the door.

"Someone died?" I asked, feigning interest.

"A very old man. Ninety years old or so. A truck was backing up and didn't see him . . ."

"Oh . . . ," I breathed, feeling a surge of compassion. "That's sad."

"Very sad. That's why they need to let off steam."

"I understand," I said, trying to give him leave.

He gestured at our table with a circular motion of his index finger.

"Your coffees are on me."

"No, you don't have to do that," I protested.

"I insist."

As he turned around, I caught a glimpse of his rawboned profile. It reminded me of another man. I saw Louie everywhere, sometimes only fleetingly, others with more persistence. That was one of his powers over me. There he was, in the features of some random face, like a mask being passed from one man to another. Thus I was able to console myself a little over his absence, by conjuring his image everywhere I went.

The mirage only lasted second. Yet in that time, a whole scene flashed through my mind. I imagined myself getting up from my chair and following the man in his paint- and cement-splattered construction garb to the grimy restrooms. Without hesitation, he walked directly to the stall. He then turned toward me and shot me Louie's familiar smile. He was waiting in there for me, a hand resting impatiently on his zipper. Once inside, I pressed myself to him and feverishly thrust my hand inside his ample pants. He was already erect, and I had no trouble extracting his hard member from its niche. It sprung forward, its foreskin retracting brusquely, his swollen tip unsheathed and moist. I was irremeably attracted to his raw scent, an acrid, almost spiced aroma. As I had done in the restroom at Café des Antiquaires, I got down on my knees and flung my lips around his violet ball of tumescent flesh.

But just as I was about to swallow his whole penis, my mouth half open, he pushed my forehead back firmly:

"Not like this . . ."

"I want you!" I begged, a wave of heat swelling between my thighs.

"We want you, too . . ."

Three of his friends penetrated the small, tiled restroom and pushed open the door of our cramped stall. They were holding their penises, but—being good laborers—they waited for a sign from their leader. The fake Louie spun me toward them, handling me like a toy. Then he gave me a decisive push in the back as his other hand slipped over my belly, tilting my pelvis and offering himself my backside. I didn't have time to protest. He gruffly planted his member inside me like a long cement column pouring into my vagina.

At the same time, the slightly bent sex of a tall black man forced its way into my mouth. The two men made no effort to coordinate with each other, and yet it felt to me like their respective thrusts were timed in an alternating rhythm, with one invading me while the other withdrew. This astonishing ballet of pistons was going to make me explode. But just as I thought I was about to orgasm, they both left me, and their two companions came to fill me where I was hungry. My new occupants were even bigger, harder, and muskier than the others before them. I didn't even want to know how many days of sweat and toil they had both accumulated over the years. I washed them with my fluids.

I thought I heard Louie's double urge them:

"Come on, you guys! Take her apart!"

His words of encouragement set off a barbaric explosion in my two orifices, which were already ablaze and dripping with a sweet nectar.

The intruders immediately responded to my unmistakable flow of desire, swelling to new proportions, on the verge of coming. They pulled out of me with the discipline of men following instructions and spurted thick gushes of translucent semen over my ass and lips and cheeks. Their nectar was soon joined by that of their masturbating friends, who were groaning like sated animals.

I hadn't come, but I was excited to have given them such pleasure.

THE CONSTRUCTION WORKER'S SILHOUETTE disappeared from the raw light outside, suddenly bringing me back to reality. How could I fantasize about such things while someone was confiding in me?

As the man rallied at the bar, his coworkers greeting him like a champion—"Oh, Z's tastes have apparently changed!"—Madame Delbard stood and looked as though she intended to leave me with the rambunctious troupe.

"Wait!" I reached out a hand to stop her.

She remained speechless, and I had just enough time to grab my phone and find a photograph to show her. The Christmas tree appeared and was almost as clear as in the original. David the child was perfectly recognizable. I turned the screen toward Madame Delbard, who contemplated it, her eyes lifeless.

"Do you recognize this little boy?"

Her veiny eyes scrutinized me as if trying to figure out what kind of trap I had set for her.

"It's David Barlet," she said reluctantly.

"And there . . . that child with the face scratched out?"

With each passing second, she lost a bit more of her composure.

"No, I . . ." She raised her eyebrows.

"Could it be your daughter?"

"No!" she cried, on the verge of pushing past me and leaving. "I don't see why they would be in a photo together before the orphanage!"

She lost it then, suddenly aware of the incredible confession she had just made. She had betrayed herself. She had needed to get it off her chest. Realizing this, I pressed:

"Do you mean to say that they knew each other before their romance ever began?"

Feeling that I was nearing a KO, I helped her sit down. She didn't resist, a round, childlike tear rolling down her cheek, which was fat and red like that of a porcelain doll.

"They met in Saint-Broladre. Yes . . . ," she whispered in a blanched voice. "They are both orphans."

That explained the improbable difference in age between the two Barlet brothers. That also explained David's neurotic obsession with Aurora—to the point where he had been determined to make a woman who simply looked like her happy, in a way that Aurora had never been.

"Do you mean to say that they grew up together?"

She nodded silently, her thoughts clearly elsewhere.

"Do you know how long they lived together?"

I knew that each year they'd spent together in that miserable place must have solidified their bond of affection. I understood that they'd been grafted to each other by pain, like Siamese twins.

But Florence waved an exhausted hand at me and slowly made her way out of the café. I didn't try to stop her this time. It was clear that I wouldn't get another word out of her. The photograph of the Christmas tree would remain a mystery.

15

MAY 31, 2010

The cardinal rule of journalism cannot be learned in school. Even my mustachioed professor had kept silent on it. The idea is simple and can be stated in one sentence: Reality is not your friend. In no case, in no way.

When you first start out, you dream of getting good scoops and making headlines. You naively think of facts as an orchard whose ripe fruit will spontaneously fall into your hands. All you have to do is include them in your article. But nothing could be more wrong. The truth resists you. It rebels against you, mocks you, does anything it can to escape you. In the field, reality is a gigantic trompe l'oeil, and screens of illusion stand as obstacles.

The obstacle of the day seemed insurmountable:

"Saint-Broladre?"

The employee at Ille-et-Vilaine's branch of the Department of Social Services was sputtering on the other end of the line.

"Isn't that the main orphanage in the area?"

"That was a long time ago, Mademoiselle . . . It's been closed for more than twenty years!"

Obstacle number one.

"Oh . . . But can't the archives still be consulted?"

"They're here, along with everything else related to family affairs and adoptions in the area."

"I see. Would it be possible to consult them?"

"It depends on what you're looking for. They're all here, in Rennes."

"I'm looking for a file on two children who lived in Saint-Broladre in the seventies."

"Are they your parents?"

The difference in age between the Barlet brothers and me often led to such misunderstandings. Would it be wrong of me to lie? I considered it but figured I'd eventually have to provide proof of my identity, so I stretched the truth.

"No . . . but one of the two is my brother-in-law."

"In that case, there's nothing I can do for you. Unless you get a court order, of course."

Obstacle number two.

I sighed, took a deep breath, and went back on the offensive.

"Just one question: Whatever happened to the orphanage?"

"The building?"

"Yes . . . does it still exist?"

"I think it was abandoned. There were plans to make it into a luxury hotel, but they fell flat, and the building is now in ruin. It's too bad, since it's such a beautiful architectural piece."

That night I did a little research online and learned that the Saint-Joseph orphanage—as the Franciscan nuns who had built it in the early twentieth-century had named it—was a beautiful example of northern Pas-de-Calais architecture. The nuns themselves originated from that region by the Strait of

Dover. Several old postcards depicted the majesty of the inner courtyard and the little steeple adorning the main building.

AFTER FLORENCE DELBARD'S HASTY DEPARTURE, I wandered for much of the afternoon through the neighborhood surrounding Rocabey Cemetery. I zigzagged through its deserted avenues, ruminating over the information that Aurora's adoptive mother had given me.

Walking was not only a form of distraction; it also helped me organize my thoughts more clearly. Still, I stopped at two different brasseries to quench my thirst and snack on sugar crepes, while using my phone to research some of what I had learned that day.

Louie had been silent since his message with the log-in information for his blog. I didn't know whether he was respecting the distance I had put between us or if that distance suited his own clandestine activities.

Before returning to the hotel, I sat on a giant mooring covered in a thick layer of flaky black paint. I let myself be hypnotized by the movement of the cranes over the Duguay-Trouin docks, the most accessible area of Saint-Malo's merchant port. Everything seemed so simple here in this game of giant cubes. Everything fit together so well. There were no surprises, no traps.

THE CLUB SANDWICH I HAD delivered to my room was not nearly as good as the ones Ysiam prepared for me at the Hôtel des Charmes, but it did provide me with the sustenance and calm I needed right then. I took a restorative shower and wrapped myself in a bathrobe that smelled of detergent. Biting into the toasted bread and its juicy ingredients, I turned on the small flat-screen facing the bed and watched the news with a distracted eye. A headline suddenly caught my attention, making me choke. I coughed loudly, my eyes glued to the newscaster:

"Twofold development in the Sauvage-Barlet Gallery affair, in which Louie Barlet, elder brother of media conglomerate CEO David Barlet, is under legal scrutiny. He was officially indicted this afternoon by the public prosecutor's office in Paris on counts of exposing minors to pornographic content and inciting minors to engage in such practices . . ."

That explained Louie's silence. Given the hour, he must have been preparing his counteroffensive with his lawyer and inspecting the evidence that the prosecution had against him with a fine-tooth comb, looking for any procedural point they could argue.

" . . . prison time is looking increasingly likely for Louie Barlet, especially since he has already come under fire in the past for aggravated exhibitionism."

The incident in the car that David had mentioned had been true. It was a line on his judicial record. The idea that my future husband had a criminal record was hardly romantic, and I am not one of those women who swoon over bad boys.

I took a long sip of sparkling water in an attempt to relax my throat.

"But according to the news site Mediattack, the most damning evidence against Louie Barlet does not come from his past but from his present activities, which are, to say the least, scandalous . . ."

I spilled my glass when I saw, along with millions of other French viewers, a screenshot of the Elle & Louie blog.

But Louie Barlet was not just a piece of news to me, as

he was for all the other TV viewers. The man who was being thrown to the wolves was *my* man. *My* love. He belonged to me and me alone. He was part of my skin, my breath, my DNA.

"This is from a website on which the man in question openly flaunts his dissolute relations with sex workers. He even posts live videos of his activities . . ."

The worst part of this newscast was when Mediattack's editor in chief, Alain Bernardini, appeared and began rambling on about everything his team had discovered.

The man was none other than that professor I had so admired when I was a student, a man whose integrity and freedom of thought I still respected. There he was, acting as my enemy. What a disappointment. I was floored by his opportunism and eagerness for the spotlight.

Thanks to the hotel's free Wi-Fi, I was able to check various social networks and measure the devastating effect of such a defamatory campaign. Even the most forgiving commentators—all of whom hid behind pseudonyms—lamented Louie Barlet's public display of his private life and his depraved behavior. His dissolute lifestyle was not the issue. What drew the most criticism was the fact that he promoted it to young people. Unsurprisingly, Antoine Gobert and his lieutenants at PRSPS were first in line to speak out against Louie and to congratulate themselves on what they saw as their first victory against a man who symbolized the decadence of modern society.

I HAD TROUBLE SLEEPING THAT night. Despite the air-conditioning, my dreams were tormented by fever. I was haunted, first by David, then Bernardini, then Gobert, then Salomé, all of whom winked at me mockingly. *You see*, my fever seemed to be saying, *it's not difficult to make them say what you want them to say.*

In the morning, I decided to leave the hotel and go back to Brown Rocks, the Barlet family house in Dinard, located on the other side of the bay.

It was a beautiful day. The taxi took the coastal road through Saint-Servan, and the half dozen miles separating the two coastal towns were a continual delight to the eyes. The driver, who dropped me off on the western edge of Malouine Point, at the end of a street flanked with sumptuous, early twentieth-century villas, seemed surprised that I wanted to stop at that abandoned house, but he pocketed my generous tip and refrained from saying anything.

My return to that house could seem morbid since I now knew that I was the doppelganger of the woman who had died just below. But I was hoping to discover other crucial clues, like the ones that had helped me find Florence Delbard. Luckily, I had thought to bring the giant rusty key with me.

As I had done the year before, I immediately went to work dusting the furniture and floors and airing out the vast rooms. A northerly wind rushed through the house. Typically, that wind was cool and rejuvenating—that is, when it wasn't announcing a storm.

I had had a hearty breakfast and decided to work through the day without stopping again. I explored every facet of the villa, even more carefully than I had done the year before with Sophia. I left no closet and no drawer unopened. I inspected every slat of parquet and every portion of hollow-sounding wall, looking for another hiding place like the one I'd found in Louie's office. I checked particularly suspicious zones several times, places like the bedrooms on the second floor. But

I found no treasure. There were a few old tchotchkes whose value had vanished long ago, along with the house's occupants. Apparently my sagacity and five senses were not enough.

Lacking any new clues, I decided to reexamine the family photos I had found the previous year inside an old dresser. Aside from some hangers and dull knives, the house offered no good tools for prying open its drawers. I went down to the shed on the far side of the garden, near a small staircase that led to the sea below.

The shed was more of an old wood-and-granite lean-to, with a rusted sheet-metal roof. It looked pretty shabby compared to the sumptuous manor above. A broken padlock hung from its door, a sign that someone had forced his or her way inside. I figured that any valuable objects had disappeared long before. I pulled at the latch on the door and entered a dark kingdom of decrepit junk. In the middle of this jumble of stuff emerged a central piece, around which all the piles of things seemed to have been stacked over the years: a small motor-boat in varnished wood. It reminded me of Riva's famous boats from the fifties. It was in poor condition, and I couldn't iden-tify the model with any certainty. Peeking under the mass of objects surrounding the boat, I noticed that its hull had a hole on its right side.

"Well, well . . . What happened to you?" I murmured, placing a hesitant hand on the flaky varnish.

Though the object was mute, the answer was obvious: it had run into something head-on, no doubt a rock peeking out of the waves. The size of the gaping hole on the starboard side hinted at the seriousness of the accident. Considering the damage, I was surprised that the seacraft was here, that it hadn't sunk. But perhaps the accident had taken place near the shore. Perhaps the Riva had gotten stuck on the rock that had ripped into it. Perhaps, then, the strength of high tide had managed to dislodge it from the rock and push it toward the beach.

But the most pressing question was this: Why had the Barlets kept this damaged boat?

The indescribable mess promised other interesting discoveries, and I continued my search, the tool to pry open the drawers now far from my mind.

Contorting my body and ducking as objects fell from the mountains of junk, I managed to slip behind the Riva and make my way to the back of the shed. The thing was squat and square. It sat directly against the beaten earth and was covered in rust: a small combination safe. I was no more an expert in safes than in speedboats, but I could tell that it was very old— bronze paint flaked off it like dead skin. Without really hoping for anything, I tried to turn the toothy dial. Nothing exciting came of this gesture but a slight pain in my right hand.

"Hmm . . . You're not being very cooperative."

Picking locks was not one of my talents, and I had no idea how I would manage to open the safe by myself. But I didn't want to give up. One doesn't hide a safe if its contents are meaningless. And even though I doubted that its thick metallic shell contained anything of financial value, I sensed I would find something important inside.

To make up for my weaknesses, I inspected the beast from all sides and noticed, on its right side near the ground, a more pronounced area of oxidation, where the wall of the safe seemed partially eaten away and thinner. I randomly grabbed an old watering can and used it to bang the deteriorated area. The alloy quickly gave way, creating a tiny hole. I wouldn't be able to do much more with my makeshift tin tool. Nor did I see anything else on hand that could help me, not even a hammer or sledgehammer.

I'd had the foresight to keep the taxi driver's card, and he arrived at the gate less than fifteen minutes after my call.

"Is there a home improvement store in the area?"

It was midday in the middle of the week, and the road and big-box store were both nearly empty. Round-trip, including the time it took to purchase a small blowtorch for about thirty euros, took less than an hour.

I returned to the shed and kneeled down in front of the safe as though I were prostrating before a religious idol. I read the instructions, put on my sunglasses for protection, and fired up the blowtorch, whose blue flame began attacking the corroded metal.

I was amazed by how effective it was. Each time I wielded it in the safe's direction, the fire licked at its wall with a short and dense tongue, eating away at it bit by bit. The border of the small hole glowed a beautiful and luminous red. Soon it was the size of a large coin. After twenty minutes, it resembled the lid of a jar. And in less than a half hour, it looked like I'd be able to reach three digits inside the safe—my index finger, my middle finger, and my thumb—and use them like tongs to extract its contents. I only hoped that whatever was inside would be small enough to make it through the hole.

Before proceeding, I had to wait for the hole to cool down. I was seized by the irrational fear that an animal driven mad from confinement would attack my probing hand. Clearly, that did not happen. Instead, I felt the smooth surface of a hard folder. Deeper still, my hand grazed across several others, though I couldn't be sure of their exact number. It took a while for me to get everything out of the safe. I made use of everything I thought might be useful in the house, including several pairs of chopsticks.

I used the flashlight app on my cell phone to verify that I hadn't left anything in the safe.

I brought the blackened papers to the room where Sophia and I had slept the year before, and I spread them out on the bed around me. I was exhausted from my efforts, and as I drifted off into a deep sleep, I noticed that the following names had been penciled onto each folder: *David, Aurora, Parents*.

My eyelids were heavy, but I instantly recognized the handwriting: it was Louie's.

16

Sleep paralysis is a phenomenon that occurs on the fringe of consciousness, during REM sleep. In addition to muscular atonia, it is known to produce visions in those afflicted that blend diurnal reality with the spectacular quality of dreams. In other words, it could be said that during such episodes, characters and situations leave the realm of the imagination and appear in the real room of the person sleeping. What I found disturbing was that the fake Louie I had seen in Z, the construction worker, could appear at any moment, even while I was sleeping. Louie had come to occupy such an important place in my libido that any stimulation—even the basic phenomenon of the heat being turned up around me—invited him to appear. He was like a hologram that appeared in the sexiest scenes one could imagine.

And since I was lying on a bed, half naked and surrounded by papers annotated in Louie's handwriting, he materialized in this room, where a few of David's old trophies were collecting dust.

He approached me, his index finger over his mouth, urging discretion. Only then did I notice that he was naked, his tattoos exposed, the tip of his sex gleaming with a pearl of desire that fell onto my thigh. He dipped his finger into the pool of semen and, without asking my opinion, smeared his fluid over my vulva, painting each fold of pink flesh, which reddened and became engorged with blood. I didn't wait for his order to spread my thighs and offer him total access to my nether regions. He spent several long minutes titillating me, dipping his finger from time to time into my natural spring, careful not to touch my clitoris.

A silhouette appeared behind him. The person was blurry, the head surrounded by a strange halo, and I couldn't make out who it was. I could have sworn, however, that it was a woman, a naked woman, whose large and heavy breasts, along with her triangle of pubic hair, betrayed her gender. Louie didn't seem surprised by the intruder. He seemed to have been waiting for her, and without looking in her direction, he held out a hand to her. The woman placed a rectangular object in his palm, which he immediately put between my thighs. It was a small mirror, and he oriented it so that I could admire my crotch.

Then he placed my right hand on my sex, urging me to caress myself. This game reminded me of a note he had sent me several months before in which he had given me a detailed description of the time I had first discovered my vagina. It was as though he had been trying to get me to think back to the origins of my sexuality. To the place where it had all started, to the time when I had become aware of the secret that lay between my legs and of its clandestine beauty.

"Go on," he whispered to his other partner.

The woman approached the bed from the right and stopped in front of my ear. Her pubis was next to my face, her abundant curls almost tickling my nose. From this distance, I could smell the scent of her sex, whose similarity to my own made my head spin. I slowly raised my eyes and looked at her face, which was identical to my own. It was Aurora, and she was alive, as though she had never drowned at sea.

I was neither shocked nor surprised when, following an instruction from our shared lover, she began to caress herself. I stopped my own self-touching for a moment, but I was so turned on by her that I immediately started rubbing my sex again. I was the perfect double of her pleasure; I was in perfect harmony with her sensations. Who else could possibly understand what she was feeling?

My eyes wandered from her vulva to my own, and this mirrored sight excited me even more.

Most intoxicating was Louie's attitude. He remained completely motionless, feasting his eyes on the spectacle. His eyes alone appeared to be his center of stimulation and pleasure. He gazed deeply, penetratingly, into our gaping vaginas, and the sensation was more satisfying than the most tumescent of penises.

Bit by bit, my doppelganger and I accelerated our pace. We were in perfect synchrony, and it was intoxicating. Her gestures mimicked mine with photographic precision. We came at the same second, in the same spasm, with the same complicit cry. A strong wave of pleasure crashed through my body, and the sensation was so raw that I closed my eyes for a moment to manage the shock.

When at last I opened them, I found myself, dressed and alone, lying in the middle of rumpled papers.

I had only gotten a few hours of restless sleep. My eyes were puffy, and I stood with difficulty. I was stiff, the muscles in my legs as sore as if I had just gone on a several-hour run.

The darkened window told me that I had napped through the afternoon and into the night.

I was hungry and considered going out to a restaurant. But I was also impatient to read what all those documents contained. I consulted my smartphone.

The connection wasn't very good, but I still managed to pull up the page for the Elle & Louie blog. Since my man had just proclaimed his love for me in my dreams, I could allow myself to challenge him on his territory.

I entered the log-in information he had given me, and I was soon directed to an admin page.

I could think of a thousand ways to describe the evening's fantasy—and the ecstasy I'd felt—for his blog's readers. But there was only one way that really made sense.

Louie and I had developed a kind of code, a secret language that only he and I could decrypt. In essence, it was based on the use of sensual gestures. Its syntax varied, depending on the message we wished to send each other. Much like sign language, our erotic Volapuk was a blend of gestures that either expressed a complete intention or a letter of the alphabet. "I love you" was therefore a light touch of the left nipple and a circular tickling with the index finger, and the stronger the sentiment, the longer the gestures lasted.

My dream could therefore be translated into the following message: "I love you" (nipple pinch), "I miss you" (mouth open in anticipation of a deep kiss), "I need you" (a whole finger gently inserted into the vagina), "I want to see you" (fluttering eyelids at the moment of orgasm), "I can't stand this situation anymore; I await your reply." Others reading this message would see it as nymphomaniacal. But if he was at his computer, he would understand. He couldn't be deaf to my call for attention. To be more explicit, I titled my post "Return to Room One." And I signed it with the diminutive he sometimes used in private with me: Belle.

Once I had finished the message, my stomach was rumbling more than ever, but it was too late to find something to eat in town. Midnight had covered the coast in its torpor. In the kitchen pantry, I was lucky enough to find an old box of spaghetti that had been expired for at least ten years, and I enjoyed a dinner of penne rigate—without salt, butter, or sauce.

Having finally filled my stomach, I turned my attention to the task at hand.

The first document to catch my eye was in the file marked *Parents*. It was an article that had been torn out of a newspaper. The scrap of paper didn't include the name of the periodical, but the date was present in the header: July 7, 1990. I read the boldface headline: *Fatal speedboating accident in Dinard*. An old, grainy, black-and-white photograph showed Andre and Hortensia Barlet on the Riva. They looked happy, and I figured it must have been taken the summer before the accident.

Residents of Dinard were sad to learn of the death of Andre and Hortensia Barlet last night. Andre Barlet, CEO of a media group, had a special place in his heart for our town. In the 1960s, he bought Brown Rocks, one of the jewels of Malouine Point. It became the Nantes-born couple's official residence, and they liked to say that the town boasted "the elegance of [their] birthplace together with the wildness of the Breton coast." They spent most holidays here.

The fatal accident took place yesterday, at around four p.m., while they were boating in the Saint-Malo bay on their Riva speedboat. According to our sources, their son Louie, an inexperienced boatman, was at the helm when it happened. The boat was moving too fast to avoid a rock. It was eviscerated, and two of its occupants were thrown overboard. Protected by the wheel and the boat's windshield, Louie Barlet survived the crash, though his knee was badly injured. The lifeless bodies of his parents were quickly pulled out of the water and rushed to Saint-Malo's medical center, where they were pronounced dead. The prosecutor's office in Rennes has opened a preliminary investigation into the two deaths, but everything seems to point to this being an accident that resulted from a navigational error.

All Dinard residents who wish to show their support for the Barlet family are invited to attend Andre and Hortensia's funeral on July 9 at eleven a.m. in the Saint-Enogat de la Rance church. This will be followed by a burial at the Rocabey Cemetery in Saint-Malo.

This was not the first time that I had been confronted with Louie's lies, either through another person or a material object. But now, with this article, I was so disgusted by his slithery untruths that I thought I might throw up my pasta dinner. I spent several long seconds in a prostrated position, my hands pressed into my stomach in an effort to quiet the cramps shooting through it. Contrary to what he had told me on several occasions, he had not hurt his knee while trying to save Aurora from drowning. It had been injured in a fatal accident that had killed both of his parents with one fell swoop; an accident for which, according to this newspaper clipping, he was directly responsible.

Why had he conflated Aurora's suicide with this tragedy? To hide his role in the death of his parents? Despite the late hour and the waves of exhaustion crashing into me—an unfair struggle between my eyelids and gravity—I only allowed myself a short break before plunging back into the mass of papers on my bed. I had a feeling that they would contain even more shocking evidence; otherwise, why would Louie have hidden them in the back of the shed?

When I had finally gathered enough strength, I got to work. Instinctively, my hand was drawn to a set of documents that Louie had marked *David*. They were his adoption papers from Social Services in Ille-et-Vilaine, dated November 28, 1976. They confirmed once and for all that David had been born on January 5, 1969. He was therefore not Louie's biological brother. Otherwise, the adoption papers did not reveal anything that Florence Delbard hadn't told me that morning: David had lived at the Saint-Broladre orphanage before the Barlet family had adopted him.

Reviewing the dates, I was once again struck by this stunning discovery: he and Aurora had known each other when they were small children, well before they had supposedly met and fallen in love as teenagers in Dinard.

I still lamented the lack of details with respect to David's biological origins and the reason he had been put up for adoption in the first place. The adoption papers made no mention of any such details.

Only when I broke a nail on the paper clip attached to the top left-hand corner of the stack of papers did I notice the photograph. I inspected it and cried out in surprise:

"What's this?"

It was a photograph of a crude carving on a blue wood

beam: a heart, inside of which the initials *A* and *D* were united with an ampersand. Aurora and David.

Another lie. Louie had told me that he and David had met Aurora when they were adults. "I was twenty, and David nineteen," he had said. And Rebecca had corroborated his story . . .

I could have tried to find new excuses for Louie, but I didn't see the point. The salient question now was this: When had Louie found out? When had Louie learned of the powerful bond between his adopted brother and Aurora? Had it made him jealous? Still, as Rebecca had recently told me, that prior relationship hadn't kept Louie from stealing his brother's wife for a time. Nor from taking me from David. Me, Aurora's perfect double.

The strata of yellowed and dusty papers were overwhelming. But based on this last fruitful find, I decided to focus my attention on photographs and paper clips. My perseverance paid off, and soon I uncovered a page that concerned the ultimate protagonist of this affair, the person who was the object of the Barlet brothers' desire, attentions, and secrets: Aurora.

I ignored the text for a moment and gazed at the picture attached to it. It was a portrait of a young woman, still a teenager, who was posing in a way that looked familiar. This was a picture of me! Or an almost identical image of how I'd looked in the picture Sophia had taken of me on her phone, and that Louie had seen . . . You know the rest.

This photograph demonstrated our almost supernatural resemblance better than any other that I'd seen. The same look, the same smile, the same attitude. I was looking at my clone. I imagined how Louie must have felt, seventeen years after Aurora's death, when he'd come face-to-face with my picture. He must have been amazed! Rebecca hadn't kept quiet about me out of jealousy; rather, she had wanted to soften the inevitable impact that my existence would have on the two brothers.

At last, I looked at the associated document. It was an official paper with the name of an insurance company in the header. Specifically, it detailed Aurora's health insurance policy. At first I was confused by the presence of such a banal piece of administrative paperwork, but when I saw the date on which it had been issued, I almost choked: January 1, 1992. I repeated it several times out loud to myself, trying to wrap my head around it. January 1, 1992. Two years after Aurora Delbard, David Barlet's wife, had died. And that wasn't the insurance bureau's only mistake. The letter was addressed to 118 Avenue Mandel, the Barlet couple's former apartment, where Louie had been living at the time. What was significant for Louie about this piece of paper? Aurora's health plan could revive the dead. What a story!

Before going to sleep, my head heavy and full of thoughts, I checked the blog. I wouldn't be able to sleep without knowing whether Louie had replied to my coded message.

My chest became constricted and my breath shortened when I saw a new post on the home page. It was by Louie and was soberly titled "The Room." It took up where I had left off. But I found his sapphic prose clumsy, which was unlike him. And it was a departure from his usual fantasies.

> *The girl standing leans over the other girl. She grabs one of her breasts and squeezes it as if to make it explode. The girl who is lying down winces in pleasure and pain.*

But this weakness in style wasn't the worst part. No, I was most disappointed by the fact that he hadn't used any of the syntactical elements of our private language. Not even a hastily groped breast to reassure me of his love.

"It can't be him . . . It can't be him."

I murmured the phrase over and over as I drifted to sleep. Louie was not the author of those lines. He never would have passed up an opportunity to dialogue with me in our secret language. He never would have so coldly ignored my requests. Never . . . ?

17

June 1, 2010

She left? Left where?"

Such is life: we spend it asking stupid questions of people who don't know the answers. That is perhaps what makes journalism such a noble pursuit: it's a lost cause. Did I say earlier that the truth evades our efforts to know it? That was an understatement. It slips, it runs, it flees our grasp. Everything escapes our perception.

The neighbor lady didn't recognize me at the gate. From where I was standing, I was able to make out her bottle-green slippers and a kind of shirtdress with giant purple flowers. She was walking so slowly that it took her a good thirty seconds to reach me, when at last her face lit up with recognition.

"Oh, Madame Delbard's niece! Did you find her?" she asked, with a little too much curiosity in her voice for my taste.

"Yes, I did . . . but I forgot to ask for her new cell phone number."

"Oh, yes . . . her cell phone."

She nodded as though I were talking about a new spatio-temporal transporter. Something that she had heard about on television but that would never enter her granite home while she was still living there.

"Have you seen her?"

"I think she got home in the late afternoon yesterday. After that, I don't know. I heard her door close after the evening news."

So around eight thirty or eight forty-five, depending on the station and the length of the commercial breaks.

"And you didn't notice anything this morning?"

"No, nothing. Usually I hear her espresso machine vibrating against her kitchen wall. But not this morning. She may have left."

She kept tabs on her neighbors not because she liked it but as a way of filling time. In the end, she didn't know much about the people who lived nearby. For her, they were just an indistinct mass of everyday sounds and hasty hellos exchanged from her porch.

Still, everything seemed to indicate that Florence Delbard had taken off, no doubt to avoid more embarrassing questions.

I thanked the old woman, took my leave, and called my taxi friend, whom I met a few minutes later on Chaussée du Sillon. His car was comfortable, his musical choices bearable, and his silence perfectly suited to my mood. The weather oscillated between rain showers and fleeting rays of sunshine, shaping and reshaping the landscape in such a way as to give one the impression of visiting different places. Fifteen minutes later, the taxi driver dropped me off in front of Brown Rocks.

"Shall I wait for you?"

"No, thank you. If need be, I'll walk. It'll be good for me."

SINCE I HADN'T BEEN ABLE to question Florence Delbard again, I dived back into the pile of documents I'd found in the safe, looking for anything I could find on Aurora and David's shared childhood. I wondered where the picture of the heart with the initials had been taken. In Saint-Broladre? The close-up shot was tightly framed, and it offered no clues to help me pinpoint its location.

Unfortunately, there were very few photographs in that jumble of papers.

However, I did find a second article on the Barlet parents' death. It was published a few days after the events had taken place, and it included more details on the local police force's investigation. It contradicted the initial report in one way: although he had remained on the boat when the accident had occurred, Louie had lost consciousness and his body had floated out of the boat with the tide. He had been wearing a life jacket, and his inanimate person had floated through the bay, carried by the currents. A fisherman had been on his way back to the port and had rescued Louie. He had taken him to the emergency room.

"And what if we continued this over breakfast?" I asked myself.

Hmm. Solitude was not good for me. So as not to go crazy, I gave myself twenty-four hours before I had to return to Paris.

The main beach in Dinard is only a ten-minute walk from the villa. I remembered the waiter who had been so attentive last year when Sophia and I had come out here.

By chance, he was working, though he was a little chubbier than I remembered.

"I recognize you . . . You've eaten here before, haven't you? You were with someone else, I think. A girlfriend. A brunette . . ."

With his free hand, he traced the graceful waves of Sophia's hair, that trap in which the hearts of so many men got entangled.

"Yes. She'll probably be back. She loved the area."

I ordered an orgy of pastries and a glass of freshly pressed orange juice. And since the terrace was half empty, I took advantage of the waiter's loquacious personality.

"Have you lived here for a long time?"

"Since forever," he replied, puffing out his chest. "I am a pure Dinardais, pure as lobster juice."

"Do you know about the speedboating accident that happened here about twenty years ago? . . . Two people died, and one man was wounded. A fisherman rescued him."

The waiter looked like he was in his forties. If he had been living in the area at the time, he would likely remember the accident.

"Of course! The fisherman who rescued the guy with the messed-up knee is an ex of my sister. Well, they weren't together very long. Yvon threw more bottles into the sea than he managed to pull crabs out of it, if you see what I mean . . ."

"Where is Yvon now?"

"Happily for everyone, he gave up fishing at the same time he stopped drinking. He works at a boat repair shop in Quelmer."

"Is that far?"

"No, it's in Troctin Bay, on the right, just after the dam on the way to Saint-Malo. It's a nice walk," he added. "Do you want me to call him and let him know you're on your way?"

"No . . . that's okay, thanks."

He headed back toward the kitchen with his empty serving tray, leaving me to devour my morning feast in a peace that was only interrupted by the distant sound of waves and a few seagulls' cries. Savoring my delectable and buttery croissants, I let my gaze wander over the Plage de l'Écluse, the main beach in Dinard. It was a month before everyone went on vacation, and the stretch of sand was still calm—a far cry from how it would be soon, with beach towels crowding one another and covering the entire expanse.

Left of the shore, at the foot of an immense hotel and just before the beginning of the coastal path, stood a row of changing booths that stretched over the developed part of the shore. The structure was made of speckled concrete and covered with little slate tiles. Its boxes were separated from one another with engaged columns, and each door was identical: white wood with a small window featuring star-shaped latticework. I figured that the only people who could afford such a privilege were the well-to-do families one often saw here, with their tribes of well-coiffed blond children. Once I had finished my last bite, it was that thought that made me inspect the area more closely.

Of course, all the doors were locked. But as I neared the end of the row, at booth number sixty-eight, I noticed a small scratch in the opaque paint, which usually kept curious eyes from spying on the bare bottoms of naked bathers. Still, the booths were not in direct sunlight, and I couldn't see inside very well. I caught a glimpse of the wooden walls inside, the paneling worn down by sand and salt, and a blue hue that I instantly recognized. It was the same blue that I had seen in the photo. Aurora and David's heart had been carved here, somewhere in one of these booths, behind one of these doors, perhaps even behind this one. I was suddenly panting for breath. The thought that it could have been right inside that booth made my heart squeeze, as though a part of me were in there, too. A repressed part of me that was bubbling toward the surface.

THE WAITER WAS RIGHT. QUELMER was nearby, and the way there pleasant. And the pedestrian path over the Rance River was a delightful curiosity for visitors. Then, the slope became rather steep. I turned right and followed a number of lush little roads that led me down to the hamlet. There, a dead-end road gave way to a slip, where myriad ships in various conditions were moored. Little trawlers ready to go out to sea sat beside skeletal wrecks covered in rust and algae. Debris was scattered all around, but despite this vision of disaster, the view of the sunny bay was pretty. A few paces from where I was standing, an ornithology enthusiast clad in khaki clothing and a cap was leaning over a telescope. The little islands in the Rance River were brimming with birds, some of them rare species. The area was a kind of natural haven for them. Great-crested grebes, dunlins, Eurasian curlews, brent geese, and so forth. The variety of plumage was worth a look for those interested in such things.

"Excuse me . . . Is there a boat repair shop here?"

"Yes," he said, without looking up from his lens. "But personally, I'd call it a cemetery."

Several feet away, I saw a decrepit and barely legible metal plaque that confirmed his statement: LOÏC KERVAZ—BOAT REPAIR. But there was no sign of Loïc or anyone else in the open-air repair shop. I looked around and at last found a wooden shed from which was emanating the thin sound of music. The door was wide open. As I drew near the shed, a man wearing a seaman's hat emerged. He looked annoyed to run into an intruder. Quickly eyeing me, he pulled on his red beard and asked, without so much as a hello:

"Who are you?"

"I . . . I'm looking for Yvon."

"What do you want from him?"

"I wanted to ask him some questions."

"You from Social Security?"

"No. I'm the fiancée of the man he saved twenty years ago."

"I don't have anything more to say on the matter," he said, shrugging his shoulders, his tone gruff. He turned back toward his hovel and said, "I've already told that story a dozen times."

Yvon may not have been a drinker anymore, but he still had the telltale features: swollen nose, bloated eyelids, and rosacea. Not to mention his unaccommodating personality, which I guessed was not just reserved for intruders like me.

At least that's how I found him.

"I'll buy you a drink, if you want . . ."

He stared at me as if I had just simultaneously offered him heaven and hell.

"Do you really think you can buy me with that?"

He was rude, and I was afraid that anything I said might convince him to send me packing.

"No . . . It was just a thought—"

"Come in," he interrupted, pointing inside his shack. "In any case, there's nowhere to drink around here."

His shed was an incredible dump. It was at once an office and a mechanic's workshop, with piles of paper strewn pell-mell and motor parts dripping with oil. It smelled of gasoline and stale tobacco.

He turned off the radio, and from under his desk, he withdrew an unlabeled bottle of brown liquid and two jars, the cleanliness of which was doubtful. Authoritatively, he poured a small amount of drink into each glass and handed one to me.

"Drink that for me. A local guy distills it. It's way better than that crap they sell in supermarkets."

I tried to hide my disgust and took a small sip of his infernal beverage. It burned my throat like detergent, but I was surprised by the smooth malted flavor that tickled my taste buds.

"Not bad, eh?" he gloated, winking.

I smiled politely.

"Not bad."

"So what do you want to know about this guy?"

"Louie Barlet, that's his name."

As I always did whenever I pronounced his name, I said it curtly and with the fiery look of a female protecting her male. He considered me, his face now serious. Then he took two long sips of his drink, almost emptying his glass completely.

"Barlet . . . I should have remembered that name."

"Why?"

"Because that was an eventful year for the family."

"Because of the accident?"

"Not just . . . Your friend wasn't the first one to splash around in the bay on a stormy day."

It was my turn to search his craggy face for clues. He looked ten years older than his real age.

"I'm not sure I understand . . ."

"At the time, I had a little boat I used for fishing for crabs and spider crabs."

"What does that have to do with the Barlet family?"

"Seamen tell each other everything. When something happens to one of us, the others will know about it before the day is done. And about six months before the speedboat accident, one of the guys saved another boy from that same family."

"David?"

"Maybe . . . He was the cousin or the brother of the other one . . . I don't remember."

"His brother, yeah. What happened to him?"

He raised his eyebrows to say he didn't know.

"We never knew . . . Seems he was trying to save his girl. My friend rescued him from the bay below Malouine Point. But I think the girl drowned."

I was speechless. According to what David, Louie, and Rebecca had all told me, Aurora's husband hadn't been in Dinard on the night of her death, Christmas 1989. Their stories had corroborated one another. They had all claimed that David, whom Andre had recently named as his successor, had gone to Paris to attend to an urgent affair. Why had they all lied to me? Why had Louie cast himself in the role of Aurora's failed savior? And for what obscure reason had David agreed to pass himself off as the husband who'd abandoned his depressive wife during one of her worst episodes—and at Christmastime? Why this strange inversion of roles? To hide Louie's involvement in his parents' death? I had trouble imagining David being okay with that, considering their fraternal rivalry and the fact that Louie wasn't even his biological brother . . .

However, their versions of events complemented each other so well that they had to be the fruit of their combined efforts. A kind of pact, I thought to myself. Their lies, together with the alcohol, were exploding in my head. When had they concocted this story, and for whom?

"Do you know if David Barlet was hurt?" I asked, emerging from my glass and my thoughts.

"I think so, but superficially. He gashed his hand, or maybe it was his thigh . . . I don't remember."

I took a deep breath and swallowed the rest of my moon-shine before asking:

"His forearm?"

"It's possible."

I thanked him with about as much warmth as his un-friendly attitude and troubling revelations inspired in me. Then I headed back toward Brown Rocks, feeling disoriented.

Among all their lies, there was one that I found more dis-tressing than the others. When I had discovered the existence of the silk armband on David's left forearm, everyone had told me that it hid the scar from his suicide attempt after Aurora's death. If David had never slashed his veins, then was I still to believe in his despair? I tried to ignore the horrible thought that this new information suggested: Had David been the one to push Aurora into the violent sea rather than the one who'd thrown himself in to save her?

"DR. POULAIN? IT'S ANNABELLE LORAND."

"Hello. How are you?"

"A little better, thanks."

We hadn't spoken since Mom's funeral. He'd gone back to his practice in Nanterre, and I to my new life in Paris. But I knew that he had a soft spot for my mother, even now that she was dead. When all was said and done, he had been the last one to try to save her when she was last hospitalized. And I still had his number in my cell phone's memory.

"I'm sorry to bother you, but I have a favor to ask."

"What is it?"

"Could you verify whether or not someone was admitted to the hospital for a suicide attempt?"

"That depends . . . When was this?"

"About twenty years ago."

"Oh, that's a while ago . . . Where?"

"I'm not sure. Either in Brittany, Saint-Malo, or Paris, in the 16th or 9th Arrondissements."

"Hmm . . . Not easy. Hospital admissions records weren't uniformly digitized twenty years ago. And the archives often just stayed in their original boxes. But I could try," he offered in an encouraging tone.

He was nice enough not to ask about the aims of my research. I must have once mentioned to him my passion for journalism, and that appeared to be enough to satisfy any curiosity he might have had.

I gave him David's full name and social security number. I tried to be patient, drawing out my walk back to the house as long as I could. I was absently window-shopping in Dinard when he called me back twenty minutes later.

"This doesn't mean that Monsieur Barlet never tried to commit suicide," he said cautiously, "but I couldn't find anything to confirm or deny it from any of the hospitals in those areas—public or private."

He had taken the initiative to expand his research and include the two years after Aurora's death. That eliminated the possibility that the suicide attempt had taken place in the long-term wake of the event. So unless David Barlet had hidden his grief, he had never tried to take his own life. His suicide attempt was as fake as his fortune was real.

18

June 2, 2010

While trying unsuccessfully to contact François Marchadeau on his professional line at *The Economist* and then on his cell phone, I reviewed everything I had learned over the past twenty-four hours. Strangely, I was less disturbed by my discoveries, which I had already in some way intuited, than by the idea of what might be motivating the protagonists in this family story. Particularly Louie.

The man I had come to know over the past year wouldn't make files filled with secrets on each of his family members. It all raised more questions on his relationships with them, notably with his adopted brother, David. Together, the pieces of this puzzle reminded me of the kinds of traps businesspeople and politicians set for their opponents. Since none of the information contained in those documents had yet been leaked, I considered another option. These files were being kept as a safeguard or fire wall.

Against whom was Louie trying to protect himself? Why had he stockpiled this arsenal of mass destruction? The obvious answer was his brother. But why? Inversely, could the fact of David's adoption somehow put Louie in peril?

"Marchadeau speaking."

"Hi, François. It's Elle Lorand."

"Elle! A pleasure to hear from you!" he said, with exaggerated enthusiasm. "Have you thought about my offer? Are you calling to give me the green light?"

"Sorry, no . . ."

His immediate silence told me that I had just rained on his parade, but he tried not to show it and asked:

"To what do I owe the honor, then?"

"I'm in Dinard. At Brown Rocks."

"Glad to hear you're on vacation," he said ironically, his tone friendly. "But how does that concern—"

"I'm not on vacation. I'm going through the Barlet family archives. I mean, what's stored here."

"Have you found anything interesting? Brown Rocks . . ." He sighed, suddenly nostalgic. "I haven't set foot in that place since David and Aurora's wedding."

Sometimes I forgot that the two friends had known each other for so long. Of course Marchadeau had met Aurora. He had also probably noticed that I was her double on that night when he'd first met me and I was still working as a Hotelle. The night I had met David.

"I've found some *very* interesting information," I hinted. "That's why I'm calling. I'd like to share some things with you . . . scoops, I should think."

"If it's more gossip about David's professional life, I think I've already told you that I'm not interested," he said dryly.

"It's not professional. It's personal. And contrary to what you might think, I'm not interested in thwarting his plans. I couldn't care less, really."

"What do you want, then?"

"To understand his relationship with Louie."

I thought I heard a *slurp* from a snifter before he said:

"I wish you luck. Others have tried and failed, you know."

"Like who?"

"Like Rebecca Sibony, for instance."

"Rebecca doesn't count. She's been in love with Louie for more than twenty years."

"That's true. You have that in common."

My reply was curt. I would swoop down on the first person who said anything remotely unflattering about my man:

"What do we have in common?"

"Her bias for Louie."

I didn't like the direction he was taking our conversation. He was being dismissive, as though he thought my relationship with the elder Barlet brother was coloring my perspective.

"You don't want to hear what I have to tell you?"

"I do . . ." He sighed. "Call me when you get back to Paris."

I COULD ONLY REMEMBER A few dark and blurry images—and an echo of strong, virile cries—from my first visit to the Brigantine, Saint-Malo's only gay, libertine sauna. But I was sure I hadn't left my phone number with them, since Louie was the one who had organized the evening. I remembered his commandment: *Thou shalt explore the unknown.*

Yet that afternoon I received what was supposed to be an enticing text message from them:

Come to the castle!
An evening of surprises for all—gay, straight,
couples, single men and women. Tonight at 9
o'clock.

Rendezvous at the Brigantine, the only place for
pleasure in Saint-Malo!
Entrance: 50 € men, 30 € couples, 15 € women.

For anyone who had ever been to the Brigantine, it was
hard to imagine that it could live up to such a promise. Hidden
in a sheet metal warehouse in the middle of an industrial zone,
the place didn't lend itself to the kinds of elegant and sophisticated fantasies preferred by most women. Regulars at the Brigantine were accustomed to hard, no-frills fucking. Sex without
preliminaries, stripped of decorum and affect. One entered its
facilities, satisfied oneself with the first body that presented
itself, and left. There, one was reduced to one's primitive state,
becoming nothing but a desiring body. Given that, the whole
premise of the evening described in the text message seemed
like a lie. Come to the castle? More like, come to the back
room!

I doubted that the invitation was random. Louie was
somehow involved, I knew it. Once again he was sending me a
message, however awkward and crude its form. But what did it
mean? How was I to understand this invitation to debauchery?
Had he followed me to Brittany? Was this a kind of rendezvous, as I had mistakenly believed the last time I'd gone to the
Brigantine?

With that thought, my stomach contracted, my chest
squeezed, my sex softened. My vagina was ductile. Desire
stretched and twisted it like laundry whenever I thought of
Louie's scent, his soft skin, his hard member. And what if he
was there this time? What if he used the occasion to make
love to me and dispel my doubts? And what if our night at the
Brigantine was as hard, as sweet, as mad, and as good as the

time I had let him into my home—and backside? Wasn't this the place to start over?

The part of me that was dying of desire saw this as a way to satisfy it. Another part of me didn't want our bodies to meet again so long as our minds weren't in harmony. From a more pragmatic and trivial point of view, I had only brought two sweaters, two pairs of old cotton panties, and a pair of jeans with me from Paris. Nothing very sexy or dressy.

I couldn't decide, and each argument for or against was fleeting. Louie knew the effect he had on me.

A shiver blossomed between my buttocks, an involuntary pucker seizing my anus. It ran through my crotch, tickling my perineum and lips. The temptation was too strong. A sudden burst of inspiration sent me searching through Brown Rocks's closets.

Bingo.

In the first bedroom, I found three dresses, which I sensed had once belonged to Aurora. One with flowers for bike rides in the warm wind, one with a daring neckline for cocktail parties. And a last one, which was tucked between the other two—it was black, with a bustier and a skirt of superposed flouncing panels, one embroidered, the other made of a light gauze. The dress was short, and it accentuated my curves in such a provocative way that I almost blushed at the sight of myself in the mirror.

I was so nervous about wearing Aurora's old clothes, in a way breathing life back into her, that I forgot to put on any underwear.

"Where to?" my taxi driver asked in a playful tone. He was clearly happy to see me again, especially in that outfit. "The home improvement store?"

"I'm going . . ."

I was suddenly embarrassed to give him the address for the gay sauna, convinced that he would be familiar with its reputation. If there was one thing that Louie's erotic lessons hadn't yet managed to erase in me, it was my public modesty toward sex.

"I'm going to the industrial zone."

"The commercial area near all the warehouses?" he asked, surprised. "But everything is closed at this hour!"

"I have a meeting. Someone is going to pick me up, and we'll leave from there."

"Okay, no problem," he said, although he sounded skeptical.

Who could I be meeting in such a place at this hour?

The taxi drove without stopping until we reached Saint-Malo. After the third roundabout, the area began to look vaguely familiar, and I asked the driver to drop me off.

"Are you sure you're okay? Do you want me to wait with you until your friends get here?"

"No, thank you . . . I'm fine."

"Okay . . . Have a good night."

Little did I know that the surprise evening planned by the Brigantine for its heterosexual clientele would actually correspond to the scenario I had just painted for my taxi driver.

After walking up the avenue flanked with hangars and warehouses—a long, deserted, poorly lit street—I was relieved to see a small group of people waiting outside the sauna's entrance. Outfits were skimpy, and makeup heavy. And the lascivious embraces of some of the couples clarified any doubts one might have had as to the purpose of their presence.

Just as I was joining the group, a minibus arrived, its

driver honking the horn and beckoning us to board. When he climbed out of the vehicle, I recognized his bald head and bodybuilder's physique from my last visit to the Brigantine.

"Ready for life in the castle?" he trumpeted in a playful tone.

"Can we wait a little longer?" asked a pretty, buxom red-head who was sheathed in a white latex dress. "Lucie and Marc said they were coming, but they're not here yet."

"Don't worry. We're not leaving for another ten minutes. In the meantime, you can find a place on the bus and put your blindfolds on. There's one on each seat."

Most of the others seemed to know one another. They were clearly accustomed to this kind of experience. As I would later discover, libertine communities are usually rather small and clannish. They tend to thrive in small towns. In their eyes I must have been something of an extraterrestrial being. But I also noticed from the way they looked at me as I entered the bus that they were pleased by my novelty.

I desperately looked for Louie's silhouette among the group. I was already dreaming of our encounter, imagining his body against mine, and I contented myself with the thought that perhaps I would find him at our destination.

After doing a head count of his flock, the man with the shaved head gave the signal to leave. Riding in a bus at night, my eyes blindfolded, feeling the bumpy road beneath me, I relaxed and found the experience rather enjoyable. The feeling of self-abandonment presaged experiences to come.

The trip lasted a good half hour, and I spent the time desperately trying to remember the name of the castle near Saint-Malo. My fellow passengers were speculating around me:

"I'm positive it's the Russian's castle . . . The one that's been for sale for several months."

"Akunin's Malouinière mansion? That would surprise me . . . It's on Vau-Garni, in Saint-Servan. If we were headed west, we would hear the sounds of the port."

"Maybe we're going to Combourg. We could fuck in Chateaubriand's old castle!"

Meanwhile, I was still wondering when Louie would show up, and I was beginning to think he might not. Was he really going to leave me alone with this horde of sex-crazed individuals who hungered for emotionless and faceless physical contact?

We were all disappointed when at last we arrived and could remove our blindfolds. The castle was not a castle. It was a large building that looked like a monastery, and it was surrounded by a high, dilapidated wall that was covered in weeds.

The second letdown was that no one was waiting for us there—neither Louie, nor anyone else.

"Does anyone know where we are?" a slender brunette whispered.

No one answered, not even the Brigantine's employee, who was visibly trying to maintain a neutral expression and preserve the mystery of the place. But as we stepped through the half-open gates into a vast courtyard, I couldn't contain my trepidation.

"Saint-Broladre . . . ," I yelped in a hushed voice.

"What? What did you say?" the woman next to me inquired.

"I know where we are . . . In the Saint-Broladre orphanage."

The body of the building, the pinnacle . . . Despite the decrepit state of the edifice, it was impossible not to recognize the building featured in the postcards I had seen online.

The beefcake shot me a look before addressing the others and asking them to follow him inside.

"As you will see, children, you have never had so much space, nor so many beds, for your games!"

The main dorm, which I also recognized from the photos I'd seen, had been rearranged for the occasion. Indeed, it could easily sleep fifty occupants, and there were only fifteen of us.

The ground and walls had been cleaned. Otherwise, they had been left in their original state. Only the beds had been redone, and large candelabras had been placed at regular intervals between them on cast-iron tripods. The ambiance was more reminiscent of a haunted house than the palace in *The Thousand and One Nights*, but the little group seemed satisfied. They clucked and whistled their approval, and they soon began caressing one another.

"Excuse me," I asked my well-built friend. "Are we expecting anyone else?"

"No, that's everyone. Are you disappointed? Do you want me to bring you back to Saint-Malo?"

His question sounded slightly condescending.

"No . . . No, thanks. I'm okay."

After all, with or without Louie, my genitals excited or not, I couldn't walk away from this opportunity to explore Aurora and David's past. I left the group, which had already divided itself into a hodgepodge of couplings—men with women, women with women, men with men—and started wandering through the rest of the building.

So this was where they had met. This was also the place where they had experienced their first, childish flutterings of emotion. Of course, girls and boys were put in separate dorms. The two orphans probably hadn't slept in the same area. I went from room to room, guided by the light of the moon. I identified the dining hall, with its columns and tables, adjacent the kitchen.

I saw that squatters had once made this their home. I also visited a library, empty save a few books lying on the floor and half eaten by rats. But there was nothing—no papers or pictures, not a tangible trace—related to David and Aurora's time in this place.

I arrived at an old courtyard that had been converted into a gym. It had high stained glass windows and a small blue door on the opposite end from where I was standing. The door led to the changing rooms.

There, on the pockmarked wall, between two metal lockers, I saw this: a heart in the flaking paint and plaster. A heart that, despite the shadows, I could have sworn had been engraved by the same hand that had carved the heart in the photograph I'd found in the safe.

I peered at the engraving, my nose almost touching the wall, a curious and trembling finger stroking the grooves. The same confident line. The same arched lobes.

But although the second letter was a *D*, as in David, the first was not what I had expected. It was an *E. E* as in Elle, I couldn't help but think.

"Are you not coming with us?"

The voice surprised me, and I almost screamed.

The redhead in white latex, whose sculptural beauty was more apparent in this bluish light, stood a few feet away from me. Her features were a little heavy, but her body was as firm and lofty as Alice's. She was smiling. I hadn't heard her following me.

"Too bad . . . You already have several fans waiting for you in the dormitory."

"Really?" I murmured, more surprised than annoyed.

"I'm one of them, you know."

She eliminated the space between us with a delicious sway

of her hips. Without warning, she placed her lips on mine and grabbed my breast. Her other hand reached for my backside, squeezing it firmly, dominantly. Her palms were warm and moist against my skin.

My hesitation barely registered in my movements, but it was enough for her to grimace and take a step back.

"Don't tell me you don't want to," she said, a challenging look in her eye.

"I . . . I don't know."

Nothing was more true. I was incapable of analyzing my feelings at that exact moment. Every second, I oscillated between fear and desire, the urge to flee and the desire to give in to this woman. She was magnificent, and the idea that she might be a present from Louie had crossed my mind, then my abdomen. Then it stretched down to my vulva, which began to shiver like a frightened animal.

She must have sensed it because she slipped her right hand under my skirt and placed it on my sex, which was half open and moist—my melting fig of desire. Her perfume was overwhelming and heady, with a musky note that I guessed was her natural fragrance.

When she plunged her middle finger into me, I grabbed her forearm. I thought I wanted to stop her, but my breath accelerated and my back arched in capitulation. She started turning her finger inside me, around and around, pushing deeper and deeper into my flesh. My eyelids closed in pleasure. She pressed herself against me, and I could feel her chest against mine, her sharp breath, her pelvis growing impatient. For her I was easy prey, a snack for a female predator. She was dying of desire for me. I could smell it in the scent that wafted toward me from between her thighs and filled the space around us.

"Tell me you don't like this, now . . . ," she whispered in my ear.

In all probability, she had noticed me when we'd first gotten on the bus. And the fact that I was wet and shivering with pleasure at her every touch must have been a triumph. Conquering me was no doubt a source of pleasure for her.

She didn't know it, but I was not giving myself to her in that changing room, surrounded by memories of lost loves carved into the wall. As her finger moved in and out of me, it seemed to grow. I recognized its curve, its length, its pointed and swollen tip, its frenulum stretched so taut it might break. Every palpitating vein thrusting into my excited walls was familiar to me. No, she had absolutely no idea, but the thing inside me was Louie's cock. His member was plumbing my depths. He was making me scream.

"Yes . . . YES!"

"You play innocent, but you're a little slut, aren't you?"

I didn't hear her trashy comments. Someone else was making me come. Somewhere else, in another time. And I had no use for her dirty verbiage.

"Huh, you gonna come?"

Despite her obvious skill, she seemed surprised by the violence of my contractions. That, and the abundance of fluid that soaked her hand, arm, and the dusty floor beneath us.

I had come, but not from her, from Louie. And although Louie was absent, I now knew that I could fill that void whenever I needed to, whenever a man or woman was there to serve as his double.

19

JUNE 3, 2010

The text or the image—which is more reliable? That is a question that every journalism student asks him- or herself at one point or another. Words are weighty, they're heavy, but only images have the power to really overwhelm the reader. Only they can grab hold of the public's conscience and dismember its critical sense. The struggle between the two media is unequal. And the setbacks I had faced in the audiovisual world had put me into the camp of the failures, along with all the words that no one ever reads.

And yet it was thanks to the text that I had learned that someone was trying to sully Louie's reputation with that abject blog. In my mind, Louie was cleared of all suspicion. But if he wasn't the author of the site, then who was? Who would do such a thing, and at such a terrible moment? Antoine Gobert? As openly hostile as that man was when it came to Louie, I didn't see how he could have gotten his hands on our Ten-Times-a-Day. Unless there was a network of people working for him at the Hôtel des Charmes, which I had trouble imagining. Ysiam seemed innocent, and so did the other bellboys and cleaning ladies. There was Monsieur Jacques, but I couldn't believe that the president of PRSPS would be comfortable developing any sort of relationship with the manager of a hotel for escorts.

On the way back to Paris on the TGV, I didn't doze off during the entire three-hour trip. Even though I was relieved that Louie wasn't the person behind the blog, I was still concerned by his other lies. It all gave me a bitter taste in my mouth. Louie may not have been the perverted monster that everyone was trying to make him out to be, but the mystery of the Barlet brothers was still intact.

Tormented by these thoughts, I barely considered the events of the night before. After my encounter with the beautiful redhead, I'd kept my distance from the others. I'd waited for them to finish their orgy and for the shaved-headed man to take us back to Saint-Malo. As luck had it, he lived on the west side of the Rance River and was nice enough to drop me off at the villa. Morning had already started to dawn, and I'd had just enough time to do a final inspection of the house before packing up my treasures and making my way to the station.

I HAD PROMISED FRANÇOIS MARCHADEAU that I'd call him as soon as I arrived in Paris, but first I felt a strong urge to check in at my new home. I had only been living in my studio for a few days, and already it felt familiar and reassuring. There, I could take solace and gather strength.

"Rue du Trésor, in the Marais," I heard myself casually announce to the Parisian taxi driver whose cab I'd hailed at the Montparnasse station.

When I arrived at my building, I was surprised to see that my mailbox was already overflowing with thick A4 envelopes. I grabbed hold of my bounty, curious to see what was inside.

Each envelope contained a stack of handwritten papers. The handwriting snaking from page to page resembled the annotations I'd seen on the papers in Dinard. It was Louie's script.

But if I had been hoping for a confession or a list of excuses, I realized after reading the first few lines that this document was of an entirely different order. As though echoing my literary project, this text was hybrid in nature.

It was titled *Your Body's Alphabet*, and it consisted of literary definitions of various parts of my anatomy. They were essentially erotic shorts describing what Louie wanted to do with my body. Some of the passages were clearly taken from our happy memories in room one, although they were written in a more elaborate style than in our Ten-Times-a-Day. But most of the short stories depicted imaginary, fantastical scenes, some of which verged on the supernatural: the letter *S* blushing on my right cheek whenever I was horny; printed letters shooting out of my vagina whenever I orgasmed, forming a poem.

Here and there, I noticed discreet uses of our erotic code. Louie had peppered the text with deliciously disguised declarations of love. And my little heart reveled in it. I reread some of the passages several times. I wanted to be sure that I wasn't mistaken, that the sometimes illegible scrawl of his pen had been expressing his love.

Buttocks *(plural noun): Her posterior was so perfectly round, so wonderfully voluminous, so ideally curved, that at times that mass of firm flesh bouncing beneath her loins seemed to have a life of its own. The woman with this magnificent backside could come and go from my grasp.*

But my hands never wanted to let go of her ass; they spent minutes, whole hours resting there. In the morning, I greeted its smooth elasticity as I would an old friend: Hello, you. She had two buttocks, and I two hands. In other words, we were made for each other.

Although his love was too varied and complex to be dissected, I was able to see its innumerable facets when Louie focused on one of my attributes. He was lyrical about my ass, playful about my thighs, nostalgic when he contemplated the nape of my neck, and salacious about my mouth. These shorts weren't really about my body but about his feelings for me, and I was so overwhelmed with emotion that a thin stream of tears began to run down my cheeks, which he described as "two apples of love that never melt when I lick them, and wouldn't even if I sucked on them for a sweet eternity."

He wasn't answering his cell phone, nor the landline at Mars House. My need to see him—to speak with him, to touch him—was so urgent that I rushed to the Saint-Paul metro station.

"LOUIE? LOUIE ARE YOU HERE?"

An icy silence filled the majestic building. Part of me knew that this was my house, but I still felt like an intruder. I knocked on the door to each room before entering, afraid of disturbing anyone. The bigger the space, the more time it takes to make it your own, and I had spent too little time in this intimidating palace to have left a noticeable trace.

One thing bothered me: the rooms were too orderly, too clean; they were too quiet. Louie hadn't set foot here for several days, I could tell.

Felicity suddenly appeared and wove through my legs. I almost stepped on her by accident.

"You were left here all by yourself, my poor darling . . ."

I followed her meows to the kitchen, where I refilled her cat bowls with water and food. She purred her thanks as I continued to pet her.

"You don't know where he went, do you?"

I would have liked to think that she knew the answer and was furious not to be able to communicate it to me. But she was wolfing down her kibble, indifferent. As soon as she had satisfied her hunger, she trotted off to the living room, looking for a ray of sun in which to nap.

Incapable of being as calm as my cat, I had already gone through the house twice when the tinkling sound of a key in my bag reminded me of the room in the basement.

I made my way downstairs with a certain measure of trepidation. When I entered the room in question, I noticed that the computer console was off. There was nothing to indicate that it had been used recently, and its memory contained no new recordings. Still, I was curious, so I turned on each of the ten cameras, one by one. Unsurprisingly, the rooms in Mars House showed themselves to be empty.

But the two screens dedicated to the neighboring house showed a lot of activity. I recognized David in the bedroom. His company was surprising. Two long-haired blondes were hard at work. One was planted on his crotch. The other was offering this first woman her groin. Both were feverishly moaning.

"Yeshche!" wailed the girl on top of David, her cries growing louder with each undulation.

Meanwhile, the other woman seemed to enjoy having her girlfriend's lips on her vagina.

Their Slavic accents—I guessed they were Russian—together with their skill left no doubt as to their profession: they were sex workers. But I doubted they were Hotelles. These women definitely fit the profile of call girls from Eastern Europe, who were known for doing sex tours all over Europe. Russians, Ukrainians, Poles made a stop in every town, honoring appointments scheduled by their dispatcher over the Internet.

As I watched them with David, I remembered the Delacroix affair, which had recently resurfaced in the media—and at a critical time in David's career. Were these girls from the infamous networks of illegal human trafficking from Eastern Europe? What was the name of the production company with which the Barlet Group had found itself in bed?

The name had been mentioned on the news, but I couldn't remember it. As a reflex, I hit the red record button. Regardless of who they were or where they were from, they would be recorded on the computer's memory. Forever coming and caressing.

As expensive as homegrown French escorts were, they were no financial match to these creatures, who must have cost David a fortune. He had chosen the very best: barely legal, their skin translucent, their bodies lithe, their hair long. Their pretty little faces even looked like they belonged in a casting session for models.

But aside from the exotic appeal, I had trouble understanding David's selection. There was me, and before me, there was Aurora. He clearly had a thing for voluptuous brunettes, not these fragile waifs.

As if to contradict me, the girl who was standing suddenly bent over and directed herself toward the point of contact between David and the other blonde. Plunging her head between their two stomachs, she stuck out a pointed and rosy tongue, alternately licking the man's shaft and the other woman's clitoris. She applied herself with such concentration that her girlfriend soon came. David seemed to enjoy this turn of events, and he came on the white stomach of one woman and the purple lips of the other.

I had recorded the scene on the computer. Still, I grabbed my smartphone and took a picture of the three lovers, David's member still swollen and ejaculating large spurts of sperm on them.

The action had taken place in the bedroom, and I was curious to see what was happening in the living room. At first the room looked empty. But then I noticed a man sitting at a table, his torso hunched. His face was lit up from the glow of a silver rectangle. He was looking into the screen of a laptop. He was at the other end of the living room from the video camera, his profile visible to me. In these conditions, I had trouble recognizing who it was.

I gazed at the buttons on the computer console for a moment and soon focused my attention on a pictogram of a magnifying glass etched onto a dial. I turned it in one direction, then in another, before managing to zoom onto the person on-screen. At last I recognized who it was: Yves, the IT manager at BTV.

I had only run into him a couple of times when I was working at the station, but I hadn't forgotten his role in Alice Simoncini's termination a year before. He was the one who had walked in on David's present fiancée with Christopher Haynes, the artistic director, who had also been fired after the incident.

I took out my phone again and framed the monochrome

monitor in its viewer before taking a picture that I would submit to Fred as soon as possible. He would be able to confirm the man's identity. As for the reason he was sitting in his CEO's living room, I could not for the life of me think of a logical explanation. But I hoped my ex would be able to provide some answers.

BEFORE GOING BACK UP TO the surface, I gave into temptation and watched a few more scenes. Scanning the other recordings, I opened the videos I hadn't watched on my last visit. Aside from the troubling sense of excitement that I got from seeing these recordings, I also hoped I would eventually see the face of the male protagonist—and that it wouldn't belong to Louie. I was looking for any physical sign that might exonerate him.

Sadly, the anonymous body on the screen could have easily belonged to another man or to him. It was impossible to tell.

His partner in this scene didn't look anything like the ones I'd seen in the other videos. Her hindquarters were hefty, and there were stretch marks striped across some areas of her skin. I could tell that this was a middle-aged woman. She was more mature than the other creatures, but she still had a coarse charm. She had magnificent breasts and surprising dimples in her lower back—her signature charm, I thought.

Lying on her stomach, she was offering her backside and thighs, which were spread wide, to her lover's incessant thrusts. The camera panned over their united sexes, where a white froth suggested this had already been a lengthy session. The lens now focused on the woman's smiling profile, her sense of satisfaction apparent. She seemed to be savoring Louie, and each time he plunged inside her, she let out a prolonged moan.

Between two shots, the electronic eye paused for a moment on the two notches dug into the woman's lower back, two little dimples that reminded me of sound-holes on a wind instrument and made me think of Man Ray's famous photograph *Le Violon d'Ingres.*

Again, I took a picture of the scene with my phone.

I CLIMBED BACK UPSTAIRS TO the foyer. I wanted to leave the house as soon as possible. But first I made sure to leave enough food out for Felicity. I would have liked to ask Armand to take care of my whiskered girl, but this seemed like a particularly bad time to ring next door.

"Everyone is abandoning you, hon . . ." I sighed, stroking her silky fur.

Was I talking to her or to myself?

My cell phone vibrated, putting an end to my passing melancholy. I had a voice mail from a blocked number. It had been recorded when I'd been in the basement, where the reception was bad. A man's nasal voice, the diction clipped, rushed through what it had to say:

"Hello, Annabelle, it's Jean-Marc Zerki. As you know, I'm Louie Barlet's lawyer. I'll be brief. My client has been the target of media and paparazzi harassment since his release. On my advice, he has decided to lie low for a while. He wanted me to tell you that he is not ignoring you. But I insisted that he keep his location secret. For the time being, you will not be able to speak with him or see him. I know this must be difficult for you, but it is important for his defense and for his safety. I hope you can understand. He has received a number of threats from far-right groups. Nothing to be alarmed about, but it's best to be cautious. Oh, right, another thing: he has nothing to do with the blog that was mentioned on television. We do not yet know who is behind it, but I encourage you not to pay any attention to what is being published on that site or to any e-mails you may receive from its host. It is likely that his main e-mail accounts have been hacked. Do not reply to any messages that come from his address. Okay, I think that's all. I will contact you again soon. Have a good night."

20

June 4, 2010

François Marchadeau was wearing a dark suit. Gone were his Panama hat and relaxed air from the last time we'd met. Things hadn't been going so well for his old friend David Barlet recently. François had opted against the laid-back atmosphere of Café Marly in favor of a cozy but stiff brasserie in Place du Châtelet.

"I have a deal for you," I said straightaway, forgoing the usual preliminaries.

Slumped in his seat, his arms resting on the backs of two neighboring chairs, he wrinkled his forehead in a sarcastic way.

"A deal? Now that you're looking into the Barlet brothers, have you decided to talk like you're in a made-for-TV spy movie?" he said ironically.

"I'll write that chronicle you want on David . . . and you'll help me contact the sources I haven't been able to reach in my inquiries on the Barlet family."

He sipped his hot beverage, the label from the tea company Mariage Frères dangling from his white cup. His gaze was calm as he searched my eyes for my intentions.

"And why would I go to all that trouble when I can tell that you're already prepared to give me what I want?"

"First of all, nothing says I'm interested in doing those chronicles—"

"Come on," he interrupted. "You wouldn't have called me back if you weren't interested."

" . . . and I have information that you don't have on our mutual *friend*."

A very famous actor who worked at the theater next door entered the café just then, stepping through the red velvet curtain that hung from the double doors as though he were making his entrance on stage. A few pairs of eyes settled on him, and a wave of curiosity followed him as he made his way through the main room, his heart clearly set on a table near ours. He looked younger and more attractive in person than on television.

"Okay, I'm listening. What shocking secret did you learn that I know nothing about?"

"Nice try," I scoffed. "First, you have to promise that you'll help me."

"I promise."

I inhaled like a swimmer just before she dives into the water. Meanwhile, thunder boomed outside like a drum's beat in a theater play's last act. Then, I took the plunge:

"David is not Andre and Hortensia Barlet's son. He was adopted from an orphanage called Saint-Broladre near Saint-Malo when he was seven or eight years old. So he was old enough to remember."

"Of course he remembers," he replied in a haughty tone. "It's one of the secrets he confided in me."

I wasn't about to let him gain the upper hand. As it began

pouring rain outside and the pedestrians scrambled to find shelter, I quickly added:

"In that case, he must have told you that he and Aurora met at the orphanage."

"That's ridiculous," he boomed. "They met in Dinard, on the beach. They were sixteen or seventeen years old. Louie can back me up here. He was too jealous of his brother to forget that . . ."

I chose to ignore his assertion and instead rummaged through my bag, from which I withdrew some of the things I had found on my trip to Brown Rocks, notably the picture of the heart carved into the beachside changing room. I handed it to him, gauging his reaction.

"Is this the kind of thing people do when they're seventeen?" I asked, provoking him.

He maintained his reserve, grabbed the photograph, and looked at it for a long moment before at last reacting:

"I don't see what this proves. Your entire theory is based on graffiti? That's pretty slim evidence."

"I met Aurora's adoptive mother in Saint-Malo. Florence Delbard."

Glossing over the details, I described our meeting, Madame Delbard's confession regarding Saint-Broladre, and her hasty departure—a clear effort to avoid further questions on David's relationship with her daughter.

"From what you're telling me, this woman sounds crazy. It seems like she would have told you anything to make her daughter sound important . . ."

So, for him, a weeping mother was crazy?

"And I don't see the big deal about David and Aurora having met before they were sixteen. That's not exactly a scoop!"

His refusal to accept the truth was starting to annoy me. I grabbed my phone and pressed its tactile screen a few times, opening the file that contained the picture of David and the faceless girl in front of a Christmas tree.

"Who is that?" he asked, sitting up in his chair, his expression suddenly serious.

"Good question. David is easy to recognize. But the others . . . All I know is that they're not Delbards or Barlets. And considering David's age in the picture, I'd say it was probably taken *before* he was put in the orphanage."

He paled, and I understood that I had just scored a decisive point. He was clearly troubled. It was almost palpable. But I would need to show him more than that to get him on my side.

Two tables from ours, the famous actor sprung from his chair when a young and fashionable singer who was about thirty years his junior entered the brasserie, her hair drenched. Seeing her, he put on the smile that had become his trademark—along with his emphatic tirades and televised scandals. He greeted her by putting a protective arm over her shoulders, a gesture that several cell phones immortalized with their cameras. Their relationship must have already been made official, and they were putting on a show.

"Do you seriously think that this girl might be . . . ?"

Marchadeau's question hung in the air. He was indifferent to the vaudeville show being enacted a few feet away.

"Aurora? It's impossible to say for sure. But yes, I think she's a likely candidate."

"And them . . . ," he murmured, pointing to the couple standing behind the two children. "Who are they?"

"No idea. A foster family, employees of the orphanage . . . They could by anyone."

He shared with me his few memories of Jean-François and Florence Delbard, Aurora's parents, whom he had only met once, twenty years earlier, on David's wedding day. His description of Madame Delbard matched the impression I had gotten from her during my brief interview.

"We still have a lot to learn."

"Maybe," he admitted reluctantly. His loyalty to his friend was admirable. "But regardless of what happens, you need to know that nothing can change my friendship with David."

"I'm not asking you to betray your friend. As I told you: I want you to help me understand the nature of his relationship with his brother."

"If that's all, then everything should be fine." He smiled, forcing himself to relax.

As he said this, I remembered the image of David with his two playmates, the Russian call girls. Did Marchadeau know about that part of David's life? Did he partake in some of the recreational sessions? Or was the image he had of his friend too pure and untouchable for him to see any of David's darker sides?

I considered telling him everything, but I contained myself. If I wanted to keep him on my side for a while, I couldn't tarnish the image he had of his friend right away. He would resent me for it, which would be against my interests.

But he was idly playing with my phone, swiping from one picture to the next. First I saw the photo of David ejaculating on the two Russian girls, then the one of the faceless man lying on top of the curvy redhead. He stared at them without saying a word, his jaw tight. Then he nervously pressed the home button and threw the phone on the table, as though it had suddenly started to burn his hand.

I was expecting him to become indignant, to claim that this was a plot and that the images had been doctored, but he didn't. Instead, he pushed his teacup away from himself and signaled the waiter.

"A Jack, please. Neat."

Then, ignoring the steamy pictures, he continued our conversation:

"You said something about needing to get in touch with certain 'sources' on the Barlets. What kind of information are you looking for, exactly?"

"I need access to the archives at the Department of Social Services in Ille-et-Vilaine."

"Let me guess: you're looking for the files on David and Aurora."

"That's right. Only direct family members can access them. Otherwise, I'd need a court order."

He furrowed his brow, tucked his head between his shoulders, and then said:

"Hmm . . . I know someone with an office at the Department of Social Services. I can take care of it."

"Great."

"Anything else?"

He had already refused my plea for help with respect to Louie's case, but I figured the time was now or never to ask him again.

"Yes . . . Antoine Gobert."

"What does he have to do with David?"

"In theory, nothing. But I think his relentlessness in the case against Louie is fishy, and I'd like to know the source of his rancor. I can't imagine he graduated from high school and instantly became the president of PRSPS. He must have worked somewhere before that, right?"

"Okay," my interlocutor grumbled. "I'll see what I can find. But there's no way I'm going to print anything I dig up on him in *The Economist*, do you understand?"

"I understand."

We spent the next five minutes discussing my future column. When we'd exhausted the topic, we took each other's ·leave—just as the sixty-something actor was reaching his hand up his young girlfriend's skirt. The girl squealed softly, seemingly afraid of drawing more curious eyes.

"You see . . . ," Marchadeau said, discreetly casting a sidelong glance at the nearby couple. "You shouldn't judge people who live in the public eye too harshly. When your life is under a microscope, the slightest faux pas can come back to bite you. Life is long when you're subjected to that kind of attention at a young age."

AS IT HAD AFTER MY first trip to Dinard, a visit to Rebecca again seemed necessary. After a thirty-five-minute metro ride, I buzzed the intercom at 118 Avenue Mandel. My former boss looked no more surprised to see me now than she had the first time I'd shown up at her home unannounced. She opened the door and ushered me into her one-bedroom, tenth-floor apartment. She was wearing a kind of pink sweat suit with gold topstitching.

"Come in . . . Would you like some tea?"

"No, thank you."

I stepped into her small, neatly ordered living room. It was as I'd remembered it. I noticed, however, that the boxes that had been piled up on one side of the room—Belle de Nuit's archives—had disappeared. Rebecca had perhaps destroyed them or, more likely, she had stored them in her cellar.

"So, was Salomé cooperative?"

The events of the past few days had almost made me forget that episode and the jealousy I had felt then.

"Let's just say that I got the confirmation I was looking for . . . and I made it out alive," I said, half-jokingly.

My host disappeared into the kitchen for a few moments and quickly came back with mug in her hand, a cloud of steam wafting over her face, as in an old photograph. In her way, she belonged to the Barlets' story. That was why her testimony was so important to me, even if she tended to dole it out as slowly as Chinese torture.

As I had done with the journalist, I told her about what I'd found in Brittany. I wanted to loosen up her tongue, to force her to be sincere. I showed her David's adoption papers and the picture of the heart. Then there was Florence Delbard's edifying story, and so forth.

She listened, attentively at first, warming her hands against her mug despite the stifling temperature of her apartment. Then she adopted the same nostalgic expression she had worn the last time.

"David and Aurora didn't want people outside of the family to know about the time they'd spent at Saint-Broladre."

"Why not?"

"Privacy reasons, I'd imagine. Or to avoid bad memories . . . I suppose that if I'd met my future husband in prison, I wouldn't want the whole world to know about it."

She was right; that made sense.

"But when they got engaged, their families knew they had met as children, didn't they?"

"Not then, no."

"If there's an unofficial version, then I suppose there must have been an official version of how they met."

"The truth is that they never really stopped seeing each other. The summer after they were adopted, they saw each other on the beach in Dinard. Their first meeting was random. David was on vacation with his new mom, his new brother, and Armand. And Aurora lived in Saint-Malo. The Delbard family often went to the beaches—usually Bon Secours or Le Sillon. Except that day . . . It must have been in July or August, in '78."

"Do you know why they decided to go to the beach in Dinard that day?"

"No . . . Probably for a change of scenery. Or maybe they had family in the area. In any case, from that day on, Aurora begged the Delbards to go to the Plage de l'Écluse."

"They didn't want to know why?"

"When a recently adopted child insists on something so harmless, there's no reason to refuse. So, yes, they agreed to drive a few extra miles to make her happy."

"Every day?"

"Almost every day," she confirmed. "I think Florence Delbard had recently stopped working at the time. She had nothing to do but take care of her daughter."

"At no point did it occur to her that the little boy Aurora was playing with had gone to the same orphanage as she had?"

"You know, when your little girl of eight years likes a boy who has a butler and lives in the most beautiful villa on the coast, you don't fret over it. After all, they were just children. They played well together. They didn't get into trouble. Neither Florence nor Hortensia suspected anything."

I imagined them running from one side of the Plage de l'Écluse to the other, building sand castles, playing marbles with dried balls of kelp, and retreating to changing room number sixty-eight, where they had left their indelible mark.

"Who told you all this?"

"Louie. He was jealous that his new brother preferred spending time with that girl to playing with him. That was also when Louie fell in love with Aurora. He would follow them and watch them from some hiding place. He was the first person to understand that David's relationship with that girl was stronger and older than everyone had thought."

Why was I not surprised?

"He didn't say anything to his parents?"

"He did. He told Hortensia, but she asked him not to say anything to anyone else. And Louie obeyed his mom."

I found that touching. I was also moved by the thought that my man had lived for so many years in the apartment just below our feet.

"And then what happened?"

"They continued to see each other for years, every summer and also during other school vacations—Christmas break, spring break . . . They were inseparable. Things started to get more serious when they were fifteen or sixteen. Everything happened so naturally. They already knew each other's family. Everyone thought it was so charming that such old beachside friends should fall in love and then get engaged."

"Everyone except Louie, I'm guessing."

"Except Louie, of course."

She reached into a small wooden box on the coffee table and withdrew an electronic cigarette. She sucked on it, puffing out several clouds of odorless vapor and visibly relaxing. The object suited her. It lent her a kind of nobility and mystery reminiscent of some of the famous courtesans featured at the Hôtel des Charmes.

"How did Louie react to their wedding plans?"

"Very badly. Especially since," she explained, "his secret relationship with his future sister-in-law had already begun. They were bound by passion, and he thought that nothing could come between them."

"And yet Aurora chose David." I finished her thought. "She chose her past relationship over her present feelings."

"No," Rebecca said, shaking her head. "She wasn't choosing her past when she decided to get engaged to David . . . I would say it was the opposite."

"I'm not following you . . ."

"She chose power, Elle."

Power?

"When Aurora and David got married, Andre had already named David his successor," she continued.

"What did that have to do with Aurora?"

"For David, his father's choice was like revenge. And it was for her, too. By standing at his side, she thought she would share in his glory and erase her own wounds. They were both out for revenge on life."

Saint-Broladre. The orphanage. The hazings and their uncertain future.

When Louie had lost to David, when he had lost his position at the head of the Barlet Group, he had also lost Aurora. And by choosing David, she had won a prize that would give her everything she needed to repair a broken childhood. At least in all appearances.

Without saying a word, Rebecca stood and went into her

bedroom. When she reappeared, she was holding small envelope, which she handed to me, with visible emotion.

"What is it?"

"Their wedding invitation."

I carefully opened the envelope and withdrew the card, which had yellowed with time. I could feel it vibrating between my fingers, as if the words printed on it were about to shoot out at me. It took me several seconds to get accustomed to the calligraphy, which was so elaborate that it was almost illegible:

Florence and Jean-François Delbard
Hortensia and Andre Barlet
are pleased to announce the wedding of their children,
Aurora and David
which will take place on **Saturday, the eighteenth of June**
1988, at three o'clock
at Saint-Vincent Cathedral in Saint-Malo.
The young couple invites you to a reception following the
service, to begin at six thirty, at the Maisons de Bricourt
restaurant,
1 Rue du Guesclin in Cancale.

June 18. On my second birthday.

I didn't see a way I could use my smartphone to take a picture of this precious relic. Instead, I tried to memorize the important information—date, time, place—before handing the invitation back to Rebecca.

"Had the Barlets and the Delbards spent much time together, before the wedding?"

"Not really, no. Andre saw the Delbards as provincials,

and Aurora's father considered David's parents to be Parisian snobs . . . although he privately congratulated himself on his daughter's good marriage."

The wedding had been quite something: a ceremony in the cathedral, the reception in a Michelin-starred restaurant—the most renowned eatery on the Côte d'Émeraude—and no doubt hundreds of guests.

"And after, did they keep in touch?"

"After Aurora's death? To my knowledge they only ever saw one another again at her funeral. Not really a time when people talk about their children's young lives, if that's what you're thinking."

True. Although Rebecca's life had been lived in the slow lane—at least compared to that of the Barlet family—she was observant. She was shrewd, and that was why she was Louie's best friend—even if she had always hoped for more.

"You were saying that Louie took their wedding plans badly . . ."

"That's an understatement. He came back to me then. I should have kept up my guard."

She spoke without bitterness, pinching her thin lips.

"Back then, his life was made up of alcohol, women, and travel . . . ," she went on.

"And an accident."

She looked at me coldly, directly. She'd understood my reference, but she rejected the insinuation.

"It *was* an accident," she said, enunciating each word for emphasis.

"The articles from back then say that Louie didn't really know how to drive a boat," I said, exaggerating a little. "If that's true, then why did Andre let him take the Riva's helm?"

"Why not?" she said, shrugging, and without much conviction.

I gave her a moment to inhale her mix of essential oils, before continuing:

"If he has such a clear conscience, why did Louie hide the accident from me? Why did he lie about the origin of his knee injury?"

"Because he does feel guilty about it. Be honest: Would you tell the man that you loved that you'd killed your parents? Even if it was an accident?"

That made sense, but it still didn't explain why he had claimed to have tried to save Aurora when really it had been David.

When I told her about what Yvon, the boat repairman, had said about the accident, she simply shrugged.

"Fishermen are all alcoholics. The one who saw David that day must have been drunker than usual."

She was on the defensive, and I saw that I wouldn't be able to get any more information out of her.

I decided to show her my hand and withdrew Aurora's insurance papers from my bag. She wouldn't be able to escape my questions.

"Have you seen these before?"

Her eyes flitted back and forth from the papers to me. She was scared, even panicky. She closed her eyes for a moment and got a hold of herself.

"No . . . I've never seen those in my life."

"But this is the Barlets' address, here, in this building."

"It is . . . but I'm not their doorman or butler," she said, her tone strained. "I've never paid attention to their mail, not when David lived downstairs, not when Louie did."

But her shrill reaction said otherwise. She must have spent years inspecting the contents of their mailboxes, like a starved woman looking for the smallest signs of encouragement.

"These papers were sent more than two years after Aurora's death," I said, "and they were addressed here, where she once officially resided, with David."

Rebecca bit her lip, as if looking for a logical explanation.

"They never found her body," she said at last. "It took many years before she was officially declared dead. That probably explains the mistake. So long as there was still hope, David and the Delbards had no reason to terminate her insurance policies."

Again, she'd come up with a rational explanation, one that made moot any other questions I might have for her.

"Rebecca . . . why are you only telling me all this now?"

Why not a year before? Why not when I had chosen the elder brother over his younger brother?

"Louie didn't want you to think that he loved you because of your resemblance to *her*, as had been the case with his brother . . ."

Over the past few months, Louie had insisted that he had first been attracted to me because I looked like Aurora. But soon, his feelings had grown, and he had fallen in love with me, Annabelle, and me alone.

As I was leaving, I felt a little less in the dark about that infernal trio, but I still had so many questions. And before Rebecca closed the door behind me, I asked:

"Do you know if David was ever in love with anyone else?"

"As a child, you mean?"

"Yes, at the orphanage, for instance. Before Aurora."

E + D. I was thinking of the initials I had seen in the locker room at Saint-Broladre.

"Maybe." She sighed. "But I don't remember."

"An Emmanuelle? An Élise? An Élodie? Anyone whose first name began with an *E*?"

"Honestly, I don't remember. Sorry."

Before leaving the building, I spent several minutes on the floor beneath Rebecca's apartment, my ear glued to the apartment door that had recently belonged to Louie. But eventually one of the residents got off the elevator, and I was forced to leave.

THE STORM HAD PASSED, CLEARING the sky for a radiant but stiflingly muggy day. My armpits and groin were damp, my top sticking to my chest, and my forehead pearling with sweat as though I had a fever. Still, I decided to wander through the neighborhood as a way of clearing my mind and sorting through all that I had just learned.

Nothing distracted me, not even the luxury cars lining the sidewalks, when suddenly my phone rang:

"Elle? It's Marchadeau."

I was surprised to hear from him so soon after our meeting. His voice was firm and determined. His tone was no longer as reticent as it had been just a few hours before.

"Yes?"

"I have something on Gobert."

"Oh . . . What is it?"

"Well, before he became president of PRSPS, Antoine Gobert worked for a long time in the private sector as a certified accountant."

I was progressively coming out of my state of lethargy. My interlocutor cleared his throat a couple of times in embarrassment, but that didn't clue me in to the significance of this information.

"He spent almost twenty years working for Sofiba, a financial office that is one hundred percent affiliated with the Barlet Group."

I was speechless, incapable of reacting, and Marchadeau finished me with these words:

"According to Delacroix's lawyer, he left the company less than a year ago. And the cherry on the cake: Gobert was the one who provided David with the incriminating evidence on Delacroix in the East-X Productions affair."

21

François Marchadeau had delivered his information on Antoine Gobert in a neutral tone that newscasters use to sound professional, as though he'd been commenting on the stock market or the weather. And yet I sensed that he thirsted for truth as I did. What had made him change his mind? Had it been the shock of seeing those pictures on my phone? I had trouble believing that. He knew David well enough to understand that his friend was not an angel. After all, both men had first met me when I was working as a Hotelle . . .

Nevertheless, I was certain that his discovery had just blown his mind as much as it had blown mine. He knew without a shadow of doubt that the link between Antoine Gobert and David implicated his friend in the conspiracy against Louie. For the first time, Marchadeau was catching a glimpse of his friend's true nature. And while he bitterly came to terms with this shift in perspective, I was quietly celebrating his reaction, which was the best news I'd gotten in weeks. I was also a little angry with myself for having succumbed, however briefly, to

David's insidious charm. He'd almost had me believing that he was working for his brother's interests.

I wasn't surprised to encounter so much duplicity from my ex. But the fact that he kept setting new lows was a source of frustration. I would have liked to see good in him, to see his love for his brother. And I wished he would stop lying to me for once.

"This is all my fault . . . ," I murmured into the phone's receiver.

"Your fault?"

"If I hadn't left David at the altar, he wouldn't be trying so hard to destroy Louie."

I didn't really believe in such a simplistic explanation of things. My conversation with Rebecca as well as everything I had found in Dinard proved that their issues far preceded me. I was just another character in the soap opera of their life.

"What are you doing right now?" I asked point-blank.

"I'm at the magazine. Why?"

"Could you get away for an hour?"

"I'm practically the boss here. I can leave as often and for as long as I want."

I was surprised that he hadn't put up any resistance. This new information was clearly a blow to his confidence in his unwavering friendship with David. They'd been friends for twenty years, he'd told me. He belonged to a generation that reveled in such expressions, as though the words alone could vaccinate them against disappointment or betrayal. It seemed he no longer believed in such pledges of eternity.

A HALF HOUR LATER, HE signaled me from the intersection of Rue Saint-Lazare and Rue de la Rochefoucauld, a respectable and prudent distance from Duchesnois House and Mars House. On the metro ride back to my neighborhood, I had managed to send Fred the picture of the man in front of the computer. Less than ten minutes later, he'd confirmed what I'd already guessed:

> Yeah, that's Yves. What's he doing at Duchesnois House?
> I wish I knew.
> Do you think he's the one who hacked into Louie's e-mail accounts?
> Maybe.
> Yves isn't the only computer whiz at BTV. My friend Francky is even better, and he hates his boss. Do you want me to ask him to check into the computer in question?
> That would be great, thanks!
> No prob ;-)

François Marchadeau had gotten rid of his jacket and tie. Two large sweat stains darkened his light-blue shirt around his armpits. Despite this faux pas, he still looked aristocratic and elegant. I wasn't attracted to him, but I couldn't help admiring the bravery of this man who would reject his class affiliations not just out of anger but also because of his love of the truth.

I guess I originally got into journalism to be like that.

"Are you inviting me in for tea?" he joked as a way of hiding how tense he was.

"No . . . Follow me," I said, gesturing for him to follow me inside the house on the left.

He didn't say another word until we'd arrived in the

basement control room. I could tell from the way he admired the house that he was impressed with the restoration work Louie had had done. Thanks to his upbringing, he was predisposed to like this kind of decor.

It only took me a moment to turn on the computer console and find the video.

David and the two slender blondes appeared on one of the monitors, going at it as wildly as they had before. One of the two was encouraging her colleague to suck David's member more ardently: "Davay! Davay! Eto otstoy!"

I had pressed the red record button too late, and the best parts were missing, but the positions and the accents were explicit enough.

"When is this from?" Marchadeau asked in a flat voice.

"Yesterday afternoon."

"Have you shown this to anyone else?"

"No . . . you're the only person besides me who has seen it."

He inhaled deeply, ran a trembling hand through his sweat-soaked hair, and asked:

"Do you know what these images would mean for David if they ever left this room?"

Obviously: They proved that the CEO of the Barlet Group was deeply enmeshed in the trafficking of illegal hard-core porn actresses from Eastern Europe. It would surely have an effect on Stephen Delacroix's appeal. And above all, depending on the timing, it could ruin the merger with GKMP and drive down the Barlet Group's share prices. It could mean disgrace and even financial ruin. The loss of his dearly won inheritance, which he had so deftly managed. All that from a couple of blurry shots that looked like any of the tens of thousands of pictures one can see on porn sites.

"Why do you think I showed this to you?"

"Hmm . . . ," he grumbled. "Well, it's not like you had much of a choice."

Indeed, he had first seen this recording by accident on my cell phone.

"In your opinion, what should we do?" I was asking for the opinion of an experienced journalist.

"For now, nothing. This is the safest place to keep this kind of arsenal."

I agreed, nodding. Then, as I was reaching to shut off the computer system, he stopped me, his hand moist but firm.

"Are you sure there's nothing else I should see on this machine?"

"The rest doesn't concern you."

"Don't you think that's for me to decide?"

He was forcing me to spell things out for him, so I said, in as dignified a voice as I could manage:

"The other videos aren't of David."

"Of whom, then?"

"They're of . . ." I hesitated. "They're of Louie. And some of his mistresses."

"Really?"

Surprised by his insistence and annoyed by his skepticism, I searched the computer and found a video I had already seen.

Marchadeau watched without saying a word, his face expressionless. When it was over, he asked to see another, then another. He watched them in silence and with the same impassive expression. Then at last his hand shot toward the commands and he pressed the pause button, freezing an image on-screen:

"There."

It was a shot of the cameraman's lower abdomen and the base of his swollen penis. I hadn't noticed it before, but it was all shaved.

"Do you notice anything?" he asked.

"No. Should I?"

"Don't tell me you've never seen David completely naked?"

"David?" I asked, choking.

He zoomed in on the pubis, and I noticed a small birthmark that was no bigger than a bean. Its shape reminded me of the tattoos that Stéphane had given Louie and me on the night of our engagement party.

"That angioma in his pubic hair is his hallmark. He never showed it to you?"

"Never . . . ," I breathed, stunned.

The birthmark likely disappeared whenever he let his pubic hair grow. But I was surprised that David had never mentioned it when we were together.

And how did Marchadeau know about it, exactly?

"David and I have been showering and changing in the same locker rooms for more than twenty years," he was quick to assert, as if reading my thoughts.

I was dazed, and he used the time to explore the treasures on the computer's hard drive. I mutely watched the videos with new eyes. To think that I had doubted Louie . . .

One mystery was still bothering me: How had David's personal movies gotten onto his brother's video surveillance system? Who had put them there, and why?

With a slam of the pause button, the sound of which bounced off of the ceiling's archivolt, Marchadeau tore me from my thoughts.

"What's going on? Is that not David?"

Ignoring my question, he played back the tape, then stopped it again. Finally, he acknowledged my presence.

"Yes . . . that's David," he confirmed, his tone deathly.

He stared wearily at the monochrome screen, letting the video play. Then, I recognized the middle-aged redhead whose snapshot I'd taken before. Without consulting me, Marchadeau replayed the sequence a second time, and I didn't dare interrupt. The woman's curves were made for love. She had a face that suggested both the deadly charm of a witch and the grace of a Madonna. And Marchadeau clearly knew who she was.

But who was this woman to him?

I WENT BACK UPSTAIRS, LEAVING him in the basement to contemplate what he had just seen. Meanwhile, I fed Felicity and got a couple of dresses from my room that were better suited to the muggy weather.

"Elle? It's Fred."

His voice thundered through the house.

"What is it?"

"Umm . . . You asked me for a favor, remember?"

I regretted my icy greeting and quickly asked in a nicer tone:

"Right, sorry. Any news?"

"Yeah! Francky says that the IP address of the computer that hacked into Louie's accounts corresponds to David's professional laptop."

"Are you sure? It seems crazy that he would take that kind of risk with his own compu—"

"It's more complicated than that. Yves used a bunch of foreign intermediaries to hide David's identity. But Francky was able to trace it all back to him anyway."

"Did he find any proof?"

"According to what Francky told me, it's impossible to get proof remotely. The only way is to get screenshots from the actual computer that was used to do the hacking."

In other words: from David's computer.

I raced down to the control room. Without disturbing my associate, who was still gazing in astonishment at the screens, I switched on the monitor linked to the camera on Duchesnois House's living room. As luck had it, the brand-new laptop I had seen before was still there. Its screen had been lowered, a sign that no one was presently using it.

"What is it? What are you doing?" Marchadeau asked in a hushed voice.

"I'm going to need you."

"Me?"

"Yes. You're going to call Chloe and ask to speak to David."

"Why?"

"To make sure that he's at Barlet Tower now."

The second video camera showed that he wasn't in his bedroom. But he could be anywhere in his several-thousand-square-foot mansion, though it was unlikely given that it was a weekday afternoon.

"And if Chloe gets a hold of him for me, what should I say?"

"I don't know. Improvise . . . You know how to do that better than I do."

He didn't appreciate my insinuation that he might ever engage in dubious journalistic practices, and he swallowed loudly before suggesting:

"I lent him a book in English on GKMP's history. I could pretend that I need it for a piece I'm writing."

"Perfect. Then, call Armand. Ask him to meet you with the book somewhere in Paris. Don't make it too close to the house, since I'll need time."

MARCHADEAU WENT BACK TO THE ground floor to make his calls, and I used his absence to rewatch the scene that incriminated David, the one in which his birthmark was prominently featured. Its resemblance to Louie's and my matching tattoos was decidedly troubling. But I didn't suspect Louie of anything since I had been the one who had come up with the design. The coincidence was perplexing. How had I not noticed this aspect of David's anatomy? Had I kept an unconscious memory of it that had resurfaced when I'd thought of the idea for our twin tattoos?

The sequence presently playing on-screen was the most unbridled sex scene yet in this erotic pandemonium. The woman wore a white mask reminiscent of the one Louie had given me to wear in the past. Although she was anonymous, the redhead was mesmerizing. She had a very narrow waist, wide hips, an ethereal backside, a stomach with just enough curve for a hand to rest on it, plump and perky breasts, delicate shoulders. Her curvaceous body was made for pleasure. She was a pinup, a woman whose looks far surpassed all ordinary conceptions of beauty.

Her vagina, which was palpitating around David's erect member, was made to the same standards. It wasn't simply pretty or well proportioned. It seemed perfect to me.

Louie's reading list for me included a work by Dr. Gérard Zwang, *Le Sexe de la femme*, in which the author delineates a surprising standard for vaginas. According to him, a good cunt must correspond to the following proportions: three and a half inches for the vulva, which he divides into three equal parts—the clitoris, the nymphae, and the vaginal canal. To this, he adds three and a half inches for the mons pubis. The result is a harmonious edifice measuring seven inches and extending from the upper pubic hair to the perineum.

The vulva of the woman on the screen was one of the best examples of human genitalia that I had ever seen. In addition to adhering to the criteria outlined by Dr. Gérard Zwang, it was also well coiffed, perfectly pigmented, and shining with excitement. I stared, contemplating this woman's charms. For the first time, I understood the male fascination for what we have between our legs.

David was quickening his pace, though without withdrawing his tip from this red-hot perfection, when—

"Annabelle? Are you there?"

Marchadeau's voice drew me out of my contemplation. I hit the stop button, shutting off the computer console, but I was still moved by the scene I had just watched. My panties were damp against my skin, and I quickly readjusted them before joining Marchadeau.

"So?" I asked casually, my cheeks pink.

"David is in the middle of a conference call with Seoul, and Armand is meeting me at Le Zimmer in a half hour."

"Perfect."

All we had to do was wait for the butler to leave the house next door before we could start the next phase of our plan.

FIVE MINUTES LATER, FRANÇOIS MARCHADEAU left to meet Armand, and I sneaked into Duchesnois House with the key that the butler had insisted I keep. I hadn't set foot inside David's house since I'd aborted our wedding and run to see my mother in the hospital. Mom had died that day. And my intrusion felt doubly wrong.

My heart was beating with fear, and when I stepped into the living room, I was flooded with memories. The coffee table was covered with newspapers trumpeting David's glory. The most recent publications applauded his business savvy and his conquest of the Korean media giant.

The laptop was on the dining table, as I had seen on the surveillance tape. I raised its silver lid, and the monitor instantly lit up, a log-in window appearing in the middle of the blue screen.

"Shit . . . ," I grumbled to myself. "A password."

What did I think? That, like that bewitching woman's vagina, the machine was going to let me gain access to David's secrets without putting up any resistance?

"Fred," I hissed into my phone.

"What do you need?"

"I have a problem . . . I'm sitting in front of David's computer, and I don't have his password."

"Right. Have you tried the obvious possibilities, his birthday, stuff like that?"

"No . . . I don't want it to shut me out."

"Don't worry. On most systems, there are no limits on the number of attempts you can make. Go for it."

So I tried my luck several times but without success: *January 5, 1970*; *January 5, 1969*; *010570*; *010569*; *Aurora*; *Aurora-Delbard*; *SaintBroladre*; *BrownRocks*. Each time, the machine gave me the same reply.

"Nothing's working . . . Could you ask your friend Francky? Cracking passwords must be child's play for him."

"Yeah, but he's not here."

"Can you get a hold of him?" I asked, insisting.

"He went home to code. And when he does that, it's impossible to contact him."

I had hit a wall. David would continue to make use of his brother's electronic identity. With disastrous consequences.

WITHOUT THINKING, I CLIMBED THE marble staircase, moved by an inexplicable feeling of curiosity. Perhaps I wanted to see the room where David had shown himself to be a more passionate lover than he had ever been with me.

As usual, everything was impeccably organized. The bed was made, and not a single item of clothing had been left lying around. For some reason, I decided to look into the closet.

One obvious truth instantly struck me.

"She doesn't live here!"

Not one dress, nor one bra, could be found amid his boxers, white shirts, and suits. Despite their wedding announcement and the grotesque video that had gone viral, it was clear that Alice hadn't moved in with her fiancé. David had been trying to promote a respectable image of himself, with a wife and future children. But was it all for show? Had he and Alice come to some sort of an agreement, complete with generous financial compensation?

Beneath an unstable pile of sweaters, I noticed the corner of a rigid piece of paper.

I jumped.

A silver cover.

"Bastard!" I hissed between clenched teeth. "So you're the one who's had it this whole time."

I grabbed the Ten-Times-a-Day from the pile of soft cashmere, and I riffled through its pages to see if anything had been torn out or added. Nothing. Its contents had been pillaged, our intimacy violated, but the book was intact.

I considered taking the book back home with me but decided against it. The damage had been done, and I figured that this notebook would be more useful to me if I left it in my enemy's hands. If I took it, he would know that I had been here and that the jig was up. I could gain an upper hand, however slight, if I let him underestimate me. And that is exactly what I intended to do.

22

The betrayed tend to react in one of two ways. Either they give up, adding infamy to misfortune, or they stand up and fight those who have wronged them. Happily for me, François Marchadeau had chosen the second option, and he was now working with me, this time without any conditions. He had agreed to help both with my research on the Barlet family and in my efforts to rehabilitate Louie's image. He saw the second task as a way of getting back at David.

SINCE WE WERE NOW IN the same camp, our interests aligned, it was time to give him all the information that I had in my possession. I wouldn't keep anything to myself . . . or almost anything.

Less than an hour after leaving Duchesnois House, I found him where he and I had taken refuge from the storm earlier in the day. He was leafing through the book Armand had returned to him, seated amid Le Zimmer's wood paneling and red wall hangings, a teapot with a yellow-and-gold label from Mariage Frères on the table in front of him.

"He's always treated that poor girl like a rag doll," he muttered angrily when I told him about how none of Alice's personal effects could be found at David's house.

Was he talking about David's new fiancée?

He went on, his words bitter:

"This wedding is as phony as Alice's promotion. The Koreans must be reassured," he said, brandishing the book, as though a fleet of Asians would fall from its pages. "The markets must be reassured. And history has proven that an unmarried CEO makes people nervous."

"So, for Louie, for David, what do you propose?"

He shook his head, swallowed some hot tea, then suggested, his tone faintly sententious:

"Nothing for now."

"Nothing?"

"It's too early to do anything."

"But we have everything we need to take David down!" I argued.

"To make him waver," he corrected, wagging his finger at me. "Not to make him fall. If we unveil everything we have on him right now, he'll have all the time he needs to prepare his defense before Delacroix's appeal is heard."

"And when is that?"

"The date hasn't been set yet. But probably in a few weeks, if not a few days."

He was trying to make me understand that, from a legal point of view, the Barlet-Sauvage and Delacroix affairs were connected. If we managed to push back Louie's trial, we could use that extra time to discredit David during Delacroix's appeal. If we could show that David was directly involved in an international pimping network and that he was secretly working with Antoine Gobert, then he would have no choice but to order Gobert to rescind his suit against Louie. It would be almost effortless. All we had to do was wait.

I furrowed my brow, and François gave my forearm a friendly and almost paternal squeeze.

"Believe me. David's lawyer is one of the best there is. If we go to battle armed only with videos that would, in any case, be inadmissible in a court of law, we'll get slaughtered."

"Who is this big star?"

"Jacques Bofford. He's been practicing law for thirty-five years. He's defended the biggest criminal and financial cases of the past two decades."

"If we give Zerki what we have, do you think he'll stand a chance against Bofford?"

I was talking about the proof we had on David, that he had been plotting against his brother and specifically about the computer hacking.

"Zerki's first internship was with him. Bofford taught him everything. His skills are but a pale copy of Bofford's talents. I saw them in action years ago, on an old case that involved David, when the student was still under the master's tutelage."

"If I understand, we're waiting for Delacroix's appeal to be heard. And in the meantime, we'll keep preparing for battle?"

I was sulking. I didn't like his conclusions, even if they were reasonable. He was making us out to be so powerless. François contemplated me for a moment, and then a smile spread across his face.

"Don't be childish. You know that my strategy is our only realistic option."

Since our great offensive attack had to be put on hold, he suggested that we get back to basics and reexamine my research: Aurora, the Barlet brothers' rivalry, all the lies and murkiness surrounding those three people.

"I don't mean to be rude, but considering Louie's liability, and the rearrangements he seems to have made with the truth when he was young . . . there might still be a lot to discover. If we don't want Zerki to get killed on the first day, we'd better give him as complete—and clean—a picture as possible."

"Just one question," I said, annoyed by what he was insinuating. "Do you know Louie very well?"

"Not really. We've met a few times at dinners and parties. I'm . . . Well, I was one of David's closest friends. That's not exactly the best way to get to know his brother. You know what I mean."

Although I had my doubts about Louie, too, I couldn't let a stranger trample the reputation of the man I loved.

"So then why do you think it's okay for you to talk about him like that?"

He leaned toward me, seizing my hands and almost knocking over his cup.

"Let's be completely honest: I'm a cuckold, and you're a woman in love with her man."

So the redhead he'd seen in David's arms had been his wife. That explained his sudden decision to help me.

"In other words," he went on, "I want to see everything heinous that this family is hiding. And you want the opposite. You don't want to tarnish the image you've made for yourself of Louie, and I can understand that. But our goal is still the same. And on the way to achieving it, we'll most likely have to come face-to-face with some things that we would rather not see."

The reference to the compromising pictures of his wife was plain.

"That's how it's going to be, Elle. We either have to accept that or give up now and let justice follow its course—and just pray that things turn out okay. It's your choice."

He coughed nervously. He was clearly still shaken up from what he had seen that morning.

"But you already knew all that," he went on. "Otherwise, you wouldn't have come to me for help."

He was right. I defended Louie on principle, but I had agreed to open my eyes to his true nature.

Marchadeau contented himself with a halfhearted smile from me. Despite his occasional gruffness, the man was lacking neither in psychological depth nor finesse.

WE SPENT THE REST OF lunch and a good part of the afternoon going over what I had found in Dinard and Saint-Malo. I was surprised by the fact that David had hidden most of his past from François, even after more than twenty years of friendship, ever since they'd first met at HEF.

Like most of us, David had several lives, which he deftly compartmentalized. In fact, he was obsessed with keeping his various lives walled off from one another. François therefore knew almost nothing about David's childhood in the orphanage. Until then, Marchadeau had attributed the rivalry between the two brothers to jealousy, a result of their upbringing. He'd thought that Aurora's role in their rivalry had been minor.

But what I told him that day—including the strange lies whereby the brothers had swapped roles in the two dramatic incidents of '89 and '90—showed him that the love triangle between Aurora, David, and Louie was the source of their bitter disputes. And it was rooted in their early childhood.

Probably at a time that preceded Hortensia and Andre Barlet's adoption of David.

"Were you there at Brown Rocks?"

"Do you mean, for Aurora's accident?"

"Yes, or when Louie crashed his parents' boat?"

"No. I wasn't there for either. As you were saying, David was a master compartmentalizer. The few times I was invited to Dinard, neither his parents nor his brother were there."

He was also unaware of other things, like Aurora and Louie's secret relationship "before and after" David and the young woman were married, according to Rebecca.

"I can understand why Louie and Aurora's affair was kept secret. But I can't comprehend why David hid his time with Aurora in Saint-Broladre."

"Neither can I," he said. "I don't see why they were so embarrassed or ashamed as to hide it so scrupulously."

"Especially since so many people seemed to have known. At least three people: Louie, Hortensia Barlet, and Florence Delbard."

He nodded silently, pensively running his hand through his gray-flecked hair.

"Did you manage to get in touch with your contact at the ministry, for the files at Social Services?"

"Not yet. It's tougher than I'd imagined. My friend can give me access to the files, but I'll probably have to go to Rennes in person, in which case I'll take the opportunity to do a little research of my own in Dinard."

The two towns were separated by about forty miles on the D137, a national road also known as Liberty Way. But Louie and I would have preferred truth to freedom.

"The strangest detail"—he sighed between two sips of tea,

grabbing one of the papers spread out over the small bistro table—"is this mistake with Aurora's insurance."

I told him the explanation Rebecca had given me, and he shrugged his shoulders angrily.

"That's bullshit!" he roared. "If someone disappears amid circumstances that could obviously lead to her death—which is clearly the case when someone drowns—the public prosecutor can declare her death immediately. There is no waiting period."

"And what makes you think that's what happened in Aurora's case?"

"Easy: I attended her funeral less than a month after the accident. In France, a funeral cannot take place without a death certificate."

Conclusion: The insurance company had to have been informed that number 2 70 06 35 063 056 19 was no longer of this world. Marchadeau didn't believe Rebecca's explanation that there had been some mistake a couple of years later.

"Yeah, but . . . it wouldn't exactly be the first time that an insurance company made a mistake."

"Hmm . . . ," he grumbled, unconvinced.

I examined the insurance papers again, and this time I noticed the address and phone number of the company, Mutaliz, at the bottom of the page and in fine print. I wondered if they were still good.

Without warning my new associate, I dialed the number.

"What are you doing?"

"Being a good journalist. I'm calling them."

"You're crazy! What are you going to tell them? That you have a dead woman's papers?"

"I can do better than that . . . ," I bragged, smiling. Then I held my hand up to silence him.

After a promotional announcement, a human voice answered:

"Thank you for calling Mutaliz. How may I help you?"

"Hello. I have a policy with you."

Marchadeau looked up at the ceiling, incredulous and annoyed. To prove to him that my methods would bear fruit, I turned on speakerphone.

"Could you please state your account number and your social security?"

I read the numbers from the page in front of me.

"Aurora Delbard?"

"Yes, that's right."

"Perfect. What can I do for you, Madame?"

"My card expired a month ago, and I still haven't received a new one."

"I see . . . Let me check into that for you. One moment, please."

As I waited, the frenetic sound of a keyboard resonating from the speaker, Marchadeau gestured his disapproval: a finger gun on his temple, his hand pretending to slit his throat, and so on.

"Madame Delbard?" the phone operator asked. "I don't understand. According to my records, your new card was sent on May 1. It should have arrived by the fifth."

I almost choked. From the other side of the table, François stopped gesturing and looked at me, his gaze empty and icy. For Mutaliz, Aurora Delbard was still alive. She had died over twenty years ago, and yet, in their eyes, she was as alive as I was. They still sent her insurance cards. And she—or someone pretending to be her—still paid her taxes and fees.

A few seconds passed before I could speak.

"Madame Delbard . . . are you still there?"

"Yes, yes . . . Sorry."

"If you would like, I could have another card sent."

"Yes, please do, thank you."

"I'm just going to confirm your address. Do you still live at 5 Square d'Orléans in the 9th Arrondissement in Paris?"

I hesitated for a moment. Should I give her my address? What good would it do me to receive the insurance card? What would it tell me that I hadn't just learned?

Marchadeau withdrew a pen from his jacket and scribbled Aurora's address on the back of the expired insurance papers. It was a journalist's reflex.

"Yes, that's right," I said absently.

"Perfect. You should receive your new card in five to six business days."

She terminated our conversation with a stock phrase. I was speechless.

AFTER LEARNING THIS ASTONISHING NEWS, Marchadeau and I, both stunned, spent a few more minutes together before taking each other's leave. Just enough time for him to confirm that, to his knowledge, the address didn't correspond to any of the Barlet family's properties, past or present.

We then left the eatery and made plans to see each other again whenever one of us had any new information.

"Oh! Wait . . . ," I said as I was leaving him.

"What is it?"

"The picture on my phone . . . I erased it."

"Thanks," he said with a sheepish smile.

SINCE THE WEATHER WAS NICE again and my studio not far, I decided to walk home. The terraces on Rue du Trésor were filled with tourists idly sipping cocktails. But my mind was preoccupied with one goal: to take refuge in my little apartment and mull over everything I had just learned.

I was haunted not by the question of *why* but of *who*. Who was the person who had been making it look as though Aurora were still alive? I had read enough crime novels to understand why someone would pretend that a person had died. But why would someone do the inverse? What was the point of maintaining a ghost's paperwork as if she were still alive?

Happily, my mailbox contained something that took my mind off these thoughts. Something sweeter, something I had been longing for. Louie was not simply the object of my investigations. He was not an abstraction or a character in a multiact drama, over which the media and lawyers constantly argued.

I missed him, and every day that sensation smarted a little more. Just as he had filled pages describing the different parts of my body, I could list the various physical symptoms that I had been feeling in his absence: stomach cramps, muscle contractions, eyelid twitches, nipple hardening, vaginal spasms . . . but I quickly abandoned this game. I wasn't in the mood to write.

I've already mentioned that Louie haunted me. His ghost visited me, and sometimes, in my waking dreams, he possessed me. This time, I was the one to call out for him, to make myself into a priestess devoted to his glory. I would do anything for his presence.

My apartment felt warm in the afternoon sunlight, and I spread out naked on my bed, arranging Louie's descriptions next to each corresponding body part. I wanted his words to caress me. His text was still a draft and some parts still had to be written. But to me, these lacunae were promises of future times together. Future pleasures.

Nipple *(noun): What amazes me most about your nipples is their capacity to change physiognomy, depending on how they are touched and also in function of subtler factors like a slight variation of temperature or a gust of cool wind.*

All I had at my disposal were my hands. My fingers wandered over my breasts, confirming this description. My aureola darkened, my nipple hardened, and I could see little mounds of excited skin. I knew that even the slightest contact would send electric waves throughout my body.

Bosom *(noun): The breath of life expands the human chest, and in the woman, it is here that desire can first be seen.*

I could feel my bosom blushing beneath my palms, as though Louie's hands were grabbing and squeezing my breasts. My breath grew shorter as the heat from my chest slowly traveled to my lower body, the tissue and mucous readying themselves for invasion.

Perineum *(noun): The perineum is discreet. It keeps its cards close to its vest. Buried between your thighs, it often escapes attention. But one fleeting caress, one single kiss, a simple touch will set it and the surrounding area afire.*

I lightly stroked this strip of skin with my index finger, and it felt like Louie was touching me from a distance. My thighs gave way; my loins hollowed themselves out; my sex opened wide. It was hungry, greedy for the two fingers I plunged inside myself.

But it wasn't satisfied, and I was no longer in the mood for reading.

Fist *(noun): Closed fist, clenched fist, threatening fist. With a little art, sometimes what is considered a weapon can become the most powerful instrument of pleasure.*

I don't remember ever having introduced my entire hand inside myself. I did it that night, convinced that it was Louie driving his vengeful fist through my loins and tearing me apart. I tilted my pelvis forward, creating a straight path for my fist, and I discovered the depths to which I was capable of filling myself. Once my hand was completely inside me, I clenched my fist tightly into a swollen ball of flesh, pushing into the spasmodic inner walls of my vagina.

Slowly, I unfolded and retracted my fingers, making my fist beat like a heart. I quickened the movement, my vagina expanding with each new contraction. I was a woman in the ecstatic thrall of her lover's fist. And the more the fist palpitated, the more I saw Louie. He was on top of me, one hand covering my mouth to smother my cries, his other hand inside of me. He was victorious. He had captured the citadel, conquered the city.

When I came, my fingers spread out in one motion. The pain was intense; my stomach clenched; my cry tore through the silence of the night. My orgasm covered his fist like a glove.

23

I didn't know how to reply to Louie's lexicon of my body. I didn't want to send him the random notes I'd been saving in my cloud over the past several days, though they were an early draft of the text you are currently holding between your hands. It seemed too early to show him what I'd been writing, particularly since I hadn't finished my investigation. I didn't want him to misunderstand my motivations. I didn't want him to think I was being snoopy when my primary aim was to get closer to him.

Circumstances were keeping us apart. I wondered if this was the ultimate test of our feelings. Was there any test more difficult than distance and the impossibility of communication? Wasn't this more intense than what any libertine experience could offer? And the ghost that kept inviting itself into my life, that fantasy man, wasn't it the most complete form of the one I loved, Louie?

5 SQUARE D'ORLÉANS

The only thing I managed to do that night in my studio was an Internet search of that address.

Before leaving me earlier that day, Marchadeau had taken

me in his arms, a sudden expression of emotion that had left me limp and speechless. I knew that this awkward gesture had come more from his need to receive comfort than a wish to offer me support. The scent of his sweat mixed with his cologne had nauseated me a little, but I hadn't had the heart to push him away. I needed his help, and this hug was the least I could do.

AS I SHOULD HAVE GUESSED, the first search results were for real estate agents. They vaunted the English charm of this luxurious neoclassical square, which was designed by Edward Cresy and inspired by John Nash's work. To my amusement, I learned that the land on which it had been erected had once belonged to a certain Mademoiselle Mars, who'd abandoned it when she moved to Rue de la Tour-des-Dames.

But what was truly interesting were the famous people who had lived on the Square d'Orléans, from the 1830s to the present day: Alexandre Dumas, Eugène Delacroix . . .

While scanning a page, my eyes were drawn to the number five: *We've been living in Orléans Square for two days, house number 5, on Rue Saint-Lazare. The apartment is very nice and comfortable, but it is still empty.*

I skimmed through several paragraphs before I learned who the author of these lines was: George Sand. The "we" became clear a few lines down, in these jealous and scornful words: *For his part, the maestro is working hard and preparing (also on Orléans Square, house number 9) a magnificent salon to receive his magnificent countesses and delicious marquesses.* That maestro, of course, was Chopin.

If Aurora had ever lived in that house, she must have had substantial resources. Means *and* motives to live there alone. But I already knew that in the days and weeks following her wedding, she had left Saint-Malo to live in the apartment on Avenue Mandel, where David used to reside.

Once again, something didn't make sense. The only idea that came to mind was that Jean-François Delbard had perhaps made some kind of real estate investment in the capital. The prestige of the area made for a good investment. And notaries did make enough money to purchase that kind of jewel. Aurora's father was perhaps cultivated enough to appreciate the significance of the house. Still, I was troubled by the fact that the house in question was situated on the Square d'Orléans, just a few paces from Rue de la Tour-des-Dames.

It was already night, and I didn't see what I could do right then. For the moment, all advances in this investigation seemed to depend on François Marchadeau. I suppressed my mounting impatience and my desire to contact him—he was probably just boarding the TGV for Saint-Malo—and I decided to concentrate on the column I had promised the associate editor of *The Economist*.

Writing about David as though I still shared my life with him felt like a fairly subtle form of temporal and emotional imposture. Following Marchadeau's good advice, I quickly jotted down a typical day in the life of David Barlet. I titled it "Twenty-four hours in the life of David B., CEO and media mogul." I didn't leave anything out, not even the brand of toothpaste that he used. My prose was cold, clinical, the text filled with brand references, not unlike the work that made Bret Easton Ellis a literary success.

David wakes up every morning at six twenty-five—not fifteen or thirty, twenty-five exactly—to the strident sound of his Cerruti 1881 alarm clock. He doesn't stretch or laze in bed. He isn't reluctant about starting his day. Instead, he jumps out of bed, moved by the unshakable desire to tackle the obstacles and difficult decisions he will face for the next twelve hours. The next half hour is divided into carefully timed five-minute intervals: a five-minute shave with his Louis Vuitton razor; a five-minute shower with his Roger & Gallet bois d'orange shower gel; five minutes to put on his suit (bespoke or Paul Smith); five minutes to do his hair and spritz himself with one of the five or six colognes sitting on a shelf in his bathroom, his preference typically leaning toward classics like Guerlain's Habit Rouge or Dior's Eau Sauvage; five minutes to drink a cup of Malongo Blue Mountain coffee, eat a bowl of Quaker Oats with lactose-free almond milk, and gulp down a glass of freshly squeezed orange juice, which his butler prepares for him every morning; finally, five minutes to sync his iPhone 5 with his MacBook Air and grab a few files he took home with him last night. It is now six fifty-five, seven at the latest, and David B. is ready to conquer the world.

I wrote two full pages, painting a picture that was sure to elicit repulsion in my readers, even if some of them would envy certain aspects of David's life. Who would ever want to live such a robotic life, such an affectless succession of chronometric gestures?

I didn't care. That life was far behind me. And the story was of little interest to me since I had to gloss over the only parts worth any attention: how David's twofold status as a younger brother and adopted child had instilled in him a spirit of conquest that knew no bounds and a sense of morality that was as blurry as his origins.

I quickly reread my work—I've always trusted the spontaneity of a first draft—and I sent it to fmarchadeau@leconomiste.fr. I was sure to attach an acknowledgment-of-receipt form. I also sent him a text message to tell him that the first installment of my column would be waiting for him in his e-mail in-box when he returned to his office.

He replied almost instantaneously:

Thanks. To be published in the next issue. Don't
forget to let me know what you want to use as your
pen name. FM

IF THE PAST YEAR HAD taught me anything, it was that putting one's fate into the hands of a single man was madness. It was foolish, negligent, and I would never do it again. Even out of love, even if the hands in question belonged to Louie. Asking for his hand in marriage, organizing our engagement party—those had not been acts of self-abandonment but of conquest. I wasn't offering myself to him; I was assailing him. To be sure, I would do anything to make him mine, but I wouldn't blindly agree to endure anything from him.

The same went for Marchadeau. The fact that I had made him my partner in no way barred me from following my own leads, developing a strategy, and acting on my own intuitions. And nothing said that I had to tell him everything.

You home? Drink at the TrésOr? Soph

My friend and I hadn't spoken since our phone call before I'd left for Saint-Malo. It felt like an eternity. I had no intention of sharing everything that Marchadeau and I had discovered that day, but I missed her. Her cheerful nature and especially her way of being at once sweet, playful, and funny.

OK. In 20 mins?

She arrived at the overcrowded terrace twenty minutes late, just as I was finishing my first Monaco. Her floral summer dress flattered her curves.

"It may not be your perfect dress," I commented, referring to her quest for the holy grail of dresses, "but you look good in it."

"Yours isn't bad either."

I didn't know what to say to her compliment: I hadn't had time to wash since my return, and I'd thrown on the black dress I'd borrowed from Aurora's closet. A dress stolen from the past.

"Does Fred know you go out in that kind of thing?" I asked, trying to deflect attention from me and back onto her.

"Fred is jealous no matter what I do or wear. I don't need to tell you how he functions."

"So your strategy is to add fuel to the fire?"

"Exactly. No point in getting worked up about him . . . might as well enjoy myself."

"True love, I see . . ."

From across the table, her expression was a blend of sweet and sour. I only hoped that Sophia was as clear with Fred as she was with me about her limited ambitions when it came to their relationship. The poor guy had already faced enough disappointment these past months.

"By the way . . . I saw my anonymous man again," she said.

"Saw" wasn't exactly the best word. And I could tell that

these blind rendezvous did more for her than a thousand dinner-and-a-movie nights with Fred would ever do.

"Still no clues?"

"No . . . Wait, yes, actually. This last time, I'm almost certain he was wearing a hat."

"A hat?"

"Yes, a summer hat. Straw, you know the kind. He put it on a chair, and I sat on it, and he . . . Errr, I won't go into the details."

That kind of modesty was so unlike *my* Sophia. It made me think that what she felt for this man went beyond the sexual. He was a refreshing whiff of adventure in her otherwise difficult life, which consisted of desperate month ends and ugly compromises.

I was wondering why she hadn't harassed me about my trip to Brittany, when two male figures stopped at our table, two pairs of moccasins planting themselves on the terrace's cobblestones. The man on the left held out a self-assured hand. He was lean, with slicked-back hair, a double-breasted suit, and a white shirt that revealed his hairy chest. His metallic voice was familiar:

"Good evening . . . Jean-Marc Zerki."

Sophia and I greeted him. The lawyer gazed briefly down my friend's dress before regaining a professional attitude.

Beside him, Louie seemed much less at ease, despite his being taller than his lawyer and better dressed. Still, he gave me a look that managed to express both his distress at seeing me again under such circumstances and the fact that he missed me. Our eyes, which devoured each other in private, didn't know how to behave in public. I looked away first.

Sophia looked uncomfortable, too. She and Louie had

clearly come up with this meeting plan together, and she was shooting me looks that begged forgiveness.

But when we stood to make room for the two men at our table, Louie started considering me with different eyes. He looked me up and down, his expression turning from surprise to contained anger. He had recognized the dress, twenty years later.

"Shall I leave you guys?" Sophia asked, desperate to get away.

"No, stay."

To express my irritation with her, I pressed into her forearm with the weight of my body. She readjusted her dress on her chair, her expression contrite, as if she was only just then realizing how indecent it was.

I was furious with her, but I also needed her. I had no intention of telling our visitors about everything I had discovered in Saint-Malo, and her presence would help distract their attention. I could avoid mentioning the contents of the safe at Brown Rocks and what I had learned from them. Instead, I concentrated on everything that could be useful to Zerki in defending his client. My voice was tight with emotion; my spine trembled. My man was so near, but I couldn't hold him in my arms. Slowly, I began by telling them about Gobert and his connection to David.

"We've known that since the beginning," the lawyer cut me off, rubbing his neck in irritation. "David has Gobert eating out of his hand, and he's trying to discredit his brother. Okay. But that doesn't solve anything. No court of law would be satisfied with such meager evidence."

"In that case . . . I have something better for you."

A gust of wind swept through the terrace, as if to represent the truth that was about to clear up their doubts and reservations. It lifted Sophia's and my dresses, to the delight of some of our juvenile neighbors. Louie kept his eyes on my face, his expression full of both desire and reproach.

Since it was Louie who had asked me to hide any compromising evidence, including the key to the basement surveillance room, I assumed that he knew about the films. But why, then, did he seem so surprised when I told him what I had seen on the screens? The dozens of videos of David with his countless mistresses, all set in the various rooms of the Hôtel des Charmes.

"Yes, of course I know about the cameras," he said, straightening to give the illusion of composure.

His skin must have started to warm with emotion because I caught a familiar whiff of lavender and vanilla, which sent a shiver of desire through my whole body.

"But contrary to what one might think, neither David nor I had the system installed."

"Who did, then?" Sophia asked with her usual directness. "Big Brother?"

Louie turned toward my friend, giving me a view of the left side of his neck and his climbing rose. I couldn't tell if it was an effect of the hour's subdued lighting, but the rose seemed to have become blurry, as though the ink under his skin had already started to fade.

"In this case, I think 'Big Father' would be a more appropriate term," he said with a tight smile. "Our father was the one who had the whole electronic mess installed."

That explained why the equipment was so dated, the screens monochrome, the plastic worn, and the commands rudimentary.

Zerki, who had been quietly listening, inserted himself into the conversation:

"Why?"

"No idea. To keep an eye on David and me, I would imagine. Or the staff. Dad was a little paranoid. He was convinced that the competition was spying on him. He may have installed it to inform him of any intrusions and to glean sensitive information."

"Since the time when you inherited Mars House, you've never been curious to see what was stored in its memory?"

"No," he said, turning toward me. "Just as it never occurred to me that there was any link between that crazy system and the rooms in the Hôtel des Charmes. As you know, I am a man of letters rather than images."

The allusion to his *Alphabet* and his recent correspondence made my cheeks and throat flush. Suddenly, I wished we were alone. I wished that his flesh and blood could meld with his ghost and that together they, that single erotic being, could make love to me. Our bodies had grown accustomed to communing with each other several times a day. Over the past few weeks, they had been cruelly kept apart. Our long night in Malmaison now seemed so far away . . .

I shook these images out of my head and continued with my line of questioning:

"You never tried to watch anything, even with David Garchey?"

"I gave him access to the control room. When I first told him about it, he was really excited. I let him play with the material . . . He told me he hadn't found anything very interesting."

I remembered how the young artist had been reticent and then excited to show me the secret room on the night of the

1827 housewarming party. I wondered what had happened to him and his creations after Captain Lechère and his henchmen had stormed the Sauvage Gallery.

The lawyer suddenly turned to his client and addressed him in a grave and almost solemn tone:

"The question I am about to ask you, Louie, is very important: Do you think that David knows about the surveillance room? Does he know that his house is being filmed?"

"I don't think so. When we were kids, we lived in Duchesnois House. We weren't allowed to go into Mars House. We must have only set foot inside maybe twice over the course of ten years, and our father was with us both times. I only discovered the existence of the basement control room when I inherited Mars House and was given the keys. That was about a year after my parents' death. David has never accompanied me on the rare times I've gone down there."

"You've never spoken with him about it?"

"Never."

"And you've never heard him mention it?"

"No."

He seemed sure of this point.

There was always Armand. If Andre had confided in the old butler, then it was possible that Armand had mentioned it to David. But without really knowing why, I had a hard time believing that idea.

As for Louie, despite his efforts to minimize his involvement, I was certain he had used the computer console and its electronic eyes at least once . . . when he had spied on me. Thanks to the cameras, he had become better acquainted with my sexual behavior than anyone else. And that had allowed him to write the anonymous notes in which he'd unveiled my secret fantasies and raw pleasures. *That wasn't how he was going to make me come undone*—he had read the words from my sighing lips.

But if he wasn't the one who had been keeping tabs on the Hôtel des Charmes with those cameras, then who had? Who had been targeting David? Who could be so sickly fascinated with him? Who had taken the risk—a calculated risk, I assumed—of leaving the videos on the computer's hard drive?

"Why did you keep it?" I asked at last, torn between this flood of questions and the desire welling up within me.

"Excuse me?"

"The surveillance system . . . You could have had it removed while you were remodeling the house. Why did you keep it?"

The nervous contraction of his jawbone was a sign of his irritation. He was twisting the silver knob of his cane as though he wanted to change it into a magic wand and make us disappear.

Oh, my Louie. You are never as handsome as when your face takes on the features of a hunted animal. You never make my heart melt as much as when you seem to be in desperate straits. I would give anything to save you.

And even though my question was legitimate, I see that it hurt you. You would have preferred me docile, ardent, my love unconditional. You don't understand that beneath my attack is the desire to love you, all of you, including the dramatic and shadowy parts of your life.

"I don't know . . . I told myself that maybe it would come in handy one day."

"Well, I think you've proven that now," Zerki said, congratulating himself for dissipating the tension. "With those videos, we have what we need to take on your opponent."

Everyone understood that this evidence—especially the

video of David with those two girls from Eastern Europe—would be enough to exonerate Louie in the eyes of justice and of the public.

However, as Marchadeau had done, Louie's lawyer attenuated his enthusiasm:

"Still, I advise caution and discretion. We need to keep this evidence confidential until Delacroix's appeal."

He repeated the tactic that the journalist had suggested earlier to me, explaining the tiniest of procedural details that were to come, punctuating his speech with somber and pointed looks, like a teacher admonishing his students.

I listened to his pompous speech like a good girl and kept myself from mentioning the investigation that Marchadeau and I had undertaken. Finally, while everyone appeared to be meditating upon the man's words, I said:

"We have another advantage over David."

"What?" Zerki asked, surprised.

"The blog . . . I mean, his idea of it."

"What do you mean?"

"He still thinks that he has me fooled into believing I'm corresponding with Louie."

"If we can't prove that David is really the one behind the blog, then it won't do us any good."

"True. But I think I know a way to unmask him."

In a few simple sentences, I told them about Fred and Francky, my duo of technological guardian angels, and the obstacles we had encountered.

"If I'm understanding what you're saying, the only way to implicate David in the blog is to crack his password and gain access to his computer."

"Right."

"And that can't be done remotely?" Sophia asked.

The cane, the one with the eagle's head on top, was flying faster and faster between Louie's hands, almost falling to the floor each time he twisted it around. He made no effort to hide his exasperation—he was barely even managing to contain it. And the more it grew, the more distance it created between us. The gulf between us was unbearable. All I wanted was to fill it with a kiss. And an infinite number of other things.

We were digging through his family secrets, and it was clearly causing him pain. Perhaps he was also bothered by the dress. I must have looked like *her* more than ever—me, the pale ghost of his long-lost love. Or perhaps after all these years, this imminent and final battle with his brother was fraying his nerves.

"According to Francky, his laptop is armor-clad with all kinds of firewalls and other protective measures. It would be almost impossible to get in from the outside."

"Concretely, what are our options?"

"Make him think that he's still calling the shots. And gain access to his computer when he's not there."

"Another break-in." Zerki sighed.

"I'm not breaking in . . . I have the keys."

But my childishly triumphant attitude did little to convince or calm Louie. He quickly stood, knocking into the table and almost spilling our drinks, and hissed at me:

"I forbid you!"

"You forbid me?" I repeated, scarlet.

"You heard me. You may not put yourself in contact with David again!"

And yet . . . I hadn't told him about the night I'd had

dinner with his brother, and how we'd briefly become friendly with each other again.

And yet . . . I wouldn't mention the thousand euros David had lent me, and that I hadn't paid back.

And yet . . . I hadn't brought up everything I had learned about the two brothers when I was in Saint-Malo and Dinard, the press clipping, the birth certificates, the photograph with the heart, and the insurance papers . . . That whole murky past of which one image, the picture of a Christmas tree, was particularly evocative.

"I won't be interacting with him," I argued limply, crushed by his anger. "I'll be going to his *house*. It's not the same thing."

"For me, it is!" he exploded. "It *is* the same thing!"

He turned on his heels, his cane brushing past our glasses, which were still trembling from the earlier shock, and he quickly disappeared into the street's shadows, the sound of his limp accentuated by the uneven cobblestones. A shadowy version of the Sun King, Louie, the man I loved so much.

The others on the terrace, all several sheets to the wind, looked on in horror as I stood, teetering, one hand leaning into the bistro table for support, and cried into the night:

"You can't escape it! Do you hear me? You can run . . . but you can't escape it!"

Escape what? Me? My anger? Or a complete and perhaps even definitive explanation? A tearing down of all the screens that his painful past had erected between us.

24

Fury—no, exhaustion. Or something else. Weariness, the sharp feeling that, of all the battles lost before they are even fought, the most hopeless is perhaps the battle to change other people. People can't be changed. Especially not Louie Barlet.

"Elle! Elle, shit, come back!"

Zerki's voice joined Sophia's:

"Come back! He doesn't know what he's saying. He's not well . . ."

I left them there, rejecting the consoling embrace of my friend and the formal pleas of the slick-haired lawyer. After a few awkward steps, I took off my ballerina flats and started to run. I wanted to escape the irksome lawyer and my treacherous friend as fast as I could. I raced up the seventy-five steps between the foyer of my apartment building and my studio on the seventh floor, and at last I collapsed on my bed. I cried and cried until I couldn't cry anymore, until all the tears had been wrung out of my body. Barefoot, my heart raw.

Saving Louie from his brother, saving Louie from himself

. . . It was the same task, and I was beginning to think that it was too much for me. I was only Annabelle Lorand from Nanterre, whom circumstance had put in a studio in the Marais. It was unreasonable to think that by myself I could rectify such a complicated and heartbreaking past, with all the accidents, deaths, broken lives, resentment, and fantasies. I now understood my limits. And even if I had Marchadeau to help me, it wouldn't be enough to untangle this mess.

AT ONE POINT, LOUIE'S SHADOW tried to force open my door. I resisted. At least my mind did. I longed to feel him against me, in me. I could no longer make do with substitutes, be they in the shape of my fist or that of another's fingers. I was done with mirages. I wanted him, the real Louie. My sex was dilating with hope, when:

I know it's late. But can I call you?

I was less bothered by François Marchadeau than I was surprised. I hadn't been expecting to hear from him until the next morning at the earliest. And given the time, he must have only just arrived at the station in Rennes. I pushed the callback button on my touch screen phone. He answered almost instantly:

"Marchadeau speaking."

"Hi, François. It's Elle."

"Elle! I didn't wake you, did I?"

It was only when I glanced at the clock on my microwave that I understood I had dozed off. It was 11:47. I had slept for almost an hour.

"No, no . . . No worries. Are you at the hotel?"

"Not yet. I'm in the Social Services archives in Rennes."

"At this hour?" I breathed, alarmed.

"My friend's girlfriend offered to let me in tonight if I wanted. I figured I'd head over as soon as I got in. That way I can leave for Saint-Malo early tomorrow morning."

I recognized the traits of a field journalist, which he had been in the early days of his career. He was maximizing every minute and every source.

Despite this professional fountain of youth, he should have sounded wearier after having embarked on such a tedious task, especially at that hour. But his tone was light. He sounded almost excited.

"Did you find something?"

Stupid question.

"One might say," he breathed, being willfully enigmatic. "But what's especially interesting is what I didn't find."

"What *did* you find?"

"All of David's adoption papers!"

He was taking sadistic pleasure in slowly revealing his news, one tiny piece at a time.

"And?" I succinctly urged him to continue.

"He was born on January 5, 1969, as we already knew. And he was adopted by Andre and Hortensia Barlet on November 28, 1976, when he was seven years old."

"Okay . . . but, like you said, we already knew all that."

I heard the sound of a page turning. I imagined it was thick and heavy, the kind of page typical of thick archival catalogues.

"He entered Saint-Broladre on March 11, 1972, after spending a few weeks in temporary foster families."

"And does it say how he got there?"

"No. His intake papers make no mention of how his parents died. All they tell us is their name."

"Their name?" I yelped, impatient.

"If I am to believe what is written here, David's biological parents were called Monsieur and Madame Lebourdais."

I bolted upright in my bed. I knew that name . . . but I couldn't remember how. Nothing came to mind. No faces, no memories. Why was it so familiar?

My eyes desperately searched the darkness of my studio, as though some piece of decoration might help. Nothing. I had the answer on the tip of my tongue, my ears, my eyes, and yet . . .

"Lebourdais?" I repeated at last.

"Yeah, why? Do you know that name?"

"I . . . I don't know. I'm not sure."

He was breathing heavily into the phone.

"You're familiar with the name, but you don't know why . . . Am I right?"

"Yes . . . That's exactly it."

"If it helps, you should know that more than eighty percent of our short-term memory is based on visual input. So when you can't remember something, think back to everything you've read or seen over the past several days. Magazines, books, posters, television commercials . . ."

In many respects, and particularly when it came to this kind of practical advice, Marchadeau reminded me of Alain Bernardini, my mustachioed journalism professor. I wondered if they knew each other. They had probably seen each other a few times since the world of print journalism wasn't very big.

Applying this mnemonic device, I thought of everything

I had recently laid eyes on. Even junk mail, even the menu at Café de la Plage in Dinard.

"It can be something as seemingly insignificant as a road sign, a name or address on an envelope," he continued, in an effort to stir my memory.

"The letters!" I suddenly cried in a hushed tone.

"The letters? What letters?"

"At the Hôtel des Charmes . . . There's this woman who's been receiving letters there. Ysiam, the bellboy, has given me her mail by accident a few times."

"Who is this woman?"

"I don't know what she's doing there. But I remember her name now. Émilie Lebourdais."

"Émilie Lebourdais," he repeated. "It can't be a coincidence. That's not a very common last name."

Bit by bit, the blurry memory became clear. I remembered Ysiam's white teeth, his smile as he handed me the fat manila envelope, then my own surprised expression when I saw that one of the letters inside was not addressed to me. The mistake had occurred twice, as if someone were making sure that I remembered the name of the addressee: Émilie Lebourdais. The corporate name of the hotel had been written on one of the envelopes, I remembered now. I mentioned this detail to Marchadeau, who read a lot into it.

"That wasn't a mistake. This woman is somehow part of the hotel's hierarchical structure. Your Ysiam had no idea who she was?"

"None. He told me that he'd never seen her. But the first time he accidentally handed me her mail, he'd grabbed it from one of the cubbies behind the reception counter, which makes me think that she must often pick up her mail at the hotel."

"Maybe she has a kind of permanent mailbox there," he conjectured. "And that gives me an idea."

"What?"

"I think we should do a complete inventory of the Barlet family's real estate assets: who possesses what, according to what terms, and who inherited what from—"

"Considering their wealth, I don't think that's going to be easy."

"You're right. But something tells me that's where we should look. I mean, if David had inherited Mars House instead of Louie, then we never would have seen those videos."

His logic seemed fuzzy, but nothing he said was exactly wrong, so I decided to trust his instincts—he was a seasoned journalist, after all.

"But I agree with you," Marchadeau continued breathlessly, his excitement like that of an eager hunting dog. "We probably will be confronted with murky evidence. It'll be difficult to get a clear view of the whole picture."

"Why do you say that?"

"Because, as the East-X Productions affair seems to indicate, the Barlets aren't strangers to financial sleights of hand, like offshore shell corporations."

I took the fact that he wanted to dig so far into the obscure depths of the Barlet empire as proof of his determination and commitment to uncovering the truth.

"You said earlier that you were especially interested by what you didn't find. What did you mean?"

"Right," he breathed. "Guess whose file I didn't find?"

"Aurora's?" I guessed shyly.

"Exactly. Social Services has no record of an Aurora Delbard."

"Are you sure? What about under another surname? What were her biological parents called, for instance?" .

"No, that wouldn't do us any good. All the children are listed under the names of their adoptive parents. For example, here it shows David *Barlet*, not Lebourdais. In any case, I checked to see if there was an Aurora Something-or-other between 1975 and 1978 . . . I didn't find anything."

I wished I were there with him right then and could check the files myself. Just in case. It was late; he was probably tired. He may have overlooked Aurora's file. It might have simply escaped his gaze, hidden itself from his attempt to flush it out from that forest of broken childhoods.

There was no record of Aurora Delbard in those archives. Officially, she had never been adopted. I remained speechless for a long moment as I considered all the possible reasons for so many people with such divergent interests to lie to me—Louie and David Barlet, Rebecca Sibony, and Florence Delbard.

There was a knock on my door, and I quickly hung up with Marchadeau.

"Elle? Elle, are you sleeping?"

Sophia.

When at last I decided to open the door, she told me that she had been pacing through the neighborhood, trying to decide whether to come to my studio. In the end, she had decided to climb the six flights of stairs of my building to see me. She was worried about me. She apologized, using her contagious humor like a balm to soothe my wounds.

"Hey! I almost forgot . . . You're engaged!"

"Yeah . . . and?"

"And that means you're going to get married, hon. This time for real!"

Nothing seemed less certain. My chances of marrying Louie one day seemed as hypothetical to me as my chances of marrying David had been the year before. But I didn't have the heart to contradict her, especially when she was trying to make amends. I forgave her and let myself give in to her energy and contagious smile.

"In conclusion?"

"In conclusion, we haven't yet had a bachelorette party for you!"

The idea was as strange to me as if she had suggested celebrating Christmas in June. But I guessed that she was using this tradition as an excuse to tear me away from the ocean of worry into which she had seen me sinking day by day—even if it only lasted a few hours, the time to have a drink and a dance.

"Do you want to do it now?" I asked, surprised.

Yes, now and until dawn. We'd go wild. Our only limits: our resistance to alcohol and male attention.

I wasn't any more in the mood to party than someone with a funeral to attend, but I gave in. Feigning excitement, I ended up convincing myself that a frivolous night out with Sophia might put an end to my endless fretting, at least for the night.

SOPHIA IS ALWAYS UP-TO-DATE ON the latest trends and hottest locales. That season, Pigalle was back in fashion, and it felt good hanging out in its sexy bars and nightclubs, where the sexual orientations of the clientele were always ambiguous. We ended up at a lesbian club on Rue Frochot, near the Moulin Rouge.

"Umm . . . Soph, do you think this is a good idea?"

The entrance was swarming with women of all ages, either coupled off or in groups, everyone a bit tipsy. Some of them whistled as we approached, and I even heard a "Yum!" and a couple of "Hmm, pretty!" As we disappeared into the club, I felt their eyes on our asses.

"What?" my guide asked. "Are you scared of a girl hitting on you?"

Scared, no. But was it something I wanted? No. Although I knew that girls tended to be subtler in their game of seduction than men. And my bruised ego could use a little flattering. But I didn't want to be hit on that night, regardless of the source, be it a man or a woman.

"Come on!" she goaded, pulling me deeper inside. "I'll be your chaperone. And if somebody bothers you, I'll give you a big wet kiss!"

That's what I loved about Sophia: she was natural, protective, and comfortable enough with me to say that kind of thing without blushing. She was always flirting with that ambiguous zone where friendship and desire meet, though she never acted on it.

Calamity Joe, which was once the Fox and before that the Moune, had been redecorated and renamed and closed and reopened by new owners countless times. The crowd inside consisted of well-dressed thirty- and forty-somethings. Most had done their hair and makeup to play up their femininity. Some wore outrageously high heels, had exaggerated bosoms or endlessly long hair, using every artifice at their disposal to flatter their natural beauty as much as possible.

I STARTED HEADING TOWARD THE bar, but Sophia yanked me in the other direction. She looked like she knew the place well—I didn't dare ask if she'd been there before, and with whom.

After wandering through a maze of doors, we arrived at a dimly lit corridor onto which opened a multitude of small rooms, some of which were occupied, others empty. As we made our way through the hallway, the function of these private boxes slowly became clear to me. Instead of tables or chairs, they all featured a kind of waist-high tatami mat that was covered with large bath towels. Inside, couples of naked women—some joined by a third party—embraced each other in a symphony of sighs and gentle moans. We weren't the only ones interested in watching these scenes. Even when the occupants had locked the door to their little cell, one was invited to peep through the wooden latticework of the moucharaby.

"Go ahead . . . ," Sophia whispered, smiling and pointing at a window. "Don't be scared. They want to be watched. Otherwise, they would have stayed at home."

Silently, I peeked into the room nearest me and saw three brunettes with perfect bodies pleasuring one another according to their desires. I was fascinated by their fluidity and grace as they transitioned from one position to the next. They looked as though they were rehearsing for a ballet recital. Aside from the few X-rated movies I'd watched with Fred long before, I had never seen women alone together. I was drawn to the softness of their touch, the consideration that they seemed to put into each movement. It was nothing like the brutal, almost violent scenes of heterosexuals making love, at least from the perspective of an outside observer.

Still, I noticed that this group had a leader. The eldest among them, a fifty-something with a firm body, was giving silent signals, directing the trio from one position to the next. She was also the one who penetrated the others. She used her fingers, a giant black dildo, or even one of her lovers' hands, which she transformed into tools. She decided which orifice was to be penetrated, how much force to use, and how long it would last.

While all three were resting on their backs, she positioned herself to slip her index and middle fingers into each woman's cunt, both within reaching distance of her long and lean body. She was surprisingly slim for her age. The other two, whose heads were lying by the elder woman's feet, then dug their fingers into their guide's dripping vagina. Their bodies convulsed with pleasure, and I stared for several long moments, captivated by this swell of trembling flesh.

Without realizing it, and despite the fact that I was dressed, I had slipped a hand between my thighs. I was torn between the desire to feel happiness with them and the shame of giving in to this new experience.

A hand touched my shoulder, and I jumped.

"Come on . . . Let's get something to drink," Sophia said, bringing me back to my senses.

Why had she shown me this scene? What had she hoped it would stir in me?

The image of my friend doing a peep show a few months before flashed through my mind, her fingers caressing her vulva as the allotted fifteen minutes came to a close.

SHE GRABBED MY HAND AND pulled me toward the bar, where an even motleyer crowd was gathered. As we made our way across the dance floor, I could have sworn that hands grabbed my waist and ass.

"What will it be, girls?" the barmaid asked; she was laced into a tighter corset than the one I had worn the night of the housewarming party.

"Gin and tonic?" Sophia suggested.

I was nodding approval when a chubby blond silhouette appeared in my field of vision between two beanpoles, who were clearly hitting on her. The blonde seemed unperturbed and was obviously trying to decide which one—and perhaps she was secretly hoping for both.

"Shit . . . ," I hissed as Sophia handed me my glass.

"What is it?"

"You see that girl there? The kind of chubby blonde?"

"What, is she your type? Do you want me to get her for you?"

"No, come on! It's Chloe!"

"Chloe . . . ? Am I supposed to know who that is?" she asked sarcastically, before taking a sip of her clear drink.

"David's assistant!"

Her hair was down, her glasses off. She was wearing a tight sheath dress, and since we were outside of Barlet Tower, I'd barely recognized her. She was almost pretty like this. I wondered if she let loose here. Or was she carefully timing exactly how long she spent with those two creatures before she sent them packing?

"That's huge!" Sophia cried, her voice drowned out by the music and general brouhaha. "Do you think David knows his secretary is a carpet muncher after hours?"

I chose to ignore the derogatory expression, but I couldn't take my eyes off the scene.

"That would surprise me. At the station she's known for being an uptight and desperate singleton. The kind of woman who eats her cat's leftover food straight from the bowl."

That was only a slight exaggeration of how people saw her at the office. She was her boss's punching bag, and no one considered that her private life could extend much beyond the errands she had to run for David.

Without warning, I cleaved through the crowd toward the pudgy blonde.

"Hello, Chloe!"

She couldn't have been more stunned to see me than if I had been David himself. Her eyes darted through the dimly lit room, looking for an escape.

"Hi . . . Hello."

"It's nice to see you!" I said, beaming.

"Yes . . . ," she stammered.

Grabbing my elbow, she led me away from the little group and begged in a hushed tone:

"Elle, I . . . David can't know that I was here."

"Hmm," I said, deciding to torture her a little longer. "It's true that David isn't very progressive. For him, a couple should be made up of a man and a woman, accompanied, if possible, by blond children."

My dig at Alice was plain.

"I know . . ." She winced. "That's why I'm begging you not to say anything to him."

"Don't worry," I said, smiling widely. "Mum's the word."

Sophia, who was flabbergasted by my initiative, finally joined us with our two glasses.

"So? Are you going to introduce me?"

"Chloe, this is Sophia, my best friend. Sophia, this is Chloe, David's assistant . . . and a regular here, from what I gather."

"Oh, cool!" Sophia cried, eager to play along.

Chloe waved her hand in protest and looked as if she were about to have a panic attack:

"No, no, no . . . It's my first time here," she insisted.

"Now, don't be modest," I countered. "And since Chloe is really nice, in addition to being a lesbian who is so comfortable in her own skin . . ."

She visibly colored, and I thought my provocations might make her explode before I got to my point.

" . . . she's going to give us a complete report on David and Louie's real estate assets. Isn't that nice of her?"

"What?" Our victim choked.

"I think you heard me."

"But . . . I can't do that! If David found out, he would fire me—immediately and without severance."

"Mmm, true . . . ," I agreed, a hint of cruelty in my voice. "That is a risk."

"I don't even know if I can get access to—"

"Of course you can," I interrupted, clapping a hand on her shoulder. "You have access to everything."

My sidekick had a brilliant idea, one that clearly gave us the advantage: she held up her cell phone and took a picture of Chloe and me, two specimens against an incriminating background.

"Awesome!" Sophia cried, still playing her part. "David is going to love it!"

The young blonde saw that she was trapped. Stunned, she pursed her lips to contain her nausea. Then she whispered in my ear again:

"Okay . . . I'll give you what you want. But I want that picture deleted. And you and your friend are going to sign a document promising not to mention my presence here."

"Perfect. You have our word. As for you, don't dawdle. You have twenty-four hours to give me what I want."

"Okay, okay . . ." She was now wearing the servile expression she used at the office. "I'll do my best."

"I don't doubt it."

BLACKMAIL IS UGLY. PERSONALLY, I disapprove of this kind of tactic and of those who use it.

Still, I left the club arm-in-arm with a beaming Sophia and wearing a triumphant smile. Feeling a renewed desire to fight, I burst out laughing, which seemed to expel all my pain.

25

JUNE 5, 2010

Gin and tonic at Calamity Joe.
   Mojitos at La Fourmi.
Vodka at Le Floors.
Coffee and calvados at Rendez-Vous des Amis.

THE END OF THE NIGHT in Pigalle may not have been as exciting as what we'd seen in the small rooms at the club, but all the drinks did momentarily make me forget my torments. Light-headed, I floated in a downy and pleasant ether, screaming with laughter at Sophia's crude jokes and flirting with waiters.

I didn't quite realize I'd taken off my shoes until cobblestones replaced the warm asphalt.

"Are you sure? Do you want me to drop you off?" Sophia asked to be nice as she jumped into a taxi.

"No . . . I want to walk. Go home. You have work tomorrow. I have nothing to do until the evening."

Nothing awaited me that day as the first rays of light shone onto Place de Clichy. No man—mine was lying low like a thug on the lam. No work. Nothing urgent. No projects. Nothing to push me into action. I could have wandered for days on end, an aimless bohemian. No one would have noticed.

It was in this kind of situation that I missed Mom most. I missed her unwavering affection. I longed to hear her soothing voice tell me that everything was going to be okay. As for Louie, I pined for him and his arms, which I wished would take me far away from the present hazards.

THE ROUTE FROM PLACE BLANCHE to the Marais is neither the shortest nor the most recommended at such a late hour. But with my head still spinning and the ground massaging the soles of my feet, I wasn't scared. I wandered calmly through the streets. Paris was waking up, and I was reminded of the flute in a Jacques Dutronc song that Maude used to love.

I was only just beginning to sober up. As I walked down the Rue des Martyrs, purposely avoiding the Hôtel des Charmes, my thoughts began to run wild.

Was it because of the lingering alcohol? Or the scene with the three women that Sophia had pointed out to me? Was it because I missed Louie? In any case, my body and mind felt like they were being pulled in all directions. That dawn, as the city silently opened up to me, I could have given up on everything, namely my promise to myself to uncover Louie's true self before committing to him. I would have set aside all my principles for one hour of raw physical love with him. Sex was our language, and I didn't want us to be deaf and mute to each other anymore. I wanted to talk, talk, talk!

Louie had taught me that torrid encounters inscribe themselves into the memory of a place, into the rock and cobblestones, and that we can draw on that resource. But I was now discovering that the opposite was also true. I was leaving a trace of my desire for him on all the walls, porte cocheres, and windows that I passed. My loins, my thighs, my sex longed for him so much that I could have screamed.

TRACE NUMBER ONE: AT THE intersection of Rue des Martyrs and Avenue Trudaine, I saw us getting on the carousel that sometimes occupied the square's triangle of pavement. I was gripping a horse's hindquarters while he feverishly rammed into me, his graceful hands kneading into the nape of my neck as though he were afraid he might fall.

His sex seemed as hard to me as the metal bars we clung to for balance. The perilous position made his ardor grow. I would have begged him to stop if I hadn't felt the walls of my vagina begin to quiver around him and drip with the first signs of pleasure.

TRACE NUMBER TWO: AT ADDRESS number 54, in the stunning orange-and-green molten-glass window of a dry cleaning shop, I spied myself stretched out over an immense ironing board. Someone had just ironed, and the board was still steaming. The skin of my buttocks was red from the steam, and I opened my thighs for my man to plant himself between them. I gripped the sides of the teetering ironing board as he thrust into my hungry sex. With each movement, we almost fell into the piles of linens.

TRACE NUMBER THREE: AT THE angle of Rue Manuel, a naked Louie kneeled before me. One of his hands snaked up my stomach and reached toward my chest, pinching my nipples. The other hand glided between my legs and inspected the state of my vulva. He started by brushing his fingers across my lips and sopping nymphae, and I could tell from the intensity of his gaze that this gesture gave him great pleasure. He prolonged the movement, testing my desire. His fingers trembled with impatience, but he was waiting for me to seize his hand and urge him to plunge it inside me—I soon did.

The fact that we were in the middle of the street didn't seem to bother him. On the contrary. And as his right hand worked its way in and out of me, his left hand abandoned my breasts and wandered toward my buttocks, where his inquisitive index finger shot toward the bull's-eye of my anus. Reflexively, my sphincter muscles contracted; then they slowly began to relax. Louie's long finger made its way up the narrow canal, which swallowed it up, inch by inch. The two sources of pleasure suddenly became one, and deep inside my stomach, it almost felt as though his hands were touching each other through my flesh. My throat let out an irrepressible wail, and without quite realizing it I fell to my knees.

WHEN I STOPPED DAYDREAMING AND the roads of New Athens no longer seemed like one long fresco of Louie's and my shared passion, I realized that my footsteps had taken me to Rue de la Tour-des-Dames.

I figured that since I was there, I should refill Felicity's food bowl and grab some clothes.

As I was walking up the street, I noticed a man on the other side coming out of one of the houses. I picked up my pace and soon recognized the butler's heavy step. My first surprise was to see him coming out of house number 1, Mars House, and not number 3, Duchesnois House. The fact that he had a key troubled me. How had he gotten it? Did Louie know that

Armand went into his house, or was the butler acting on orders from David? I was reminded of Armand's emotional hug a few weeks earlier, and it occurred to me that the old man might simply have gone to the house next door to water the plants and feed my cat.

My second surprise was that he did not go back to David's house but headed in the opposite direction. After a few jerky steps, he turned right onto Rue de la Rochefoucauld. I followed him from a respectable distance, getting close enough to make out a plastic bag that seemed to contain an assortment of envelopes of different colors and sizes, along with a number of vague objects and foodstuffs.

"Where are you going this early, Armand? What thankless mission have you been tasked with this time?" I whispered to myself.

When he got to Rue Saint-Lazare, he turned left. So as not to draw attention from any passersby on their way to work, I put my shoes back on. Armand turned left again, onto Rue Taitbout, with hardly a sidelong glance at the Art Deco post office building.

A few paces farther on, at 80 Rue Taitbout, an elegant porte cochere opened onto an opulent private passage. Armand disappeared into the opening. When I arrived at the entrance, I read the golden capital letters over the door: SQUARE D'ORLÉANS.

My heart pounding, my breath jagged, I ran on tiptoes to follow him. After a narrow passageway and a first small courtyard, I at last reached the square, which lived up to the flattering descriptions I had read of it online. It was so stunning that I had to force myself to tear my eyes from it in order not to lose Armand. He had reached the gurgling fountain in the center and was walking around the surrounding trees. With all the white buildings and antique colonnades, one could have easily thought oneself in one of London's toniest neighborhoods—Chelsea or Mayfair. The illusion was perfect, and I really felt myself transported.

On the other side of the calm and lush square—which unfortunately had been invaded by a number of luxury vehicles—the man walked under a second gateway and was swallowed by its shadow. Once my eyes had adjusted, I saw him stop in front of a building entrance. He punched in the code or pressed the intercom button—I couldn't say which—and stepped into the foyer with surprising vivacity. By the time I arrived in front of the emerald-green double doors, it was too late. I jiggled the door handle—nothing. Armand had escaped me.

Since I didn't hear anyone in the entryway, and there was no sound of an elevator, I figured he had taken the stairs. That is when I noticed the marble plaque under the archway: *George Sand lived on the second floor of this house from 1842 to 1847—The Society of the Friends of George Sand.* On the other side was hung the number five.

5 Square d'Orléans.

Although I didn't have any proof, I was convinced that Armand was visiting the Romantic author's former apartment. I tried to see if there was any movement on the second floor, but there was nothing. Nothing but the usual sounds when a host greets a visitor: doors opening and shutting, voices, laughter . . .

"FRANÇOIS? FRANÇOIS, IT'S ELLE."

As I slowly made my way back to the square's entrance, more perplexed than ever, I felt a strong need to tell Marchadeau about what I had discovered.

I quickly summarized the facts, including the disastrous

meeting with Louie and his lawyer and my late night out. His thick and raspy voice told me that I had woken him. I, too, was in cruel need of sleep.

"He went to 5 Square d'Orléans. Are you sure about that?"

"Positive."

"Hmm . . . ," he grumbled. "It would seem that everything is beginning to add up."

"How so?"

The journalist was having trouble waking up because he had continued his research late into the night. From his hotel room in Rennes, he had called his most trusted informants, particularly those who had access to tax records, like notaries and tax inspectors, whose commitment to confidentiality tended to be less than inviolable, provided they were given a little incentive.

"Andre Barlet bought George Sand's former apartment on the second floor of 5 Square d'Orléans at an auction in May 1977. The sale was made by Master Cornette de Saint Cyr himself."

The most famous auctioneer in Paris. Even a philistine like me knew that.

"Not long after David was adopted," I noted.

"Exactly."

The corduroy-clad butler had therefore been visiting someone with ties to the Barlet family. But why the devil had that address been used for a dead woman? Who had made that decision? Had David been so morbid in his desire to keep his dead wife's memory alive as to create a kind of mausoleum for her?

François was clear on one point: at no time during his twenty years of friendship with David had the latter ever mentioned such a prestigious asset.

"Did you find out who's lived there since they bought it? Have they rented it out? Or lent it to people?"

"No. The people I managed to contact are only interested in the fiscal implications of property. Not in what people do with an asset once it's been purchased."

"I suppose your contacts helped you make a list of the Barlet family's other properties . . . ," I said, encouraging him to tell me what else he'd learned.

"They did. There are the two properties on Rue de la Tour-des-Dames. According to Andre and Hortensia Barlet's wills, Mars House went to Louie and Duchesnois House to David. That much we knew."

"It's weird if I think about it . . . ," I thought aloud.

"Why?"

"Because Armand once told me that Hortensia Barlet had inherited Duchesnois House from her parents."

"So?"

"So . . . you don't think it's odd that it went to the adopted son, while the house that had been more recently acquired went to their biological son?"

"You're right. That might explain all the quarrels between the brothers regarding family property."

He let out a long sigh, and I heard him leafing through a stack of papers, the rustle of which was interspersed with sounds of him yawning. Finally he spoke again:

"When they died, the Barlets' estate included Brown Rocks in Dinard, the apartment on Avenue Mandel and its dependency . . ."

Namely, Rebecca's small one-bedroom apartment on the tenth floor of the seventies-era building.

" . . . several studios on the Côte d'Azur," he went on, "as well as two other buildings. And, with the exception of the two properties on Rue de la Tour-des-Dames, which I mentioned earlier, all of these properties are managed by a real estate investment trust in which David and Louie own equal shares."

"Really? Two other buildings?"

The breadth of the family's assets was not a surprise to me. What amazed me was that they were the first people I'd met who owned several buildings in Paris. For a girl from Nanterre, that fact was as astonishing and magical as if they had owned the Eiffel Tower or the castle in *Sleeping Beauty*.

"The first of the two buildings is the Freighter on Rue de Miromesnil, which housed the Barlet Group until the tower was built . . ."

I heard him quickly riffling through the pages again. He was clearly annoyed not to find the information he sought.

"And the other building?"

"I'm looking, I'm looking . . . but I'm not finding anything in what was given to me. It's infuriating."

At least my bluff with Chloe wouldn't be useless. I told Marchadeau about my strategy, and we soon hung up, promising to inform each other as soon as either of us learned anything new.

IT WASN'T YET SEVEN. HARASSING Chloe now wouldn't do me any good. I was overexcited despite my all-nighter; I was champing at the bit. To kill a couple of hours, I found a café near Place Saint-Georges that opened early, and ate some pastries.

I dozed off several times—mini siestas that only lasted a minute or two—and I spent the rest of my time watching passersby as they made their way to the metro station.

I noticed a poster for a period drama that had been filmed here the year before on a nearby advertising column. It was going to be released soon under the enigmatic title *The Stranger from Paris*. *The past killed her present*, read the catch phrase. The image above featured the movie's star, an actor wearing a soft hat from the forties, standing next to a woman's shadow. My eyes were drooping, and in an effort to stay awake I thought of one of my last clients when I was a Hotelle. "Wait . . . Didn't I see you five minutes ago in Place Saint-Georges?" he'd asked me.

That was impossible.

He must have been confusing me with someone else.

AT EXACTLY NINE O'CLOCK, I dialed Chloe's number, on the nineteenth floor of Barlet Tower, to which I was sure she was just returning after a trip to the coffee machine. Her morning was no doubt already in full swing.

"Chloe? It's Elle Lorand."

"Elle?" she stammered, paralyzed with fear.

"I was calling for any news . . . And I hope the rest of your night went well. What a place, right?"

The venomous allusion rendered her speechless for a moment; then she breathed into the telephone receiver, her tone stressed:

"I . . . You told me I had twenty-four hours!"

"Well, let's just say that things have gotten more urgent since we last saw each other at Calamity."

"But I can't . . . I'm at work."

"Exactly. You're in the perfect place to find what I'm looking for."

"Okay . . . Okay, I'll see what I can do."

"That's more like it. You have one hour."

"One hour!"

She coughed as if I were squeezing her lungs with my own hands.

"Yes. Otherwise, that wonderful picture that Sophia took last night will be sent to David's phone. With the GPS coordinates, of course . . . to clear up any possible doubt."

Before abandoning her to her task, I told her that I was particularly interested in that second building owned by the Barlet family. Fifteen minutes later, not a second more or less, Chloe sent me a text message whose tone was as cold as an iceberg:

E-mail with complete list of Barlet properties sent to your personal account.

2nd building on intersection of Rue Pigalle and Rue de la Rochefoucauld. Address: 55 Rue Jean-Baptiste Pigalle.

That's all I can do for you.

Please erase the picture and this text message ASAP.

Chloe

I quickly paid my bill, left the café, and as I walked, I reread the message several times.

The intersection of Rue Pigalle and Rue de la Rochefoucauld. Address: 55 Rue Jean-Baptiste Pigalle. I knew that address! I had lived there for a whole year. That enchanted, erotic year that had sealed my love for Louie once and for all.

Yes, that building was quite simply . . .

"The Hôtel des Charmes," I whispered to myself.

26

Imagine a giant bag of marbles released onto an ice-skating rink and you'll have an idea of my thoughts at that moment. My ideas were bouncing around without rhyme or reason and seemed to vanish as soon as they were formed.

THE IDEA THAT LASTED THE longest, before evaporating, was that David perhaps used his birth name, Lebourdais, as an anonymous way to manage the Hôtel des Charmes. Perhaps he'd added the female first name as a way of further masking his identity. The letter *E* that I had seen carved into the locker room in Saint-Broladre resurfaced in my mind like a sign: What if he had simply borrowed this first name from a childhood romance? *E* for Émilie?

That explanation would certainly clear up a few things— why the Hôtel des Charmes had become the place of choice for Hotelles, how Andre Barlet had managed to install cameras in the rooms. But it also raised more questions than it answered.

Louie had lied by omission when he'd neglected to tell me that the hotel where our love had first blossomed actually belonged to him and his brother. And he couldn't have been completely oblivious to the cameras, the one-way mirrors, and all the other spy-related devices in the hotel rooms.

And how could the brothers know about those devices without knowing that they were connected to the video surveillance system in the basement of Mars House? That would make no sense.

I THOUGHT THROUGH THESE IDEAS over and over again, in the hope that the situation would become clearer. Wandering through the streets of New Athens, going through every detail again and again, I felt like Eliza Doolittle in *My Fair Lady* as she tries to iron out her Cockney accent. I thought of questioning Monsieur Jacques, but he would probably cover for his bosses, as he'd always done.

I also refrained from calling the two brothers, contenting myself with a text message to Marchadeau. Had he known that the sheets belonged to his old friend that one time I'd offered myself to him?

His reply to my message was sober. He informed me that he was on his way to Saint-Broladre, which he hoped to explore more thoroughly, this time in the light of day.

I WAS REMINDED OF AN eighties song that Mom used to sing while cooking when I was a kid. The lyrics went, "I don't want to go home, I don't want to go home alone." That was exactly how I felt, only without the colorful and fun vibe of eighties pop songs.

My studio on Rue du Trésor may have been my sanctuary, but I knew before I got there that this time it wouldn't be able to offer me more comfort or answers than the streets of this hostile world. Anyway, I've always liked feeling slightly out of sync and being able to watch as those around me hurry from one place to the next. Inversely, I enjoy rushing through the streets when everyone else is strolling. The Parisian morning was now teeming with activity. As I watched people come and go, their stress visible in their hurried strides—an anticipation of the criticism they would surely soon receive at work or school—I couldn't help but take pleasure, however cruel, in the contrast between them and me.

ONCE AGAIN, MY MAILBOX WAS stuffed with mail. Several manila envelopes were void of postage, a sign that they had been hand delivered. In addition, the postman never arrived before ten or eleven, and that was still hours away.

I shivered momentarily at the thought that Louie had perhaps come looking for me here the night before, after Sophia had convinced me to go out. Perhaps he had come to apologize, to make peace, to reunite our two bodies and soothe the pain of separation. As happened each time I thought of him, a pleasant and painful tingling sensation ran through my body, from my chest to my sex. Louie was in my DNA. He was dormant under my skin, and the slightest thought could reactivate him. My whole body was now agitated with desire.

I CLIMBED UP THE SIX flights of stairs to my apartment as quickly as my tired legs would allow. As soon as I was inside, I ripped open the envelopes. I thought at first that there must have been some kind of mistake, because some of the definitions were of body parts that Louie had already described in his *Alphabet*. But as I impatiently skimmed over the sheets of paper, I realized that there was no mistake.

Rather, Louie had added further elaborations on some of his previous entries. In particular, I noticed that none of this new text spoke of *my* breasts, *my* buttocks, *my* middle. Rather, they described *his* body parts. He expressed his regret through each part of his anatomy. His whole body was asking for my forgiveness. His whole being was beseeching me to relinquish my plans against David. He was forbidding me from entering into contact with his brother. He was begging me not to do it.

Even if his contrite prose reassured me as to his feelings, even if each of my erogenous zones burned with desire for its male counterpart, I knew that I could not back down. If I wanted the two brothers to take off the masks they wore, then I had no choice but to confront them. It wouldn't be easy. The mystery was becoming more elusive the further I advanced through their territory—Brown Rocks, the two properties on Rue de la Tour-des-Dames, the Hôtel des Charmes, and 5 Square d'Orléans. One thing was certain, however: everything was connected. It all went back to one source, somewhere in the meanders of the Barlet family's past.

If I could figure out which of the two brothers was filming the rooms in the Hôtel des Charmes from Rue de la Tour-des-Dames, then the tangle of lies would begin to unravel. My aim was not to determine which of the brothers was good or evil. Louie had done his fair share of wrong. I simply wanted to understand what it all meant for him. And I wanted to help him win at trial.

I WORRIED THAT MY USER name and password to the blog might have been invalidated, but as luck had it, they worked.

User Name: elleandlouie

Password: hoteldescharmes

When I got to the admin page, I wrote the following note, supposedly addressed to Louie:

Rendezvous tonight at ten, in the room of your choice. It will be pitch-black, no light allowed.

I figured David would see the message and assume that the room in question was at the Hôtel des Charmes. He would be tempted to come in person since the darkness would preserve his anonymity. Sophia and her invisible lover were the ones who had given me the idea. And I was counting on Sophia, along with Fred, to catch my ex-fiancé red-handed.

"SO, YOU WANT US TO hide in front of the Hôtel des Charmes and follow David inside?"

She was completely flabbergasted when I described my plan to her over the phone, but she didn't protest for long. Happily for me, she considered this an opportunity to make up for her betrayal of the night before.

"Okay," she agreed, playing along, her tone now conspiratorial. "And what if Louie is the one who shows up?"

"If he sees my message and thinks it's for him, it's up to you guys to intercept him. If you don't manage to do that, then come what may. To be honest, I wouldn't be opposed to a little game of truth between the two brothers."

That was only half true. I feared that kind of confrontation almost as much as I hoped it could shed some light on things.

"And what should we tell Louie to convince him to leave?"

"I don't know. That the fire alarms went off."

"Hmm . . . Not very believable."

"Oh, well, you'll figure it out . . . Improvise!"

Less than an hour later, I received an answer to my invitation. As I'd hoped, David was taking the bait. But he was still wary:

Let's meet somewhere else first. Nine forty-five. At Two Moons. It's near the hotel. Rendezvous in the Jacuzzi.

I called Sophia for help.

"Two Moons!" she exclaimed, laughing nervously.

"What? What about it?"

"Oh, nothing, hon. It's only the biggest swingers' bathhouse in Paris. At this time, it's worse than the metro at rush hour. I mean, in terms of a *discreet* location, it couldn't be worse."

She seemed to know a lot about it. I knew that her private life was wilder than mine, but still, I felt uncomfortable.

David's request to meet there was a game changer. It was public; there would be lots of light. It would be difficult to get him to admit to plotting against Louie. If he appeared at the club, it wouldn't constitute an admission to his having created the blog. But he probably wasn't planning on showing up in person—he didn't want to blow his cover.

As for me, I realized that it would be difficult not to join in the libertine games. My experiences at the Brigantine and in Saint-Broladre during "castle" night had taught me how open and direct people were about sex in those kinds of places. Regulars were forward, to say the least. It only took a few minutes before you found yourself mixed up in a more or less dubious gathering, one hand on someone else's crotch, while another person groped yours. You practically had to defend your own body. And my own lack of experience in this kind of situation made me nervous.

"It's also the cleanest club in Pigalle," Sophia said, trying to reassure me. "Most of its patrons are very respectful couples."

As respectful as the tall redhead in Saint-Malo? I refrained from retorting.

I SPENT THE REST OF the morning and a good part of the afternoon rereading the notes I'd taken for my memoirs, correcting certain passages, checking facts or events that seemed contradictory, comparing my memories from yesterday with the facts of today.

What had motivated me to work on that then, Louie's writing or the fact that Marchadeau had liked my first chronicle? I felt completely uninhibited while typing at my computer. The words came naturally, spontaneously, fluidly. Only the more daring passages gave me pause. Not that I felt embarrassed. On the contrary, I burned to relive those moments. And since I still had to wait for Louie and endure the ardent fire of desire, I ended up feeling so disturbed that I broke my pen. When I write about sex, I can't help thinking—and feeling—that these are sensations I want to experience now, right away, posthaste.

I interrupted my work to give myself the pleasure that circumstance was denying me. I even tried my vibrating panties, a present from Sophia for days of sexual desperation. And this was just such a day. But it tickled and pricked more than it satisfied.

AFTER DINNER, I WAS PUTTING on a midthigh-length dress—without underthings—when something suddenly occurred to me. I still wasn't sure how my plan for the evening would turn out. If David knew that I was in possession of the videos with the Russian girls, or if he suspected that I was, he might decide to erase them that night. I hadn't forgotten that Armand had access to Louie's house.

But I was already running late. So, as I stepped out into the street, I called Sophia again.

"Soph, I have one more favor to ask you."

"If it's to ask Fred and me to go with you to Two Moons . . . my answer is no!"

I burst out laughing. And Lord knows, I wasn't in the mood for jokes.

"Don't worry. I'm a little nervous, but—"

"What do you need?"

"Could you go to the Hôtel des Charmes right now?"

"Right now?" she whined. "But I thought that—"

"Hold on, I'm not done. Go see Ysiam. He has a copy of my keys. Then come to my apartment and get the keys to Mars House. They're on my nightstand."

"And then?"

"And then go straight to Rue de la Tour-des-Dames, to Louie's house, and down to the control room I told you about—"

"In the basement?"

"Yes, in the basement. And then copy the last video recorded on the computer console. It should be easy. The videos are organized according to date. The most recent recordings are at the top of the list."

"But I can't do all that by myself!"

"Bring Fred. I'm sure he has a USB flash drive, which will be useful."

She wouldn't have time to do all that *and* make it back in time to the Hôtel des Charmes to help me out . . .

In other words, I would probably be alone there when the time came. That is, unless Fred flew through the city on his rumbling motorcycle. Or unless I took my time in the temple of Parisian debauchery.

TWO MOONS LIVED UP TO its reputation. That much was clear as soon as I arrived. The entryway was framed by two gigantic black bouncers with shaved heads and clenched jaws. Behind them, two immense Thai- or Indonesian-inspired statues stood guard in front of a carved wood door. Once inside, a small counter welcomed visitors. A not very polite young woman, who avoided eye contact, handed me a white towel, an orange cotton sarong, and a Velcro armband with a pocket of condoms.

"How much do I owe you?"

"Nothing. Today we're open to the public, and it's free for single women."

Without saying another word, she pressed a button that unlocked the red door on the left. Inside, I was simultaneously struck by the heat, the wooden decor, and the relaxed atmosphere of the bar and adjoining room, where several partially naked couples in sarongs were quietly talking over cocktails. The night hadn't even kicked off yet, and the place was already very crowded.

Another staff member, this one a hair smaller than his colleagues outside, noticed that I was new and signaled at me to take the stairs. The second floor featured an impressive locker room, where men and women of all ages, skin colors, and physical appearances were undressing or putting their clothes back on—all with the greatest sense of nonchalance. The atmosphere was relaxed and friendly. Some of the couples were joking with other couples; others were checking one another out and making plans to meet later, in the sauna or the Jacuzzi.

"Are you alone?"

A middle-aged brunette, who was rather plain—save her ample chest that stretched her T-shirt to its limits—stood before me. Behind her, there was a scrawny man. He was shorter than she was, and he had a goatee and a number of tribal tattoos—an effort, perhaps, to give himself some character.

"Yes, I'm alone . . ."

"This is your first time, isn't it?" she said with an exaggerated smile. "If you want, we can show you around. It would be our pleasure."

"Thanks, but—"

"No commitment, of course!" she was quick to add. "I mean, we both think you're really attractive, but we don't want to force anything."

I hadn't even entered the ring, and already two kitten-like wildcats had descended upon me.

"No, that's really nice of you . . . but I have to find my friend."

"Okay," she said, smiling in disappointment. "No worries. We'll be here for at least the next two or three hours. If you want to meet up with us, you can find us in the main room upstairs, at the back."

"Okay . . ."

After getting something to drink at the bar—mango juice—I wandered for a while through the ground floor, a long and narrow room with plenty of alcoves and recesses. Large sofas were placed in the middle of the room, and a gigantic screen offered the more reserved visitors an uninterrupted flow of X-rated videos. I sat on a sofa and enjoyed the scenery for a while. I saw a young couple from the projects, twenty-somethings with tons of piercings and tattoos, chic sexagenarians.

Some passersby shot me meaningful looks. Women were prime targets since there were so few, especially young and pretty ones. That was why I hadn't needed to pay. People undid my sarong with their eyes and stared at my generous curves. I noticed one graying man who seemed particularly interested in me, despite the blond beauty at his side. I didn't get a good look at her until they were walking away. She looked young, and something about her reminded me of someone.

I followed them for a bit, to the giant Jacuzzi surrounded by artificial rocks, where couples were embracing and splashing around. I didn't have a choice anymore: if I didn't want to stick out, I would have to do like everyone else and undress completely. Five or six pairs of male and female eyes delighted in my striptease. Under their gaze, I felt like Venus melting into a steamy whirlpool bath.

A giant sign on the wall formally prohibited sexual practices in the hot tub. Only kissing was allowed, and my neighbors were taking full advantage of that. All around me, people kissed with wild abandon. One couple remained impassive and seemed content with the feeling of the jets against their buttocks: the sixty-something and his blond creature. She stared at me with increasing intensity and ended up slowly crossing the Jacuzzi, fighting against the bubbles and the current.

"Hi, I'm Olga."

That very pronounced Slavic accent . . . That pristine Russian face, that nymph-like, budding body, those tiny breasts—

three or four times smaller than mine . . . She was one of the girls in that hard-core scene with David!

"Hello," I replied, my voice trembling.

"I'm here for our rendezvous."

Behind her, the couple that had tried to pick me up in the locker room was ignoring the sign. The man slipped an eager hand between his partner's thighs. The woman closed her eyes and opened her mouth in pleasure.

Now I understood the reason for this preliminary meeting: David wanted to make sure that I came alone, and he'd sent Olga to escort me to the Hôtel des Charmes.

"Okay . . . Now that you've found me, what's next?"

"He wants you to have a little fun here before following me to the hotel."

To have fun? Or to be humiliated? David had imagined this evening with these depraved merrymakers as a way of ensuring that he had the upper hand. It was clear to me that if I wanted to see David tonight and get him to confess, I would have to accept the rules of his game. At least up to a certain point.

Without asking my opinion, Olga grabbed my hand and pulled me out of the hot tub.

"What about him?" I looked at the man who'd been accompanying her. "Is he staying there?"

"Him? He's a client."

She emerged from the water with incredible ease, her hand still holding mine, and led me upstairs to an area opposite the dressing room. The lighting was more subdued, the temperature hotter, and the majority of those wandering around were completely naked. Like my libertine leader, everyone seemed comfortable and nonchalant.

"The steam room, the sauna," she said, pointing as we made our way down the corridor.

Wooden partitions and doors soon replaced the glass surfaces, opening onto little rooms that reminded me of the ones Sophia had shown me at Calamity. Here again, moucharabies offered direct but discreet views onto what was going on inside. This arrangement also let sound through, and moaning accompanied our passage down the hallway. Groups of curious onlookers were stationed in front of some of the rooms. Some individuals were content to get an eyeful; others, unperturbed, were masturbating.

"Fuck her . . . Fuck the little slut hard!" growled a man holding his penis at the couple behind one screen.

At the end of the hallway, the last room of this maze was unlike the others. It was bigger, and there was no latch to lock the door. Anyone could enter and join in on the action. This was the room for uninhibited participants, swingers without limits. When we arrived, we saw an indistinct pile of bodies. It was a kind of moving tableau. It moaned; it screamed; it blazed like hot lava.

But as I looked more closely, individuals began to emerge out of that mass of heads, penises, cunts. A gigantic man caught my attention. He was ramming into a petite brunette's ass, and as he took this woman doggy-style, he somehow managed to lick the vulva of another woman who was standing next to him. Meanwhile, he had also stuck his whole hand into the vagina of a third woman, who was lying on a slightly elevated mattress. And this last woman, for her part, was swallowing the disproportionately large penis of a very small man.

"Go ahead!" Olga said to me, pointing to the group.

"What?" I stammered.

"You do what you want. You suck, you fuck, you put your hand . . . what you want, but you must go," she ordered me, in a dry and matronly tone.

"What if I don't want to?" I countered.

"If you don't want, no rendezvous at the hotel after . . ."

I understood the ultimatum, turning my gaze back to the group heaving a few feet from where I stood. I timidly resolved to join the group, but I didn't know how to approach this magma of flesh and palpitating desire. The piercing cry of an orgasm—Where did it come from? From whose throat? From which sex?—made me freeze for a moment. Then, I kneeled next to a couple engaged in tame missionary sex.

I shot what I hoped was a congenial look at the man and his partner; then I slipped a hand between the two and tried to reach the woman's tumescent clitoris. I rolled my finger over it, and her reaction was explosive, electric. The woman's hips lifted suddenly, pushing the shiny penis out of her before her partner could thrust it back in. Her entire lower body was shaking. She was on the verge of orgasming, and I felt strangely proud of myself for the effects of my touch. I pressed her little button more vigorously; its elastic resistance tickled the flesh of my middle finger.

"Looks like you found your friends."

The female voice came from behind me without warning, its tone one of relief rather than reproach. I recognized the couple from the dressing room. They were both smiling at me, and the man was masturbating, his eyes boring into mine and his hand holding his penis as though it were a cane or a pipe.

Their intrusion might have made me ill at ease, but I took it as the best of possible outcomes—the one from which I'd emerge mostly unscathed.

Without taking my finger off the girl's clitoris, I turned my torso, raised my eyes toward Monsieur Changing Room, and brought my lips to his purple gland. He quickly understood and thrust his swollen flesh into my mouth. Despite feeling a little disgusted—he tasted bitter and musky—I adjusted my teeth and tongue to better accommodate him.

"I knew we would be friends, you and I," his wife rejoiced out loud.

She took her turn, and after a strange contortion of her body, she lay on her back and put her head beneath my bent legs, her mouth next to my vulva. I wanted to tell her to stop, but her husband's member was in my mouth, and I couldn't speak. With each passing second, the husband became bolder and his thrusts so deep that they almost suffocated me.

These two knew their stuff. The wife soon began licking me with long, vigorous strokes of her tongue. At times, she would cover the surface of my vulva, which welcomed her openly; at others, the tip of her tongue shot into my nymphae or clitoral hood. The fleshy gag invading my mouth muffled my cry when she suddenly planted the entire length of her tongue into my vagina.

Through half-open eyes, I saw Olga, whose discreet smile and batting lashes told me that she approved of my initiative. An idiotic question from Lord knows what talk show suddenly sprung to mind: "Is sucking cheating?" And what about being sucked? How unfaithful was I being to Louie by consenting to all this?

I was appreciating Madame Changing Room's know-how when suddenly she straightened and pointed an authoritative finger toward my sex. She had apparently decided to offer me to her husband.

But I wouldn't let them decide for me. Letting myself be taken was out of the question. Abandoning the two women, I faced the man. I hooked my arms around his thighs and thrust my head toward his pubis with increasing violence. I continued until I could feel the tip of his penis jamming into the deepest recesses of my throat. He was a prisoner of my movements. I was going so fast, with such intensity, that he couldn't have left my mouth even if he'd wanted to.

"Slow down, dear," Madame Changing Room advised. "At that pace, you'll exhaust him in two minutes!"

Her prophecy soon came true. In a few moments, after a couple of contractions, the first drops of a hot and viscous geyser formed on the tip of his glans. Reflexively, I stepped back, and the man's semen spurted through the air, a few drops landing on my cheeks and lips.

"Oooooh . . . ," he moaned. "You give really good head."

I took the compliment with a smile and stood, massaging my sore knees. Then I left the satisfied couple and met Olga.

"That's done . . . You got what you wanted. Can we go now?" I asked with a defiant look.

27

Anger mixed with frustration makes for a strange feeling. I hadn't come. I'd complied with his orders. I was furious. Not so much with those who had enjoyed my favors as with myself. I could have, I *should* have, refused such depraved conditions.

I FOLLOWED THE BLOND OLGA, her slender silhouette barely clad in a tiny, transparent white dress. With one hand, she was tapping a message into her phone. I assumed she was signaling David. I had passed his test, and his accomplice had completed her mission. The hour of true combat could now begin. We could enter the ring.

Pigalle was teeming with tourists and provincials, who formed a cosmopolitan and heterogeneous crowd. Indeed, the neighborhood was a true melting pot.

"It's cool here, isn't it?" Olga asked, suddenly affable. "I like all the different people!"

Was I to understand that she liked interracial penetration?

In any case, that's what all the males ogling her seemed likely to suggest as foreplay.

I kept my wicked thoughts to myself and checked to see that my camera was still in my bag, its battery charged.

As we left Boulevard de Clichy and rounded Place Pigalle, we passed in front of the imposing facade of the Folie's Pigalle, a nightlife institution on the Right Bank. All that was left before we reached our destination was a short walk down Rue Jean-Baptiste Pigalle. It would only take two minutes, if that.

Everything was happening so fast, I thought to myself as we started down the street's gentle slope. There was no way Sophia and Fred would be able to meet me in time. The situation was now beyond my control, and as I stepped into the small square below the Hôtel des Charmes, the one with three spindly charm trees, I almost felt as I had on my first visit there more than a year and a half before.

Each of my steps was heavy with pain, disappointment, and memory. To think that it wasn't so long ago that I had never set foot in this neighborhood! I had undergone so many new experiences here . . . But one stood out from the rest: here, I had experienced my first time with the man of my life.

"Are you okay? Are you sick?" Olga asked, worried, noticing that I was lagging.

My plans here tonight might betray not only Louie but also my own memories. But my thirst for truth prevailed over all else; in spite of myself, it was leading me toward decisive revelations.

"I'm fine . . . Let's go inside."

As we made our way through the lobby, Monsieur Jacques barely raised his eyes from his registers. Now that I knew the true identity of his employers, I understood the concierge's attitude toward me—something between guile and deference. Ysiam was not at his usual post by the elevator, and we took it by ourselves to the top floor of the building. I was probably least familiar with its blood-red corridor, having only been there once, to the Marie Bonaparte room. For me, it retained its mystery, giving free rein to my unconscious, which wandered beyond my control, as in its own garden.

Olga ordered me to turn off my phone. After verifying that I had done what I'd been told, she led me to the door facing the Marie Bonaparte. Unlike the other doors, this one was not red but black, and as I stepped into the room, I tried not to see that as a bad omen. As I had commanded, the room was pitch-black, thanks in part to a heavy curtain placed in front of the entryway.

My breath grew heavy. With each passing second, my inhalations became more febrile, my exhalations shorter and more jagged. My legs were shaking. In spite of myself, my chest heaved and my nipples hardened.

Olga left without a word. Several minutes passed, and I took advantage of this precious moment of respite to go over my plan again: let David enter the room so that he wouldn't suspect anything; undress myself and invite him to do the same; touch his most sensitive zones, from what I could remember (torso, pelvis, scrotum, glans); wait until he was sufficiently excited; finally, take out my camera and quickly take a picture of the blog's true author.

A simple plan, impossible to mess up. Unstoppable.

MINUTES WENT BY AS SLOWLY as molasses. Waiting was torture. Was David going to stand me up? Had Olga's report awakened his suspicions? Ten minutes had gone by, and I was about to leave the room when a faint movement in the shadows made me jump. My pupils may have been dilated, but I couldn't see a thing. I could have sworn, however, that I'd noticed something move in one of the corners . . . Suddenly, thundering music filled the room, hitting me as hard as a punch in the face. Whereas Louie was always looking for ideal erotic music, David was clearly trying to unsettle me with this song, with its violent electric guitar chords and its insane drumbeat. Death metal, hard-core death, death something or other . . . It was morbid and brutal and seemed to be setting the scene for carnage rather than love.

A second later, four shadows emerged from the four corners of the room, as if from the sonorous fury itself, and came toward me. I sensed their rapid motion, but before I could react, they had already grabbed hold of my wrists and ankles with an iron grip. I screamed and fought, but they quickly lifted me off the ground as though I weighed less than a wisp of straw. Leather cuffs were then wrapped around my four limbs, and I heard a metallic click. When they released me, I found my body stretched and suspended three feet above the floor. I felt like a fly caught in a web. All that was missing was the spider who, I was sure, would come out and eat me.

Their mission accomplished, the four silhouettes exited, indifferent to my desperate cries:

"You can't leave me here like this! I called the cops!"

I knew that bluffing was useless. My last hope was Sophia, and I had sent her on a mission impossible. I reminded myself of the time I thought her errands should take. Best-case scenario, she could arrive around . . . eleven thirty. And if my calculations were correct, it was now about eleven, which left thirty minutes during which David could do with me as he pleased.

As if sensing my fears, David entered the room. I would have been incapable of identifying someone by sight at that moment, what with the tears streaming down my cheeks. I recognized him by his cologne. Then by his voice, which was one in a thousand, and which sounded exactly like that eternally young French actor . . . But this wasn't Gérard Philipe. David wasn't Le Cid or Fanfan la Tulipe. He was just the man who had wanted to destroy my fiancé and trick me in the most abject manner imaginable. David, my tormentor.

"Well, look what we have here."

"What?" I bellowed, trembling, paralyzed with pain and fear. "What's happening?"

"The two of us, in this hotel room. God knows how many guys you've fucked here," he sneered, insulting me. "Maybe all of Paris. But there was only one who was foolish enough not to have had a bite of you here—"

"Fuck! What do you want?"

I squirmed as if possessed, but my contortions only succeeded in tightening the leather bonds, which dug into my skin and tore my hyperextended muscles.

He didn't reply. I heard him rummaging through the room, then felt him draw near me, between my legs.

"To enjoy the view, for starters."

"What?"

I was frozen with fear when a flash from a camera—*my* camera, I supposed—blinded me.

"You're completely insane!" I yelled, terrified. "Sophia and Fred are going to be here any second."

"With pleasure. Your little friends are most welcome! I'm even surprised that they didn't come with you."

Surprised? How could he be surprised? He hadn't known anything about our plans.

"I have to say that your accomplices disappoint me," he continued in the same condescending tone. "Yves knew from the start that someone had broken into the system. He even made your weekend hackers believe they'd gotten into my machine undetected."

So David had known all along that I was on to him. That was how he'd been able to avoid my trap. And to prevent my friends from showing up and helping me, he'd taken the precaution of sending me to Two Moons with Olga.

My body swayed in my trap, which sent an incredible shooting pain through my limbs.

"David, this is really bad," I said, hopelessly trying to reason with him. "Kidnapping, torture . . . This won't turn out well for you."

"I only see a game between two consenting adults, and it's not very different from the other games you've played in this very hotel with Louie. And so willingly."

"I'm sorry . . . ," I begged. "Is that what you want to hear? Okay . . . I'm sorry for everything: the failed wedding, the rendezvous here with your brother . . . Everything!"

The din of the music forced us to scream, and it occurred to me that the soundproofing in the room must have been perfect. Otherwise, someone would have heard us.

I didn't realize it, but he'd moved and was now standing by my side. He whispered into my ear:

"You don't understand . . ."

"Understand what?"

Then, slowly, he began to run his hand over my body, which was pulled as taut as a wire. Idly, almost painfully, it swept over me, from my thighs to my lips.

"I could find a thousand ways to torture the two of you and it still wouldn't make up for Louie's treachery."

My stretched limbs were pulling on my diaphragm and compressing my lungs. I was having trouble breathing. Speaking became another form of torture, and each word tore into my chest.

"I repeat . . . I'm sorry about our wedd—"

"But I don't give a damn about our wedding!" he boomed, cutting me off. "Do you really think that a man like me has trouble finding a suitable wife? Seriously, Annabelle, just look at you!"

He broke into a cruel laugh.

"Elle, honestly . . . If you think that my ego can't handle being rejected by a little girl from *Nanterre . . .*"

He spat this last word with all the contempt he could muster. I thanked heaven that Mom had never met this horrible individual.

"You've got it all wrong, poor girl! I whistle, and girls much prettier and smarter than you come running! Do you understand?"

He started whistling, as though a battalion of subservient beauties were about to step through the door and prostrate themselves at his feet. Drunk with pride, he was pathetic, ridiculous.

"Okay," I said, as calmly as possible. "So what's your problem? How exactly has Louie betrayed you?" Thanks to Rebecca, I knew of at least one way, and it was perhaps the most painful betrayal: his brother's secret relationship with Aurora.

"Come on! Tell me! I have nothing better to do right now. We have all the time in the world."

I surprised even myself by discovering that I still had the resources to provoke him. But he didn't appreciate my courage.

He must have pressed a button of some sort because the music suddenly stopped. And from where he was now standing, a few paces closer to the door, he whispered softly, in a kind of lament, the timbre of his voice strange:

"He ruined everything . . . He always has to soil everything that's mine. That's all. Louie only knows how to do one thing: to steal what others possess, or to demean what he can't have."

"Aurora? Is that it? Are you talking about Aurora?"

The rush of his footsteps toward the door was his only reply. He knocked twice on the door behind the curtain, opened it softly, but instead of leaving the room as I had expected, he stepped aside to let pass several silhouettes, about three or four—no doubt the individuals who had put me in such an uncomfortable position.

I silently hoped that they would untie my limbs, but instead they violently grabbed my breasts, buttocks, and thighs, kneading and beating them like bread. I was the dough in their childish games. A woman to mold.

My sense of panic was turned up a notch when I realized that David was about to leave the room and effectively abandon me to the whims of his wild and ruthless minions. It was obvious that this erotic fantasy was about to turn into a gang rape.

However, the first thing to present itself between my legs was cold and as hard as steel. Another thing that surprised me was the religious silence in which these anonymous people worked. They didn't insult me or swear at me. There were no exhortations to fuck me harder, faster, to humiliate me. They weren't being ritualistic. Rather, it seemed that they were carefully following a list. An instruction manual.

"David! David, no! Come back!" I screamed as loudly as my aching lungs could manage.

The thing drove into me, but it was less painful than I had feared. It was a midsized dildo, and one of the faceless hands was pushing it mechanically in and out of me. There was no concern for how I reacted. I was an object.

When a monstrous dildo came to replace it, pushing aside my nymphae and driving into my vagina, I barely even felt it.

I was numb, and I believe I must have lost consciousness.

28

JUNE 6, 2010

When I awoke, I found myself in the Josephine, my beloved room one. I was as surprised to be there as I was to feel alive. I stretched my limbs, my head heavy and my muscles sore. I moaned. How had I gotten here? Who had brought me? And in what state? If several men had taken advantage of me in that dark room, no doubt for several hours, then why was my vagina the only part of my body that wasn't hurting?

I NOTICED SOUNDS COMING FROM the adjacent bathroom. Only then did I understand that I was not alone, and that the person performing his ablutions had spent the night with me. I prepared myself for anything, for David or one of his henchmen to emerge, a triumphant smile on his face. Who could it be? What would David have considered to be the most humiliating option for me?

But what worried and anguished me most was that I was still a prisoner. Had Fred and Sophia abandoned me? Had someone convinced them to stand aside when they'd arrived at the Hôtel des Charmes?

A final and terrible idea crossed my mind: Were they working for David? Had he bought them? What was loyalty for Fred compared to his job at BTV?

Suddenly, the sound of water became louder. The mystery man was now taking a shower, and the sound of his whistling floated toward me. I could have sworn I recognized the same notes that David had whistled the night before in the darkness of his torture chamber.

It made sense that David would have returned to abuse his thing. That is, unless he thought that abandoning me to a third party, like when I was a Hotelle, would be a better way of sexually debasing and objectifying me—making me into a gadget to be passed around between men, like any other toy.

I wasn't sure which of these two possibilities would be worse.

"David?" I called out in a hushed tone. "David?"

When at last I heard the bathroom door creak open, I yelped in surprise. Perhaps too sharply. Part of me must have thought he was only a dream. The stranger froze, hesitating as to whether to come to my side. I imagined his hand tense on the door handle, his breath suspended.

After several interminable seconds, the bathroom door finally opened. The body that appeared before me was naked, and the first thing I noticed was a budding rose tattooed over a freckled shoulder.

"Louie?" I gasped.

There he was, facing me, his sex half erect, a smile smeared across his face. A smile, but I couldn't tell if it expressed contentment or worry, empathy or severity.

Stunned, I sat up in the Josephine's bed.

"No, no, no . . . ," I cried, shaking my head, horrified and trembling. "Don't tell me—"

He rushed toward me, his expression tender.

"Shh, darling. Everything is all right."

"What are you doing here? What . . ."

He wedged himself next to me, pressing my side against his soft and warm chest. He rubbed my shoulders, my neck, my hair. I could have stayed like that forever, being cradled by his reassuring presence and his smell of lavender and vanilla.

But I hadn't forgotten our fight. I hadn't forgotten that he'd forbidden me from searching into David and his past. The last time we had taken leave of each other, we had both been angry. And then the next time I saw him it was after David had kidnapped me. I deserved an explanation, I think . . .

"I didn't see your message on the blog until last night at eleven," he said.

"It wasn't meant for you."

"I know. But I was worried that your trap wouldn't work. David is always at least a step ahead. When we were little, he always won at chess."

I found his admission of weakness touching, and I invited him to continue with a more conciliatory look.

"I knew that in order to meet your conditions, he would probably draw you up to the top floor. The rooms there are the only ones in the hotel that can be made pitch-black."

"And then?"

"David had already left by the time I arrived. As for the guys who were there, they didn't put up much of a fight. They were simply S and M fetishists whom David had found in clubs and generously paid. They were interested in money, not trouble."

He had saved me from them. And his account fit with the impression I'd gotten that David's henchmen were simply doing their job.

"Did they . . . ?"

He guessed what I wanted to ask.

"No . . . They didn't have time. But if you want, we can file a report for attempted rape."

I shook my head weakly.

He placed a tender hand on my forehead and concluded, sincerely relieved:

"You seem better."

"Yeah . . . except for my wrist and arm," I said, pouting. "And what about Fred and Sophia?"

My question seemed to surprise him. He squinted his brown eyes, the thin lines around which intensified his gaze.

"They weren't there."

"Are you sure?"

"Positive. Or they'd left already."

And left me to my torturers?

"What time did you arrive?"

"I don't remember. Not before eleven thirty."

The time when my two friends should have been coming to my rescue. And if they had arrived after Louie, they probably would have asked Monsieur Jacques about me, and he would have told them where Louie had taken me.

If they never showed up at the front desk, then . . .

A shiver of dread ran through my whole body. Fred. Sophia. I couldn't believe that they would betray me and leave me in the hands of my enemy.

It was too much. I needed calm, quiet, time to reflect.

"Could you take me home, please?"

"To your studio?" he asked, surprised. "You don't want to come back to the house?"

Contrary to what I had been expecting, the previous night

hadn't revealed anything new about David or Louie. And I wouldn't learn what I needed to know to untangle this web if I fell back into Louie's arms—as tempting as that was.

I wanted Louie more ardently than ever. But I wanted him free and proud. I wanted him by choice. I wanted him un-shackled from everything past and present that was holding him down. I saw that, despite Louie's love for me, he was, like his brother, a slave of their fraternal feud. He was trapped in his role, by both bitterness and old memories.

If I agreed to go back to Mars House, I would probably never leave its comfort and tenderness. I would be intoxicated by sex and passion, and I would give up on ever learning the answers I still so desperately wanted to know.

HIS TAXI DROPPED ME OFF on Rue du Trésor. Our kiss was brief but filled with passion. I took it as a promise of our future reunion.

As I reached for the door handle, he stopped me and drew me toward him. His arms wrapped around my waist, forming a delicious prison. It took all my will to tear myself away from him.

"I can walk you up . . . ," he suggested, tempting me. "Just for a minute."

He could give me all the comfort I needed so much right then. And make love to me.

But once again, I chose truth over desire.

"No, really," I said, refusing his offer with a forced smile. "I need to be alone."

Oh, I would have sold my soul to spend a few hours with him. But it wasn't time yet. And I couldn't find the words to explain that to him.

"Rest well, then," he whispered.

"Yeah, you, too."

I was closing the door of the dark sedan, the latest in flashy German luxury vehicles, when I thought I heard him softly add:

"You especially. You're going to—"

Me especially? What did he mean by that? What was he predicting? What had he been saying when the door had slammed shut? You're going to . . . need it?

I wanted to ask him and moved to reopen the door, but the powerful vehicle was already speeding off, leaving me there, distraught, on my strip of cobblestone.

WHEN I RETURNED TO MY studio, I thought to turn on my phone, which I had switched off under Olga's orders the night before. Its battery was low, and I had to recharge it for about ten minutes before I could consult my messages: one voice mail and two e-mail messages.

The first was from Sophia. Her voice sounded strange, perhaps altered by stress or fear: "Elle, it's me . . . I mean, us. I'm at the police station with Fred. I don't have much time to talk. We did what you asked. But as we were leaving, two police cars arrived to search Louie's house. We were arrested for breaking and entering, attempted theft, and a few other awesome charges . . ."

The charges were absurd: they shouldn't have been arrested for breaking and entering since they'd had my key. As for theft, I highly doubted that the police found the CD or the flash drive that they'd lifted. "I don't know when we'll be able to leave," she went on. "I tried to contact Louie but couldn't reach him. In any case, we won't be able to meet you as planned. I'm . . . I'm sorry. I'll call you back when I know more."

I was about to call Zerki and ask him to help my friends when I noticed who had sent the two e-mails. Marchadeau, who had been silent for twenty-four hours, was finally resurfacing. I figured he must have put his hands on something important. The two messages were from the night before. They'd been sent one after the other, a few minutes past midnight.

Strangely, they both had the same subject—"Found this in a locked box in the basement of Saint-Broladre"—and the body of both messages was blank. What could he have found in the dust and rubble of that old orphanage? A box in a basement . . . ? Was it possible that some of the archives had been abandoned and left there this whole time?

I feverishly opened the attachment, which took a couple of seconds to load. I zoomed in on the document until the text was large enough to read. The header indicated that this was a Saint-Broladre intake form dated March 11, 1972, for a little girl who was barely two years old. Her birth name was Émilie Jeanne Laure Lebourdais. Born June 1, 1970, in Dinard.

I repeated her name to myself several times, as if to convince myself of what I was seeing.

"Émilie Lebourdais . . ."

Like the woman who received her mail at the Hôtel des Charmes. Émilie like the letter *E* carved into the locker room at the orphanage.

"Émilie Lebourdais . . . David Lebourdais."

The two names whirled through my head. The logical conclusion of this information was tickling my cortex, which was about to explode, but one piece of the puzzle was still missing.

"David Lebourdais, Émilie Lebourdais . . . the same surname. Admitted on the same day: March 11, 1972. A brother and a sister."

Saying it out loud felt like slowly uncovering a secret.

The little Émilie he'd so adored, the little Émilie who was so dear to his heart, whose name played an important role in the hierarchical structure at the Hôtel des Charmes . . . That little girl was his sister. What had become of Émilie Lebourdais when her older brother, the young David, had become the Barlet family's second son in November 1976? Under what new identity had she reappeared?

Alas, the intake form didn't say.

Breathing hard, I opened the attachment in the second message from Marchadeau. It was slow to load—the file was probably bigger. As it slowly appeared, its colors emerging, I recognized the image: it was the picture of the Christmas tree. But this time, it was the original. No one had scratched it out. It was intact.

I could now see the missing face, and the pretty little girl standing next to David in her plaid dress wasn't unfamiliar to me.

Because, despite the gap of twenty years, despite the mystery that still engulfed her, that face was my face. Or, rather, it was Aurora's face.

Or, rather, it was Émilie Lebourdais's face.

David's sister. And his former wife.

29

Oh, staggering power of screens. Oh, maddening magic of television. Oh, numbing effect that washes my worries away and reboots my stressed-out mind.

My first reflex after learning this chilling new information was to turn on the television and let myself be lulled by the insipid drone of morning programming. I idly flipped through the channels, only interrupting my veg-out session to leave a message for Zerki, asking him to help Sophia and Fred out of the mess into which I'd gotten them. I clicked through music videos and inane shows and twenty-four-hour news channels.

I caught a brief mention of the Barlet Group–GKMP merger between two sports segments. A bald economic reporter spoke of the positive effect that this announcement had already had on the share prices of the two companies: "The Barlet Group's share prices are up 9.7 percent since May 1, and GKMP's shares have seen a jump of 11.2 percent over the same period, which has been its largest percentage of growth over the past three years . . . Suffice it to say, the markets are welcoming this merger with open arms."

I had a completely different kind of equation on my mind: $E + A + D =$ the truth. Three separate identities, but only two physical people. I wondered if there existed a mathematical symbol to express uncertainty with respect to one of the elements of a formula.

WHEN AT LAST I EMERGED from my torpor, I turned to my laptop computer for answers. As I did so, the thought crossed my mind that Yves the computer genius could have easily hacked into my e-mail account.

I typed "Émilie Lebourdais" into Google and was not surprised that, like "Aurora Delbard," the name offered few results. Only one was really relevant. It was a link to a real estate investment trust called Tour-des-Dames, which listed Mademoiselle Émilie Lebourdais as one of its minority shareholders, the majority shareholders being David and Louie Barlet.

It was a small discovery, but it suggested one important fact:

"She's still alive . . . ?" I asked myself, my voice trembling.

Why else would she appear as a shareholder? A quick check confirmed that the page had been updated at the beginning of the year. The inclusion of her name on the site as a minority shareholder in the Barlets' real estate investment trust could therefore only mean one thing: Émilie Lebourdais, alias Aurora Delbard, was still in this world, as of January 2010.

Like a missing pixel in a picture, this piece of information shed light on the "Delbarlet" family portrait. If the people who had coined that name had only known how fitting it was!

That was why all the accounts of Aurora's death were so contradictory.

That was why Florence Delbard had been so uneasy about discussing her daughter's death.

That was why my former client had thought he'd seen me on Place Saint-Georges—he had really just run into my doppelganger.

Although this revelation shed light on matters, there was still so much I did not know. I wondered who could have removed Émilie-Aurora's adoption papers from Social Services; who among the guests at Aurora and David's wedding on June 18, 1988, knew that they were witnessing an incestuous union; and why so many of those involved in this family drama had pretended that Aurora had drowned herself.

In the midst of this bewildering maelstrom, some questions were more pressing than others: If Aurora was still alive and living near Rue de la Tour-des-Dames, in Paris, then why had David and Louie spent all these years searching for her double? Everything that I'd believed was unraveling.

If Aurora was still alive, then who was I to them?

One last thought haunted me more than the idea of an insane love affair between two orphaned siblings, more than the madness of a man marrying a woman of his own flesh and blood in order to repair childhood wounds: the thought that Louie, *my* Louie, was somehow involved . . . But what had been his role?

Rebecca had told me that Louie had been the first person to suspect David and the young Aurora's prior relationship. He knew their secret, then. And perhaps David had organized the whole spectacle in order to hide his sister and wife from the world. But had Louie helped?

It seemed likely. As I had now suspected for some time, the events of December 25, 1989—the circumstances surrounding the "fatal accident"—had resulted in an agreement between the two Barlet brothers. But why? How could Louie, whose sincere love for Aurora at the time I did not doubt, have agreed to such a pact? Instead, shouldn't he have done everything in his power to stop that unnatural union and take the woman he loved from his brother?—from *their* brother, since, in the eyes of the law, David was as much Aurora's brother as he was Louie's?

What's more, their fraternal relationship had quickly deteriorated after the accidental death of their parents, and Louie no doubt had had thousands of opportunities—and at least as many good reasons—to speak out and reveal the couple's unspeakable truth to the world. I imagined the media sensation that that would have created: *David Barlet (CEO of the Barlet Group): incest, lies, death . . .*

Meanwhile, Louie could have gotten back together with the woman he loved and regained his rightful place at the head of the Barlet empire.

The fact that he hadn't said anything made no sense. All's fair in love and war, isn't it? And I couldn't believe that they had come to some kind of truce that had lasted twenty years. Neither one had let the past go. In fact, there must have been a reason why neither brother had considered getting remarried, despite both having engaged in countless conquests—that is, until I came into their lives.

If they had both managed to uphold some sort of pact, it had been in the service of mutual interest, perhaps a terrible secret. I didn't see any other possible explanation. But what was that secret?

I WAS INCAPABLE OF VISUALIZING this tentacular problem as a whole, so I consulted the picture of the Christmas tree on my phone, hoping for inspiration.

"Monsieur and Madame Lebourdais," I said to myself.

I now knew the identity of the two anonymous adults. They had to be Émilie and David's parents. The picture had probably been taken a few weeks or months before the siblings had been admitted to Saint-Broladre. What had happened to the Lebourdais couple between Christmas of 1971 and March 1972? How had their children wound up in an orphanage in such a short amount of time?

It was too soon to formulate a hypothesis. I simply reviewed the elements that their adoptive parents had been able to provide me. Florence Delbard had told me to my face that she didn't know anything about Aurora's life before her arrival at the orphanage. But could I trust her? She had pretended that her daughter was dead—to the point of making fake visits to the cemetery! Was it possible that she didn't know?

I LOST MYSELF IN THE dizzying forest of signs for the rest of the morning. Everything was taking on new meaning. Even Louie's latest tattoo project seemed like a telltale sign. *S* and *F* framing the rocks where Aurora had supposedly died. But the letters no longer sounded to me like the motto "Semper fidelis," but like the Latin for sister and brother: "soror" and "frater."

All of this information was churning through me like a chemistry experiment gone wrong. My head was full of opaque froth. The elements were there, right before me, but I couldn't make sense of anything. Whom was I to believe? Whom should I call for help?

Louie? He would deny the evidence. Rebecca? She would try to hide and evade the truth. Sophia? Marchadeau?

A phone call decided for me.

"Jean-Marc Zerki speaking. Louie told me about your friend's troubles. The girl I met the other day."

Captain Lechère must have told Louie that his team had come across two surprise guests while they were searching Mars House.

"Happily," the lawyer said placidly, "the police found no evidence of breaking and entering. Nor were they able to prove that your friends had destroyed evidence, which is what the police had suspected at first, considering your relationship with the two."

Destroying evidence, no. But removing certain things from the police investigation was another matter. And I hoped Fred had managed to transfer the file onto his flash drive before they'd been caught!

"Are they going to be released?"

"In theory, this afternoon."

"Do you know which files Lechère's men found on the computer console?"

"Unfortunately, not yet. And they've cordoned off the house until the first hearing. We won't have access to the computer until then."

That wasn't good news for Louie's legal troubles. Zerki's entire offensive strategy relied on the infamous Russian videos. Without them, it would be much more difficult to show David's culpability and exonerate his older brother.

I SLEPT DEEPLY FOR THE next several hours before I grew restless and my dreams strange. Louie's pages were scattered throughout my small apartment, and in my dream they suddenly gathered together, as though moved by an invisible wind. Each page had taken the shape of the organ it described, forming our two bodies in a stunning paper construction.

Since we could not physically make love, we would "make words."

BUT SOON, EACH DESCRIPTION VENTURED away from its neighbors, and rather than seeking out its counterpart of the opposite sex—Louie's pectorals against Elle's chest, for example—as one might have expected, it followed its strongest desire and sought out whichever body part it presently found most tempting. Louie's mouth glued itself to my buttocks, one of my nipples stroked his scrotum, and our genitals united in a surprising feat of levitation. Dismembered as we were, the possibilities were endless. We were no longer limited by the natural movement of our joints or our degree of flexibility. The magic of writing transformed us into erotic acrobats.

Is it what I would have wanted if Louie had actually been present with me in that room? The tender tip of my tongue titillated the button of his anus, which was so sensitive that even the slightest touch made the paper sphincter contract. A rimming for my man with the rose.

I could have sworn I heard the sound of flying papers rustling with ecstasy. When it couldn't take it anymore, his nose charged toward my vulva. Playing with it like a toy, the nose caressed my nymphae and the area surrounding my lips with its straight and noble bridge and its nostrils. Then, without warning, its slightly curved tip shot into the entrance of my vagina. Hungry for my scent, it dived as deeply into me as it could. The small member in the middle of his face thrust in and out of me, sometimes disappearing completely between my thighs, until I softly and sweetly came. A pure and abundant liquid flowed out of me . . . It was ink.

Another phone call tore me from these pleasant dreams. The sheets of paper all fell at once, resuming their usual inert position.

"Shit! Thank you, God, you picked up!"

"Soph, is that you?"

"I'm with Fred. We're just leaving the station in the 9th Arrondissement."

"How are you?"

"Like I usually am after a night being grilled by a couple pervy cops and an alcoholic."

"Crap, Sophia. I'm sorry."

"Next time you need a favor, forget I'm your best friend, will you?"

I knew that if another opportunity presented itself, she wouldn't hesitate for one second. But I understood her frustration.

"What happened, exactly?"

"What I said in my message. Except that before we were nabbed, we managed to copy the video onto Fred's phone. They didn't think we'd be able to transfer it there! They didn't even look at our smartphones."

"That's crazy."

"Right . . . These super cops are a far cry from *CSI*."

"And what about the rest?"

"We erased everything. Neither David nor the police will be able to access anything. The only images that are left from the computer system are the ones we have."

"Perfect!" I exclaimed. "Soph . . . I don't know how—"

"Thank Fred. Without that geek, the cops would have gotten their hands on everything."

How ironic that the fate of my new man was in my ex's hands . . .

"We're about to meet Zerki at Café des Antiquaires," Sophia went on. "We have to give him the file we took. Then we're headed to my place, where we'll shower and fuck like rabbits . . . Then we're going to sleep for two days solid."

"That seems like a good plan to me," I said, laughing softly.

"And you? You okay? The lawyer told me that Louie played the providential hero."

"Yeah. He . . ."

Lied about everything. Covered for his incestuous brother. Gave up the woman he loved for David. Jeopardized his union with his new love—me.

But how could I say all that over the phone?

" . . . he was great," I sputtered.

OF THAT MUCH I WAS sure. He was great. I just didn't know how I fit into the equation. Had he done it all for me? Was his heart really available? When Aurora was dead, or when I thought she was, she had cast a shadow over our relationship. But now that she was alive . . . wasn't she more of a rival?

At that moment, my fiancé's name appeared on my phone's screen.

"I have another call," I informed my friend. "It's Louie."

"Answer."

"No, that's okay. He'll call back."

He did call back, several times over the course of the afternoon. But I refused to answer his urgent messages. In the end, he gave up, his calls first becoming more sporadic, then ceasing altogether.

WHAT WOULD MOM HAVE SAID in such circumstances? What simple and affectionate solution would she have whispered into my ear, she who always knew exactly how to help?

Go home, dear.

Maude Lorand had an adage for every possible situation in life. But for her there was one saying that fixed everything: "Go home." Take refuge; go back to the fountainhead. Find yourself again, *you*.

A tear formed in the corner of my eye when I remembered that I'd sold her house in Nanterre. *My* house. And that now my only home was this studio, with its impersonal walls, in a city where I would always be the "girl from Nanterre," as David had put it. Now that the excitement of independence had worn off, I wondered if I would ever really feel at home here.

"Go home . . . ," I repeated to myself out loud.

Suddenly, everything made sense.

I bolted upright in my bed, my sheets still damp beneath me from my feverish slumber.

30

June 7, 2010

"Do you still live at 5 Square d'Orléans in the 9th Arrondissement in Paris?" The woman's voice from the Mutaliz helpline was still ringing in my ears.

GOING THERE BY MYSELF WAS probably a terrible idea. I should have, in the following order: (1) demanded an explanation from Louie, David, or even Rebecca; (2) followed Armand back into the building on his next visit; (3) in any and all cases, enlisted Sophia to be my faithful Sancho—she never hesitated to tilt at windmills.

Why didn't I do any of that? Even today, with hindsight, I couldn't say. No doubt because we can only face our biggest fears alone. Like heroes in horror movies, we defy logic, and instead of calling the police or waking our spouse or turning to the neighbors for help, we go down to the basement to meet the monster alone, and the monster ends up devouring us—everybody knows that.

I left on foot, alone, with the image of Mom in her kitchen on Rue Rigault to keep me company, a Maude who kept whispering the same words to me over and over again—"Go home, dear." After two days of indecisive torpor, I was now headed to the neighborhood of the Église de la Trinité.

A pleasant evening was setting in over the capital. A storm had cleared the air, and the atmosphere was conducive to strolling and enjoying the scents of the season—flowers, light perfumes, hot sandwiches . . .

As I walked, I tried to remember the various historical anecdotes Louie had shared with me during one of our strolls through the city. In particular, I thought of his theory on how, regardless of your present mood, Paris could match it, through one of the details in its landscape.

As I passed in front of the libertine bathhouse on Boulevard de Sébastopol that I had visited a few weeks before, my thoughts took a different turn. An array of naked bodies filled my mind. Whenever I tried to chase them away, they immediately returned. And each time, their features grew sharper. There was clearly no getting rid of them.

Two individuals began to stand out in the imaginary crowd: Louie. And Aurora.

What if I walked in on them in a compromising position? And what if, whenever Louie mysteriously disappeared, he was leaving to meet my double? Rebecca had been clear on one thing: they had been lovers both "before and after" Aurora had married David. Why would Aurora have ever put an end to her secret relationship with Louie? Had they ever stopped seeing each other?

I tried to push the images out of my mind but couldn't. They were so lifelike, it seemed as if I could touch Louie and Aurora, as if I could smell them and feel their skin shivering, their hearts thumping. The thought was as painful as a torrent of lava, and I couldn't get it out of my head. I had a morbid fascination for that other woman, who was like me but not. And although she was twenty years older than I, in my imagination, her body was unaltered by time. Louie cupped her breasts, which were just as firm as my own. Even her sex, its full labia majora and delicately pink nymphae, hadn't aged and looked like mine. When Louie suddenly introduced his middle finger into her, I jumped as though she were I. And then he softly pressed that grainy bulge that gave me so much pleasure.

"Don't stop . . ." Aurora sighed, just as I had so many times before.

As I walked by the Strasbourg–Saint-Denis metro station, the streets filled with a cosmopolitan crowd, street peddlers and traffic, I imagined Louie inserting a second finger inside of her and working his two digits like a piston. The idea made me stumble, and I realized I'd lost my bearings.

Where was I headed again? Was it really such a good idea to go and see the realization of my worst fears?

AFTER WANDERING FOR A WHILE longer, I took one of the Grands Boulevards, ignoring the chic brasseries, as well as the theaters with their loud posters. I barely even noticed when I passed the Jouffroy Passage, where Louie procured his antique canes.

I walked as if in a dream, as if the GPS of my feelings had taken control of my legs and decided which route to take—straight on Boulevard Montmartre, which became Boulevard Haussmann; then right on Rue Taitbout, past Rue la Fayette, where I began to feel a slight incline in the street.

How long had I been bobbing through this ocean that was

the city? I arrived at 80 Rue Taitbout, the golden letters of the Square d'Orléans gleaming in the sunlight.

What was sex like for them? Did Louie make love to Aurora the same way as he made love to me? Or, despite the resemblance between us, did he treat us differently?

I tried to imagine them spread out over a Persian rug, Louie lying on his mistress's back—his favorite position after he and I made love. His long and slender sex explored the fissure of the buttocks beneath him, diving at last into Aurora's vulva, which was wet with desire. Crushing his partner under his weight, he bit into her shoulder, the nape of her neck, and even her face; and I could feel the tip of his teeth on my own round cheeks.

From time to time, he slipped his hands under Aurora's stomach, and depending on his present desire, he spread apart her white and delicate thighs, creating a wider passage for entry. Or sometimes he teased her vulva and hypertrophied clitoris.

She murmured: "Louie . . . My Lou . . ."

I froze in front of the square's imposing entrance, staring at an ornamental detail I hadn't noticed on my last visit here. The gilded number eighty appeared on both sides of the door, and there was a third that separated the two words: SQUARE 80 D'ORLÉANS. To me, the three eighties were like three protagonists in a love triangle. I could think of three such triangles with a link to this place.

Sand, Musset, and Chopin.

Aurora, David, and Louie.

Louie, David, and me.

And in a few seconds, I would be able to add a fourth to that list: Aurora, Louie . . . and me.

$3 \times 80 = 240 \ldots 24$, which was my age, I realized, losing myself in absurd superstitions.

"Are you looking for something, Mademoiselle?"

An elderly gentleman with an old bulldog had stopped a few steps from where I was standing. In his tweed cap, his jowls drooping almost as much as those of his dog, he could have easily been mistaken for Jacques Prévert.

"No . . . Actually, yes," I immediately corrected myself. "I'm meeting someone, but I've forgotten the code to her house."

"You don't have her telephone number?" he asked, surprised and slightly suspicious.

"I do . . . but my phone is almost dead."

I waved the object in question, taking care to hide the screen, which showed that the device had actually just been charged.

"Oh . . . And where are you going, if you don't mind my asking?"

"Building number 5."

"Five? But that's where I live!" he exclaimed, as though the banal coincidence suddenly made us old friends. "Who is it you're going to see?"

I hesitated, knowing that my entry into the building depended on how I answered his question. I couldn't get it wrong. But was I there to see Émilie Lebourdais or Aurora Delbard? Or some combination that I couldn't anticipate, like Aurora Barlet? After all, that had been her name when she'd officially disappeared from the face of the earth.

Go home. Go back to the fountainhead. In other words, follow my one lead, Mutaliz, whose address on record for Aurora *Delbard* was 5 Square d'Orléans.

"Aurora Delbard . . . ," I said, almost as a question.

"Oh, okay." His expression was suddenly less friendly.

"Is there something wrong?" I asked as I followed him toward the first courtyard.

"No, nothing wrong," he said, shrugging. "It's just that . . ."

"Yes?"

"Well, we don't see her very often. I've lived here for ten years, and I haven't run into her more than three times. The last time was several years ago."

"She goes out a lot . . . ," I said, defending my double. "And she often works odd hours."

The man seemed satisfied by my lies. I had, after all, told them with conviction.

But after we'd passed the fountain and its melodious gurgle, and as we were nearing our mutual destination, he turned toward me, his expression curious.

"You look like her. Are you her sister?"

"No . . . Her cousin," I lied again.

"Oh, I was going to say . . ."

That you look related, I finished his thought for him in my head.

When we reached the glass doors, he turned his back to me and punched in the code, careful to hide the path of his index finger over the keys. He was nice, but he was also prudent.

Inside, I thanked him and took the staircase on my right. He was waiting for the elevator, a wrought-iron antique, and looked surprised to see me sneaking away.

"Aren't you going upstairs? Which floor, again?"

His remark proved that he hadn't seen Aurora very often and that he knew almost nothing about her.

"No, that's nice of you, thanks. I'm just going to the second floor."

He nodded, his droopy face bobbing, and at last he left me to my exploration. I climbed the wide and deep stairs, each step cushioned by a thick red carpet with floral motifs. The walls seemed to sway a little, and the situation felt so surreal that I would not have been surprised to meet a couple clad in tails and crinoline—ghosts from the building's flamboyant past.

However, with the exception of the screeching elevator, the building was utterly silent. When I reached the second floor, I noted three doors. I couldn't remember Marchadeau's description, and none of the doorbells had names on them.

I tried my luck on the one that was closest, to my right, pressing the old, black Bakelite button for several seconds. I waited, my ear practically pressed to the door. But there was no sign of life on the other side.

The second door was across from the elevator. I pressed the doorbell and waited for a while before hearing the click-clack of heels on the parquet and then the creak of hinges. The door opened onto a tiny grandmother, the kind one only sees in fairy tales, with spectacles, a gray bun, and a shawl.

"Oh . . . I'm sorry, Madame. I have the wrong door."

"There's no harm done, Mademoiselle, no harm."

I could tell that she hoped to take advantage of my mistake and engage me in conversation, of which she must have had precious little. But I apologized profusely and quickly turned to leave, abandoning the poor old woman to her solitude.

In case Aurora was watching me through the peephole, I climbed four or five steps and waited for thirty seconds before tiptoeing back down to her floor.

The door on the left had to be the one. I pressed my ear against the panel of varnished wood. I heard a few deeply resonating musical notes, the product of an instrument and not a recording.

"Chopin . . . ," I whispered to myself.

It was being played with a jerky hand, but between the snags I recognized the nocturne that Louie and I had heard during our first meeting.

The music stopped and started from time to time, repeating a couple of measures each time it picked up again.

Were they making love through music? Was this melody Louie's ideal sexual score? The music for which he had been tirelessly searching?

And what if Aurora and Louie's ultimate fantasy was . . . me, Aurora's erotic doppelganger? And what if the events of the past year had all been leading up to this: bringing the three of us together in the same bed?

I had the brief sensation that they were both standing on the other side of the door, she with her face crushed into the wood, he glued to her body, his sex planted inside her, both acutely aware that a thin oak board was all that separated us. I could almost hear Aurora sighing as he moved in and out of her, as he pinched her nipples and pressed her clitoris. Feeling their body heat so near, smelling the combined scent of their genitals and skin, almost made me faint. And as I tried to regain my composure, I accidentally pressed the palm of my hand into the doorbell.

The piano stopped at once, and with it, the imaginary scene in my head. I waited a moment and thought I heard soft steps nearing the door. A hand turned the knob in an awkward movement.

There was still time to escape, to hustle down the staircase and never think of Aurora again. I could accept Louie as he was, with all his madness and mystery.

"Hello . . ."

The voice came from a ten-year-old girl who was wearing a pale-blue dress and a matching headband.

I immediately saw the confusion in her eyes. She stared at me incredulously, panic tarnishing her childish features. I was there, in front of her, but I was also behind her at the piano.

Speechless, I examined her nose, her eyes, her mouth, anything that might bear a sign of resemblance, however slight. Was it possible that they'd borne a child together?

Suddenly, she turned toward the apartment's interior and weakly called out:

"Mademoiselle!"

No, Aurora wasn't her mother.

A voice called back from the other end of the hallway; though slightly deeper perhaps, it could have been my own:

"What is it, dear? Is it your mother?"

Next, I heard a few worried steps; then a woman in a white dress appeared in the hallway. She reached a hand to open the door wider and see what had upset her student.

She might have yelled, rolled her eyes back in alarm, and thrown me out of the building. But she didn't do any of that. Instead, she half smiled to herself as if to say, *At last, we meet.* She contemplated me for a few seconds, with one hand on her student's head, before at last gently asking the child to leave:

"Go home, Louise. That will be all for today. Tell your mom that I'll keep you fifteen minutes longer next time. Okay?"

"Yes, Mademoiselle."

The little girl shot me one last terrified glance and then disappeared down the stairs, leaving me face-to-face with the piano teacher. My reflection in a mirror.

I was surprised to see how much time had spared Aurora,

or should I say Émilie? But even more unsettling was the contrast between her smooth features and the intensity of her gaze, which made her look like she was a thousand years old.

"I'm . . . ," I stuttered, incapable of constructing a coherent sentence.

Meeting Aurora was more than a shock. I didn't know how to define it yet, but I already sensed that this moment would reshape my existence, as well as my most deeply held beliefs. It would determine my future. Indeed, this was not a prosaic encounter between two quasi twins. This was the reset button for my whole life.

Again, I found her attitude disconcerting. Instead of inviting me to come inside, she smiled, nodded her head, and then closed the door on me. Just like that. Without so much as an explanation. She didn't even try to learn about who I was, to understand me, or simply to compare notes.

As nonviolent as her behavior had been, it felt as if she had just punched me. She locked her door, and I immediately broke down, hot and heavy tears rolling over my cheeks. KO'd before I'd even been able to put up a fight.

Once I'd regained a little bit of energy, I let out a deep cry, like the wail of a wounded animal. I slammed a heavy fist into the bottom of Aurora's door, then another, then a hundred more. A wild and muffled drumbeat. But no sound from inside betrayed any reaction. She was completely indifferent to my pain.

THE SAME COULD NOT BE said for her neighbors, many of whom came down from the floors above, including my old friend, this time without his dog. Some had come to help and inquired into what was the matter. Others threatened to call the police. But from the depths of my despair, I noticed that no one mentioned Aurora or any other occupant of her apartment. No one dared ring her doorbell.

What were they afraid of? Did they realize that the apartment was occupied and that the woman wasn't a ghost?

A teenager with a rugby player's build helped me outside, and I continued by myself through the leafy square. Behind me, the neighbors' indignant exclamations faded. And through an open window, I thought I heard Chopin's nocturne, this time played with confidence.

The recluse of the Square d'Orléans had gone back to her indolent life and sent me back to mine.

I REACHED THE TOP OF Rue Taitbout without really knowing how I'd gotten there. I wandered aimlessly for a while through the neighborhood. I was a zombie, as though Aurora had emptied me of substance.

I was so distraught that I barely noticed when the long and slender carriage of a car stopped beside me, its tires screeching. Two doors opened, and the individuals who emerged lunged at me without saying a word. I couldn't identify who they were since, as I was late to notice, they were wearing masks. They plucked me off the sidewalk and forced me inside the car. In their hands, I didn't weigh more than a garbage bag. And in that moment, that is about what I thought I was worth.

The limousine sped away from the curb, throwing us around in the back like three packages. Despite being jostled, my kidnappers were careful and exact in their gestures. Before I could scream, a giant syringe was inserted into my mouth, its contents trickling down my throat. Painfully, I swallowed whatever it was, incapable of spitting it out.

A moment later, I fell into a deep sleep, my head clamped in a chemical vice, all possible resistance muzzled by the substance. Yet despite my queasy dreams, I was happy that these strangers had taken me away from my nightmare. In a way, I was happy to let go.

31

Slowly, I opened my eyes, one eyelash at a time, so as not to overwhelm my retinas, just enough to prove to myself that I had come out of the chemically induced coma.

I TURNED MY HEAD RIGHT, then left, to see where I was. But I was not yet fully conscious, and I was incapable of situating myself in space or time.

My field of vision was reduced to a small and fuzzy tunnel, and I could barely see anything. My head was throbbing, and I couldn't concentrate.

The room in which I found myself seemed big. It was dark, with a few spots of light emanating from candelabras on the ground. The black-and-white-checked floor, along with the Empire furnishings—whose varnish shone in the darkness—served as an important clue. And since the dimensions of the room were smaller than those of Josephine's castle . . .

"Château de Bois-Préau . . ."

The small castle was situated next to Château de Malmaison and had been completely remodeled under the Second

Empire. Its decor was almost identical to that of its prestigious neighbor. I hoped I was right. Otherwise, I would have no idea how to figure out where my kidnappers had taken me.

Its high windows were covered with heavy black curtains, which hid any clues from the world outside.

Seized with panic, I squirmed. Something tugged at my wrists, and I realized that I was attached to the arms of my red satin chair.

Happily, I wasn't naked, which is what I had feared after my traumatizing experience with David and his henchmen. Still, someone had taken off my clothes and dressed me in a long white nightshirt.

I tried to break free, but the knots holding me captive resisted my attempts. Aurora, that woman I had surprised in her apartment a few hours before, did she know about this macabre scene? Or was she somehow responsible for it?

On the other end of the room, a door set into the wall creaked open just enough to let a shadow through. The shadow approached me, its gait slightly unbalanced. When it was halfway across the room, I saw that it was a man in full regalia—a white silk tailcoat with gold embroidery. A mask covered his face.

When he was just a few steps from my chair, he veered right and pressed what must have been a remote, because two immense crystal chandeliers were suddenly illuminated, and the room filled with blinding light. I recognized with certainty now the salmon hue and the antique decorations of the ballroom of Château de Bois-Préau, such as I had seen them in photographs.

An instant later, I felt the man's presence beside my ear, and his warm voice uttered these reassuring words:

"Don't worry. I'll untie you now. They were just to keep you from falling."

"Louie . . . ?" I stammered.

The fog lifted from my eyes, and I no longer had any doubt as to the man's features.

"Everything is going to be all right."

"Why . . . Why are we here?"

The smile on his face widened enigmatically. Louie's smile, which had shown me *his* Romantic Paris. I wondered what new mystery he wanted to introduce me to that night, but he refrained from saying anything but these cryptic words:

"I hope you will forgive my method . . . but I think that sometimes the end justifies the means."

He could have told me anything. In that moment, I was just so happy to hear his voice. To smell his scent of lavender and vanilla. To have my fears muffled by a cocoon of sweet memories. However, as he untied the straps, freeing my arms one by one, a less docile—or perhaps less drugged—part of me rebelled.

What was this masquerade all about? Why had he kidnapped me when I'd left Aurora's apartment? Had he had me followed? I had been refusing his calls, but did that justify that kind of behavior?

He moved away from me again, toward one of the doors behind me, conveniently escaping my questions.

"Everything is going to be all right," he had just said. But what did he mean by "everything"?

"Come!" he ordered, beckoning me to join him.

I barely managed to stand on my legs as I made my way toward him, my steps hesitant and the tiles cold beneath my feet. It occurred to me that, for the second time since I'd known him, he was walking without the help of a cane.

He pushed open a door that was decorated with a lyre and a bouquet of flowers and led to a small adjoining room. There, in the middle of the period furniture, stood a mannequin dressed in a long ivory silk dress. Despite my state, I instantly recognized it: the Schiaparelli wedding dress, the one that had been made for Hortensia, the one that I had almost worn a year earlier to marry the younger Barlet brother.

"It can't be . . ." I sighed, stupefied.

I had regretted sending it back to David after I'd taken it off that night in the Josephine and offered myself to Louie. Armand had come by the Hôtel des Charmes to pick it up a few days later, and he had clearly taken it upon himself to restore it to a pristine condition.

"It needed a few touch-ups, but I think it's as beautiful as the day of my parents' wedding," Louie said triumphantly.

"I . . . I can't," I managed to stutter.

He pretended not to understand.

"Do you not like it?"

"Louie," I breathed wearily. "We're not getting married . . . not now."

"And why not?"

He smiled at me as radiantly as on the night of our first kiss. It was as sweet and as affable as each smile had been from him over the past year. He seemed so sure of himself, so sure of his charms.

"You're not serious, are you?"

"I don't think I've ever been so serious," he replied after a long pause, his tone suddenly grave.

That sublime dress would now be a symbol of my promise to myself: I wouldn't marry him so long as I hadn't freed him of his secrets.

"I love you. You love me, too, I know it."

"We can't get married," I insisted, indignantly this time. "It would be completely insane!"

He grabbed my arm, more passionately than threateningly.

"Really? Is that what you think? Weren't you the young woman who asked me to marry you just a month ago . . . The woman who organized an engagement party for us next door?"

His eyes bore into mine, imperiously demanding a reply.

"That was you, wasn't it?"

"I . . . I saw *her* tonight" was my reply, a non sequitur. "I saw *her*, Louie."

That piece of information, though delivered with insistence, didn't seem to bother him. And based on his unflinching, stoic gaze, I saw that he understood who I meant.

"I know . . . I mean, I've had my suspicions. But believe me, it's not important."

"Really . . . It's not?" I choked.

How could he speak so casually about his former love? How could he shrug her off, when Aurora had conditioned every aspect of his existence, including our meeting?

"If I had wanted to"—he sighed—"I had a thousand opportunities to marry her. And yet *you* are the woman who is here tonight. With me."

I didn't know how to respond to that, I who had always thought of myself as a casting error in the glamorous and sophisticated world of the Barlet family. The double of a woman whom I had always suspected had never completely left his life.

He was accepting me, even though I had avoided almost all of the tests he'd hoped to see me pass before our union. I had been so absorbed by this insane quest for truth that I had neglected the very basis of our love, the fusion of souls and of pens that found its strength in the alliance of our bodies.

ON OUR WAY BACK TO the ballroom, Louie brusquely turned toward me and eyed me with intensity.

"Our guests have arrived. They'll be upon us any second."

"Louie, I—"

He pointed at the Schiaparelli, which shone magnificently under the light of the chandeliers. The dress was a symbol of the vows he hoped I would take with him, in just a few minutes.

"So . . . will you put on that dress or not? You have to tell me now, Elle. And you should know that, whatever you say, I will never ask the same question again."

This was at once the sweetest and most odious ultimatum. Was it right to choose this passionate love even though it had already broken up one wedding and reignited a family feud?

"Yes . . . My answer is yes. I'm going to put it on."

Or, rather, I was going to put it on *again* and pray that this time it was the right choice.

Then, without saying a word, he made his way to the other side of the living room and opened one of the double doors. Two slim silhouettes entered and trotted toward me.

"Good evening," purred the two young women in concert.

The hairdresser/makeup-artist was brandishing brushes and a flattening iron, while the stylist hid behind a box of pins and a pair of scissors.

Poking and prodding me like a doll, their expert hands quickly fitted me in my dress, adjusting it over my waist and full bosom; they coiffed my hair into a cascading updo and then painted my face with a few delicate brush strokes.

They flitted around me like Cinderella's sparrows, and in less time than it took me to transition from feeling tormented to amazed, they had finished their work. They held up two pocket mirrors for me to admire myself. The transformation was spectacular. These two girls were true fairies, and their skillful hands had turned me into a princess.

Louie eyed me keenly, his quiet look one of admiration and pride. Then he flung open the doors on the other side of the room, inviting a crowd of guests to enter. They were all wearing masks and dressed in evening wear that was as modern as Louie's tails were old. A man in domestic's livery and with a head of gray hair—Armand?—hurried toward me with a chair that was identical to the one on which I was sitting. He placed it beside me without so much as a word. Another factotum set down an Egyptian-style pedestal table supported by two back-to-back sphinxes, and on which, I noticed, was sitting a giant purple velvet box.

The guests approached us in religious silence. A moment later, Louie took his place in the chair next to mine.

"Thank you . . . ," he whispered at me, tears in his eyes.

As he said that, a young, curly-haired brunette came to stand at my right.

"Hey, princess! And thanks!"

She was thanking me, too? For what?

"Thanks?" I asked.

"Yeah . . . Without you and your craziness, I never would have had the opportunity to wear it twice."

Sophia adjusted the cleavage of her dress, which I immediately recognized: her ideal dress. Her adjustment had raised her chest to an indecent degree, and the male contingent of the guests had noticed. Among them, I recognized Fred's blond crew cut and François Marchadeau's balding temples. This latter's gaze was devouring my friend more avidly than anyone else. Nothing seemed to indicate that David was present.

Strangely, everyone, including Sophia, was acting as if this was all normal.

"Soph," I asked, leaning toward my friend, still groggy, "when were you invited?"

"For tonight? Completely randomly. There was a group text-message this afternoon, something along the lines of 'Hurry over to Rueil-Malmaison in your evening wear.' Fred and I were in bed . . . We didn't get the message until the last minute!"

Rebecca's slim body was now making its way toward us. She took her place next to Louie. She was followed by a man in a dark suit and a blue, white, and red sash. He was no doubt the only civil officer who had agreed to officiate such a last-minute affair and in such a place.

The city worker glanced over the room and its occupants as he took his place a few feet from where we stood, his hands resting on his potbelly, which poked out from between the two sides of his open jacket.

Suddenly, between the dresses and suits, I saw Mom's floral shirt. She smiled at me in the sweet way that only she knew how, and I distinctly heard her murmur:

"He loves you. And you love him."

My throat tightened, and tears sprung to my eyes.

The man with the sash came forward another step.

He cleared his throat, and his deep and round stentorian voice filled the room, silencing the public. A small crowd of about a hundred persons was now gathered.

"Good evening, everyone. Thank you for coming on such short notice to this prestigious setting. We are gathered here tonight to celebrate the union of Mademoiselle Annabelle Lorand, aged twenty-four years, a freelance journalist of 29 Rue Rigault in Nanterre, in the department of the Hauts-de-Seine . . . Is that correct, Mademoiselle?"

He shot me a perfunctory smile that left me cold. The mention of my former address was moving, and I would have given anything to have Mom present with me that day. She had missed out on both of my weddings.

I also noticed that her mirage had disappeared into the mass of guests.

"Yes, that's right, Nanterre," I finally replied, after a few insistent jabs from Sophia.

"Very good . . . Mademoiselle Lorand, then, and Monsieur Louie Barlet, aged forty-two years, director of an art gallery, and of 1 Rue de la Tour-des-Dames in Paris. Is that correct, Monsieur?"

"That's correct," Louie stated in a firm voice.

"Now, I shall state your rights and responsibilities . . ."

As the public official recited his text, his voice slack with indifference, I tried to spot other friendly faces in attendance. It wasn't easy with the masks, but I thought I recognized Alban, Peggy, David Garchey, and even Jean-Marc Zerki, who was somehow slicker than usual, his crow-black hair shining under the overhead lighting. All the others must have been friends of Louie's. So this was what my future husband's social life looked like. This was the milieu in which I would soon find myself.

" . . . husband and wife promise to be honest with each other, to renounce all lies—be they overt or by omission—with respect to their past, present, or future lives. Repeat after me: 'I promise.'"

Of course, the portly man officiating our wedding service did not say such words. But I wished he had. I wished that the words binding Louie and me to each other formed a promise of transparency.

I was going to marry Louie. Here. Now.

I could no longer run. I had already stood up his younger brother; I didn't feel capable of sacrificing the elder, the man I loved, on the altar of my persistent doubts. I couldn't reject Louie because of the shadow of a woman, even if she seemed more threatening now that I knew she was alive than when I'd thought she was dead.

"Mademoiselle Lorand, do you take this man, Monsieur Louie Barlet, to be your lawfully wedded husband?"

He must have repeated the ritualistic sentence at least two or three times, and in the face of my stubborn silence, a hysterical shudder ran through the crowd. Sophia elbowed me again and hissed through her teeth with an authoritative smile:

"Shit! Elle, say yes!"

Instead, I declared in the loudest and most self-assured voice that I could muster:

"I swear."

The potbellied officiant smirked, though he quickly regained his composure. In a professorial tone, he corrected me:

"For now, a simple yes would suffice, Mademoiselle."

"Yes . . . ," I stammered, my eyes suddenly and inexplicably filling with tears. "Yes, of course."

"Very good, thank you," he said in a joking tone. "Monsieur Barlet, will you take this woman, Mademoiselle Annabelle Lorand, to be your lawfully wedded wife?" The man chuckled lightly, his neck swelling and reddening, and then added: "No need to swear."

Louie ignored the legal representative's joke and turned toward me. He then declared in his warmest, sweetest voice, a tone I recognized from our limitless palette of intimate caresses:

"Yes. That's what I want."

His answer seemed to well up from his whole body. It made me shiver, body and soul.

"Good, good, good," the officiant said three times, as Whurman, the notary, would have done. "By the powers vested in me, I declare you husband and wife."

And, as if he had accompanied us on the journey that had led us to this moment, he added, teasingly:

"This time it's official, I swear!"

DESPITE HIS INAPPROPRIATE HUMOR, TWO or three people laughed, and a moment later, a long round of applause filled the room like fireworks on Bastille Day.

Through my tears, Louie kissed me and bit my lips. And in a weeping whirlwind, Sophia crushed me against her ample chest. At last, I understood what had just happened. Yes, this was my life. I was the teetering bride—still a bit drugged and no doubt drunk with happiness.

Louie wrapped his arms around me and whispered in my ear:

"He can't hurt us now."

David had done everything in his power to keep us away from each other, and this moment was proof that he had lost. Still, I feared that the institution of marriage wouldn't be enough to safeguard us against his wrath.

But that was what Louie believed. He had been beaming in his radiant suit ever since we'd exchanged our sacred vows.

"I almost forgot . . ."

He grabbed the box sitting atop the pedestal table and opened it without ceremony. Inside, two rings had been awaiting their blessed hour. I immediately recognized the family ring; it had been polished and our names engraved in it. Beside it, a bigger, more sober and masculine ring for Louie.

He took my hand and solemnly slid the wedding band over my finger. Then, I took my turn, and with trembling hands, I put his ring on his finger. Filled with emotion, I realized that I had at last been freed from the parasitic thoughts that had been poisoning my happiness.

Then, with an impish smile and a defiant expression reminiscent of our time in room one, I looked at him and said:

"Don't you have a final test for me?"

The idea that he had planned a traditional wedding for us was almost an insult to our passion. I imagined the guests suddenly stripping and wandering naked through the room, their collective flesh quivering. That would make for a spectacular wedding finale. But a crew was already setting up the buffet tables on the other side of the room, rhythmic music swelled around us, and some of the guests had slowly started to dance. This seemed like any other wedding reception.

"You seem disappointed." He guffawed.

"Hmm . . . a little."

He didn't let me feel disappointed for long. Squeezing my hand in his, he led me over the black-and-white-checked floor. Strangely, none of the guests interrupted us. In the foyer, Richard was waiting for us, his driver's hat covering his bald head, his expression as impassive as ever. He handed Louie one of his canes and signaled for us to follow him.

"I have something better than an erotic test for you."

As he spoke, Louie pointed to the limousine in which we had ridden to Château de Malmaison for the first time.

"Hold on . . . We're just going to leave our guests?"

Sophia, Fred, Marchadeau . . . We were the king and queen of this party, and yet we were going to abandon them all there. Was I going to run away from all of my wedding receptions?

"Where are we going?"

"That's part of the surprise . . . if you'll give me the benefit of the doubt."

He opened the limousine door for me and patiently waited for me to accept his invitation. I climbed into the luxurious passenger seat, gathering my train behind me. A moment later, Louie joined me, and Richard drove the powerful car over the driveway's gravel. We were "on our way to anywhere," as Sophia would say, toward an imaginary Cythera. My chest was swollen with excitement, and a warm wave crashed through my pelvis. Without realizing it, I was smiling like an idiot, my gaze lost in the glowing urban landscape.

At that hour—it was now nighttime—there wasn't much traffic, and it didn't take us long to reach the tunnels that led to the city at La Défense.

"You still won't tell me where—"

"Shh," he ordered gently, placing a finger on my lips. "Just relax. You'll see soon enough."

That was the moment he decided to extract a bottle of chilled champagne and two sparkling flutes from the side pocket. He expertly opened the bottle and served us both a glass.

"Madame Barlet," he said as he handed one to me, "I believe I recall that there is one thing you have never done . . . and I am delighted to offer you the opportunity to have that experience."

With those words, he took the champagne flute from my hand and placed it along with his in a receptacle made for that purpose. Our lips still tingling from the wine, he kissed me and pressed his muscular body into my heaving chest.

He was right: I had never made love in a car. As the car drove through the Place de l'Étoile, the light from the Arc de Triomphe washed over us, and I realized the true purpose of this escapade: to associate our pleasure with the most beautiful monuments of the capital. To make Paris a garden for our pleasure. To combine the stars of the City of Light with our most precious intimacy.

When we reached the Champs-Élysées, I discovered, thanks to his inquisitive fingers, that I was already wet. This was the prettiest avenue in the world, and his hand's journey inside me the sweetest incursion. We left a trace of our preliminary fluids beneath the countless street lamps, across the opulent building facades and luxury boutiques.

He knew how much I desired him. And his fingers turned slowly inside me, pushing into the mucous walls of my vagina, stretching them as far as their plasticity allowed, calibrating the intensity of his touch to the frequency of my moans. Each bump in the cobblestone road sent my love deeper inside me. If he continued for much longer, I would soon lose all control and melt in his hand. Each time we reached a red light, he paused, waiting for our vehicle to start moving again, his senses alert. As soon as the light turned green again, his fingers reapplied themselves to my genitals. We sensed the teeming crowd of pedestrians outside the tinted windows of our limousine. The idea that they were there, just a few steps from where we were making love, excited us all the more. They couldn't see us, but they could hear us. I held my breath, while my vagina, which longed for Louie, endured the torture of his absence. His hand rested on my lips and engorged clitoris. The wait was so agonizing that I could have screamed at Richard through the glass partition to burn through the red light. It might have meant running over a pedestrian, but at least we could have returned to our mad desires.

IN PLACE DE LA CONCORDE, my hand freed his already erect member. It proudly burst out of the fabric. Outside, the majestic obelisk was haloed in artificial light, the fountains at its base spraying it with water. I shot Louie a defiant look and inserted his sex into my mouth. First, I teased him and flitted my tongue over the sensitive skin of his glans. Each passage over his frenulum elicited a sigh that stimulated me more than any word could. We were passing in front of the National Assembly when I swallowed his entire member, lashing it with my tongue. It was my turn to wield the power. One thrust too many and he would come in my mouth, in a long, frothy river of white-hot foam.

WE TURNED LEFT, AND NOTRE Dame was appearing in our window, when he withdrew his penis from my mouth. He was on the verge of being KO'd. Without a thought for his own pleasure, he lifted layers of fabric from my legs and tore off my soaking panties. The delicate elastic didn't put up much of a fight, and soon the thin wall of lace flew to the floor. My genitals were laid bare under the car's orange light. And I discovered that while I'd been sleeping, an expert hand had shaved my pubic hair, which I had grown out after our engagement party. My yin tattoo, that symbol of my sex, that key to my femininity, appeared in the shadows. Louie gently kissed it. Then his lips pressed against my petals of pink flesh, which slowly began to open. He nibbled at them for a moment, tasting my sap, which was now pearling in places. He was thoroughly enjoying the sight and scent of me.

"My rose . . . ," he whispered.

If Louie could have bottled the scent of my sex, he would have made it into a cologne to wear so that he could be intoxicated by me at every hour of the day.

Excited by this first contact, he drove his tongue inside me without warning, then immediately withdrew it and lapped at my musky vulva. His tongue wandered over the same area with studied precision, and each caress felt unique.

"Higher . . . ," I begged, beside myself with all of his attention.

He complied, wrapping his lips around my little patch of triangular skin and sucking on the mound hiding beneath it. He sucked on my clitoris, then pushed it away, savoring each submersion. The powerful suction removed all taboos, reservations, doubts, distress, and modesty. And the more he sucked, the more it felt as though all of me were dissolving in his mouth. I was on the verge of madness.

From between fluttering eyelashes, I noticed that the car had stopped in front of the cathedral's vast square.

My pleasure was rising, shooting out of the car, flying toward the two towers, dancing around the gargoyles, and illuminating the stained glass windows. I was Louie's Madonna, and my happiness was his masterpiece.

"Yes!"

My cry rang out like a shot, and I thought I heard the sound of pigeon wings flapping in terror. I didn't care if anyone heard me. I wanted to scream yes to this joy. Yes to our reunited bodies. Yes to our accomplishment. Not a hesitant yes, like the one I had uttered to David a year earlier at the foot of this same monument. A full and frank assent, one untarnished by the Barlet family's mysteries.

TRULY, I WAS READY TO welcome Louie into my life and person, to make his desire mine. My eyelashes expressed what I wanted; my lips didn't have to utter a word. He straightened slightly, now between my open thighs. His member brushed against my crotch like a bird searching for the entrance to its nest. Then, he slowly penetrated me, enjoying every centimeter. We were made for that union of bodies, and for many more that same night and in the future. He was barely moving, preferring instead to feel the palpitation of his member against the walls of my vagina. Our mucuses married perfectly.

I don't know how long we stayed like that—statues of flesh, concentrating on the minuscule sensations of our united bodies. His torso was crushed into my chest and his nose was buried in the crook of my neck. At last he came, in a soft spasm.

"I love you . . ." He sighed simply.

I was about to say the same, but he declined my declaration with a tender kiss.

Then, he rummaged through the side pocket again and withdrew an envelope. With a timidity I found endearing, he offered it to me.

"What is it?" I asked, my thighs still shaking from our dance.

"Open it."

The envelope contained one single object: a key. I held it as gently as if it were a wounded bird and read the label attached to its ring.

"'Room two,'" I read aloud.

"*Our* room. A room for this married couple. The only room to which Hotelles have never been given access."

"But . . . where is it?"

Without exaggerating, I could say that I knew the topography of the Hôtel des Charmes by heart. Yet I couldn't figure out where this nuptial suite—Louie's gift to me—was located.

"It can't be accessed from the hallways. The only point of entry is a hidden door in room number one."

Behind one of the numerous mirrors in the Josephine, I supposed. I burned to see and experience it, to write even prettier and more ardent pages than we had written in room one. I thought of how sweet it would be to write to each other again, just as it was so sweet to have our bodies reunited. I was already enjoying the thought of putting the present moment into words.

I pressed myself to Louie. I was happy.

I would defend him; I would pardon him; I would love him.

CLOSE YOUR EYES NOW. OUT of happiness. Out of pleasure. Out of perfect abandon. With closed eyes, they say, nothing can escape you. You'll see. You'll see everything now.

I'll see everything.

ACKNOWLEDGMENTS

I would like to thank my agent, Anna Jarota.

Thanks also to her wonderful team: Ted, Gwladys, Marc, Anne, and anyone I may be forgetting.

Thanks to editors from all over the globe who believed in this project and put faith in me as a French writer, with all my untranslatable Gallicisms!

Thanks to all the tattoo artists who participated, in their way, during the months in which this project gestated, and particularly to the amazing girls at Dragon Tattoo.

Thanks to Alphabet Man, who is less virtual than he believes.

Thanks to my friends and their unwavering support and occasional goading, especially to Emmanuelle.

THEMATIC BIBLIOGRAPHY

For those interested in compiling a library of erotic literature of their own, here is Louie Barlet's complete list of recommendations (in chronological order, from their date of publication):

Hymn to Aphrodite, Sappho
Satyricon, Petronius
The Art of Love, Ovid
The Decameron, Boccaccio
The Canterbury Tales, Geoffrey Chaucer
The Lives of the Gallant Ladies, Brantôme
Forbidden Fruit: Selected Tales in Verse, Jean de La Fontaine
Erotic Sonnets, Giorgio Baffo
The Story of My Life, Giacomo Casanova
The Sopha: A Moral Tale, Claude Crébillon

Fanny Hill; or, The Memoirs of a Woman of Pleasure, John Cleland
Erotica Biblion, Honoré-Gabriel de Mirabeau
Le Pornographe, Nicolas-Edme Restif de la Bretonne
Philosophy in the Bedroom, Marquis de Sade
My Secret Life, Anonymous
L'Enfant du bordel, Pigault-Lebrun
Gamiani, or Two Nights of Excess, Alfred de Musset
Venus in Furs, Leopold von Sacher-Masoch

ABOUT THE AUTHOR

Emma Mars is the pseudonym of an author who lives in France.

THE HOTELLES SERIES BY
EMMA MARS

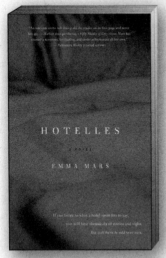

HOTELLES
A Novel

Available in Paperback and eBook

Paris, a hotel room, the middle of the afternoon . . .
So begins the story of Annabelle, a young escort in
Paris who has accepted her final proposition before
marrying the powerful and generous man of her
dreams, media mogul David Barlet. But the mysterious
handwritten notes she has been receiving—notes that
detail personal fantasies no one could possibly know—
don't prepare her for the fact that her new client is her
fiancé's brother, Louie. Through visits to the Hotel
des Charmes, where each chamber is dedicated to one
of French history's great seductresses, Louie awakens
Annabelle's body and her psyche, delivering her to
heights of ecstasy and fits of passion. He pushes her
beyond her limitations to tap into her deep seductive
power—and she discovers that true freedom comes
only when you fully surrender to desire.

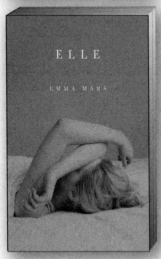

ELLE
Room Two in the Hotelles Trilogy

Available in Paperback and eBook

In a hotel room in Paris, a young woman named Elle
experiences the most exquisite freedom and sensual
pleasure she has ever known, thanks to Louis, the
man who has conquered her completely. So many
things in life have changed since they first met. Her
engagement to Louis's deceptive brother, David, has
been broken. Her mother has died. Yet Elle is wholly
fulfilled with Louis, the master who heightens her
senses and unleashes her deep, seductive power. Louis
takes Elle beyond her wildest fantasies. In sublime
self-abandonment, she discovers absolute ecstasy,
absolute sweetness, absolute desire. Then David
unexpectedly returns, stirring up painful memories
and threatening their bliss. Elle fears her education
may soon be over. . . . She does not understand that
it has only just begun.